W9-BFF-721

ENDGAME

THE COMPLETE
TRAINING DIARIES

ENDGAME
THE COMPLETE
TRAINING DIARIES

—

ORIGINS

DESCENDANT

EXISTENCE

JAMES FREY

HARPER
An Imprint of HarperCollinsPublishers

Endgame: The Complete Training Diaries

Endgame: The Training Diaries Volume 1: Origins © 2014 by Third Floor Fun, LLC

Endgame: The Training Diaries Volume 2: Descendant © 2015 by Third Floor Fun, LLC

Endgame: The Training Diaries Volume 3: Existence © 2015 by Third Floor Fun, LLC

All rights reserved. Printed in the United States of America. No part of this book may be used or reproduced in any manner whatsoever without written permission except in the case of brief quotations embodied in critical articles and reviews. For information address HarperCollins Children's Books, a division of HarperCollins Publishers, 195 Broadway, New York, NY 10007.

www.epicreads.com

ISBN 978-0-06-233276-9

15 16 17 18 19   PC/RRDH   10 9 8 7 6 5 4 3 2 1

❖

First Edition

Table of Contents

Twelve thousand years ago, they came. They descended from the sky amid smoke and fire, and created humanity and gave us rules to live by. They needed gold and they built our earliest civilizations to mine it for them. When they had what they needed, they left. But before they left, they told us that someday they would come back, and that when they did, a game would be played. A game that would determine our future.

This is Endgame.

For 10,000 years the lines have existed in secret. The 12 original lines of humanity. Each has to have a Player prepared at all times. A Player becomes eligible at 13 and ages out at 19. Each bloodline has its own measure of who is worthy to be chosen. Who is worthy of saving their people. They have trained generation after generation after generation in weapons, languages, history, tactics, disguise, assassination. Together the Players are everything: strong, kind, ruthless, loyal, smart, stupid, ugly, lustful, mean, fickle, beautiful, calculating, lazy, exuberant, weak. They are good and evil. Like you. Like all.

This is Endgame.

When the game starts, the Players will have to find three keys. The keys are somewhere on Earth. The only rule of Endgame is that there are no rules. Whoever finds the keys first wins the game.

These are the stories of the Players before they were chosen—of how they shed their normal lives and transformed into the Players they were meant to be.

These are the Training Diaries.

ENDGAME

THE TRAINING DIARIES

— VOLUME 1 —

ORIGINS

MINOAN
MARCUS

When Marcus was a little kid, they called him the Monkey.

This was meant to be a compliment. Which is exactly how Marcus took it.

At seven years old, he monkeyed his way 30 meters up a climbing wall without fear, the only kid to ring the bell at the top. Ever since then he's made sure he always goes higher than the other kids, always gets to the top faster. Always waits at the summit with a cocky grin and a "What took you so long?"

He can climb anything. Trees, mountains, active volcanoes, a 90-degree granite incline or the sheer wall of a Tokyo skyscraper. The Asterousia Mountains of Crete were his childhood playground. He's scrambled up all Seven Summits—the highest mountain on each continent—including Antarctica's Mount Vinson, which meant a hike across the South Pole. He's illegally scaled Dubai's 800-meter-high Burj Khalifa without rope or harness, then BASE jumped from its silver tip. He's the youngest person ever to summit Everest (not that the world is allowed to know it).

If only someone would get around to building a tall enough ladder, he's pretty sure he could climb to the moon.

Climbing is an integral part of his training. Every Minoan child hoping to be named his or her generation's Player learns to scale a peak. They've all logged hours defying gravity; they've all broken through the clouds. But Marcus knows that for the others, climbing is just one more skill to master, one more challenge to stare down.

No different from sharpshooting or deep-sea diving or explosives disposal. For Marcus, it's more.

For Marcus, climbing is everything.

It's a fusion of mind and matter, the perfect way to channel all that frenetic energy that has him bouncing off the walls most of the time. It takes absolute focus, brute force, and a fearless confidence that comes naturally to Marcus, who feels most alive at 1,000 meters, looking down.

He loves it for all those reasons, sure—but mostly he loves it because he's the best.

And because being the best, by definition, means being better than Alexander.

It was clear from day one that Alexander Nicolaides was the kid to beat. It took only one day more to figure out he was also the kid to hate.

Marcus's parents called it camp, when they dropped him off that first day. But he was a smart kid, smart enough to wonder: What kind of parents dump their seven-year-old on Crete and head back to Istanbul without him? What kind of camp lets them do it?

What kind of camp teaches that seven-year-old how to shoot?

And how to arm live explosives?

And how to read Chinese?

It was the kind of camp where little kids were *encouraged* to play with matches.

It was most definitely Marcus's kind of place—and that was even before he found out the part about the alien invasion and how, if he played his cards right, he'd get to save the world.

Best. Camp. Ever.

Or it would have been, were it not for the impossible-to-ignore existence of Alexander Nicolaides. He was everything Marcus wasn't. Marcus could never sit still, always acted without thinking; Alexander was calm and deliberate and even broke the camp's

4

meditation record, sitting silent and motionless and staring into a stupid candle for 28 hours straight. Marcus mastered languages and higher math with brute mental force, thudding his head against the logic problems until they broke; Alexander was fluent in Assyrian, Sumerian, ancient Greek, and, just for fun, medieval Icelandic, and he was capable of visualizing at least six dimensions. Marcus was better at climbing and shooting; Alexander had the edge in navigation and survival skills. They even *looked* like polar opposites: Alexander was a compact ball of tightly coiled energy, his wavy, white-blond hair nearly as pale as his skin, his eyes as blue as the Aegean Sea. Marcus was long-limbed and rangy, with close-cropped black hair. If they'd been ancient gods, Alexander would have had charge over the sky and the sea, all those peaceful stretches of cerulean and aquamarine. Marcus, with his dark green eyes and golden sheen, would have lorded it over the forests and the earth, all leaves and loam and living things. But the gods were long dead—or at least departed for the stars—and instead Marcus and Alexander jockeyed for rule over the same small domain. Marcus was the camp joker and prided himself on making even his sternest teachers laugh; Alexander was terse, serious, rarely speaking unless he had something important to say.

Which was for the best, because his voice was so nails-on-chalkboard annoying that it made Marcus want to punch him in the mouth.

It didn't help that Alexander was a good candidate for Player and an even better suck-up. The other kids definitely preferred Marcus, but Marcus knew that Alexander had a slight edge with the counselors, and it was their opinion that counted. Every seven years, the counselors invited a new crop of kids to the camp, the best and brightest of the Minoan line. The counselors trained them, judged them, pushed them to their limits, pitted them against one another and themselves, and eventually named a single one as the best. The Player. Everyone else got sent back home to their mind-numbingly normal lives.

Maybe that kind of boring life was okay for other kids.

Other kids dreamed of being astronauts, race-car drivers, rock stars—not Marcus. Since the day he found out about Endgame, Marcus had only one dream: to win it.

Nothing was going to get in his way.

Especially not Alexander Nicolaides.

Tucked away in a secluded valley on the western edge of Crete, the Minoan camp was well hidden from prying eyes. The Greek isles were crowded with architectural ruins, most of them littered with regulations, tourists, and discarded cigarette butts. Few knew of the ruins nestled at the heart of the Lefka Ori range, where 50 carefully chosen Minoan children lived among the remnants of a vanished civilization. Tilting pillars, crumbling walls, the fading remains of a holy fresco—everywhere Marcus looked, there was evidence of a nobler time gone by. This was no museum: it was a living bond between present and past. The kids were encouraged to press their palms to crumbling stone, to trace carvings of heroes and bulls, to dig for artifacts buried thousands of years before. This was the sacred ground of their ancestors, and as candidates to be the Minoans' champion, they were entitled to claim it for their own.

The camp imposed a rigorous training schedule on the children, but none of them complained. They'd been chosen because they were the kind of kids who thought training was fun. They were kids who wanted to win. None more than Marcus. And other than the thorn in his side named Alexander Nicolaides, Marcus had never been so happy in his life.

He endured Alexander for two years, biding his time, waiting for the other boy to reveal his weakness or, better yet, to flame out. He waited for the opportunity to triumph over Alexander so definitively, so absolutely, that everyone would know, once and for all, that Marcus was the best. Marcus liked to imagine how that day would go, how the other kids would carry him around on their shoulders, cheering his name, while Alexander slunk away in humiliated defeat.

He was nine years old when the moment finally arrived.

A tournament, elimination style, with the champion claiming a large gold trophy, a month's worth of extra dessert, and bonus bragging rights. The Theseus Cup was held every two years as a showcase for campers—and a chance for them to prove their worth. There were rumors that the first to win the Theseus Cup was a shoo-in to be chosen as the Player. No one knew whether or not this was the case—but Marcus didn't intend to risk it. He intended to win.

He swept his opening matches effortlessly, knocking one kid after another senseless, even the ones who were older and bigger. Bronze daggers, double axes, Turkish sabers—whatever the weapon, Marcus wielded it like a champion. Alexander, who'd started off in another bracket, cut a similar swath across the competition. This was as it should be, Marcus thought. It would be no fun to knock him out in an early round. The decisive blow needed to come when it counted, in the championship, with everyone watching.

The two nine-year-old finalists stepped into the ring for a final bout. Personal, hand-to-hand combat. No weapons, no intermediaries. Just the two of them. Finally.

They faced each other and bowed, as they'd been taught.

Bowing before you fought, offering up that token of respect, that was a rule.

After that, there were no rules.

Marcus opened with a karate kick. Alexander blocked it with ease, and they pitted their black belts against each other for a few seconds before Alexander took him in a judo hold and flipped him to the ground. Marcus allowed it—only so he could sweep his leg across Alexander's knees and drop him close enough for a choke hold. Alexander wriggled out and smashed a fist toward Marcus's face. Marcus rolled away just in time, and the punch came down hard against the mat.

The camp was on its feet, cheering, screaming Marcus's and Alexander's names—Marcus tried not to distract himself by trying to figure out whose cheering section was bigger. The fighters moved fluidly through techniques, meeting sanshou with savate, blocking a tae kwon do attack with an onslaught of aikido, their polished choreography disintegrating into the furious desperation of a street brawl. But even spitting and clawing like a pair of animals, they were perfectly matched.

The fight dragged on and on. Dodging punches, blocking kicks, throwing each other to the mat again and again, they fought for one hour, then two. It felt like years. Sweat poured down Marcus's back and blood down his face. He gasped and panted, sucking in air and trying not to double over from the pain. His legs were jelly, his arms lead weights. Alexander looked like he'd been flattened by a steamroller, with both eyes blackened and a wide gap where his front teeth used to be. The kids fell silent, waiting for the referee to step in before the two boys killed each other.

But this was not that kind of camp.

They fought on.

They fought like they lived: Marcus creative and unpredictable, always in motion; Alexander cool, rational, every move a calculated decision.

Which made it even more of a shock when Alexander broke.

Unleashing a scream of pure rage, he reached over the ropes to grab the referee's stool, and smashed it over Marcus's head.

Marcus didn't see it coming.

He only felt the impact.

A thunderbolt of pain reverberating through his bones.

His body dropping to the ground, no longer under his control, his consciousness drifting away.

The last thing he saw, before everything faded to black, was Alexander's face, stunned by his own loss of control. Marcus smiled, then started to laugh. Even in defeat, he'd won—he'd finally made the uptight control freak completely lose it.

The last thing he heard was Alexander laughing too.

* * *

"You always tell that story wrong," Marcus says now. "You leave out the part where I let you win."

Xander only laughs. At 14, he's nearly twice the size he was at that first Theseus Cup, his shoulders broader, his voice several octaves deeper, his blond hair thicker and forested across his chest. But his laugh is still exactly the same as it was on the day of the fight.

Marcus remembers, as he remembers every detail of that day.

You never forget the moment you make your best friend.

"Yeah, that was really generous of you, deciding to get a concussion and pass out," Xander says. "I owe you one."

"You owe me two," Marcus points out. "One for the concussion, one for the cheating."

They are hanging off a sheer rock face, 50 meters off the ground. They will race each other to the top of the cliff, 70 meters above, then rappel back down to the bottom, dropping toward the ground at a stomach-twisting speed.

Marcus has heard that most kids his age fill up their empty hours playing video games. He thinks this is a little more fun.

"I most certainly did not cheat," Xander says, trying to muster some of his habitual dignity. Most people think that's the real him: solemn, uptight, deliberate, slow to smile. Marcus knows better. Over the last five years, he's come to know the real Xander, the one who laughs at his jokes and even, occasionally, makes a few of his own. (Though, of course, they're never any good.) "Not technically, at least," Xander qualifies. He jams his fingers into a small crevice in the rock face and pulls himself up another foot, trying very hard to look like it costs him no effort.

Marcus scrambles up past him, grinning, because for him it actually *is* no effort. "Only because no one ever thought to put 'don't go nutball crazy and smash furniture over people's heads' in the rules before," Marcus says.

"Lucky for both of us," Xander says.

Normally, Marcus would shoot back a joke or an insult, something about how it's not so lucky for him, because Xander's been clinging to him like a barnacle ever since. Or maybe something about how it was luckier for Xander, because now, with Marcus as a wingman, he might someday, if he's lucky, actually get himself a date.

But not today.

Not today, the last day before everything changes. Tomorrow, they will find out who has been selected as this generation's Player. It'll surely be either Marcus or Alexander; everyone knows that. They're the best in the camp at everything; no one else even comes close. It's what brought them together in the first place. After all that time wasted hating each other, they'd realized that where it counted, they were the same. No one else was so determined to win—and no one else was good enough to do so. Only Marcus could melt Xander's cool; only Xander could challenge Marcus's cockiness. In the end, what else could they do but become best friends? They pushed each other to go faster, to get stronger, to be *better*. Competition is all they know. Their friendship is built on the fact that they're so well matched.

Tomorrow, all that changes. Tomorrow, one of them will leave this place as a winner, and embark on his hero's journey. The other will leave a loser, and find some way to endure the rest of his pathetic life. Which means today is not a day for joking. *I couldn't have made it through this place without you,* Marcus would like to say. And *no one knows me like you do.* And maybe even *you make me want to be my best self.*

But he's not that kind of guy.

"Yeah, lucky," he agrees, and Xander knows him well enough to understand the rest.

They climb in silence for a while, battling gravity, scrabbling for purchase on the rock. Marcus's muscles scream as he stretches for a handhold a few inches out of reach, finally getting leverage with his fingertips and dragging the rest of himself up and up.

"It's probably going to be you," Xander says finally, and they both know what he's talking about. Marcus can tell Xander's trying not to breathe heavily, but the strain in his voice is plain.

"No way. Totally you," Marcus says, hoping the lie isn't too obvious.

"It's not like Endgame is even going to happen," Xander says. "Think about it—after all this time, what are the odds?"

"Nil," Marcus agrees, though this too feels like a lie. How could Endgame *not* happen for him? Ever since Marcus found out about the aliens, and the promise they'd made to return—ever since he found out about the Players, and the game—some part of him has known this was his fate. This is another difference between him and Xander, though it's one they never talk about out loud.

Marcus *believes*.

When they were 11 years old, Marcus and Xander spent an afternoon digging for artifacts at the edge of the camp's northern border. It was Xander's favorite hobby, and occasionally he suckered Marcus into joining him. What else were friends for? That day, after several long hours sweating in the sun (Marcus complaining the whole time), Marcus hit gold.

Specifically a golden *labrys*, a double-headed ax. The labrys was one of the holiest symbols of the Minoan civilization, used to slice the throats of sacrificial bulls. Marcus gaped at the dirt-encrusted object. It had to be at least 3,500 years old. Yet it fit in his palm as if it had been designed just for him.

"No one's ever found anything that good," Xander said. "It's got to be a sign. That it's going to be you who gets chosen."

"Whatever." Marcus shrugged it off. But inside, he was glowing. Because Xander was right. It did have to be a sign. The ax had chosen him—had *anointed* him. Ever since then, he's believed he will be chosen as the Player. It is his destiny.

But that's not the kind of thing you say out loud.

"It doesn't even matter which of us gets picked. Without Endgame, being the Player's just a big waste of time," Marcus says now. "Though I bet you'd be a chick magnet."

"But what good would it do you?" Xander points out. "It's not like you'd have time to actually date."

This is a game they play, the two of them. As the selection day draws closer, they've been playing it more often. Pretending they don't care who gets picked, pretending it might be better to lose.

"Imagine getting out of here once and for all," Xander continues. "Going to a real school."

"Joining a football team," Marcus says, trying to imagine himself scoring a winning goal before a stadium of screaming fans.

"Going to a concert," Xander says. He plays the guitar. (Or at least tries to.)

"Meeting a girl whose idea of foreplay isn't krav maga," Marcus says. He's still got an elbow-shaped bruise on his stomach, courtesy of Helena Loris.

"I don't know . . . I'll kind of miss that part," Xander says fondly. He's been fencing regularly with Cassandra Floros, who's promised that if he can draw blood, she'll reward him with a kiss. "But not much else."

"Yeah, me neither," Marcus says. "Bring on normal life."

He's a few meters above Xander, and it's a good thing, because it means Xander can't see his sickly, unconvincing grin. A normal life? To Marcus, that's a fate worse than death.

A fate he'd do anything to avoid.

The counselors try their best to give the kids some approximation of a normal upbringing. In their slivers of free time, campers are allowed to surf the Net, watch TV, and flirt with whomever they want. They even spend two months of every year back home with their families—for Marcus, these are the most excruciating days of all. Of course he loves his parents. He loves Turkey, its smells and tastes, the way the minarets spear the clouds on a stormy day. But it's not his world anymore; it's not his home. He spends his vacations counting the minutes until he can get back to camp, back to training, back to Xander.

Deep down, he knows this is another difference between them. Sure, Xander wants to be chosen. But Marcus wants it more.

Marcus *needs* it.

That has to count for something.

Marcus is happy to pretend that he and Xander are evenly matched, that the choice between them is a coin flip. It's easier that way; it's how friendship works. But surely, he thinks, their instructors can tell that it's an illusion. That Marcus is just a little better, a little more determined. That between the two of them, only Marcus would sacrifice everything for the game, for his people. That only Marcus truly believes he's meant to be the Player—and not just any Player, but the one who saves his people.

They're both pretending not to be nervous, but deep down, Marcus really isn't.

He knows it will be him.

It has to be.

He reaches the top with a whoop of triumph, Xander still several meters behind. Instead of savoring his victory or waiting for his best friend to catch up, he anchors his rappelling line, hooks himself on, and launches himself over the cliff. This moment, this leap of faith, it's the reward that makes all that hard work worth it. There's a pure joy in giving way to the inexorable, letting gravity speed him toward his fate.

Tomorrow, everything changes.

And it can't come fast enough.

The amphitheater is filled to capacity. Every Minoan within 200 kilometers is here to learn who their new Player will be. Marcus sits in the front row with all the other prospects, remembering the last time he was at this ceremony. He was young then, too young to understand what it meant or imagine that someday it would be him.

It's strange now, thinking about his life back then. It doesn't feel real, or at least it doesn't feel like *his* life. He was a different person then, before he knew the truth about the world and his place in it. His life, the one that matters, is defined by Endgame, and by his friendship with Xander. Before them, he was just a fraction of himself. Now he's whole.

Elias Cassadine, the camp leader, takes the podium to deliver a speech about the import of this decision and the honor he is about to bestow. Marcus has endured many a lecture by Elias, and knows the man will drone on forever about the long-lost Minoan civilization and its tradition of heroes. How the legendary King Minos was actually an alien god, who chose the Minoans, of all peoples, to live among and rule. Elias will speak of Endgame as a sacred compact between the Minoans and the beings from the stars, a chance for this chosen people to rise above the rest—if their champion can rise to the challenge. He will boast about the camp's rigorous training program and the care with which the instructors have selected their Player. As if it takes some kind of genius to pick out the best. Elias will talk duty and sacrifice, and how everyone in the audience owes a debt of gratitude to their new Player. He'll blather on forever while everyone fidgets in their seat and pretends not to be bored out of their skulls. Xander catches his eye and Marcus mimes choking himself. *Put me out of my misery,* he means, and of course Xander knows it, because Xander always knows what he means. For the last five years, everything he's done, he's done with Xander. It's going to be strange, going forward alone. Yes, he *can* do it on his own, but why would he want to?

Marcus wonders whether he might be able to talk Elias into defying tradition and letting him keep Xander around. Batman had Robin, Theseus had Daedalus—why couldn't Marcus have Xander? It's a brilliant idea, and he can't believe he didn't think of it before. He's working up some good arguments in favor of it when he realizes that Elias Cassadine has stopped droning and excited murmurs are rippling across the crowd. Beside him, Xander has gone pale.

"Meet our new Player," Elias says, and Marcus is already rising to his feet when his brain kicks in and processes what he's just heard. What he's hearing now, as Elias says it one more time, almost drowned out

14

by the thunder of the cheering Minoans.

Xander's name.

Xander's name, not Marcus's.

This isn't happening, Marcus thinks, because it can't be happening.

This is just a dream, Marcus thinks, because he's had many like it—nightmares, really, but then he always wakes up.

There is no waking up this time.

This is real. The announcement has been made. The *choice* has been made, and it's Xander who steps hesitantly up to the podium, lowers his head as Elias sets the golden horns atop his wild curls. A tribute to the legend of the Minotaur, these horns are the official marker of the chosen Player, and it's Xander who will bear them. Xander who clasps his hands over his head in triumph, Xander who's been named the best. Xander who's been named the Player.

It's Xander who's won.

It's Marcus who's been left behind.

Things move quickly after that. They are all expected to leave the camp by the end of the week. Soon a new group of children will arrive to begin seven years of training and claim the camp as their own. Marcus and the others will go back to their families, while Xander goes forward. Somewhere.

"You really can't tell me where?" Marcus says. They're packing up the room they share. Seven years of memories dumped into a few cardboard boxes, taped up, and sent away. Of all these belongings, the only one that means anything to Marcus is the golden ax—and even that has lost its shine. The labrys was supposed to mean something, was supposed to mean he was chosen. Now? It's nothing but a rusty old ax. Marcus thinks that he should offer it to Xander as a gift, a way of saying without saying, *The future belongs to you.*

Instead he tosses it in a box, and resolves to throw it away as soon as he gets the chance.

"I really can't tell you." Xander pulls out a pizza box that must have been sitting under his bed for weeks. That would explain the smell. "They swore me to secrecy about all Player stuff, and I don't think they're kidding around."

Don't be jealous, Marcus reminds himself, like this is even possible. Like he's not seething with rage.

"No worries," Marcus says. "Feel free to lord it over me with your super-special Player secrets and your exotic classified missions. I've got secrets too, you know. You'll never guess what I've got hidden in this sock drawer."

"A pack of condoms you ordered online and have been hoarding for so long they've probably turned to dust," Xander says, without missing a beat. "Plus some incredibly foul socks."

He's right on both counts. It only makes Marcus angrier.

How dare Xander keep secrets?

How dare he act like everything is the same between them, like they're still best friends, like everything is fine—when everything is ruined?

How dare he win?

There's an awkwardness between them now, a stiff silence, and Marcus knows it's his fault.

"I really thought it would be you," Xander says, not for the first time. It makes Marcus want to punch him, because how's he supposed to respond? "So did I"?

Actually, that's not a bad idea. So he says it out loud. Then laughs, like it was a joke.

Xander laughs too. Fakely. It's even worse than the silence.

Marcus knows he's acting like a spoiled brat. Like a child who doesn't get what he wants and throws a temper tantrum. But it's not like Xander's any better, with this humble *aw, shucks* act, like he's not loving every minute of this. Maybe it would be different if Xander would just own it, rub his victory in Marcus's face.

That's always been the way between them—always crowing, always bragging, never apologizing.

They could afford to be honest, because they were on such even ground.

Not now.

Now every word out of Xander's mouth sounds like an apology, and Marcus sees that for what it is: pity.

"We'll still be friends," Xander says, tossing a sweatshirt in his suitcase. It's Marcus's sweatshirt, but Marcus doesn't say anything. Xander's already taken everything that matters. What's one sweatshirt more?

"Yeah, sure," Marcus says, not even bothering to sound like he means it. "Of course." Because what's Xander going to do, come home from swimming the English Channel or battling a fleet of ninjas—then go play video games in Marcus's basement? Not going to happen.

"Anyway, I've got kind of a surprise for you," Xander says.

Marcus grunts. He's tired of surprises.

"They gave me three days before I have to leave," Xander says.

"For your magical mystery tour."

"Yeah. That. Three days . . . and access to a helicopter."

Marcus freezes. Despite his foul mood, he feels his lips drawing back in a smile. He can't stop himself.

Because he knows what a helicopter means.

"So?" Xander says, hope lighting up his face. "You in?"

With a helicopter at their disposal, they can fly from the nearby Daskalogiannis airport to Nea Kameni, a remote, uninhabited island where an active volcano pokes out of the Aegean and into the clouds. They can, as they have done before, hike up to the lip of the volcano and then rappel down into the maw of the beast, feel the heat of the lava on their backs, test themselves against the most powerful foe nature has to offer. Thirty-five hundred years ago, a volcanic eruption on the island of Thera destroyed the Minoan settlement at Akrotiri and devastated communities all along the coast of Crete. The eruption spelled the beginning of the end of Minoan civilization—now, every time Marcus bests a volcano, he feels he's striking a blow on behalf of his ancestors. It's rare they can find a way to get themselves to Nea Kameni—rarer still that Xander agrees to try. He may have overcome his childish fear of heights, but he's never much liked the idea of climbing into a massive cauldron of boiling lava. Marcus usually has to butter him up for days, whine and plead and promise to do his homework, before Xander finally gives in.

Not this time, obviously.

Xander knows what he's doing, dangling this trip before Marcus. A volcano climb is the one thing he can't resist.

"No way will they let you," Marcus says, trying hard to maintain his sulk. It's tough: Even thinking about the climb has him jittery with excitement. "You think they're going to let their precious Player risk himself on a stupid volcano?"

"Leave that to me," Xander says. "If I can't handle a few overprotective instructors, how am I supposed to save the world?"

Good question, Marcus thinks.

Then he thinks:

Enough.

Yes, a mistake has been made. Yes, Marcus deserved this win. Yes, he is in despair, and his life is pretty much over. But that's not Xander's fault. And if their positions were reversed, Xander would find a way to accept it. He would find a way to be happy for Marcus, because that's the kind of person he is.

Marcus resolves to be that kind of person too.

He resolves to be happy for Xander.

Or at least do a better job of faking it.

It is easy, at the base of the volcano, to imagine they are the last two people on Earth. That Endgame has come and gone, the human species wiped off the face of the planet, the two of them abandoned to live out their days on this bare rock. It wouldn't be so bad, Marcus thinks. Blue sky and turquoise sea, days in the sand and nights by the campfire, nothing to do but race each other up and down the volcano, no one to say who won and who lost, who is special and who is not—no obligations to their people or to the future. Only the present moment, only the two of them.

The first night, sitting around the campfire, toasting marshmallows and doing their best impressions of Elias Cassadine, it's hard to remember that this won't last forever.

They've brought tents, of course, but both of them prefer sleeping under the stars. They lie on their backs, side by side, the silence between them comfortable instead of awkward. Like it used to be, before.

"What if I can't hack it?" Xander says quietly.

"It's only a couple thousand meters," Marcus says. "You can do that in your sleep. And if you can't, I'll just toss you over my shoulder and carry you up. Not like I haven't done it before."

"That's not what I mean," Xander says.

Marcus knew that.

He doesn't want to talk about it—not now, in this place where it's so easy to forget. Once they leave here, Marcus will begin the rest of his life. His loser's life. He'll never be able to forget again. This is supposed to be their escape from all of that. And Xander is about to ruin it.

"What if it actually happens? Endgame. And it's all on me." Xander speaks slowly, like he knows this isn't anything he should admit out loud. "How do they know I'll be good enough? What if they're wrong?"

"They're not wrong," Marcus says, glad Xander can't see his face in the dark. "They know what they're doing. They've been doing this for centuries, right? If they picked you, then it's supposed to be you."

"You sound so sure," Xander says. "*Everyone* is so sure—except for me. Doesn't that mean something? That I'm not sure?"

"Not everything has to mean something," Marcus says. "You take things too seriously."

"We're talking about the end of the world," Xander says, frustration leaking through. "I'm not supposed to take that seriously?"

Marcus says nothing.

"You wouldn't have any doubts," Xander says—and, incredibly, he sounds jealous. As if *Xander* has reason for envy. "You'd know you could do it. You're probably thinking right now that you could do a better job than me. Admit it."

"Maybe I am," Marcus says, because Xander is his best friend. And because it's easier to be honest in the dark. "But maybe being sure isn't always the important thing. Maybe having doubts will make you stronger."

"How?" Xander's voice is small, almost afraid. Eager for Marcus to tell him what to do. And for that one moment, Marcus truly wishes he had the answer—knew the words that would calm Xander's fears and help him believe in himself.

But he doesn't.

"I don't know," Marcus admits.

"Exactly."

The morning is crisp and clear, perfect for a climb.

Neither of them is in the mood to talk.

They pack up their ropes and carabiners, then begin the long haul to the summit. The volcano looms above them, hissing smoke and ash into blue sky. It's like climbing any mountain, but it feels different when you know what's waiting for you at the top. When, at any moment, the cavernous mouth could spit out a glob of lava that would incinerate you in seconds.

Marcus focuses on that feeling of approaching danger. He focuses on finding handholds and footholds, on pulling himself up one arm-length at a time. On the crumbling rock beneath his fingers and the heat of the sun on his back. On the loamy smell of the rock and the twitter of distant birds. On his body, pushed to its limits; on this lonely wilderness at the edge of the world. Tunnel vision: it's another reason he's so good at climbing. To summit the great peaks, you have to shut everything else out. You have to believe nothing matters but making it to the top.

He and Xander do not race, not this time. Competition seems beside the point for them now. They climb at a steady pace, Marcus leading the way. Until, impatient to reach the summit, Marcus pushes himself to climb faster.

"Thought we weren't racing," Xander pants from behind him, which only makes Marcus speed up more.

He tells himself it's only about getting to the top. That it has nothing to do with wanting to exhaust Xander, to prove to both of them that Marcus is still the best.

But behind him, Xander breathes hard, gasping with effort, while Marcus smiles and picks up the pace.

It takes them half the day to reach the summit.

Now the fun can begin.

It's like a different planet up here—a dead, arid one choked by sulfuric gases and thick clouds of ash. The gaping vent in the rock spews clumps of lava and burps puffs of oppressively hot air. They're braving this climb without masks, and the foul gases—toxic enough to eat through metal—burn Marcus's eyes and scald his throat. Small fissures in the rock called fumaroles exhale clouds of steam, and gossamer threads of cooled lava weave eerie orange spiderwebs in the rising updraft. From Marcus's perch on the rim, the lake of lava several hundred meters below is almost completely obscured by thick ash and smoke, but the red glow is unmistakable, like a second sun. The noise is thunderous, earsplitting, an engine roar that drowns out everything else. This is an alien place; humans are not meant to survive here. Marcus loves every inch of it.

"Remind me again why I let you talk me into this?" Xander shouts over the noise as they hoist themselves over the lip of the volcano.

It's what he says every time. And every time, Marcus responds with *Because you can't say no to me.*

But that's no longer true, of course. Xander is the Player: he can say no to anyone and anything he wants. It's Marcus who's obligated to serve Xander's whims.

So instead he says, "You don't want to come, just wait here." Then propels himself over the lip of the volcano without waiting to see whether Xander will follow.

It's like traveling back in time, into an age of tectonic creation and primordial ooze.

It's like descending into the mouth of hell.

Hot air closes in with a pressure that makes his ears pop. Every breath is scalding poison. The walls are rainbowed with color, chemicals glazing the rock—orange iron, green manganese, white chlorine, cheerfully yellow sulfur. The sky above disappears behind a thick cloud, and there is only the cavernous volcano, and the sea of magma below.

Marcus stares into the frothing, sparking abyss. It's easy to imagine he's staring into the molten center of the earth.

Legend says it was a volcano that erased the ancient Minoan civilization from the face of the earth, and Marcus can believe it. His people spend so much time worrying about destruction coming from the stars—but if they knew what it was like down here, they would fear the earth just as much, its destructive power immense enough to consume itself.

That's how Marcus feels now, too: bent on destruction. Consuming himself.

He swings himself down the cable and howls into the steaming pit. All his envy and despair, his rage and frustration, his disappointment in himself and his terror of what's to come, he flings it out of himself and into the churning magma below.

It feels good.

Good enough that he looks up to the lip of the opening, where Xander still perches hesitantly on the edge, and shouts, "What are you waiting for, slowpoke?"

Xander waves, then leaps off the edge, hurtling into the air. The cable stretches taut and he swings back toward the inner wall of the volcano—and that's when it happens.

Without warning. Without reason.

The line snaps.

"Xander!" Marcus screams. There's nothing he can do but watch.

Watch his best friend plummet down and down.

Watch the broken cable dangle uselessly, too many meters overhead.

Watch Xander fling out his arms, reach blindly and desperately for purchase, for something that will slow his fall.

Watch, and hope.

Xander does it. The impossible. Catches his fingertips on a jutting rock, halts his descent. He can't stop his momentum, and his body smashes into the volcano wall with such impact that Marcus can nearly hear the crunch of bone.

"Xander," he whispers, panic stealing away his breath.

Xander is dangling by his fingertips, nothing saving him from a drop to his death but vanishing strength and sheer will. It's crazy that things could turn so wrong so quickly. But the craziest thing of all: Xander is grinning.

"Little help up here?" he calls down to Marcus, barely audible over the volcano's roar. There's a lilt in his voice, and Marcus recognizes it, that adrenaline shot of pure joy that comes from facing death and surviving. "Or you going to leave me hanging?"

It's a joke, of course. It would never occur to Xander that Marcus would just leave him there.

It wouldn't have occurred to Marcus either.

Not until Xander put the idea in his head.

It will be easy for Marcus to save him. He need only climb up to where Xander is dangling and clip him on to the intact cable. So why would Xander look worried? He assumes Marcus will do exactly what he's supposed to do. He assumes everything will work out.

Because for Xander, everything always works out.

Marcus works hard, Marcus tries, Marcus needs—while Xander just hangs around, waiting for good luck to drop into his lap. *Expecting* it.

What if this time, things go differently?

What if this time, Xander's luck turns sour?

Marcus doesn't climb up the cable. He doesn't do anything. He watches.

He watches Xander's arm muscles straining, his fingers turning white as the blood leaches out of him.

Now you know how it feels to want, Marcus thinks. *How it feels to be desperate.*

How do you like it?

The desperation is painted across Xander's face. "Marcus!" he shouts, no longer kidding around. "What are you waiting for?"

There's probably panic in his voice, but it's hard to tell, over the noise.

Marcus still doesn't move.

He tells himself: Just a few more seconds. Just enough to give Xander a taste of *need*. Just enough to scare him a little and remind him that he can't always expect the world to fall at his feet, cater to his desires.

"What the hell are you doing, Marcus!" Xander screams. *"Marcus!"*

He's losing his cool.

Marcus has always been able to make Xander lose his cool.

But what does that say? If Marcus can so easily throw Xander off his game, then how can anyone think *Xander* is the strong one? If Marcus can defeat him this easily, how can Xander expect to stand up to any of the other Players? How can he carry the fate of the Minoan people on his shoulders?

It's a mistake. Even Xander admitted that much.

Letting him continue would mean risking all their lives.

I should let him fall, Marcus thinks. *I'd be doing everyone a favor.*

It's just another joke, though.

It has to be.

Because surely he's not serious about doing nothing, watching his best friend's fingers slip from the rock, watching Xander frantically try to hang on.

Even though the thought is in his head now—and the thought makes the deed possible.

It would be that easy.

To do nothing.

To let gravity take its course.

Let Xander save himself, if he can. What could be wrong with forcing the new Player to face one simple test? To prove that he's the right man to protect his people? Or give way to the one who can?

Marcus isn't doing anything wrong.

He's just not doing *anything*.

Xander sees it in his face—knows what Marcus is going to do before Marcus knows it himself. It's always been this way between them.

"You're better than this," Xander pleads.

But it turns out he's not.

After, in his nightmares, he sees it again and again.

Xander's fingers slipping, giving way.

Xander falling.

The fall seems to take forever.

It takes enough time for Marcus to realize what he's done.

To regret.

To scream Xander's name.

To watch helplessly as Xander plunges into the lake of fire.

The churning molten rock sucks him under. Marcus doesn't see the burning lava strip away his flesh, flood his lungs, melt his bones, turn him to ash. Not in real life, at least.

In his nightmares, he sees every detail.

"I don't know what happened," Marcus tells people, and this part of the lie is easy, because it's true. "He was there—and then he wasn't."

He tells the same story to everyone: The ground crew that greets him when he staggers off the helicopter. Elias Cassadine, who collects him from the airfield, patting him on the shoulder in some sorry approximation of comfort. The other kids from camp, who gossip about every gruesome detail. Xander's parents, who will not stop crying.

"His line snapped, and I tried to help him, but I couldn't," Marcus says, over and over again. "I couldn't get there in time."

And everyone—even Xander's mother, through her tears—says, "Don't blame yourself."

He acts like a zombie, shuffling through one day and the next. It's not just for show. He feels dead inside. Hollowed out. He has to force himself to go through the motions of life. Put one foot in front of the other. Remember to eat. Remember to breathe. Do not tell the truth. *Do not.*

He wants to shout it to the world, the truth of what he's done. But maybe that's a lie too. Because if he really wanted to, he would. Instead he lies, and keeps lying. He misses Xander and blames himself, and every night as he falls asleep, he whispers a plea for forgiveness and swears that in the morning, he'll turn himself in. Then morning comes, and he lies. And every time he does, it's like killing Xander all over again.

He is chosen to be the Player in Xander's place.

"Think of it as a tribute to your friend," Elias says. Marcus tries. There is no ceremony this time around. No amphitheater filled with screaming hordes, no long speech about his impressive accomplishments and glorious future.

There is only a quiet conversation in Elias's office, an offer extended and accepted.

Of course Marcus will take Xander's place, Marcus says. Of course he will do his friend, and his people, proud.

He will keep the golden horns in a safe place, and try not to wonder whether they weighed this heavily on Xander's head.

Before Marcus can slink out of the office, Elias opens a steel safe and withdraws a clay disk, about the size of an outstretched palm. Carved with a spiraling formation of strange symbols, the artifact looks ancient. Elias places it gently in Marcus's hands. The hardened clay seems to warm to his touch.

"Do you know what this is?" Elias asks.

Marcus shakes his head.

"A century ago, archaeologists found a disk in the ruins of the Minoan palace at Phaistos," Elias explains. "It was stamped with two hundred forty-one symbols, in a language never before seen and, to this day, never deciphered. No one knows what it was for or what it might mean. It's on display in a museum in Heraklion, where historians and tourists alike can puzzle over its significance. Or"—he pauses, tapping the disk in Marcus's hands—"so we would have them believe."

"The one in the museum is a copy," Marcus guesses.

Elias nods. "The Phaistos Disk, this disk, belongs to the Minoan people. It is the most sacred talisman of our line. This language you see here is the language of the gods—those beings from the stars who birthed our civilization and will one day return to put it to the test. The disk's message spells out a challenge and a promise."

"Endgame," Marcus says in a hushed voice, awed by the thought of a message echoing through three millennia.

"Endgame," Elias agrees. "The gods love the Minoans over all peoples. The starry god King Minos descended from great heights to rule our society, to help us flourish and reign. Endgame will be our chance to prove ourselves worthy of that love. It will be *your* chance. So I ask you now, Marcus Loxias Megalos, do you swear on these sacred words that you will live up to the challenge? That you will forsake all, in the name of Endgame? That from now and ever on, you will live for the game, and for your people?"

Marcus doesn't hesitate. He doesn't have to.

He has already forsaken the only person who matters to him. He has nothing left but this.

"I do," Marcus says. "I swear."

"Then so it shall be," Elias says.

And so it is.

* * *

It turns out that supersecret Player training is pretty much like the training he got before, except that now he has to do it alone. There are no other campers—there's no Xander. No one to challenge him, to push him to greater and greater heights, no one to beat. No one to celebrate his victories or console him through his losses. Only Elias, who has taken over all his training and who spends most of his time droning about what life was like back when *he* was a Player. Which is almost worse than being alone.

Marcus is kept busy, jetting halfway across the world to pit his survival skills against the Amazon jungle, infiltrating Middle Eastern warlord encampments, studying ancient scrolls with a cloistered sect of Tibetan monks, building his strength, testing his limits, trying never to stop and think, never to remember. Never to regret.

He doesn't climb anymore, not unless he has to. Whatever joy he took in it is gone.

He gets by.

More than that, he excels.

"It's like you were born to be the Player," Elias says, more than once. Words that a younger Marcus would have killed to hear. The worst part is that Marcus knows he's right.

In a way, it's Elias's fault—if he'd only realized Marcus's greatness sooner, if he'd named Marcus the Player in the first place, then everything would have been fine. Xander would still be here. Marcus tries his best to hate Elias for this, but it's hard, because Elias Cassadine is now the closest thing he has to a friend.

Imagine how hard Xander would laugh at that.

"You need a rest," Elias says one day, after Marcus fumbles with the bomb he's disarming and nearly blows them both up.

"No way," Marcus says. "I'll get it the next time. I just need one more shot."

"You need some time off," Elias says. "Take a week. Hang out with your friends. You deserve it."

There's no arguing with Elias—and certainly no admitting that he *has* no friends anymore, which is exactly what he deserves. He knows the other kids from camp hang out together sometimes now that they are off living their regular lives, telling stories of better days. But Marcus wouldn't go, even if he were invited. He knows he would make them uncomfortable, a living reminder of their failure, and of the dead. Just as they would make him uncomfortable, pretending to be impressed by his triumph when they all know he was really a runner-up. It's better for all of them if he stays away.

So the week stretches on, endless and empty. Marcus stares at the football posters on his wall and the picture of Xander on his desk, and in the silence, the stillness, everything he's tried not to think about is impossible to escape.

One night after another, he doesn't sleep. Can't sleep.

He stays up all night, staring at the ceiling.

The last day, he visits Xander's grave for the first time.

He stands before the gravestone, shivering in the sticky summer air. It's a simple marker, bearing only Xander's name and the dates of his birth and death.

So close together.

There was a funeral, but Marcus wasn't there. He was too busy with his new training regimen.

He was too afraid.

In his hand, Marcus holds the golden horns, the official marker of his selection as a Player. It's such a silly thing, a flimsy band of fake bull horns that no one in his right mind would actually *wear*—but for so long, it was everything. A symbol of the life he wanted so desperately. And then it was a symbol of everything Xander had taken from him. The band fit so comfortably on Xander's head. Even though it didn't belong there.

Marcus sets the golden horns on the stone.

"I did what I had to do," he says. "What a champion would do. That's all."

Elias teaches that winning at all costs is more than just a phrase. That Endgame is not football, and it's not war—it's not a place for rules or for honor, for loyalty or mercy. Winning means doing whatever it takes, without hesitation or regret.

Marcus is working very hard to believe it.

"I thought you might be here," a voice says behind him.

Marcus turns around. Elias is leaning against a gravestone, a strange, knowing smile on his face. He gestures toward the horns. "I hope you're not planning to leave those here. They belong to you."

Marcus shrugs, hoping Elias can't see all the emotions, the pain, churning just beneath his surface. He's supposed to be stronger than that now. He's supposed to be invulnerable. "They were his first. All of this was."

"Until you took it from him."

Marcus has trained in relaxation and control. He knows how to master his breathing and his heart rate, how to tamp down his body's reaction to stimuli and remain physiologically unmoved by panic. There may be fireworks going off in his head, but outwardly, he's perfectly calm. Elias, he has learned, always has an agenda. Marcus waits for him to reveal it.

"What happened on that volcano, Marcus?" Elias says.

"I told you what happened."

"And now I'm asking again."

"His cable snapped," Marcus says—Marcus always says. "I tried to help him, but I couldn't." He's gotten used to lying about it—he's gotten *good* at lying about it—but it feels especially wrong to do so here, in the shadow of the grave. "I couldn't get there in time."

"You're an excellent liar," Elias says. "That will come in handy."

Marcus stops breathing.

Elias bursts into laughter. "Oh, wipe that deer-in-the-headlights look off your face, Marcus, you're better than that."

Marcus tries to remember what he's been taught, remember his breathing, but it's hard to find his calm center when every nerve ending in his body is screaming.

Elias knows the truth.

He knows.

He knows.

"We're both men here," Elias says. "It's time to be honest."

"His cable snapped. I tried to help him, but I couldn't." Marcus knows he sounds like a robot, but he's capable of nothing else. "I couldn't get there in time."

Elias shakes his head, still chuckling. "Okay, then, how about I tell the truth. His cable snapped? Yes. You tried to help him? No. You watched and did nothing while your best friend hung on for dear life? Yes. You watched and did nothing while he fell to his death, then came home and lied about it, stole everything that was supposed to be his?"

Marcus swallows hard. His tongue feels huge in his mouth, clumsy and incapable of speech. His throat is clenched, his breath gone. But he manages to squeeze out the necessary word: "Yes."

"Yes," Elias says. "Yes. Good. Yes. That's a start. And don't you want to ask me something now?"

Marcus stares at him blankly. He's waited for this moment for so long, for someone to ferret out the truth, for the consequences to crush him. He's pictured this moment, but never past it. He doesn't know what happens next.

"You want to ask me how I know," Elias prompts.

"How do you know?" Marcus says obediently, although he doesn't care. He doesn't see how it could matter.

"I know because I was there," Elias says. "Many of us were. We all wanted to see for ourselves what you would do when the opportunity presented itself."

Marcus gapes at him, wheels turning. Because if Elias was there, waiting and watching, that meant he knew something would happen, which meant—

"Good, you're keeping up," Elias says. "Alexander's cable snapped because our sniper shot it."

"You were testing him?" Marcus says in wonder.

Elias sighs, obviously disappointed. "For someone who's so sure he deserves to be a Player, you're not very quick on the uptake. We were testing *you*."

The words are like an explosion; Marcus could swear the ground is shaking beneath him. Thunder roars in his ear. The muted colors of the graveyard burst so bright he needs to shut his eyes against the pain of them.

This is how it feels, when your world falls apart and remakes itself into something you don't recognize.

When everything you thought was solid melts away.

"It was always going to be you, Marcus," Elias says. "It was obvious the first day I met you. But we had to know how much you wanted it. We had to know how far you would go—how much you would sacrifice for victory."

Marcus concentrates on standing still. It takes all the energy he has to hold his muscles rigid. He fears that if he relaxes his control, even for a second, he will collapse. Or he will lunge at Elias and pummel him to death.

He thinks about relaxing his control.

Thinks hard.

Instead he forces out the obvious question. "Why are you telling me this? Why now?"

"Because it's time for you to grow up," Elias says. He takes the golden horns off Xander's grave. "Stop sulking. Stop beating yourself up— what's done is done. You made a choice, and it's a part of you now. You know what you're capable of, and that's a good thing. It's something you won't soon forget." He presses the horns into Marcus's hands. Marcus wants to let them drop to the dirt—but instead his fingers close around them, the sharp point of a horn digging into his palm.

"You're the Player now," Elias says. "*You*, not Alexander. Time to start acting like it."

* * *

It should make some kind of difference.

It should make *all* the difference.

It means that everything Marcus has been telling himself, all those lies about obligation and noble sacrifice, about doing what must be done for the good of his people . . . they're all true. If Endgame comes during his tenure—and it must come, it *has* to come, or else what was the sacrifice for?—the Minoans will have a champion worthy of them. A Player who knows exactly what he's capable of, and can never forget it.

It means death was simply Xander's fate. Letting him die, that was Marcus's.

He only did what he was supposed to do.

What he was meant to do.

This is the gift Elias has given him: his new truth.

He'll spend the rest of his life trying to believe it.

SUMERIAN

KALA

It begins in motion.

For Kala, life is motion.

Life is blazing sun and endless desert dunes. Life is duty and honor. Life is Playing and life is winning.

And winning means staying in motion. Being the fastest. Being the strongest. Being the best.

She is running.

Mile after mile, noon sun scorching the earth, sweat soaking her shirt and brow, feet *pound-pound-pound*ing the sand, muscles screaming, joints pulsing, heart thumping, brain willing *go go go*.

But she cannot go as fast as she needs, because the boy in front of her is too slow. This is a team training exercise, run in single file, let the leader set the pace, and Kala is not the leader. She pumps and gasps behind him, her breath on his neck, hoping he'll get the message. Kala hates this kind of exercise, hates having to depend on someone else to get things right.

Faster.

Behind her, the long tail of her cohort stretches along the sand. If she looked back, she would see a straight line of identical black uniforms and identically determined runners, their feet pounding in lockstep, their dreams fixed on the same distant goal of becoming the Player. But Kala never looks back.

The boy in front of her, unfortunately, follows a different rule. He turns toward her, opens his mouth as if to speak—and stumbles over his own feet. He catches himself, but not soon enough: Kala slams into him, and they both go down in a tangle of sweaty limbs.

The line of Players-in-training races on. Even in team exercises, the fallen are to be left behind.

"Watch it!" Kala snaps, extricating herself from the boy.

"It's impossible not to," he says. She is already back on her feet, but he sprawls in the sand as if lounging at the beach. His eyes pin her in place.

For a moment, all is still.

As if time has stopped.

And the world has narrowed, so there is only her.

And only him.

"Whatever," she says, then shakes it off and starts running. If she's fast enough, she can catch up with the group.

She's always fast enough.

The boy's name is Alad. That's what he calls himself, at least. His official designation is 37DELTA. All the Players-in-training are assigned numbers instead of names. They had names when they were born, just like they had families. But when the minders choose a child for training, all record of the past is erased. The children are snatched from their homes at age four, raised in a communal camp, assigned a number and a series of minders, and, very quickly, they forget there is any other way. When they're old enough to care, they choose a name for themselves.

Kala is 5SIGMA. She chose the name Kala because it means "time," and time is the enemy she plans to conquer. Time is what lies between her present in this camp and her future beyond it. Her life is a ticking clock, hours to fill and be disposed of.

She used to wonder if she would have liked her real name as much.

The minders don't like it when you say *real name*.

This is the real you, they say. *This is the only you there is*.

Blood muddies the water, they say. *Players must stay clear*.

This is why they have no family but one another.

Some of the Players-in-training in her cohort have bonded, formed tight cliques and pairings, but Kala has never bothered. She has always felt separate from them. She has always known herself to be different. It's so easy for them to accept what they've been told, to believe what they're meant to believe. They've been told they must *want* to win, they must *need* to win, and so they do. They've been told that this life, this training, should fill them up, and so it does.

They've been told not to think about the world beyond this camp, or a future beyond Playing; they've been told nothing matters beyond the game.

And so they do not; and so it does not.

It would be easier, if she could be like them. But Kala has never been filled up by this life. She remains hollow. She stays in motion so she can ignore the empty hole at her center, so she doesn't have to worry about what's wrong with her that nothing is ever enough. She runs, because every step forward is a step away from here, into a future where she will have more. At least, she has to believe she will. That someday she will know what it is to feel, to want, to need.

She has never been able to imagine what that might be like.

Until now.

She has never paid much attention to Alad. After the run, after the fall, he is everywhere. He sits beside her at meals. He manages to be chosen as her sparring partner in combat drills and her spotter in strength training. He fires beside her in target practice and grins when her perfectly aimed bullets tear the target to shreds. She nearly falls over him on the camouflage field, where he has turned himself into a creature of sand and lies still and prone in the seemingly unbroken stretch of brown. He distracts her with a wink as she's arming grenades, and she nearly blows them both up.

He distracts her a lot.

He is always watching her. When she points this out to him, he grins. "How would you know?" he says. "Unless you're watching me too."

She is watching. She notices things about him she somehow never saw before: The way his dark eyes crinkle when he smiles. The way his muscles ripple under his shirt, and the thin line of hair trailing down from his belly button when the shirt comes off. His forearms, and the way the veins bulge when he bears her weight. The curve of his neck, the line of his back, the glow of his skin in the sun, the languid grace of his movements, never urgent, always assured. His lips—quirked in a smile, pursed in a frown, tight with anger or loose with laughter, but always, always, full and soft and waiting.

She really needs to stop noticing his lips.

Alad is quiet like her, but there is a kindness to his quiet. While she is an isolated unit, closed off to distraction and connection, he is open to the world, noticing all. Noticing her. She is always in motion, but he is still. When she sits beside him, the silence filling the space between them, she can feel his stillness encompass her. When he is near, the urge to run, to fight, to *move* falls away. There is no need to escape from her thoughts, because her thoughts are of him.

And she doesn't mind.

Alad pretends not to push himself. He doesn't let the others see how hard he works to be the fastest or the best.

"Why bother trying?" she hears him say to one of his bunkmates. "It's not like it's a race. Who knows how they choose the Player?"

The truth is, no one knows. There are nearly 100 of them in this cohort. They were all born within a few months of one another, all taken from their parents and brought to this place. Many are from Iraq; others come here from Kuwait, Qatar, Syria. There is even a girl from Scotland. They have in common only their Sumerian bloodline—and their determination to win.

Only one of them can.

From these 100 rigorously trained potentials, a single Player will be selected.

The Player will train even harder, will prepare, will wait for Endgame. Those not chosen will live to serve him. And, somewhere in the desert, another cohort, several years younger than Kala's, eagerly awaits its turn, for when that Player ages out. Somewhere else, a hundred weeping four-year-olds struggle to understand what's become of their lives. They too will grow up to Play this game, and after them more children will be taken from their homes, more children will train, more children will wait.

The cycle has played out for millennia, and it will never end. Not until Endgame finally comes, and the chosen Player gets her chance to Play. No one knows when the choice will come, and no one knows why. You simply wake up one day to discover that one of your own is gone, and that is the Player. Which means you are not.

This, at least, is what they have heard.

Each of the bloodlines has its own strategy for picking a Player. Kala knows she is supposed to believe the Sumerian way is the best. But it's difficult, when no one seems quite sure what the Sumerian way *is*. Alad claims not to care, but Kala can see him straining to be the best. She can see how much he wants it, how he believes that his efforts will be enough. And sometimes the minders do pick the strongest in the cohort, sometimes the smartest. But sometimes the choice makes no obvious sense. They have picked scrawny Players and foolish ones, saintly Players who care only for their bloodline and egomaniacal Players who will Play only for themselves. The last Player was chosen six years ago, after the one before that died unexpectedly in training, a dagger through his chest. Kala remembers when the girl was chosen, remembers the swirling rumors: she was immune to pain; she was a record-breaking weight lifter; she was chosen by the flip of a coin. Kala tries not to listen to gossip, but she can't ignore the chatter about what is to come. The current Player is about to age out—a new one is needed. So the choice will come soon, they know that much. There is nothing they can do but train and wonder and wait.

And, of course, speculate endlessly about the choice: when it will come, how it will be made. This is the favorite hobby of Kala's cohorts, and they never shut up about it.

Kala doesn't play along. She's never seen the point. She likes that Alad doesn't see it either.

Friendship in the camp is not encouraged, but neither is it forbidden. And somehow, without realizing it, Kala lets Alad become her friend. They begin to count on each other; more than that, they begin to know each other. When they spar, she can anticipate his movements—recognize a feint, block a punch before he throws it. At meals, Alad now reaches without asking for her untouched saltah, at least when the stew is made with goat, which she detests. When he can get his hands on some halvah, he always snags extra for her, though never enough to satisfy her sweet tooth. They don't talk about anything that matters, but then, no one talks about things that matter. Nothing is permitted to matter except their training. Not their hopes for the future, and certainly not their faded memories of the past.

Everyone has at least a few that they hold precious and secret. Kala remembers a red stuffed elephant named Balih, and she remembers her mother's smell, a comforting waft of saffron and nutmeg.

At least, she thinks it was her mother.

She prefers to believe that.

Even without talking, Kala can sense Alad's moods. When he broods, she can almost see the dark cloud hovering over him—and when he brightens up, he nearly sparkles. He brightens often when she is near, and it makes her feel sparkly as well.

Which is ridiculous.

She tells herself that this is a natural bond between two warriors. That it will make her stronger, and strength is what she needs to endure the passage of time. That maybe this—knowing someone inside and out, needing them near, skin prickling when they are—is what it means to be family.

Kala doesn't know much about family. But she knows family doesn't make your stomach flip when they smile. Family's touch doesn't feel like an electric charge.

Kala doesn't believe in lying to herself, so she is forced to admit: it is not family, and it is not friendship. It is something more.

And something more is definitely forbidden.

Kala swings the ax in a wide circle. It cracks hard against the staff of Alad's ax. Her teeth clack together with the impact.

Alad feints left, swings right, Kala anticipates him, blocks the attack. She always anticipates him.

He is fast; she is faster.

"You're dragging today," he teases her. An undercurrent of tension hums in his voice. He's lost three bouts in a row, and he's about to lose this one too.

They both know how much he wants to win.

"I'm just taking it easy on you," Kala says, and pretends this is a joke. She leaps gracefully as he swings his ax at her ankles. The blade whirs harmlessly beneath her feet. Kala twists in the air, head over heels, landing behind him, her ax already in motion.

He dances away just in time. The blade slashes at his tunic, tears through the thin cotton. She can see his anger rising, has come to recognize the telltale signs. The sweat beading at his neck, the twitch of his ear, the way his grip tightens on the ax. He's not angry at her—never at her. He's angry at himself.

She attacks; he blocks.

She attacks again; he blocks, swiftly and surely.

But she can feel his ax give way to hers when she bears her weight against it, and she knows his arms are tiring.

She wields the ax like it's weightless. Like it's an extension of her arms. She spins and dances, whirls and leaps. In her hands the blade is a quicksilver, a blur of deadly motion.

"I'm just waiting for the perfect moment to make my move," he says, and jabs at her. She grins at his boast as she darts from reach.

She can hear the gasps beneath his words. He's tiring. She could fight forever.

Instead she swings the ax up hard, then turns it at an abrupt right angle, spins around, knocks his feet out from under him. That fast he is on his back, the tip of her ax pressed to his chest.

He smiles up at her, and she can see what it costs him to lose, and to bear it. "You're beautiful when you're a sore winner," he says.

"I didn't say anything," Kala protests.

"You're thinking it." He winks.

She clasps his hand and pulls him to his feet. Every time they fight, he hopes to win, but she knows he never will.

It's not that he's a lesser fighter. It's that he's too eager to win. Too needful. When Kala takes a weapon in her hand, she gives way to the emptiness at her center. She needs nothing but to make clean cuts, to let the ax or dagger or sword do its job. She lets herself not care— because she has come to understand that in battle, caring gets in the way.

She's glad Alad doesn't ask for the secret of her triumph. She doesn't want him to know how easy it is for her. Especially now that she sees there is another way. Now that she sees what it is to be desperate, to *need*. She envies his heat, draws close to him as if to warm herself on his fire.

She wonders, sometimes, if her fighting will suffer. But it's easy to put that fear out of her mind.

There's a certain advantage in knowing how not to care.

They sleep in bunkhouses—one for the boys, one for the girls—as it has always been. Little more than cabins of hard clay, with narrow cots and cubbyholes for their belongings. They have very few belongings: knives and swords, of course, tangles of circuitry, and favored toxins. Some girls fashion jewelry from wire and polished stones, and everyone eventually figures out how to scam personal pleasure items out of the minders. Stuffed animals, when they were small, then puzzles and games, now comic books and football banners. They all have their own laptops, of course, and while access to the internet has been disabled, they were all taught to program, to hack, to build and rebuild the circuits from scratch, before they were 10 years old—if they want to punch through a firewall and connect with the world, no one can stop them.

Their laptops are frequently searched for contraband material; their belongings are itemized and approved. There are no locks, no doors, no privacy, but none of this is needed. After all, they have no secrets from one another, or from their minders.

Or, at least, they are not supposed to.

Those who keep secrets learn early to keep them in their heads.

This is where Kala keeps her shreds of memory, the scents and colors of a family that has probably long since forgotten her. No one knows how carefully she has pieced together these fractured shards, trying so hard to make some comprehensible picture come into view. She doesn't know why it matters to her and to no one else. Maybe because she's missing a piece of herself. She believes that if she knew them, could find them and face them, she could fill the puzzle in.

This is her most dangerous secret.

It has, for so long, been her only secret. After tonight, she will have two.

Kala sleeps beneath the southernmost window. The moon is already setting when Alad appears at the opening, the stars bright. Something has kept Kala awake. Like she knew he was coming. She is ready.

They have spent years practicing the art of subterfuge, so it is nothing for her to ease out of bed and launch herself silently through the window. The other girls never stir in their sleep. It occurs to her that she may not be the first to have had a midnight caller—how many girls have tiptoed past her cot, slipped open the door or climbed out the window? How many have breathed in the night air and the musky scent of nerves and need, clasped hands, and run into the night?

She prefers not to know. She doesn't want to think of this as something usual, *common*. There is nothing common about the way she feels when Alad takes her hand and looks at her, so full of fear and hope, nothing usual about their soft footsteps padding across the camp until they reach a secluded clearing, within the perimeter of the base but still far beyond prying eyes. The camp is built on an excavated lake bed, one of the few areas in this arid corner of the country where clay and stone interrupt the endless miles of sand. There is nothing here but the scratchings of spiders, the bare rock, and the two of them.

Kala should be nervous. Of being caught—of *not* being caught, and whatever happens next. But when he cups her chin in his strong hands, when he whispers, "I couldn't wait any longer," when she closes her eyes and some powerful force draws their lips together, it all feels too right for worry.

It is like running. No thought, only motion: only breath, only heartbeat, only the body and its needs.

Except there is no motion now.

She has never felt more still. She never wants to move from this place, from his arms.

"You're so beautiful," he tells her, and she goes tense, because she knows it to be a lie. She knows her green eyes are too wide apart and her slim, muscled body is all sharp lines and hard edges. Her black hair is hacked off close to her scalp, which makes her ears look huge. These aren't things she minds, but they are things she knows.

Then he continues.

"You're like a living weapon," he says quietly. She can feel his lips move against the skin of her neck. "A blade. Shining in the night. The way you move, the way you *strike* . . . it's like liquid starlight."

She understands now. When he says *beautiful*, he means *strong*.

Where he finds strength, he sees beauty.

In this, most of all, they are the same.

"I was afraid you wouldn't want this," he whispers. "Me."

She is afraid of how much she wants it.

Him.

Their kisses are urgent, their embrace furious, hands and lips exploring uncharted territory, skin warming to the touch, burning with contact, with need.

Kala has always wondered what it would feel like, the connection to another person, the thing called love, but she has never really understood it.

Somehow, her body knows what to do.

After, they talk.

Not like before, when they talked like everyone else, about nothing. Now, it is like a door has been thrown open. Kala has never even realized that she wanted to talk, to give voice to all her carefully hidden thoughts. She's never seen the point. But she must have wanted it, because talking with him is almost as satisfying as being with him. Every word is a release.

They meet every night, and lie together under the stars.

Everything Kala knows about love she learned from the movies. Or at least from the movies they are allowed to stream on their computers—and the ones the minders don't know they stream.

The minders consider some movies to be good practice for learning foreign languages; the Players-in-training consider it good practice for the life they will someday live beyond the barbed wire of this encampment.

In the movies, when a boy and a girl lie together beneath a jewel-studded sky, the boy charts the constellations for the girl and awes her with his understanding of the cosmos. Kala and Alad memorized the map of the sky when they were children. For those who know what is to come, there is no beauty in the stars, only danger.

He cannot awe her. Everything he knows, she knows, and vice versa. So they talk about what they don't know.

"What do you think it's like, growing up in a family?" she asks him.

"Total hassle," he says. "You're always trying to make curfew or getting grounded, you have to do the dishes and take out the trash, and I bet you'd get in real trouble if you set off a grenade in the backyard."

Kala sighs happily, thinking of the homemade explosives she tested yesterday, which turned an old equipment shed to a heap of ash. "I would miss grenades," she admits.

"Besides, they're sort of like family," he says. "The minders."

She laughs. "They're *nothing* like family."

"And how would you know?"

"You remember the day your first minder left?" she asks, and she can feel his muscles tense beneath her fingers. "That's how I know."

By this point, they have been through dozens of minders, some lovable and some forgettable, some who changed their lives and some who seemed determined to ruin them. No minder stays with them for more than a few months—it's the best way to prevent personal attachments from forming—and eventually their faces begin to blur together. But no one forgets their first.

When the children are brought to the camp at age four, each one is assigned a minder. Kala's was a round woman with a stern voice but a ready smile: Hebat, which means "lady of the skies" in the ancient language of their people. Alad's was Kingu, "the great emissary." Kala barely remembers this time, but she remembers feeling frightened and alone, clinging to Hebat's skirt with chubby toddler fists. She remembers how Hebat wiped her tears when she cried and helped her blow her nose when she was ill. Hebat taught her how to speak Persian and Sanskrit, to dress herself and tie her shoes, to brush her teeth and wrap her hair into braids. Hebat read her to sleep at night, and by eagerly looking over her burly shoulder, Kala taught herself to read too. Hebat was her entire world—and then, one day, Hebat was gone.

Gone without saying good-bye.

Gone without leaving any word of how to contact her.

Gone for good.

Everyone's first minder leaves like this; it is the first important lesson Players-in-training must learn. No one person matters; no personal attachment lasts. After that first year, they are placed in a series of ever-shifting groups—different units within the larger cohort, different minders, different camps. She and Alad have been in the same grouping for a few weeks, and Kala already lives in fear that he will be taken away from her. Nothing and no one stays the same here for more than a few months. The only constant in life is Endgame.

Kala has never spoken of her first minder to anyone. "Mine was Hebat," she says now. "I really thought she loved me."

"We all thought that," Alad admits.

"I know that now, obviously. But for years, I felt like such an idiot." Something else she's never said aloud. But it feels like she can tell Alad anything. Or at least almost anything. "Like it was this secret shame. That I'd fallen for her act. Imagine that, five years old and already beating myself up for not seeing through the bullshit."

After Hebat, Kala was different. That was the first sliver of ice in her heart. The beginning of the cold, the empty. After Hebat, she had *wanted* not to feel, had wanted to forget her beloved minder and the parents who came before. She was angry and alone, and so she taught herself not to care. By the time the anger faded and the loneliness grew, by the time she needed to care again, she no longer remembered how.

Maybe if she found them again, the ones she'd left behind . . . maybe if she could remember the faces of her mother and father, she could remember everything else she'd lost.

She needs to be whole again, now more than ever. Because now she has him.

"It was a good lesson," Alad says. "I bet you never fell for anyone's bullshit again."

"It was a cruel lesson."

"To prepare us for cruel lives. To harden us."

"Maybe I didn't want to be hard," she says.

He presses his lips to the smooth flesh of her stomach, and even though there is nothing beneath it but rigid muscle, he says, "I bet we can still find a few soft spots. If we try."

Sometimes, it's better not to talk.

They avoid each other now, during the day, so no one will suspect the thing between them. It's agony to stare at him from across the room while she should be working on her ancient Sumerian translations, wanting to brush aside the lock of hair that's fallen across his eyes, knowing she can't. But it's the delicious kind of agony, like pressing on a bruise. It distracts her from her training. She's slowed down, and people notice.

"What's different about you?" Britney asks one night, as they brush their teeth, and Kala nearly laughs with delight. She likes the idea that there is something different about her, that the other girls can see her happiness painted on her skin, a badge of honor.

"It's a mystery," she says, and Britney shakes her head and then, for good measure, her booty. (Britney named herself after her favorite American pop star and never lets anyone forget it.) She's used to Kala keeping her secrets to herself; they all are.

But this is the first time Kala wishes she didn't have to.

Alad is terrified of what will happen if the minders find out. Kala, on the other hand, can't bring herself to worry. "What's the worst they can do to us?" she asks him, tickling the spot behind his knee where he's especially sensitive.

"I don't even want to think about it," he says.

But she has thought about it. A lot. The worst they can do is disqualify her from being a Player. Would that be so bad?

She's played hard because she's liked how it feels to win, because it's a good way to pass the time. The others are all so desperate to be selected, to gain the recognition, to earn the chance to save their people. For Kala, all of that has always rung hollow, like everything else. Player. Endgame. Bloodline. Nothing but words, no more or less important than any others.

Now she has something real.

Now she knows what it is to really care, and she knows what she wants. All she wants.

Alad.

Let them discover the truth. Let them send her away. What does it matter to her, as long as Alad goes with her?

And she knows he would.

He loves her as much as she loves him.

She can tell.

"I wish we could stay here all night," Alad tells her, in the place she has come to think of as *their* place, the clearing dusted with pebbles and moonlight. "I wish I could wake up beside you."

"Someday," she says, then stops.

They never talk about the future.

"Someday this will be all be over and we can be together for real," he says.

She wants to freeze this moment in time and live inside it forever.

"Tell me," she says. "Tell me a story." She nuzzles her head into the curve of his shoulder and presses her palm to his. She likes that their hands are exactly the same size. That they know the same languages and can perform the same complex algorithms and multivariable equations with the same lightning speed. That he is slightly stronger but she is slightly faster. This is not how it is in the movies, but that doesn't matter. She thinks this is the way it should always be.

"Once upon a time, there was a handsome boy and a beautiful girl." His voice is like honey, slow and deliberate. "They grew up together, but even though the girl was very smart, she was slow to notice the obvious."

"Which was?"

He grins. "Which was that the boy was amazing. A prince among men."

"I bet the girl wasn't too shabby herself."

"You bet right," he says. "The girl was . . . she was a miracle."

The word sits between them. He does love her, she knows that now, without a doubt. It's not just the things he says; it's the way he says them. The way he looks at her when he does.

She wonders if that would change, if he knew her secret—if he knew what she's done.

"The boy and girl were forbidden to be together, but they found a way," he continued. "Every night, they came together and—"

She puts a finger to his lips. "It's not polite to kiss and tell."

He clears his throat. "And had a very nice time. Then, one day, the boy was chosen as his generation's Player."

"Oh, the *boy*?" she says.

"Naturally."

She gives him a teasing shove. "Sexist pig."

"Oink."

"If you think just because you're the guy, you—"

"May I continue with my story?" he asks her.

She can't play mad for long. She doesn't care who is named the Player in this story, any more than she does in life. She doesn't care about the game; she wants to know what happens after. "You may," she says.

"*Anyway*, the boy was chosen to be his generation's Player, not because he was a boy, which is a stupid thing to assume, but because he was a magnificent example of the human species, quite possibly the apotheosis of the race."

"And modest too."

"Exactly." Alad strokes her as he speaks, his fingers trailing back and forth across her body in time with his words.

"The boy and girl were separated for a time . . ."

She wants to make a joke here, to keep the mood light, to prove to him and to herself that the story isn't real, but she can't do it. The thought of being separated from him, it's like a physical ache. Like imagining someone amputating a limb.

"But their sacrifice was worth it," he says. "Because the boy acquitted himself admirably as a Player, and when his tenure was over—"

"Uneventfully."

"When his completely lacking in eventfulness tenure was over, he was showered with all the rewards that accrue to a Player past his prime. Fame, fortune, power."

This much, she knew, was true. Former Players had their pick of the good life—the rest of their bloodline saw to it that they got whatever they wanted, as thanks for their years of duty and sacrifice. Players-in-training got no such advantage: You were sent on your way with a small bank account and a forged high school diploma, and you hoped that would be enough. You spent the rest of your life on call to any Player who might need you—except for the ones who came crawling back, volunteering to be minders, because they could imagine no other life. But actual Players? It was like winning the lottery. Assuming you survived long enough to cash in your ticket.

"Totally free of responsibility and obligation, the boy and girl moved to a beautiful mansion in Abu Dhabi. They got married and had two very handsome sons, and promised each other they would never be apart another day in their lives. And they lived happily ever after."

Kala rolls over on her side so she can get a clear look at his face. "So do you really want that?" she asks.

"What, marriage? Kids? Yeah. I know we're young, but eventually . . ."

"No, not that. I mean, yes, that, I'm glad you want that, because . . ."

She shakes her head. Everything's getting muddled. Until tonight they have never talked about the future, and now suddenly it's all laid out before her, a street paved with gold. It's so much, so fast. And there's so much he still doesn't know about her. "I mean, do you really want to be chosen as the Player?"

"Of course I do." He sits up, looks at her like she's a stranger. "Don't you?"

She sits up too, and takes his hands. It's good to hold them, but not as good as it is to be held by them, to curl her body into his embrace and feel cut off from the rest of the world. "I guess? I don't know, I never gave it much thought."

"Yeah, I can see how that would be, given that it's *our entire purpose in life*. And has been since we were born."

"Not since we were born," she says quickly. Because that's the whole point.

"Get picked as the Player and you get *everything*," he says. "It's not just an honor; it's being set for a lifetime. You watch so many movies— but do you know what the world's really like? The world outside Hollywood? It's hard and it's expensive and it's getting shittier every day. Yeah, I want to be the Player. I want the chance to save the world. And after, I'll have enough money and power to live life the way I want to live it." He gives her hands a very gentle squeeze. "And protect the people I love."

Love. It is the first time either of them has said the word.

Except that Players don't love. Everyone knows this. Those chosen to be the Player are broken of the habit of love, and they never regain it. Even those who live on to old age choose to die alone.

He must tell himself that he will be different. Kala has noticed this about human nature: everyone likes to believe they are the exception to the rule.

She's not going to argue with him, certainly not after he's used that word. Letting someone believe whatever he needs to—maybe that is also love.

"It was a good story," she tells him. "Really good."

"How about you?"

"I'm not really much for stories," she says.

"No, I mean, what do *you* want?"

She reaches for him, with pointed purpose.

He laughs and pushes her away. "Aside from the obvious, I mean."

Now is the moment. She can lie to him, make up some trivial desire, some stupid thing like a motorcycle or a Nobel Prize—or she can show him the part of herself that she's been keeping secret all this

time. Say it out loud, this truth that she's never exposed to the light.
She can trust him enough to hear her dark desire, the desperate wish
at the base of her life, and love her anyway.

Maybe he will even understand her dream.

Maybe he will share it.

She turns away from him and, for good measure, closes her eyes. She
doesn't want to see his face when she admits it.

"I want a family," she says.

"What, like kids? You know I want to give you that. I mean, not
anytime soon, obviously, but—"

"No," she says, though it would be easy enough to let it go. "I mean,
yes, I want that too, someday, but that's not what I mean. I want *my*
family. The people I came from. The people they took me away from."

"Oh."

She can't read his voice, and after a long moment of silence, she
can't stand it anymore. She turns back to him. He searches her face,
and she loves him for trying to understand. But she can see that he
doesn't.

"Don't you ever think about it?" she says. "Where you came from?
Who you belong to?"

"Why would I think about that? They gave us away, Kala."

"We don't know that," she says. "We don't know anything. What
makes you so sure it was their choice? Has anyone ever given *us* a
choice?"

She's ready now, charged with anger. If she can just make him see
it, then she can tell him everything. About the late nights spent
hacking through the camp's firewalls, searching for back doors to
password-locked archives, decoding encrypted files. About what she's
spent so long looking for—and what she's found.

About how she hasn't done anything about it, not yet. Hasn't known
what to do, until now.

Now, they can do it *together*.

"You know why it has to work this way," he says, and it almost sounds like he's chastising her. "You don't give toddlers a choice. You make smart choices for them, for their own good. For *everyone's* good."

"And now? We're not toddlers anymore, Alad."

"And now we choose to do what needs to be done to protect our people," he says. "Or at least *I* do."

You sound like a robot, she wants to tell him. *You sound brainwashed.*

"This is bigger than us," he says. "This is the end of the world. The survival of the race. If our birth families didn't want to give us away, then they were being selfish. Some things are worth a sacrifice."

"What if someone tried to take me away from you?" she asks.

"That's never going to happen."

"But if it did?"

"I would never let anyone take you away from me," he says, voice deadly serious. "I promise."

But a promise is more than just the word. They both know he can't promise her anything, not really. Their lives have no space for any promises except the promise they've made to the cause. The promise they were forced to make.

She doesn't point this out to him. She doesn't want to argue, or to talk about duty or families or promises anymore. For once, she doesn't want to talk at all. She kisses him to win his silence, and keep it. Easier not to hear the judgment in his voice, the doubt.

There's no doubt in his touch.

And in the quiet of his arms, she can imagine that, deep down, they are the same.

It happens the next day. There's no warning, no portent in the sky or tension in the air, some flashing neon sign to indicate *This is the day everything changes.* There's just a tap on her shoulder as she cools down after her afternoon run, a whisper in her ear that she's wanted in the central office.

Her first thought, her only thought, is that they know about her and Alad. Because what else could it be?

Stepping into the office is like crossing into a different world. The only part of the camp with central air-conditioning, the room offers no hint that it's in the middle of the Rub' al-Khali, the biggest sand desert in the world. The room's air is crisp and cool, its lines sleek and modern—they could be in a luxury high-rise in the heart of Abu Dhabi. Except that, through the window, the desert stretches on and on.

Three minders are seated along one side of a conference table: Adar, who runs the weapons range; Ninsuna, who oversees discipline; and Zikia, who teaches military strategy or, as she puts it, how to win. Unlike the other minders, Zikia has never stayed at the camp for more than a week or two—but also unlike the others, she always comes back. Hardened by training and age, Zikia seems molded from steel. Her expression is sharp enough to cut. It is from Zikia that Kala has learned to appear weak when she is strong, and appear strong when she is weak.

But this depends on knowing the difference between face and mask, and in this moment, Kala does not. She feels strong and weak in equal measure.

If Zikia is here, summoning her, then this is bigger than she expected. This is real trouble.

"5SIGMA," Zikia says, giving her a sharp nod. Kala has always liked the tough old woman. An aging former Player, she is good at mustering charm when she needs to persuade, but there is always steel in her eye. Kala appreciates that, unlike the other minders, she does not pretend to care about any of them.

Kala stops midway between the minders and the doorway, and waits for them to speak her transgression, and her punishment.

As long as she and Alad can stay together, nothing else matters.

And they will stay together.

He promised.

Zikia pulls her lips back in a chilling smile. "Congratulations," she says. "You've been chosen."

It's so far from what Kala is expecting to hear that it takes her a moment to understand. "Chosen for what?" she asks, and then the foolishness of the question sinks in. What else is there to be chosen for? What has there ever been?

"You will be our Player."

Now all three of them are smiling. They have the look of jackals watching the weakest member of a herd fall behind, biding time before they pounce.

"I don't understand," she says.

"Six months from today, the current Player will age out," Zikia says. "At which point the honor will fall to you."

Kala told Alad she didn't know whether she wanted to be the Player. That wasn't a lie. It had seemed so unlikely, and so huge, even her imagination couldn't encompass it.

Now that the moment is here, she knows exactly what she does and doesn't want.

She doesn't want the responsibility.

She doesn't want a new life that's even more restricted, more circumscribed by obligation, more dictated by the needs of others.

She doesn't want to sacrifice herself, even for the survival of her people.

She doesn't want to spend years waiting for death to rain down from the sky, knowing that when it does, she will have to act.

She wants to cry.

But Kala has been well trained. She has been molded into a warrior, a flesh-and-blood weapon, sleek and strong and always in control. She is not capable of falling apart, even when she wants to.

When she speaks, her voice does not tremble. "Can I ask you, ma'am, why me? Britney is a better fighter, Farzin is much better at military strategy, and—" She cuts herself off just before she can say his name. Alad wants this so much, for himself.

What will he think when he finds out she's taken it from him?

"You can ask, but we're under no obligation to answer," Zikia says. "All you need know is that we have faith in our choice. Yes, along some vectors, others are superior to you. But you are the only one capable of Playing the game as it needs to be Played. It must be you."

The message is clear: the choice is theirs, not Kala's.

No one is going to ask her whether this is what she wants. This is what it *is*, and she's meant to accept it.

"Tomorrow you and I will begin your training."

"Begin?" she says. Her mouth is working of its own accord. Her mind is frozen. Stunned. "I've been training for my whole life. Training *is* my life."

"You don't know true training," Zikia says. "But you will."

"Pack up your belongings," Adar says. "Tomorrow you leave this place."

"Wait, leave? What? To go where?"

"We can't tell you that," Zikia says. "And Kala, we trust that you'll keep this discreet—better the others not know of our decision until you're gone. People can be . . . unpredictable."

"I'm not even supposed to say *good-bye*?" she says, her voice catching on the word. There's only one person she would care to say good-bye to.

And she can never say good-bye to him.

"It's even more important, now, that your only attachment is to the matter at hand," Zikia says. "If you've got anything here that matters to you, any*one*—trust me when I say, it's better to sever that cleanly, while you can."

The way Zikia is looking at her, the way she says *anyone*, it's as if she knows. That there is a someone. That the someone matters.

But she can't know. If she knew, she would never have chosen Kala to be the Player.

Maybe if Kala admits it, the minders will change their minds.

But she can't speak.

"You have sixteen hours to wrap things up," Zikia says. "We leave at dawn."

There is nothing to pack. There is only one thing in this place she holds precious, and he won't fit in a backpack.

So she goes about the rest of her day as if nothing has happened. She forces herself not to panic, not to rush into Alad's arms until they can be alone. They have until dawn. That's plenty of time to plan.

Kala has spent years learning to power through pain and fear. She's an expert at deception, and so it's nothing for her to lie to her cohorts, to put on a happy face, to go to sleep beside them as if she'll be there when they wake.

Even as she lies in bed, staring into the darkness, she keeps up the mental wall. The minders have trained her to visualize an actual wall, hundreds of feet high and thick with steel, as strong as it needs to be to keep unwanted thoughts at bay.

It's only when Alad appears at the window that the wall begins to crumble.

It's only when they've reached their special clearing, and he takes her in his arms, that she tears the whole damn thing down and lets herself break.

"What? What is it? Kala, what's wrong?" Alad is panicked, desperate, searching her for wounds, for something that would explain the quivering mess in his arms. Kala is not like this; Kala is never like this.

She's never fallen apart before, and so had no idea how much strength it would take to piece herself back together. She clings to him, holding herself up, holding herself *here*. "It's me," she says, when she can speak. Snot and tears flow freely, and she almost laughs, thinking about how pretty crying looks in the movies. There is nothing pretty about this. "They picked me."

"To what?"

"To Play."

He is holding her up—so when he lets go, she staggers and nearly falls. Suddenly it's as if there are miles of space between them. As if today's decision has carved a fissure through her life: *before, after.* They stand on opposite sides of a chasm, staring across.

"Congratulations," he says in a wooden voice.

"No. No congratulations!" If she can make him understand, the space will close again. It will have to. "There's nothing to congratulate. I don't want this! Who could want this?"

He flinches, and she would take the words back if she could. Even though they are true. She sees what her life will be now, how it will no longer be her own. He wouldn't want this, if he knew how it felt.

It feels like falling.

"I wish it had been you," she says, reaching out to touch him. He pulls away. He can hear the lie in her voice, she knows. He just doesn't understand it.

She could never wish this for him.

"So this is it," he says. "This is good-bye."

No one knows how Players are chosen; no one knows where they disappear to when they are. But everyone knows they come back different.

They come back hard.

The Players are all, at some level, like Zikia. They can be kind, charming; they know how to make their eyes twinkle to get what they want. But there is ice in their hearts. Kala would like to believe it's impossible, that it could happen to her—that this mysterious training will strip away the fundamentals of who she is, will take away her ability to love just as she's found it again.

But she is a girl raised on stories of alien invasion and imminent apocalypse.

She knows nothing is impossible.

"Run away with me," she says. The words are out before she realizes she's going to say them, before she realizes it's what she wants to do. That she's never wanted anything more.

"What?" he says, stunned dumb as she was a few hours before.

"Let's just go," she says, excitement building. Hope building. "We can leave tonight. Get away from here, away from *them*; screw being the Player and their stupid Endgame." This is *possible*, she realizes—more than possible, this is necessary. This is the answer, the miracle she's been waiting for, as if a solution would drop out of the sky. She's smarter than that. Miracles only happen when you make them happen. Maybe the same is true for lives.

"And exactly where are we supposed to go?" Alad asks.

They both know that the Sumerian reach is wide and powerful. If Kala defies their edict, they will hunt her down. They will punish.

"There's nothing out there for us," Alad says. "Our lives are here."

"*Your* life," she says. "I'm leaving here tomorrow no matter what; the only question is if I go where I'm told—or where I want."

"It's a few years, Kala. You can do that in your sleep. A few years and then it's behind you and you can have everything. We can have everything." He puts his arms around her and she can breathe again. Will he still want to hold on when he knows the truth?

Because there's no time left.

She has to tell him.

"There is something out there for me," Kala says. "I . . ." She swallows. It's beyond forbidden, what she's done. It's unthinkable. "I tracked down my family. My birth family. I know where they live. I know everything about them."

"And you didn't tell me?" His voice is unreadable. But he is still holding on.

"I couldn't. I knew what you'd think, that it was, I don't know, weak. Stupid."

"Nothing you do is weak or stupid, Kala."

"I wasn't even going to do anything about it, not at first," she admits. Now that she's broken the floodgate, the words spill out of her. "I just wanted to *know*. But now . . . I need to see them. I can't stand it anymore, having them out there but not *knowing*. Not seeing their faces. I know you don't understand it. I know you don't feel this way, that no one does, that I'm the freak, but I can't help it. It's always felt like something was missing, and something *was*. Them. They're a part of me. Like you're a part of me, Alad. I have to go. I have to. But I don't want to go without you. I never want to go anywhere without you again. Come with me, just to see them, and then we can go anywhere, do anything we want. We can make our own choices, for once. Make our own lives."

He says nothing.

He doesn't look at her.

So this is how it ends, she thinks.

She tells herself: *I can go without him.*

She tells herself: *I don't need him.*

She tells herself: *I don't need anyone.*

But then his ice melts and his smile breaks through and he lifts her off the ground and buries his face in her hair and whispers "yes, yes, yes," and she knows that this is the only answer she could have survived.

They will go two hours before dawn.

She is reluctant to leave Alad, even for the time it takes them to gather supplies—water and weapons and enough cash pilfered from the minders' cabins to get them where they need to go. But it will be faster if they separate, and the faster the better.

She waits for him by the rendezvous point, fifty yards south of the guard tower, steeling herself for him not to show. Seconds tick past, then minutes, and he doesn't come, and he still doesn't come . . .

And then he does.

They have chosen the guard tower staffed, at this hour, by Dilshad and Javed, because everyone knows that Dilshad regularly sneaks away from her post to play poker with the kitchen staff, while Javed spends his shift down the internet porn rabbit hole and wouldn't notice if a freight train blasted through the gate.

Kala and Alad are a little more subtle.

It takes no more than a snip of the right wire to disarm the electrified gate. From there, it's easy. They can scale barbed-wire fences in their sleep. Alad goes first, flinging himself up and safely over the barbs like a gymnast on the uneven bars. He snatches hold of the other side of the fence to break his fall, then climbs down the rest of the way. Safe. Free.

She loves to watch him move, watch his muscles ripple and flex. Even now, when a wrong move could set the sirens blaring and the guards running, she allows herself a moment of wonder. Impossible to believe that he belongs to her—that they belong to each other.

Then it's her turn. She climbs halfway up the fence, pushes off with her legs, vaults her body up and over the barbed-wire rim, tumbling head over heels, then makes a blind grab and wraps her fingers tightly around chain link. She dangles midway up, six feet from the ground. This close to freedom, climbing is too slow. She pushes off again, sailing through the night air. *This is how it feels to be free,* she thinks. Like flying.

She lands gracefully, the force of impact vibrating through her bones, and without pause they are both running, across the desert, into the night, eager to put miles between them and the camp before anyone notices they're gone. This is the plan: Run until dawn, then find a suitable hiding spot, a cave or a dried creek bed, somewhere they can wait out the searchers who will come with the sun.

They don't speak, or even look at each other. Instead Kala falls into step behind Alad, watching his smooth, even gait, the steady pumping of his arms, the sweat dripping down that familiar curve of neck, thinking of the first time she really *saw* him, and how little she knew, before that, of what it meant to be alive.

These are the rumors—this, they say, is what happens when you shirk your duty, foolishly try to escape:

They come for you.

They *find* you, wherever you hide.

They blindfold you, tie you up, toss you into an unmarked van, hold you at a secluded location until you've learned the errors of your ways.

Learning comes through brainwashing.

Or through starvation.

Or through torture.

They cut off fingers; they pry out teeth. They waterboard and electrocute. If they suspect you've given away the secrets of your training, that you've spilled dangerous information to the wrong party, they cut out your tongue.

At least, these are the stories.

All the stories concern Players-in-training, children who are of little value to the big picture. There are no stories of what happens to Players gone rogue. It is simply not done.

Or if it is done, the penalties are too awful to speak of.

Kala believes none of it. These are bedtime stories, used to scare children who might otherwise contemplate running from the closest they have to a home.

But she does believe they will come for her. So it's a good thing they've taught her so well how to hide.

And, if it comes to that, how to fight.

Her family lives in Abyaneh, one of the oldest villages in Iran, home to fewer than 200 families—and on many days even more tourists, looking to commune with a Persian past. It is in the center of that country, more than 1,500 kilometers away, and will require crossing north across the Yemeni/Saudi Arabian border, finding passage across the Persian Gulf, and then making their way into the heart of Iran.

She knows these facts about her family, and many others: She knows her mother's name is Roshan Jahandar and her father is Parham. She has a nine-year-old sister, Mina. She knows her own name, her name at birth—Simin, which means "delicate" and surely was meant for some other girl. She whispers it to herself sometimes, at night, trying to imagine who that girl might have been, whether somewhere inside Kala she still exists. She knows her father is a doctor and her mother a writer of online instruction manuals. She knows she has her mother's green eyes and her father's lopsided ears, and her sister has precisely the same shade of hair. The files she's broken into have many facts, and the internet has supplied many more. But nowhere in the files, or in the gigabytes of data floating in cyberspace, are answers to the questions that really matter, the facts she needs to know.

Whether her parents remember her; whether they wanted to give her away.

Whether she was loved; whether she is missed.

What it means to be a daughter, to have a mother and a father.

What it means to have a family, and whether this one still belongs to her.

They travel only at night, navigating by the stars, making their way slowly across the desert, tracking miles across the dunes from dusk till dawn. Days are for curling up in dark places and whispering each other to sleep. They have learned how to find hidden rivulets of water beneath the earth, and how to slow their metabolisms to stretch the length of time they can subsist without. They are trained to spot traces of life, to sniff out human trespassers in the wild and track them down. And so it is that on the third night, as their water is running out, they find a bedouin camp. While the travelers sleep, Kala and Alad rifle through their supplies, taking what they need. They also take two camels. After that they make better time, and soon they have reached the Shaybah oil fields, meaning they are well across the Saudi Arabian border and only a few kilometers from the United Arab Emirates.

The oil field has its own airstrip, and it is child's play to steal a plane. Kala drops the flight crew one by one with a series of toxic darts, while Alad takes out the pilots with a simple choke hold. She is about to slit their throats, just to be sure, but Alad stays her hand.

"It's not necessary," he says. "We can do it without that. And if we can, we should."

They can. They do.

Kala reminds herself that they are starting a new life now. She will have to learn to be soft.

They dump the pilots on the runway. They have both logged hours in the flight simulator on several models of plane and helicopter. Kala settles into the pilot's seat with Alad beside her and, with a roar of the engine, eases the plane off the runway and into the air. In no time, they are in the emerald city of Abu Dhabi, gaping at skyscrapers and tourists dripping with jewels, luxuriating in the air-conditioning of their spacious hotel suite. A stolen credit card number has bought them a palatial spread, complete with a Jacuzzi and all the water they can drink.

There is the temptation to stay. At least for a little longer.

"I can't believe we're doing this," Kala says to Alad, as she's said so often. "We're really doing it." She needs to keep repeating it, to make herself believe. Every time she falls asleep, she worries she'll wake up back at the camp, only to discover this has all been a dream.

"We really are," he tells her, as he always does, and then kisses her. He always does that too.

They hack the Emirates Airline site and assign themselves two seats on a flight to London, leaving the next morning. They do this under their own names—then claim two more seats on a flight to Tokyo under the names Enki and Enlil, the Sumerian gods of earth and air. If the minders are searching for them, these are the bread crumbs they will find. Kala hopes they will assume the London tickets are fake—too obvious, too easy to track—and uncover the Tokyo flight. Then the wild goose chase will commence.

In the meantime, Kala and Alad will acquire fake passports, charter a boat across the Gulf, and then—because everything is safer in a crowd—ride endless buses north into Iran, at least until they reach Ardestan. There they will steal a car, or perhaps, if whim overtakes them, two motorbikes, and venture into the countryside.

She's covered her tracks in the camp's computer system. The minders will have no reason to guess where she's going—no reason to think she's trekking into her past rather than her future.

Even if they somehow do, she'll be gone before they have time to figure it out. She doesn't need to *stay* with her family, doesn't need to bring danger to their door.

She just needs to see them.

To know.

"Don't worry," Alad says as their bus bumps along endless miles of dusty brown landscape. Someone a few rows behind them is carrying a crate of chickens, whose squawk is nearly as bad as their smell. "We'll get there soon."

He thinks she's impatient, but the closer they get, the slower she wants to move.

What if she hates them? What if they hate her?

Worse: What if they are simply strangers? If she steps through the door and feels nothing? If the thing she's been looking for her entire life turns out not to exist? She's been searching so long for that missing piece—but if she doesn't find it here, she won't find it anywhere. And that hole at her center, the one even Alad can't fill, will be empty forever.

These are the fears that keep her awake at night. But then Alad will murmur something in his sleep, or roll over and curl an arm around her, and her worries fade away.

Nothing can go wrong now.

The village is smaller than she imagined. There are, along the way, cell towers and satellite dishes, all the necessary trappings of modern life. There are, in the heart of the town, befuddled tourists gaping wide-eyed at the red soil and the colorful traditional garb. But as they creep through the village's terraced streets, it's easy to imagine they've been transported back in time. It feels so remote here, untouched by time—the kind of place you would seek out if you wanted to hide from the world.

This is what Kala thinks as she stands on the front step of the house that could have been her home. Maybe they came here to forget her; maybe they came here to get away.

The houses have no addresses—they stopped in the café to ask how to find the Jahandar family and half the room was able to tell them. A mile north of the grocery at the end of town, where civilization is reclaimed by nature, they will find a small blue cottage surrounded by fig trees. Everyone says: "And tell them we say hello." Her family is popular in this place, that's clear. They are loved.

Here is the house. Here are the trees. Here is Kala, discovering what it means to be afraid.

The files couldn't tell her why her family was chosen to donate a child, why *she* was chosen: whether they gave her away willingly, whether they volunteered. They moved to this village one year after she was taken—or given—and have been here ever since. *What were they escaping?* Kala wonders. *Memories, or me?*

"Maybe this is a bad idea," Alad says, because surely he can smell her fear. He's giving her a graceful out. "You don't have to go in."

"We came all this way . . ." She hates how her voice sounds: so small, so defeated.

"And we can go farther," he says, eyes lighting up with the possibility. "We keep talking about the future, Kala—but why wait? Let's start it tonight. Now. Let's forget about the past and start the rest of our lives."

They have agreed to go to Paris next, because the movies say it's the most romantic place on earth. Alad is right, they could go right this moment, bring their future to life.

She loves him for suggesting it, for offering an out that carries no shame.

He can see she is afraid, and he doesn't hate her for her weakness. She loves him for that too.

"You think they forgot me?" she says.

Alad brushes a finger across her cheek. "I think no one could forget you."

Inside, there is music playing.

No, not music—scales, stumbling up and down the keys. Kala

imagines a child's unsteady hand.

She imagines a sister.

She knocks on the door.

"Can I help you?"

Kala recognizes the woman's face from the photos in the files. A couple of inches shorter than Kala and many inches rounder, she has the weathered skin of someone who's spent too much time in the sun. She looks like a nice woman, but she looks like a stranger.

"Yes?" the woman, the *mother* says, growing impatient. There is no recognition on her face. "What is it?"

Kala had always thought she would feel something. That some pheromone or long-dormant memory would spring to life at the sight of her mother, that love would spontaneously appear. She knows better than that—knows it is a fundamental law of nature that something cannot spring from nothing.

But isn't it also a law of nature that mothers always know their children?

Shouldn't there be something of her infant self in Kala's face, something that calls this woman to her, makes her *see*?

And if not, if there's nothing left, then what is she doing here?

"Maybe we should go," she murmurs to Alad. He takes her hand. Maybe he's about to pull her away; maybe he's going to convince her to stay. She'll never know. Because at that moment, a small girl runs into the room. She peers around her mother's bulk to get a glimpse of the visitors, favoring them with a gap-toothed smile.

The mother looks nervously between the child and the strangers, and Kala wonders whether she's thinking about the last time a set of strangers came to her door, expressing too much interest in her child.

"I ask you one more time, who are you and what do you want here?"

There is so much to tell, but Kala is capable of squeezing out only a single word. The word that, for the first time, feels like it belongs to her.

"Simin."

The woman goes still. Color drains out of her face, and she calls for her husband, or tries to, but her voice rises no higher than a whisper. "Get your father," she croaks to the child. *"Now."* The child scurries away, but the mother does not take her eyes off Kala. She does not move.

"Simin?" she says, finally, her voice wobbling on the second syllable. "My little Simin?"

Kala has waited so long to say it: "Mother?"

Then there is screaming, and there are arms around her and a mother's tears and a father's laughter and somewhere in the symphony of joy a child's nervous squeal and Kala breathes in the scent of saffron and nutmeg and finally understands, *This is what it means to come home.*

It's like watching herself in a movie. This can't be real, this scene she's dreamed of so many times, all of it coming true exactly as she imagined. Dreams like this aren't supposed to come true.

But: Here is her father serving her and Alad a heaping bowl of lamb stew; here is her mother weeping and weeping, smoothing her hair and peppering her forehead with kisses; here is her sister, fearless and bright, already in love with the handsome young man who brought her big sister home.

They are brimming with questions about what her life has been, but she doesn't want to talk about that. She has questions of her own: about the life that she missed, the family she never had, the person they hoped she would be—but those questions are so big, she doesn't know how to begin to ask.

For now, she just wants to soak them in. To live inside this feeling, like she's swallowed the sun. This feeling that, she realizes, must be happiness. The feeling of living a life you've chosen, with the people who are meant to belong to you.

They've just finished dessert and are sipping steaming mugs of chai when she hears the thunder in the distance.

Which is strange, because the night is clear.

It's only when she catches sight of Alad's expression that she realizes that it's not thunder.

It's a helicopter in the distance, coming closer, maybe more than one.

Kala has been trained to act fast. She has been raised to be a hero, to save her people.

But when it counts, she is too slow.

She is on her feet as the men smash through the windows and the door. She is screaming "Get down get down" as they raise their guns. She is flinging herself at her sister, to shield the girl from harm, as the first shot goes off. She is a frenzy of motion . . . but all of it too late.

It's over almost as soon as it begins.

And there's a hole at the center of her mother's head.

And her father's.

And her sister's.

Their bodies are motionless. The floor is thick with blood. Alad is frozen in a corner, watching.

Someone is screaming.

Kala realizes it's her.

She forces herself to stop, and then there is only the thunder of helicopters overhead. There are the four men with guns, and the woman who led their charge.

Zikia, who has come to claim her.

Kala was so sure she wasn't followed. So sure they wouldn't figure out where she was going. So sure she'd been careful.

She was so careless with her family's lives.

"Players cannot be compromised by attachment," Zikia says. "You know that. Caring is weakness. Love is threat."

"How?" she says, because she must know what she's done.

"Well done, Alad," Zikia says. "You've shown us all your true colors."

Kala turns to him, the boy she loves, the boy who is her entire world, knowing it's impossible.

Knowing nothing is impossible.

"Alad?" she says, and in that word is a plea: *Tell me this woman is lying. Tell me you wouldn't.*

He doesn't.

He says, "I'm sorry."

There has always been an empty place at Kala's center. It was filled, for a moment. But now, with those two words, the emptiness consumes her.

"I had no choice," he says. "You were betraying the cause, I had to tell someone, and they said if I told them where we were going, they'd let you off the hook, they'd let me be the Player, and you know how much I wanted that, you didn't want it at all, and that just wasn't fair." He's babbling. It's background noise to her, barely audible above the buzzing in her ears, the echo of her sister's laughter. "They would have found us anyway, eventually. You know that. I thought it would be easier this way. That we could both get what we wanted. I didn't know what they were going to do, Kala. You have to believe that. You have to forgive me. How could I know?"

There is, somehow, a weapon in her hand. A Caracal pistol, her favorite. Compact and deadly. Just like her.

"You gave yourself away to a fool," Zikia tells her. It is Zikia's gun, and Zikia's hand on her shoulder, its gentle pressure telling her what she needs to do now. Who she needs to be now. "Your misguided attachment blinded you to the truth of him, and look what it's done."

Caring is weakness.

Love is threat.

"Kala," Alad says. Pleads. "Kala, I love you. I only did this for us. For our future."

She can smell the blood, its iron tang. This is what she will think of now, when she remembers her mother. Not saffron, but blood.

Not the life she could have had, but death.

"Kala, *please.*" Alad's voice breaks.

Kala is only a word she chose to call herself. It is not real. No more real than Simin, that leftover from a child's dream. Kala means "time," the destroyer of all things. There are those who say Kala is the name of the god of death.

She is 5SIGMA. She has always been 5SIGMA. She sees that now. She sees the way forward.

She pulls the trigger.

Blood blossoms at the center of his forehead. His eyes go wide, then empty.

She has always had excellent aim.

"Good," Zikia says. Then: "I'm sorry it had to happen like this."

"I'm not," Kala says, and is already in motion, stepping past Zikia, past the bodies of the people she will force herself to forget, past this present and into her future. She will not pause to cry, or to regret.

She has been scooped out, emptied of the capacity for tears, and of the weakness that goes with them.

She will move forward. She will forget Alad, forget her family, forget love, forget what was or what might have been, focus only on what is.

Playing.

Winning.

Surviving.

There is nothing else.

MU
CHIYOKO

All day, every day, Chiyoko belongs to her people. Her life, her time, her choices, none of them are her own. She lives for the Mu, the thousands who share her ancient bloodline and will rely on her to save them if Endgame comes. It is both obligation and honor; it is a promise she made before she was old enough to understand sacrifice. A promise made on her behalf, before she was born. The stars spelled out her fate six days before baby Chiyoko made her way, red-faced and gasping—but never crying, never that—into the world. She was training for her role before she was old enough to understand what training meant, that training was anything other than life. She has never had friends, never had hobbies. She has never doubted the person she would grow to become, the things she would be capable of, the obligations she would serve, because her uncle told her what would come to pass, and she knew no other way but to believe him. She begrudges none of it. The Mu are her people and she is their Player. Her days belong to them.

But her nights are her own.

By day she endures an isolated, regimented existence, her every minute accounted for. She is a precious object, to be protected at all costs. Yes, the training is rigorous and often puts her life in danger—she's leaped from airplanes, scaled skyscrapers, infiltrated military installations, walked through fire—but those are calculated risks, *efficient* risks. They serve a purpose. When she is not enduring missions, preparing for an end that might never come, she is meant to be safe at home, under her uncle's watchful eye. If and when Endgame begins, she will be the champion of her people. But until then, her uncle never tires of reminding her, she is a 13-year-old girl. A 13-year-old girl who can tie a hundred different knots, load a machine gun in three seconds flat, disarm a man three times her size. But she cannot do something so simple as open her mouth and ask for help.

Chiyoko lived 13 years as a Player-to-be, and accepted the limitations of that life, having never known any other. But 10 days ago, on her 13th birthday, she ascended. Player-to-be no more. She is now the Player, the one and only. She has placed her hands on the ancient scrolls, the ones that tell of the near obliteration of the Mu by their alien overlords. She has sworn to protect her people in the event that these merciless beings finally return. The Mu were saved once, by the cruel grace of the creatures from the stars. Only Chiyoko can save them again. This she swore to do—silently, with a slow nod of the head that her uncle understood. She could hear several of the elders on the Council of Twelve muttering, as if a promise were not a promise unless spoken aloud. As if her entire life had not been a promise of service to them and their needs.

She thought things would change after the ceremony. That upon coming of age she would live a freer life, able to make her own choices. She was wrong.

If anything, her uncle's rules have gotten more oppressive. She is still a precious possession, now more precious than ever. Her skills, her energies, her days—these belong to her people, her uncle reminds her, as he pushes her ever harder.

Chiyoko lives to please her uncle, the only one who believes in her without reservation. She delights in meeting his expectations and exceeding them. So by day she lives the life he sets out for her.

By night she flies.

Rooftop to rooftop, soaring over the streets of Naha, a creature of the dark. She runs up the sides of building, vaults over walls, lets momentum carry her up, across, away. She never hesitates at the edge of a roof: to hesitate is to fall. She flings herself at edges, leaps across chasms, holds tight to those seconds aloft, defying gravity. In those seconds, suspended between roofs, tens or hundreds of feet above the ground, she can be free.

Her trainers called it parkour, and they taught her well. No one knows how much she took the training to heart, that she has made the night city her own.

Chiyoko has always been good at secrets.

Some nights she spies on her neighbors, alighting on a balcony or windowsill and stealing glimpses of a stranger's life. More often she enjoys her solitude, letting her mind drift into fantasy as her body takes flight: She is a vampire; she is a superhero; she is a monster. She is an anime vigilante, flickering in two dimensions across a cartoon sky. She wonders what they would make of her, these innocents, if they caught sight of her silhouette streaking across the low-hanging moon. Whatever it might be, it couldn't be stranger than the truth. That she *is* a superhero. A vigilante. That she is fated to save the world. Or at least her people. And she's been taught to understand that they are all of the world that matters.

In the day, while she trains with her uncle, she bears this responsibility without telling anyone of her doubts: Can she do it? Is she strong enough? If Endgame comes, will she survive? She keeps her fears to herself, and lets no one guess how much she dreads Endgame, how much she hopes her time as the Player will pass without incident. That the days and years will slip past until she ages out of eligibility and the fate of the world slides onto someone else's shoulders.

At night, the doubts disappear. They have no more hold on her than gravity.

She feels it as she leaps fearlessly into shadow: certainty. A sureness that she is the one, that Endgame will come, and come soon. That she will rise to meet it.

Part of it, surely, is the solitude of night, its promised escape from the doubting eyes of the Mu. Out here in the dark, there is no one to wonder how a girl who can't speak can do anything else. No one to treat her like she is broken, damaged, stupid, *wrong*. No one to smile and pretend to believe her uncle, believe she is up to the challenge, while their gaze shines with the truth of their skepticism.

No wonder it's easier to believe in herself when she can be invisible. But that's not all of it.

That may be what sent her into the night for the first time, but it's not why she stayed, or why she can't stay away.

Soaring from building to building, she becomes one with the dark. A shadow slipping across the sky, she feels connected to the stars as she never does on the ground. Only in motion, in the air, can she hear them singing to her. Whispers on the breeze, chimes in the night, a message meant only for her ears.

We are coming.

We are coming.

We are coming back.

Alone in the dark, she imagines she can feel their presence, their watchful eyes, those beings from the stars. And their eyes hold no doubt. They know she is the one. They know she will be ready.

This is why she defies her uncle's wishes and sneaks into the night. She needs these booster shots of confidence. She needs that belief that comes only in darkness, to get her through all those hours in the light.

But tonight is not about confidence or freedom.

Tonight is about learning her fate.

Tonight she scales the barbed-wire gate surrounding Satoshi Nori's estate and climbs his ivy-carpeted walls. She perches lightly on a sill and activates the transmitter she long before hid in his sitting room. The transmitters are long-range, and she could have eavesdropped on this conversation from the comfort of her own home. But she prefers it here, with the wind sharp on her cheeks and the Mu Council of Twelve bickering in hushed tones behind the bulletproof glass. Twelve of them, one for each of the original 12 tribes of Mu that stood up to the creatures from the stars. As reward for their rebelliousness,

11 of the tribes were wiped from the Earth. One line remained, one charged with remembering the price of defiance. The Mu have been obedient servants ever since, playing their role in the game, warning the ancient bloodlines of humanity about the Endgame to come. Millennia of tradition and servitude, all resting in the hands of these 12 old men and women. These are the 12 who have placed the burden of her people on Chiyoko's shoulders, and among them now are those who would try to take that burden away.

They may refuse to face her, but they can't stop her from facing them. They may treat her like a child, but they're fools if they think she's going to act like one, letting decisions be made for her, letting conversations fly over her head that will decide her future.

Satoshi Nori is the de facto leader of the Mu—he is neither the wisest nor the boldest among them, but he has the most money, and that counts for plenty.

Chiyoko has been listening in on him for more than a year now. Which is how she knows his to be the loudest voice speaking up against her, arguing that a girl like her—a *defective* like her—should not be the Player, no matter what the signs may say.

Unlike her elders, she has never much cared what Satoshi thought. But maybe she should have. Because this afternoon she overheard her uncle agreeing to attend a meeting of the council, a meeting in which they would hear Satoshi out once and for all.

The Council of Twelve meets, as a rule, only once a year. An unscheduled meeting is agreed to only under grave consideration—if her uncle agreed to attend, he must have had good reason. He must have believed Satoshi would say something worth hearing.

Her uncle's eyes are the only ones that have never lied to her. His faith in her is bone deep, and it is what sustains her through every doubting day. Or so she has always thought.

Maybe she is foolish after all.

Chiyoko clings tight to the wall, disappearing into the darkness. She closes her eyes against the wind, and listens.

"The girl is weak," Satoshi says. "After so many generations, you would have us trust our people's survival to this defective thing? This mute?"

It's nothing she hasn't heard before.

"You would have us cast away a hundred generations of tradition, defy the word of the gods, all on your opinion?" Chiyoko's uncle says. "Chiyoko's voice may be weak, but her spirit is strong. She is our Player, whether you like it or not."

This, too, is familiar territory. No one questioned Chiyoko's annunciation as Player-to-be—not until she was five years old and it was clear she would never speak. For three millennia, the elders have anointed a Player in the womb, and that child has grown up to Play. Never has this tradition been violated. Never has the child proven unworthy. But three millennia is a long time. There are those who believe that maybe, finally, the elders have made a mistake. That maybe it's time to dispense with tradition and apply common sense. Choose a Player who will be whole. The argument has raged behind Chiyoko's back for a decade.

It is as if they think that because she cannot speak, she does not hear. So tonight's argument is familiar—but then it takes an unexpected turn.

"This cannot continue," her uncle says. "This dissension, the lack of faith. It's too dangerous."

"Then we are in agreement," Satoshi says.

"You said you had a proposal?"

"I propose we offer our people a Player they deserve, one without defect or disability. Akina Nori."

Chiyoko barely knows the girl. The Mu rarely socialize with one another, finding it safer to assimilate into Naha society and keep their bond hidden from prying eyes. On those rare occasions when their children came together, Chiyoko was always ignored. She played silently by herself, while the others chattered together. But she knows enough about Akina Nori: The girl is beautiful, athletic, wealthy. She is also Satoshi Nori's daughter.

"Imagine my surprise," her uncle says, and Chiyoko can hear the wry smile in his voice.

"She's a good candidate," Satoshi says. "Top of her class, and the most accomplished fighter I've ever seen."

"You've never seen Chiyoko."

"In fact, I have," Satoshi says.

Girls like Akina don't learn how to fight. Not unless they're being trained for something. Groomed for something.

"I have support," Satoshi says, and there is a murmuring among the elders, a murmuring that sounds like agreement. "You would be surprised to know how much."

"I have support as well," her uncle says. "But I agree with you—this cannot continue."

Chiyoko nearly loses her grip on the sill. The wind is suddenly colder than it was, biting sharp and angry at her flesh.

She never asked to be the Player. Never thought to wonder whether she wanted it.

But she finds now she does not want to lose it.

Who would she be without it?

Who would she be without her uncle's belief that she is special, that she is the one?

Who would she be but a broken girl who only feels whole in the dark?

Then her uncle speaks again. "I propose a test," he says. "A challenge. Chiyoko has a training mission coming up. Survival in the wilderness. I intended to test her against the elements—but I see no reason not to pit her against an enemy as well. Akina will have the element of surprise, the superior firepower; Chiyoko will have her training and the will of the gods. Let us leave them to their own devices and see who lives."

A woman gasps, and Chiyoko recognizes this as Satoshi's wife. Akina's mother.

"Chiyoko will know none of this?" Satoshi says.

"You have my word," her uncle says, and all the Mu know what this is worth.

"You would send your own niece into an ambush?"

"I have no fear that she can take care of herself," her uncle says, and relief surges through her. This is how much he believes in her. Enough to risk her life on her skill and his certainty. "Can you say the same for your daughter?"

"Satoshi, think about this," Akina's mother says. Her name is Lia, and Chiyoko knows her to be a fearsome woman, all sharp vision and sharper edges. There are those who whisper that she is responsible for much of Satoshi's success and all his decisions. She doesn't sound fearsome now. She only sounds afraid. "This is our daughter."

Satoshi says nothing.

"If you have no faith in her, how can you expect our people to defy the gods' will and follow yours instead?" Chiyoko's uncle says.

"If Akina kills Chiyoko, then you'll accede to my wishes?" Satoshi asks. "You and yours will acknowledge that she is to be our next Player?"

"She will have earned her place. And if it is Chiyoko who survives, there will be no more of this," her uncle says. "No more questioning, no more dissent. You will accept the gods' will. You will accept Chiyoko."

"If she survives."

"Yes. If."

Chiyoko leaps from the sill and lands noiselessly on the dewy grass. She takes no pleasure in the flight home, racing down streets and grazing roofs. She doesn't enjoy the silence or spare a glance for the crystalline stars. She allows herself no thought, no emotion, not until she is safely enclosed in the dark of her room. Surrounded by evidence of her uncle's love for her: The books he has brought her. The weapons he has given her. The mural he painted on her wall, a serpentine river to remind her that she is like water: deceptively peaceful, quietly strong, dangerous when underestimated, often deadly.

Chiyoko's uncle has always believed in her. He has raised her, all these years, while her parents travel the world, monitoring Mu business and Mu fortunes in other countries, ensuring that the people—and its secret, ancient mission—will live on. Like Chiyoko, they have a responsibility to their bloodline, and she cannot begrudge them that. She knows they love her. Even if there's a part of her that wonders whether it's easy to love her from a distance. With thousands of miles between them, they don't have to be confronted by her silence, her failure. She, in turn, doesn't have to be reminded of their disappointment.

Her uncle has never been disappointed. He speaks up for Chiyoko, who cannot speak for herself. As a child, when she cried herself to sleep after a hard day of training, only to wake up screaming silently from a nightmare, her uncle was always there, waiting. He knew. He told her of his time as a Player; he told her it was an honor, and that she would do her people proud.

She still has nightmares.

Sometimes, in the dreams, she can speak. She never remembers the sound of her voice when she wakes up. But sometimes she can almost hear the echo of her scream. Always, when she wakes up afraid, he is there to calm her, as he is tonight. He brushes her hair from her forehead and sets a soft kiss on her brow. "Whatever happens is meant to happen," he whispers. "That has always been the way."

This is the philosophy that allowed the Mu to recover from near extermination. This is what has enabled them to serve the murderers so faithfully over the millennia, to ensure that the other peoples of Earth would serve them too. *Whatever happens is meant to happen*—alone, it is the motto of a defeated people. But the Mu are not defeated, only disciplined. And so there is a second part to their philosophy, just as essential as the first.

Do whatever must be done to prevent it from happening again.

Whatever must be done. That has been the core of Chiyoko's training, and she knows it to be the core of her uncle's being.

Whatever must be done, no matter who it may hurt, no matter what might be sacrificed.

Her uncle isn't the only one who knows how to read silence. Over the years, she has gotten very good at reading the lines of his face, the worry in his eyes, and she knows what he is thinking now.

He's thinking that Satoshi might be right. That Akina might win. That he has just agreed to sacrifice his beloved niece to a larger cause, and that it is hard, but it is right.

He's sending her into an ambush, but that's not what hurts.

What hurts is that he's worried she won't come back.

Know your enemy.

This is the first rule of battle, a necessity of victory.

And so, in the few days she has left, Chiyoko sets out to know Akina Nori. She will not make contact with the girl, not until absolutely necessary. She will lurk in the shadows, watching, waiting for Akina to reveal her secret self, the indulgences and weaknesses that will seal her fate.

Her uncle's basement houses a workshop filled with gears and circuitry, GPS chips and microscopic lenses and microphones. Chiyoko has logged many hours down there, designing surveillance equipment to suit her needs. Recording devices disguised as pens, hair clips, lucky rabbit's feet; infrared cameras the size of a pinhead; nearly invisible trackers that can be shot into a target's neck, with a small sting easily mistaken for a mosquito bite. In the lush gardens of her father's estate, Akina slaps at her skin and suspects nothing, feels nothing, certainly not the tiny ridge of a GPS signal emitter.

It's easy enough that it feels almost like cheating, but Chiyoko has been trained for a game that has no rules except one: win at any cost. This is what she intends to do.

Akina isn't careful. She lives her life on the surface, almost as if she wants Chiyoko to see.

Chiyoko sees Akina train in a lavish gym on her father's grounds, sees her practice aikido, muay thai, sanshou, capoeira, and jujitsu, sees her skills with the wooden dagger, the battle-ax, the curved kujang, the shuriken, and several semiautomatic machine guns. Akina is good—Chiyoko is better. Where Akina fights expensive instructors in well-equipped facilities, Chiyoko has battled real enemies on urban battlefields across Japan. Akina, Chiyoko can tell, has never truly had to fight for her life. Paid instructors will always hold back, always pull a punch if it threatens to wound. Chiyoko has stabbed thugs on an empty subway platform in the bowels of Tokyo; she has speared gangsters in a deserted alley of Nagasaki. She has danced away from bullets and kicked knives out of grimy hands. She has fought knowing that no one, not even her uncle, would step in to save her—fought for her life and emerged understanding what is needed to survive. She sees this is a lesson that Akina, spoiled by the luxury and illusion of safety, has never had to learn.

Chiyoko sees that Akina is stronger with her right arm than her left, and has a hamstring strain that acts up when she pushes herself too hard. She sees that Akina is handier with a revolver than with a rifle, and nearly hopeless with a crossbow, her arrows always flying a few centimeters to the right of her mark.

She sees Akina laboring over ancient texts and struggling to translate the words of their ancestors, and sees that she is smart, but not brilliant, and that Satoshi Nori sees this as well, but pretends not to. She sees Akina put away her training gear and her books so that she can go to school or watch a movie or hold someone's hand in the dark. In some ways, they are not so different. They have the same pale skin, the same shoulder-length black hair with bangs cutting a razor-straight line above their eyebrows. When Akina is training, she wears the black robes of a samurai, just like Chiyoko. Watching her from a distance, Chiyoko can almost imagine she is watching herself. But when Akina steps out into the world, she is a girl transformed. Chiyoko's closet is filled with identical black skirts and white shirts. This is her costume for daily life, how she hides her superhero self away. She is a black-and-white movie, drab and easily missed, trained to fade into the background.

Akina is Technicolor. She paints her lips cherry red and her eyelids gold and silver. Akina streaks her hair with neon blues and greens, tugs rainbow socks up past her knees. One day she will drape herself in pure pink pastel princess gear from head to toe, with sparkling tiara to match; the next she will go goth girl, black and bloodred nails and lips, a walking darkness that somehow still shines bright. Every day, Akina remakes herself anew. As if she is always choosing, and choosing again, who she would like to be.

Chiyoko's life has been a tunnel, funneling her toward a single goal. Every choice is measured against Endgame, and so no choice at all. Now she sees what it might be like to live another way.

Sometimes, especially in the quiet before the dawn, Chiyoko thinks that if she only wanted it enough, she could will herself to speak. But what would she say? What would *she* choose?

Chiyoko has always wondered if there are some things that cannot be known unless put into words. If this is why she has never quite known her own heart.

Her tongue is intact, her lungs hale, her throat unmarked. Okinawa's best doctors have been unable to find a single flaw. She is designed for speech—but somehow, still, destined for silence. As if the gods themselves stole her words, unspooled them from her in the womb. She remembers being very young, clapping chubby hands, banging stubby legs, anything to be heard. To be known. She remembers the faces of her elders: Anxious. Hopeful. And, finally, disappointed. They did their best to hide it from her, but Chiyoko has always been good at watching. Understanding.

She tried for them, harder than she tried for herself. She remembers that too. Opening her mouth. Willing herself to scream.

There was only ever silence. So it has always been; so it will always be. Chiyoko cannot have what she wants. So she has trained herself to want what she has.

She is that strong.

She was designed for strength too. And that *is* her destiny.

But sometimes, even now, if only for a moment, she is weak.

Chiyoko presses herself into the shadows of a school and watches Akina Nori, and even though she knows this butterfly of a girl is nothing to be envied—shallow and preening and fated to die—she cannot help herself. She wishes; she wants; she imagines, just for a moment, a life that cannot be.

Akina flips her hair and laughs. The melodic trill comes so easily to her that she does it again. Akina talks with her voice but also her hands, fingers dancing through the air as she tells her friends story after story. They turn toward her as if warming themselves in the sun.

Chiyoko has no friends. No school, no stories. She has a family that cares for her and a room full of beloved books. She has a destiny, and all this is meant to be enough.

Akina has a life.

Akina has a boy named Ryo, who she calls Ri-Ri, even though he claims to hate it. She tickles his neck and he laces his arms around her waist and lifts her off the ground. She whispers in his ear, and even Chiyoko, hiding so close, listening so closely, cannot hear what she has to say.

Chiyoko follows Akina for three days, traipsing back and forth across the city, from the school with its eager audience to the Naha Main Place with its endless corridors of stores, from the mangrove woods where Akina slides her body against Ryo's to the family estate where she talks herself out of trouble for breaking curfew. Soon Chiyoko understands everything she needs to know about the enemy. Akina is used to getting what she wants—life is easy that way, for those who are able to ask. Akina never searches the shadows, never catches a glimpse of movement, of Chiyoko's eyes blinking in the dark.

Chiyoko is good at hiding, at turning invisible. It has saved her life more than once, and very soon it will save her again.

Akina, it is clear, has never turned invisible. Wouldn't know how.

Akina is soft, Akina is spoiled, Akina expects to win, and because of that, Akina will die.

So there is no reason to envy her, Chiyoko reminds herself.

No reason at all.

They come for her in the hour before dawn. Ten masked figures, all in black, all with swords and guns. Chiyoko likes that there are so many of them. It is a sign of respect from her uncle. He knows any fewer than that and they would have no hope against her.

Foolish, though, that they expected to catch her asleep.

She wakes as the first soft footstep crosses the threshold of the house, two floors below. By the time they burst through her door and window, she has hidden her shuriken and her favorite knife beneath her thermal gear, along with a compass and several packets of water purification tablets.

"Come along quietly and you won't get hurt," one of them says, and it's times like this that Chiyoko wishes she could laugh out loud.

She comes along quietly, as she does everything. But she's not the one who gets hurt.

She is a silent whirlwind of violence, kicking and punching, slicing flesh. Cartilage crunches beneath her fist and bones crack against hard floor. She jabs a stomach, ducks a roundhouse swing, aims the flat of her hand at an exposed throat, dances past flashing knives, her body like water, flowing through the enemy unharmed. By the time they succeed in binding her hands behind her back and lashing her legs together, there are four bodies on the floor, and two moaning in opposite corners.

There is no shame in losing this fight; she is expected to lose. She suspects she was not expected to take so many of them down with her.

"Maybe they're wrong about her," a woman's voice says as something sharp pierces Chiyoko's spine. "She's a tough one."

She glimpses a needle, feels something poisonous creeping through her veins.

"You want to *tell* us how tough you are, sweetheart?" a man says, giving her a rough shake.

In the silence, he laughs. "Didn't think so."

"Show a little respect," the woman says. "She's still the Player."

He laughs again. "Not for long." He lifts Chiyoko off the floor and swings her body over his shoulder. She is no threat to him now, hog-tied and poisoned, weak and fading.

Fading.

The laughter is softer now, as if coming from a great distance.

Or else she is the one at a distance, untethered from the world, from her body, floating farther and farther away.

Her lids are so heavy. Darkness closes in.

Hold on, she wills herself, but there is nothing to hold.

There is nothing but empty dark, and silence.

And she is so tired.

"Sweet dreams, chatty," the man's voice says.

She dreams of killing him, slowly.

She dreams that he begs her for mercy, and that instead she makes it hurt.

She opens her eyes to a pounding headache and the thunder of an engine. Ropes bite into her wrists and ankles, but she slips a finger free of the bindings and that's all it takes to extricate the rest of her.

She rises on sore legs to find herself in a small cargo plane.

A small, *empty* cargo plane. Flying thousands of feet over a sea that stretches to the horizon.

With no pilot at the controls.

And a fuel gauge tipping toward empty.

Sometimes, Chiyoko thinks, it would be nice to be able to swear.

She scrambles into the pilot's seat and scans the console. She's never flown this kind of plane, but she's logged many hours of solo flight time on military transport craft and a Boeing freighter with similar controls. The radio has been disabled, as has the navigational system, but the steering is intact, and it's not hard to get a feel for the stick and ease the plane onto a level flight path.

Flight path to *where* is the question. She estimates she has about twenty minutes of flying time left, and even if she could land the plane on the open water, she wouldn't last long. She'd be dead of exposure or dehydration or sharks long before Akina got around to ambushing her. This is a survival exercise, and Chiyoko knows her uncle isn't going to make it easy on her, but he also wouldn't make it impossible. Somewhere in that endless stretch of ocean, there must be land.

She guides the plane in an ever-widening spiral, scanning the waters until she sees it. First just a speck of brown on the horizon, then, as she closes in, a spit of land dense with green. An island.

It will do for survival—just not for landing the plane.

Chiyoko levers the control stick into place with her shoe, a makeshift autopilot that will guide the plane in a loose, lazy circle around the island. Then she begins to scour the cabin for a parachute.

There is no panic. She's been trained out of that. As she sorts through crates and unscrews panels, checking every inch of the plane for the chute she knows must be secreted somewhere, she breathes at regular intervals. Calm, collected, in and out. Heart rate low and steady. No mental sirens blare. Chiyoko knows how to suppress the dumb-animal part of her brain, the part that in most people would be shrieking incoherently.

Out of fuel!

Lost at sea!

No way out!

This is part of the test: staying calm, staying rational. Children panic—Players Play.

She uncovers a parachute beneath a loose panel in the flooring and straps it to her back. Then it's merely a matter of dropping elevation, plotting a flight path over the island, heaving open the freight door, swiftly gauging the physics of momentum and gravity, calculating the relevant distance and velocity vectors—320 km per hour horizontal motion and a 9.8 m/s2 vertical acceleration that without the parachute could have her smashing to the ground at a terminal velocity of 195 km per hour—perfectly timing her bailout.

Waiting for her moment.

Waiting.

Waiting.

Jump.

She could stay here forever.

Floating.

Blue above, blue below.

A thunder of wind in her ears, the sound of silence.

The chute rippling overhead, the ground inching closer, the seconds stretching, her isolation absolute.

There is no threat here, in the air. No attack to anticipate, no enemy to avoid. No game to Play. There is only a child's dream of flight, a lazy drift through the clouds, like floating in a lake on a summer day.

It is like flying again over the streets of Naha, soaring through the night from roof to roof, that same weightless freedom, and she feels at home. Drifting through the air, one with the sky.

This is where she belongs.

This is where she would happily stay.

But she cannot fly, only fall, and inevitably the ground rises up to meet her. The game begins again.

Impact.

As Chiyoko assembles her lean-to, rigging a makeshift home from bamboo stalks and the waterproof chute, she wonders when and how Akina will appear on the island. She snorts, thinking of the girl diving out of a plane. It seems more likely she'll arrive by yacht.

Chiyoko gathers wood for a fire and then uses the lens from her compass to focus the sunlight into a spark. She strips a small sapling and fashions it into a fishing rod. Between that and the nuts and berries she's able to forage near her campground, she should have no problems with food.

She builds camp on the coast but ventures into the dense trees in search of fresh water. She finds a spring a half mile away, and there are enough small animals feeding from it that she feels confident to drink.

She waits for Akina, waits for the ambush she knows is to come. Waits for the girl she is meant to kill.

Two days pass, and this becomes her routine: Tend the fire. Forage for food; trek to the stream. Swim. Work out under the blistering afternoon sun; throw her shuriken at increasingly distant targets.

Wait.

Wait.

Wait.

She plays out the attack in her head, imagines her hands around Akina's throat, her knife in Akina's belly. She kills the girl again and again in her mind.

Kill the girl; kill the doubt.

That is the promise of this mission.

All those who have questioned her will be silent. They will be forced to accept her, and to believe in her.

In the silence that follows, she will finally, fully believe in herself.

That is the promise, and so she waits for it to deliver.

She is distracted by her reflection in the water. Just for a second— no, less than that. For a heartbeat. She catches a glimpse of herself, rippling across the blue, and smiles, so that the quiet girl in the water will smile back at her. Nothing about the girl announces her ferocity. Even here, besting the wilderness, she looks like a shy schoolgirl, nothing more. Chiyoko is easily underestimated, and that has always worked to her advantage. But there are times she wishes her exterior could match what lies within. That her reflection revealed a warrior. A warrior should never be caught off guard. Even one beat of distraction is too many, and by the time she hears the noise behind her, it is too late.

A jaguar stands before her, ready to pounce.

Two more eye her from the brush, their coats sleek, their legs strong, their teeth sharp.

She reaches for her knife, and deliberates. She could, with a flick of the hand, bury it in the nearest jaguar's neck. But that would leave the other two alive—and her knife out of reach.

She could keep her knife close, wrestle the beasts to the ground one by one—and risk being overpowered.

If she can distract or disable one of them, maybe she can outrun the other two.

Maybe.

The jaguar closest to her—too close—lets out a low growl.

She breathes. She thinks. She does not panic. She is Chiyoko, the fated champion of the Mu line. She is trained for all contingencies; she is in control regardless of circumstance. She can do this.

Somehow.

She has studied the world's most dangerous creatures. Jaguars, she knows, can run at nearly 100 km/hour over short distances. Their powerful jaws can bite down with more strength than nearly any animal on earth. Skull-crushing force, literally. They live and hunt alone—except during mating season. Now.

Just her luck.

Chiyoko never acts until she's certain of success. The jaguar, on the other hand, has no doubts.

It pounces. One hundred ten kilograms of muscle and teeth fly at her, jagged claws extended, fierce jaw open wide.

Chiyoko vaults backward, flips across the spring, lands sure-footed, and readies herself to fight—when a shot echoes through the trees, and the beast drops to the ground.

Two more shots, and the other two jaguars are dead side by side. Chiyoko spots a muzzle poking out through the leaves. And there, steady behind the scope, is Akina Nori.

I deserve this, Chiyoko thinks as she prepares herself for a final shot and the darkness to follow. She knew the ambush was coming and somehow fell into it anyway. Unforgivable. *My people deserve better.*

But the shot never sounds. Instead there is a soft thump as Akina drops to the ground. Chiyoko assumes a fight position. Surely the girl doesn't imagine she can best Chiyoko in hand-to-hand combat?

"Chill out," Akina says, lowering the weapon. "I'm Akina Nori, remember me? Satoshi's daughter? They sent me in as reinforcements, said you'd probably need some help with the whole survival thing."

Chiyoko purses her lips, trying to figure out why Akina would go to the trouble of lying. Why not just shoot when she had the chance? True, guns are inelegant, an amateur's weapon, and something Chiyoko would never stoop to herself. But surely Akina has no such standards, not when the stakes are so high.

Akina misunderstands, or pretends to. "Oh, don't get all sulky about it. You think I want to be here? I'm supposed to be front row center at a concert tonight, not in the middle of nowhere eating DIY sushi with a stick. And no offense, but it's pretty obvious you could use the help."

This makes no sense. Akina must have some kind of plan, but it's incomprehensible.

"I don't know if you noticed, but I did just save your life," Akina says. "You could at least say thank you." She catches herself then, and makes a face Chiyoko has seen too many times: simultaneously embarrassed, afraid of offending, irritated at the need to be afraid.

"Uh, I mean, you could be thankful. Or whatever."

Chiyoko presses her hands together and offers Akina a shallow bow. The girl is right: she did save Chiyoko's life. Which puts Chiyoko in her debt.

This is not good.

Nothing is more dangerous than surprise and confusion.

If understanding the enemy is the key to victory, then misunderstanding the enemy—or mistaking an act of mercy for aggression, and vice versa—is the harbinger of defeat.

For the first time, Chiyoko wonders whether she has underestimated her opponent.

For the first time, she is afraid.

Akina keeps up a steady stream of chatter as she follows Chiyoko back to her camp. "You must get stuck doing this crap all the time, huh? Weird that you're not better at it. Did they bring you over in the same kind of boat? Can we discuss the bathroom situation there? Or maybe, better yet, let's never discuss. I mean, I get the whole wild-girl-in-nature thing, but is a boat *nature*? I don't think so. Would it be so much to ask for a hair dryer? Or, I don't know, how about some moisturizer?"

Chiyoko barely listens, which isn't hard. Could the plans have changed? she wonders. Could Akina really be here to help? But she knows Satoshi Nori too well for that, and she saw him swear an oath with her uncle. There is no question: Akina is here to kill her, and it's Chiyoko's job to kill Akina first.

She could do it now.

She could do it easily.

Strike the girl from behind. Spear the blade into her neck, sever her spinal column.

It would be over before it began, before Akina had a chance to understand her defeat.

It would be over, and Chiyoko could go home, and a new life, free of doubters and doubt, would begin.

But she never acts until sure of success. This is what has kept her alive for so long. She *can't* be sure, not until she understands what has happened. Why Akina has done what she's done.

So Chiyoko will wait.

Only long enough to find out what the girl is up to, she tells herself. No longer.

One day passes, and another, and still Akina lives.

On the bright side, so does Chiyoko.

Chiyoko knows why she hasn't made a move on Akina yet. To kill without clarity always leads to more confusion, not less. But as for why Akina hasn't made a move, that remains a puzzle.

Chiyoko usually loves puzzles, but not the kind that's planning to kill her and never the kind that won't shut up.

Akina has moved her supplies to Chiyoko's camp. Or rather, Chiyoko's camp has become Akina's camp, since the other girl actually *has* supplies, and they have taken over. Akina's tent, Akina's sleeping bag, Akina's food, Akina's weapons. Chiyoko can't believe how the elders have stacked the deck in favor of this girl, almost as if they're rooting for her to win.

Which, of course, they are.

All but her uncle, and her uncle knows Chiyoko doesn't need any extra advantages to win.

Or he doesn't want her to win. But Chiyoko refuses to allow this possibility.

Camping with Akina is like living in luxury—or would be, if Chiyoko didn't have to be constantly on guard against attack. She insists on preparing all the food so Akina has no chance to poison her. When Akina goes to bed, Chiyoko slips into the jungle to sleep in the hollow of a tree, safe from midnight ambush. She wakes with the sun and eases herself back into the camp so Akina never suspects a thing.

"Want to do a little sparring?" Akina asks, the first afternoon. "I'm going crazy, just sitting around twiddling my thumbs. Aren't you?"

Chiyoko agrees, warily. But when Akina picks up her throwing stars, Chiyoko folds her arms, shakes her head.

She will fight, but not with weapons.

Not unless this is to be a fight to the death.

Akina shrugs. "Hand-to-hand, then. Have it your way. But I should warn you, I don't lose."

She does.

They grapple, mixing martial arts with street fighting, fists flying, kicks thumping against shins and stomachs, bodies flipping and tumbling, sweat streaking skin, nails scratching, blood staining, and then, all too soon, Akina is on her back and Chiyoko's hands are at her throat.

Akina gasps for breath, taps the ground three times with her right hand, the sign clear: *Stop. You win.*

I give up.

Chiyoko does not stop.

Chiyoko squeezes Akina's neck, presses her knee to Akina's chest, feels her lungs heave, feels her grow feeble as the air does not flow. A few more seconds and Akina will be dead. This will be over. Just a few more seconds of holding on.

But Chiyoko lets go.

Akina does not move, only lies there, gasping, sucking in painful breaths.

"What the hell was that?" she says, when she can speak. Her raspy voice is as perky as ever, but there is a darkness in her eyes, like something wild and unleashed. She knows what it was. She knows why. She just doesn't know why Chiyoko let go.

Chiyoko doesn't either.

She's killed before. She's killed easily. In all the times she's doubted herself, she's never doubted that she could, at the very least, act when necessary. Do what must be done.

Could it be that Satoshi is right? That she's too soft to be the Player? That relying on her would lead the Mu to their doom?

Chiyoko offers Akina her hand, helps the other girl to her feet.

It's different, killing someone who's not trying to kill you. Killing someone who hasn't yet launched an attack. Chiyoko wills Akina to act, to make a move of her own. To shuck off the shallow schoolgirl act and reveal herself as an enemy. If Akina attacks, Chiyoko will be able to defend herself. If Akina would simply *strike*, Chiyoko would not hesitate. But even after the sparring match, even after fingerprint-shaped bruises bloom at Akina's throat, Akina does not attack.

All she does is talk.

And talk and talk and talk.

"You know the best part of this stupid island? No little sisters. You know what I mean? No, wait, you're an only child, am I right? And I bet you always wanted a little sister. Onlies always do. It's because you don't realize how annoying they are. Trust me."

Occasionally she pauses to let Chiyoko nod and shake her head, but often she speaks right through the silence, as if taking charge of Chiyoko's side of the conversation as well as her own. Sometimes she does it so well, and so confidently, that Chiyoko is almost carried along by the illusion. It's nice, pretending to be part of a conversation. Most people fall silent around her, or speak slowly, as if she has a problem with her brain as well as her mouth. Akina acts like it's normal that Chiyoko doesn't speak—like Chiyoko is choosing, for now, to stay silent, but might change her mind at any moment.

"You think you want a sister until you have to buy a dead bolt for your diary and then your boyfriend's getting emails of your incredibly humiliating baby pictures when *someone* gets herself in a sulk just because she's not allowed to borrow your silk dress. Which, by the way, would look ridiculous on a ten-year-old."

Chiyoko has no diary, no baby pictures, no silk dresses. Certainly no boyfriend. But when Akina says, "You see what I mean," she almost does. Akina talks about their island, and sees beauty and magic where Chiyoko only sees utility or danger. "Like a brooding giant," she says, about a massive dark cloud sweeping overhead. While Chiyoko worries about monsoons, about damage to their camp, about storm and ruin, Akina gazes at the sky. "Imagine that, a shadow cast by a fairy-tale beast. A giant fist thrusting toward the earth, scooping us into its cloudy grasp. If I had my paints . . ." She pauses, even blushes a little. "I want to be an artist. I know, it sounds stupid."

Chiyoko doesn't shake her head, doesn't do anything, but Akina smiles as if she has.

"Okay, maybe not stupid. But silly. That's what my father says. That my paintings are as silly as the idea that I could make a living from them. He says it's time I get serious, now that—"

She stops abruptly. For once, Chiyoko wishes she could urge Akina to keep going. Something important was about to come next. An admission. But she can't ask. And Akina doesn't offer.

As Akina talks and talks, Chiyoko hears the truth behind her words, and finally begins to understand. They are at an impasse, the two of them. Chiyoko is too soft to kill Akina before Akina proves herself an enemy. Akina, it's clear, feels the same way. Each of them is silently willing the other to make the first move.

Neither makes it.

Both pretend the silent battle isn't happening. That they are not in a contest of wills that must end in one of their deaths. That this is a waiting game, weakness pitted against weakness, and that eventually, one of them will decide to be strong, and end it.

Akina is better at pretending than Chiyoko has ever been. It is the one skill in which she bests the Player, and as they wait each other out, Chiyoko tries to learn from her.

Akina lives the lie of friendship like she actually believes it's the truth.

When the storm comes, Akina drags Chiyoko out of the tent and into the rain. They whirl in circles and dance and splash. "Like being a little kid again!" Akina says joyfully. Chiyoko, who was never that little, even when she was, can't help but smile.

Nothing about Akina Nori is as Chiyoko expected, and that bothers her. She is supposed to know everything about Akina. She's been trained to understand her enemies—she knows that is the key to any Player's survival. Is it possible that watching someone, spying on their every word and move, is not enough to truly know them? How many other things has she misunderstood, in all her years of hiding and watching?

Akina talks about her parents' marriage (shaky), her schoolwork (dull), her new puppy (prone to peeing in shoes). She talks about hating the way her father tries to control her life.

"He's always telling me what to do, you know? Oh, what am I talking about, of course you know. You probably get it more than anyone. It's not like when you were a little kid you went around saying 'I want to be a Player when I grow up,' right? I mean, you must think about it, what would have happened if it wasn't you. Who you would have been if you had, like, a normal life."

But Chiyoko doesn't think about it, never lets herself. From the day she was born and did not cry, she has never been normal. How could she be owed a normal life?

She has never thought of it this way, her uncle controlling her. He only wants to make her the best Player she can be. How else would he show his love?

"Well, bright side, it's not like you're stuck doing this forever. Make it through a few more years and you get your life back. Unless you believe the whole Endgame thing is actually happening, and happening soon, but who really believes that, deep down?"

They are sitting side by side before a campfire when Akina admits this, roasting fish on twin sticks over the flames. Chiyoko has imagined nights like this, staying up too late, slipping secrets back and forth in the dark with a trusted friend. This is how girls in books live, girls without responsibilities weighing on their shoulders or death hanging over their heads.

Sometimes, on this island, she feels like she's fallen into a dream, the dream of a child hoping to imagine herself into an alternate life.

She and Akina are not friends, will never be friends.

How can they be friends when, no matter how diligently they ignore the fact, only one of them can leave this island alive?

Sometimes it's hard to remember what is the lie and what is the truth.

"You want to know a secret? I can trust you not to tell anyone, right?" Akina laughs at her own lame joke. Then leans in close and lowers her voice. "Sometimes I think the whole thing's bullshit. I mean, come on. *Aliens?* It's about as likely as the idea that there's some Temple of Mu sitting at the bottom of the Pacific. Tell me you didn't laugh in their faces the first time they told you 'the truth.'"

Chiyoko doesn't remember a time when she didn't know the sacred truth of her bloodline. It has never occurred to her that she could question what she's been told.

That belief is a choice.

"So what are you going to do? After, I mean."

Chiyoko has never imagined an after. She is the Player. That is her fate.

How can there be an after to fate?

"Seriously?" Akina says, reading Chiyoko's blank look. "No idea?" She eyes Chiyoko appraisingly. "I think you'd make a good shrink someday. You're such a good listener."

Chiyoko laughs, silently. She is not easily insulted.

"It wasn't a joke!" Akina insists. "You really are. It's not just that you don't talk, it's that . . . you really *hear*, you know?" She falls silent, and gives Chiyoko a strange look.

Chiyoko cocks her head to the side, as if to say, *What?*

"I just didn't know you had a sense of humor," Akina said.

Until now, Chiyoko didn't quite know it either.

"My father thinks I don't take anything seriously enough," Akina says quietly. The smile is gone from her voice. "But he doesn't get it. I have to laugh at it all, because I *do* believe it."

Chiyoko raises her eyebrows.

"Oh, I know what I just said. And I meant it. Aliens, et cetera. It sounds like bullshit. But what can I say? I believe it. I believe our people were all massacred by a bunch of aliens, and that if we don't stay in line, it can all happen again. That the stupid aliens are going to make it their business to be *sure* it happens again. That they set things up so that the only thing standing in their way is a freaking *teenager*. That's what my father doesn't get—if I believe all that, how am I supposed to take anything seriously? How can any of this matter if at any second, the whole world could get wiped out?"

Chiyoko nods, shallowly, to say she understands but perhaps does not agree. Endgame or not, this is the reality of life, she wants to say. Life ends. An ending doesn't remove meaning from all that comes before.

"You ever get jealous of them? The ones who don't know? I mean, I look at my friends, the ones who aren't Mu. Who don't have any idea

98

what's coming. It's so easy for them. They've got nothing to be afraid of. Nothing real, at least. I try so hard to pretend I'm like them, to make myself forget. But I can't forget."

All these days together, and Akina still manages to surprise her. For Chiyoko has envied Akina in exactly the same way Akina envies her friends.

Once again, Chiyoko has mistaken Akina's lies for truth, failed to understand that they are more same than different, that they both live under the reality of obligation.

They have both tried, and failed, to forget.

Perhaps now, it is time to remember.

Chiyoko dreams of Endgame.

She dreams of an all-consuming fire, a sky choked with smoke, a rain of acid and blood.

She dreams of skylines falling, horizons burning, scorched earth stretching to the horizon, sightless eyes and severed limbs and killing fields crowded with death.

She dreams of her uncle, his back turned to danger, and in the dream she wants to call to him, *warn* him, but there is no voice, no call, and the sky falls down on him and crushes him under its giant fist.

She dreams of the life draining out of his disappointed eyes, and of his final words.

I was wrong.

You are too weak.

And now our people will pay the price.

Chiyoko wakes in terror and, for a moment, forgets where she is. Forgets why she is damp and shivering in a pile of dirt rather than tucked safely into her own bed, her uncle's cool hand on her forehead, his reassuring murmur in her ear. Reality creeps back in slowly, and she does her best to shake off the nightmare. Her people believe in dreams, believe that the gods can speak through signs and portents in the night, but not every dream has meaning. Not every dream is truth.

Dawn is on its way. Chiyoko creeps back to the campground so she can feign sleep before Akina wakes, but Akina is gone. A trail of fresh footsteps leads back into the trees, and Chiyoko follows, cautious and quiet. The lightening sky has a heaviness to it, and Chiyoko can feel the night weighing down on her. Something has changed; something is coming.

Akina stands in a clearing, holding a satellite phone that Chiyoko has never seen.

"Yes, Father," Akina says as Chiyoko plays statue in the brush. It's been so long since she had to be invisible.

"No, Father," Akina says. "Not yet. But . . . are you sure there's no other way? She's not like you said. She's—"

Akina goes quiet, her face changing as Satoshi spills poison in her ear. Chiyoko doesn't have to hear his end of the conversation to know what he has to say. She's heard it all before.

"Of course I want our people to survive," Akina says, "but—"

Another silence, longer this time. When Akina speaks again, there is defeat in her voice. "Yes, Father. I understand. Tonight, then. I'll finish it. I promise."

Chiyoko can't help but feel relief. Reality has finally intervened, saved them both from this flight of fantasy. She'd lulled herself into believing there was a choice here: Kill Akina or don't kill Akina. Responsibility or mercy. But there has never been a choice, except the choice to live or the choice to die.

"Yes, Father, I promise. After she goes to sleep. It'll be done."

Yes, tonight, Chiyoko promises herself. Tonight it will be done.

It is a strange day, both of them pretending they don't know it's the last. The hours pass slowly, and Akina is unusually quiet. There is no chatter over breakfast, no complaint about the temperature of the water and the absence of conditioner, no trash-talking when they spar. Chiyoko misses it. She's fallen out of the habit of silence.

"What's it like, being the Player?" Akina asks her that night as they sit by the fire, watching the flames dance and the moon rise. "Do you ever wish it were different, that it didn't have to be you?"

Chiyoko, of course, says nothing. The stars are bright tonight, and feel too close.

"You must wonder sometimes," Akina says, her eyes fixed on the horizon. "What happens if you're not strong enough? If you do something wrong, and everyone dies. To have all that on your shoulders . . ."

Chiyoko wonders if she's trying to make herself feel better, repeating her father's arguments, convincing herself that Chiyoko doesn't deserve her role.

"Sometimes I think it's too much to ask," Akina says. "How can you put all that on us? We're just kids."

Not us, Chiyoko thinks. *Only me.*

Almost as if it's spoken aloud, Akina says, "They shouldn't put it on *you*, I mean."

Chiyoko shrugs. It's hard to do, almost as if Akina spoke the literal truth, and all those lives are balanced on her shoulders, weighing her down.

"Whatever, it's not like you're ever going to have to *do* something. I mean, what are the odds that this Endgame thing is coming soon to an Earth near us? Or coming ever, right? Maybe it's just the world's most sadistic bedtime story." Akina laughs, but there's no joy in it.

Chiyoko climbs to her feet. Enough of this.

"Yeah, I'm tired too," Akina says. She stands and together they damp down the fire. "It was a good day, Chiyoko. Wasn't it?"

Chiyoko can give her this: she nods.

"They've all been good days, I guess," Akina says. "Who would've thought?" She looks up to the sky, its stars gleaming like diamonds on velvet. "I'm going to miss this, I think. Will you?"

Chiyoko shrugs again, but the answer is no. She will do her best to never think of this place, this night, again.

"Good night, Chiyoko."

Akina raises her arm as if to touch Chiyoko, or embrace her, but stops it midair and settles for an awkward wave. Chiyoko waves back.

Good-bye.

Then it is just a matter of waiting for Akina to snuggle into her sleeping bag, close her eyes, and fall asleep, or pretend to.

Chiyoko doesn't bother to pretend. The game ends tonight, one way or another. She sits awake, watching the stars, counting the seconds, and when she can wait no longer, she creeps into Akina's tent. The girl lies on her back, still and peaceful, chest rising and falling in a slow, steady rhythm.

Maybe she's planning to wake early and strike at Chiyoko just before the dawn, or maybe she intended to stay awake but sleep overtook her. It doesn't matter. Chiyoko is tired of trying to understand Akina, to know her.

Knowing her has only made this harder. If she knows more, it might become impossible.

Maybe they shouldn't *put it on me,* she thinks. *Maybe I* am *just a kid.*

But she has never been just a kid.

She has never been just anything.

Her knife is a Japanese tanto, the kind used by the samurai warriors. This blade is double-edged, with an engraved handle that sits perfectly in her palm, and according to her uncle it is more than 900 years old. It is razor sharp. Her uncle gave it to her for her seventh birthday, and she has sharpened it every night since. Even here. Especially here.

Akina will be dead before she has a chance to wake. She will never know pain, she will never know failure. Chiyoko cannot afford to be merciful, but she can at least be kind.

That's the plan, at least.

But as Chiyoko brings the blade to Akina's throat, Akina opens her eyes. She does not flinch. She does not look surprised. Chiyoko realizes she's been awake the whole time. Awake and waiting.

She's been waiting for Chiyoko, for this moment, maybe since the beginning.

The blade rests on the delicate flesh of Akina's neck. Chiyoko does not bear down; Akina does not pull away. Their eyes meet.

"It's the only way," Akina says quietly. "I can't do it. I can't be what he needs me to be. If it has to be one of us, it has to be you."

Chiyoko watches her. There are so many things she wants to say—and at the same time, there is nothing to say. She is thankful to have an excuse for silence. This doesn't feel like killing an enemy.

Because she is not an enemy, not anymore.

Akina has managed to surprise her once again. Chiyoko never thought she was someone who would want to die.

"I don't want to die," Akina says. How is it that she understands Chiyoko so perfectly, when Chiyoko doesn't understand her at all? "But it's better than the alternative. There is no alternative."

Chiyoko dips her head. She needs to live for her people. She needs to live for herself. And if Chiyoko is going to live, if Chiyoko is going to Play, then Akina has to die.

All the doubts she's nursed about herself, about whether she's strong enough for Endgame, strong enough to do whatever needs to be done, they all slip away. In this moment, she knows her own strength, finally knows her determination not just to live, but to win.

This is the certainty that has always awaited her in the dark, but she knows now it will remain when daylight comes. This moment will always sustain her.

This moment, this choice, this will define her.

The elaborate ceremony on her 13th birthday, the solemn promise over an ancient text, the approval of her elders, none of it meant anything, not compared to this moment. To this knife in her hand, to the life it will take.

This is her moment of ascension.

This is how she will finally and wholly accept her fate. This is how she will truly become the Player.

The blade slides easily through flesh, through artery, and when Akina whispers "Thank you," blood bubbles from her lips, and then it is over, and all that is left is silence.

She lays the knife on Akina's body. She will dig a hole by the sea and lay Akina to rest, the knife along with her. She has loved this knife, loved its deadly power and the way it shapes itself to her grip, enacting her will on flesh and blood, tearing life from its victims. But that time is over. When she kills again—and she knows the moment will come, probably soon, and often—there will be no pleasure in it. Only necessity. She understands now, what it means to live a full life, to live outside the game, and she understands what it means to take that life away.

As, in a way, it was taken from her.

Tomorrow, Akina will fail to check in with the mainland. And so Satoshi will know, all will know, the outcome of this test. Soon Chiyoko's people will come for her and ferry her back to her life. But she will not forget what happened on this island. She will not allow herself to forget. She will return as the Player, and if Endgame comes, she will Play. She *chooses* to Play. But she will be a different Player than she was, Playing for a different purpose.

Before, she cared only about living up to expectations, escaping the disappointment of the people she loved. She Played to make her uncle proud, to make her parents love her; she Played to prove herself to her family, and to her bloodline—and there was honor in that. But now she knows better. Now she will also Play for herself, and for the kind of future that Akina dreamed of but will never have. She will endure these years as the Player for what lies at the other end—a life she has never let herself imagine, a life that holds more than duty, a life of laughter and friendship and choice. She will Play for life, and for the hope that, one day, she will have one of her own.

KOORI
ALICE

Alice lies on cold ground, pebbles digging into her back, her eyes fixed on the stars. The land is rusty and flat, hard-packed mesa pockmarked with sickly desert bushes. A flock of corellas skims across the rising moon, and a snake dozes in a dark crevice of the lean-to, but otherwise, Alice is alone. This is the back of beyond, the never-never, harsh desert bushland with no human settlements for hundreds of miles. This is the danger zone, where pitiless sun scorches unwary travelers and bones bleach in the midday heat. It is the unimaginable stretch of emptiness where feral horses run wild, kangaroos bounce across the horizon, and snakes and lizards rule an unforgiving domain.

For Alice, it is home.

She comes here when she can, when she needs to escape, and lets the earth recharge her.

She has been here, alone, for five days, hiking through the bush, slicing up dingoes with her boomerangs and roasting them on a spit, watching the stars spin, thinking. Preparing.

Waiting for the dreams to come.

It's been a full year since Alice spent this much time on her own in the bush. A year since she ventured out into the land with nothing but her buck knife and a supply of water. Five of them had set out that day a year ago, each hiking in a different direction, each hoping that somewhere in the bush the dream would settle upon them. The dream that would name them as the next Player.

Five cousins, five Koori, each a direct descendant of a former Player—

and so each privileged to try for the honor themselves.

Four of them were boys; one of them was Alice.

None of the boys were as tough as she was. None as determined. None had been pushed as hard, trained as well, taught to understand that this moment, this honor, mattered more than anything. None of them believed it would be her, the girl, the ugly girl with the chubby cheeks and the moon-shaped birthmark rising over her eye, the girl with the untamed bird's nest of curls and the dead mother. None of them but Alice, who knew she would return from her solo quest with her ancestors' verdict rendered. She knew she would return home as the Player.

So she was not surprised when the dream came, her ancestors whispering her fate in her ear. She was not surprised to wake with the red kangaroo nuzzling the hollow of her neck, sacred creature of her people offered as a tribute from the sleeping world to the waking one. She has not returned since, because she has not needed to return— her path as the Player has been clear, her training easy and almost joyful, her days driven by a purity of purpose.

Until now.

Now she's returned to her homeland, to the earth that gifted her with her duty and destiny. She's returned for guidance from her ancestors. She's walked; she's fasted; she's wilted in the heat and shivered in the night. She's waited for the dreams, and the dreams have not come. Alice has patience. She trusts the land; she trusts the spirits of her people. She waits.

She watches the stars. They feel closer tonight.

Everything feels closer tonight: the sky, the ground, her future. The time is near, she thinks. The answers are close.

She breathes.

She trusts.

She sleeps.

She dreams.

* * *

Flames streak from the stars. Dusty plains erupt in pillars of light. The sky is on fire.

Alice watches the world begin and end and begin again. She is an eye of calm at the center of the raging storm of eternity.

She is Alice Ulapala, Player of the Koori. Savior of the Koori. She is Alice the Player, but also Alice the 112th, an infinitesimal point on the unbroken line of her people. She is both at once, and also neither, also a free-floating consciousness on the sea of time, dipping into the now and the then and the might someday be.

In this place between, there is no one-thing-after-another, no cause and effect. No boundaries between past and present, between Alice and her people and her world.

This is where Alice will find her answers. From her ancestors. From herself.

This is where the spirits of the Koori dwell, all memories of past and possibilities of future mingling together, melting into an endless stream.

This is dreamtime.

Her question is not asked in words, nor is the answer spoken aloud. But as Alice slips deeper into dreamtime, as she soaks in the desire of her line and the visions of fiery future, she understands.

The future is unwritten, its possibilities branching in two directions: death and life. This moment is the hinge.

She is the hinge.

What she does now, what she chooses to do, how she Plays, this will alter the flow of events. This will carry her line forward, or end it.

Alice is Alice the 112th. She is only a single Player in a line of Players stretching back through the millennia. But she sees here, in this place that is no place, that she is the one that counts.

Alice feels the tendrils of the waking world reaching for her, pulling her from the dream.

Color and light fade away, and the heaviness sets in.

The weight of reality.

The weight of time.

She holds fast to the dream as it fades. She lets her spirit stretch through the flow of ancestors, the eternal slivers of soul of all who came before, and, as she always does, seeks out a single bright light in the shimmering stream.

Somewhere among that line, somewhere in dreamtime, lives her mother.

Or, at least, the elemental piece of her mother that slipped into eternity as her body returned to the earth.

But the line is unbroken, the stream undifferentiated. Her mother is only one of many, a single star in a cluster of galaxies, unfindable.

Alice never stops looking.

She wakes knowing what she needs to know.

She needs to stop delaying and fulfill her duty.

She needs to Play.

She radios Henry, her trainer, who's waiting on her word, the plane fueled and ready to go. She didn't tell him why she needed to come out here, or how much—but she didn't have to. Henry knows her well enough to understand why, for the first time, she has hesitated. As he knows her well enough to trust that she will return, ready to fulfill her obligations, to carry out her next mission, to follow orders. He knows her well enough to wait.

And she knows him well enough to know he hated every minute of it. Now she puts him out of his misery.

"Come and get me, mate," she says into the satellite phone, marveling that even out here in the heart of nowhere, this tiny machine can commune with the stars. Or at least a mechanical approximation of them whirling through the ether, beaming her words to an airstrip 300 miles away. "And make it snappy."

There's nothing much Alice loves about flying. Especially in this tin can of a plane.

Especially with Henry at the controls.

He's always a nervous driver, and being several thousand feet above the surface of the earth never helps his mood.

"Still the same as the last thirty times you checked," Alice teases as he sneaks yet another glance at the altimeter.

"It never hurts to be careful."

"No Player ever won by being careful," Alice says.

"And that's why I never let *you* drive," Henry points out. "Now, can I get back to outlining your mission?"

"You're the boss," she says, but when he returns to describing the target, she tunes him out. Instead she stares out the mottled window, watching the plane's wing tear through wisps of cloud. True, there's nothing to love about flying, but it's better for her than what's waiting on the ground.

"Are you even listening?" Henry asks, without looking over at her. He knows her that well.

"Maybe it'd be easier to pay attention if ya didn't yabber on so much," she suggests.

"This is important, Alice."

"Everything's *important* with you, Henry. You'd think the fate of the world was at stake or something." She grins, because that's what she does when she's nervous. Finds something to laugh about. Something to let out the pressure and remind herself that life isn't always so deadly serious. Even her life. Henry, on the other hand, doesn't crack a smile. "Sometimes I think you're missing the humor gene."

"I have an excellent sense of humor," Henry says drily. "That's why I only laugh at things that are *funny*."

"Oh, I see, you're training me to tell better jokes. Glad to see you finally realize that a good Player needs a sense of humor."

"A Player has no need to be funny," Henry says sternly. But he can't help himself. His lips quirk into a small smile. "My daughter, on the other hand, should find herself some better material. This family has a reputation for comedy to uphold."

Alice gives him a gentle slug on the shoulder. "Yeah, Dad, that's what I always say about you. You're a laugh a minute."

He pretends to take offense at the insult, and she pretends to mean it, and for a moment, everything is like it used to be between them. For a moment, they are father and daughter, the two of them against the world, laughing in the face of death and danger.

Then the moment passes. Henry hands her a dossier. "Study it. We've only got a half hour till we land."

He didn't used to be this serious. When he first started training her, he made it into a game. She was five years old and her mother was dead. They both needed something to do—some way to be with each other and to be with their own grief, without letting it consume them. Training showed them the way. Henry taught her to be strong, taught her to run and hunt and fight. He taught her to love her people, and to love life again, even without the person who had given it meaning. They trained hard, but they also laughed, a lot. They came to know each other, to understand each other and trust each other, as they never had before. They learned to be two instead of three. And they did it all without forgetting the woman they'd lost, not for a single second. How could they, when life was all about Playing, and Alice's mother had been a Player?

Not just any Player, but one of the best.

She'd broken records (and more than a few noses). She'd made a name for herself by the time she was fourteen, been beloved by her people for her courage, infamous for her fearlessness and steely nerve. She'd bested one death-defying risk after another, waiting eagerly for Endgame to arrive so she could fulfill her destiny and save the world. But it didn't matter how good she was—she'd ended up just like every other Player before her. Waiting in vain for the beings from the stars to return. Growing up, growing old, until she was too old to Play. Old enough to fall in love, take a husband, bear a daughter, get cancer, die.

Infamous nerve, fearlessness, courage—none of it helped her, not in the end.

Or rather, it did help.

Just not enough.

At first, Alice trained to forget her mother—pushing her body to its limits was the best way to escape her mind, and her pain. But later, she trained to remember. She dreamed of becoming as good as her mother, as brave and strong. The older she got, the fuzzier her memories got. Life before her mother's illness was little but old stories and faded photos. Alice had always thought that if she could really do it, if she could be named the Player, she would have a connection to her mother that neither time nor death could break.

Maybe Henry had thought so too.

Maybe he'd thought that by turning her into the Player her mother used to be, he could bring his wife back.

Maybe he still thinks so, even though now Alice *is* the Player, and she's no closer to her mother than ever.

The only thing that's changed, now that it's official, is Henry. Training used to be the thing that made them a family. But once she officially took on her role as a Player? Training took over their lives. It's all Henry talks about anymore, all he thinks about. In his eyes, she's a Player first, a daughter second. Sometimes she wonders if he even remembers he's more than just her trainer. If, maybe, he wishes he weren't.

"I don't know what you're so worried about," she tells him now. "I'll get the job done. Don't I always?"

"This isn't like the others, Alice. This is your first kill."

"Tell that to the dingoes," she points out. She once took out three with a single toss of her boomerang, a personal record.

"Your first *human* kill," he says, like she needs the reminding. Like this whole field trip to the bush, this journey into her dreams, hasn't been about exactly this moment. This mission. Her first human kill. She's mastered everything else a Player could possibly need to do.

She's an expert in 16 different forms of hand-to-hand combat, can handle ancient weapons just as well as she can an AK-47; she's leaped out of airplanes, scaled mountains, scavenged for artifacts at the bottom of the sea, deciphered coded passages that have foiled expert cryptographers for centuries. But she's never killed a person before. She's always found a way to avoid it, another way to get the job done. A better, easier, less deadly way.

Until now.

Now Henry says it's time she learns what it means to kill.

Learns whether or not she has it in her to do it.

Learns now, before her life and the lives of her entire people are at stake.

This dossier in her lap lays out the life of a man who will be dead by sunrise, if she does what she's supposed to do.

She opens the file.

Zeke Cable is a 42-year-old bank executive with a wife, a child, a three-bedroom condo in a fashionable part of Melbourne, and a studio in a significantly less fashionable one. His juvenile record shows a couple of misdemeanor charges from his days as a graffiti skate punk, but since then, he's stayed clean. No record, not even a drunk-driving charge. No signs of criminal activity or domestic abuse. No sign he's done anything deserving of death.

And she's supposed to kill him?

"What the bloody hell is this, Henry?" she growls.

"What?"

"You know what."

Maybe so, but he pretends not to. "I don't think I'm asking you to do any more than you're capable of," he says. "The target poses minimal risk to you."

"I'll say," she snaps. "You want me to shoot some random guy? Some innocent who hasn't done anything wrong?"

"Everyone's done something wrong."

"You know what I mean."

"And you know what I mean," Henry says. "He's not Koori, if that's what you're worried about."

Alice laughs angrily. "You think *that's* what I'm worried about? So if he's not Koori, it means he deserves to die?"

"It means you're not meant to care whether he dies or not," he says. "The *Koori* are your concern. No one else."

Alice remembers a time, long ago, when she was still doing target practice with her boomerang. She spotted a kangaroo streaking through the bush and was set to take it down, when her father stayed her hand. "There are those who believe roos are sacred to our people," he told her. When she asked if *he* believed this, he shrugged, and said better safe than sorry. "It's always better to err on the safe side when it comes to killing, Allie." He had called her that when she was small, and then, eventually he stopped. She didn't remember when, or why. "Killing is one choice you can't take back."

Even when he was pushing her past her limits, he was gentle with her then.

That stopped too.

And apparently he's changed his mind about killing.

Or maybe his rules are different when it comes to people.

"I thought you were going to set me out against a criminal, Henry," she says. A part of her knows there's no point in arguing, but she can't help trying. He's taught her never to give up. "A drug dealer. A gangster. A terrorist. You know, a *bad guy*."

"Like in the movies?" he says, keeping his eyes straight ahead. She doesn't know if he's refusing to look over at her, or just doesn't want to bother. "Real life isn't always so black-and-white, Alice. Though if it makes you feel better, Zeke Cable *is* a bad guy."

"Oh, yeah? What, did he cheat on his taxes? Roll a bloody joint?"

"He's dangerous, Alice. He's a dangerous man whose death is necessary for the protection of the Koori people. You don't need to know why. You don't need to see evidence. You just need to trust me, and do as you're told."

"Kill him," she clarifies.

"Yes."

"Just to prove that I can?" She snorts. "That's stupid."

"What's stupid is putting the fate of our people on the shoulders of a girl who's afraid to kill," Henry snaps. "It doesn't have to be easy. It should never be easy. But sometimes it must be done, and you have to *know* you can do it. Otherwise you might be the one to die."

"You're yabbering again," she tells him. "I get it."

"I just want to make sure you understand why I'm asking you to do this. And that you're careful." He puts his fingers to his lips and then to her forehead, as he always does before a mission, and she allows it, because before he was her trainer, he was her father, and sometimes he still is.

"I'm always careful," she tells him.

"You're never careful. And I know this mission is—"

"I told you, I get it. It's peachy," she says, not wanting to hear him hammer away at it more. Not wanting to hear her father urging her to kill. She understands that it needs to be done, and she understands that that's what being the Player is all about. Doing what must be done. The spirits of her ancestors have affirmed that this is the way, that Alice must fulfill her duty. Whether she likes it or not, it's time for her to prove herself.

To kill a human being.

Just to show that she can.

Alice hates Melbourne.

She hates all cities, the way the buildings press in on you and block out the sky, the air heavy with smog, the streets dense with people. The crush of bodies, the brute intrusion of humanity at every turn, its smells and fluids and inescapable whine. The cruelty of humanity, that pains her too, and it is nowhere more evident than in cities, where breathing bodies stretch along sidewalks and curl against buildings and are treated by passersby like inanimate parts of the landscape. Eyesores to be stepped over, brushed past—overlooked and ignored. Melbourne is meant to be one of the loveliest cities in the world, but all Alice sees is a desecration of land, a trash heap of so-called civilization where once there was beauty.

She's a creature of the land. She doesn't want to spend any more time here than she needs to.

But she's in no hurry to get the job done.

Zeke Cable lives in a bleak, modern high-rise that towers over its neighbors. The building is nearly all windows. It's not a home for someone with secrets. It's a building meant for people eager to show off, to live their lives under a spotlight, hoping passersby will envy the glow.

The doorman gives Alice the side-eye when she steps past. Even in her city drag—black skirt and impractical heels—he can tell she doesn't belong here. But she's hacked the complex's computer system and put herself on the list of approved guests for apartment 12D, so there's little he can do.

Apartment 12D is a multimillion-dollar luxury condo with views of the water, whose resident is on a business trip in Sydney.

Apartment 12D is also directly above Zeke Cable's apartment, with a convenient network of air and heating ducts connecting the two.

From her luxury perch, Alice can listen in on her target. She can watch him through the vents, see him pack his daughter off to school in the morning and burn his toast, see him rant at the sports page and kiss his wife good-bye. And that evening, she can watch him strip down to his boxers and crawl into bed beside his sleeping wife; she can unscrew a vent and ease it open; she can lower her Colt Delta Elite and orient its muzzle in the direction of his head.

Her stocky, muscled body is a cramped fit in the narrow ducts. Her grip is slick with sweat, but she holds the gun steady.

The boomerang's no good in close quarters like this, not when she doesn't have enough room for a good throw. It makes sense to use a gun.

Except she hates guns. Hates the cold machinery of them, the cold steel wall they erect between predator and prey. Hates how *easy* they make things. Her boomerangs are a part of her, an extension of her limbs. Most of the world imagines them as a joke, a child's toy, and so much the better. The best weapons are easily underestimated. Just because Alice has only wounded, never killed, just because she prefers to hunt animals over people, doesn't mean she doesn't know a good weapon when she sees one.

She has many, and treasures them all. The smooth wood boomerang she's had since she was a child, the carbon-reinforced plastic one Henry gave her for her last birthday, with its aerodynamically perfect angle and razor edge. Her mother's boomerang, carved out of bone and handed down her line for centuries, from Player to Player, a deadly gift from the past. Each is a weapon that requires dedication and skill—more than that, it demands a deep knowing, a communing with both the world and the target. It means understanding angles and wind currents and anticipating your target's next move before he knows it himself. A good throw casts the boomerang into the future, allowing the target to step into his own fate.

Guns feel like cheating.

All of this feels like cheating. There's no challenge in reaching through a vent and putting a silenced bullet in a sleeping man's head. There's certainly no justice in it.

There's no *sense* in it.

Henry has always done what's best for her, and for her training. If he says she has to kill this man—if he says it's better for the Koori if this man dies—then he must have a good reason. But there's no reason to take that on faith.

If Zeke Cable does need to die, then Alice will make it happen. She promises herself that. But first she will take the time to get to know her target, to find out what's so dangerous about him. She'll convince herself of what needs to be done.

And then she'll find it in herself to do it.

It's a good plan.

Except that she can't find the answer to her question. She can't find anything about Zeke Cable that would consign him to death. She watches him in his apartment, stalks him through the city streets, slips into his office disguised as a delivery girl, hacks his computer files, taps his phones, and finds . . . nothing.

Or rather, she finds the foibles of a middling man, one who sometimes tries his best and sometimes doesn't bother.

He's a fine father, except when he's in a temper and rages at his six-year-old until she bursts into tears. He follows celebrity gossip, but mocks his wife for watching reality TV. He also cheats on her, and keeps a studio apartment in the city for rendezvous with his mistresses, both of whom are nearly a decade younger than he is. He spends more of his workday surfing the Net than actually working and, probably of more concern to his employers, has embezzled nearly half a million dollars of company funds. He's untrustworthy and often unkind.

But that's not enough for her.

She doesn't know what would be. She doesn't know if Henry's right, if there's a softness in her that needs to be rooted out. Maybe even if Cable were a monster, an unabashed killer who took giggly pleasure in stabbing women in dark alleys or smothering small children, she would still hesitate to put him down. Would still pull back at the last second, thinking about what it means to pull a trigger, to end a life, blot out an existence for all time.

Maybe, but her father hasn't given her the chance to find out.

He's never been one for easy tests.

"We don't know what Endgame will be," he likes to say. "But we know it won't be easy."

Cable's daughter is named Lily, and at six years old she has a sunshine smile, Pippi Longstocking pigtails, and a blithe trust that the world is without shadow. She loves her father, even when he yells, and she doesn't imagine a life in which he does not exist.

Alice knows this, because she remembers being six and assuming her parents were immutable fixtures. She remembers discovering she was wrong.

Alice watches Cable's eyes sparkle as Lily locks her arms around his neck, watches him swing her through the air while she giggles and cries, "More, Daddy, more!"

Alice never played this kind of game with her own father—or if she did, she no longer remembers. When he smiles at her with fatherly pride, it is because she has set the explosives properly and demolished a building in one shot, or she has translated a difficult passage of Coptic that has foiled scholars three times her age. Never because she's giggled or smiled or put her arms around him and called him Daddy.

She's certainly never called him that.

Love doesn't have to come with hugs and giggles, she knows that.

And love doesn't make someone a good person, she knows that too.

Even bad guys have someone they love; even monsters have family.

But if she kills this guy in cold blood, which of them is the monster?

The longer Alice stays in apartment 12D, the longer Alice listens and watches and lives as Zeke Cable's shadow, the less sure she is.

She descended into dreamtime to ask the question, and her ancestors answered:

You are the Player.

This is your fate.

She has seen the two futures spread out before her, the destruction lying in wait if she chooses to abdicate responsibility, defy her elders and her destiny.

But dreams are unspecific—loopholes abound.

Who's to say fulfilling her duty means doing exactly as Henry says, following his orders blindly? Who's to say Playing means obeying? Means killing?

Sometimes she wonders what her training might have been like if her mother had lived. Or whether she would have been trained at all. Maybe, having endured those years as the Player, Shayna Ulapala would have wanted a different life for her daughter—different choices. Alice tries to imagine that. Imagine if, instead of spending every second of her childhood competing with her cousins, learning to stalk prey and strike down her enemies, studying the words of the past and the threat of the future, she had grown up without responsibility, believing there was nothing to fear. Imagine if she had played with dolls and puppies, attended a normal school, made friends and cut classes, lived life like the girls on TV.

Alice tries to imagine, but it's impossible. It's like trying to imagine herself out of existence—everything she is, everything she's ever known or cared about, is rooted in this life, this game.

Playing is who she is. Everything she is.

But she won't Play by anyone else's rules, not even Henry's.

She's been taught that the Koori are unique among all the peoples on Earth, because only they did not bow to the creatures from the stars. Only they were not pressed into servitude by these beings. They have been, will always be, freethinkers. Standing on their own. Beholden to no one.

She went through the motions of this mission, but her heart was never in it—perhaps because deep down, she knew the truth. Her truth.

She cannot do it.

She will not.

Alice returns home expecting Henry to be angry. It's why—immediately after giving Zeke Cable's employers an anonymous tip about the embezzlement, because she can at least do that much—she shut off her cell phone. She doesn't want to talk to her father until she can do it face-to-face, explain why she's disobeyed his direct orders, decided for herself to cancel her mission, because it was stupid.

She doesn't plan to use the word *stupid*, of course. She knows how to handle her father when he's angry.

Except she's never seen him *this* angry.

"Sit," he says as soon as she appears in the doorway. Somehow, she can tell from his voice and the steel in his eyes, he already knows what she's done.

"If you'd just let me explain—"

"Sit," he says, with tightly contained fury. He flips on the TV. "Watch."

There's a nightmare on the screen.

Flames and smoke and screams. It looks so much like the horror she's seen in her dreams that she has to steady herself for a moment, remind herself that she is awake, that this is life.

And when she does, the words of the newscast penetrate.

A bomb, at a Melbourne shopping mall.

An explosion, flying shrapnel, bloody children, weeping mothers, bodies piled on bodies, heads and fingers and ragged limbs.

"Don't you dare look away," her father snaps, but she can't. She is fixed on the screen.

Because it's the camera that has looked away from the carnage, has turned to the faces of the men responsible.

Three strangers, and a man she's come to know, or thought she'd come to know, as well as anyone could.

Zeke Cable.

Part of an antigovernment anarchist group, the news says, and more pictures come on the screen: the two young women she'd assumed were mistresses.

These were the accomplices.

Conspirators.

Murderers.

The group moved ahead faster than planned when an anonymous tip set authorities on Cable's trail. It was thanks to the tip that they were caught.

Thanks to Alice.

Many things, she now sees, are thanks to Alice.

She turns to her father, a white-hot fury building in her to match his own. "You knew," she says. "You knew he was going to do this. And you didn't tell me."

"I told you he was dangerous," Henry says. "I told you he needed to die."

"But you didn't tell me *why*!" she shouts. As part of her training, Alice has learned to control her emotions, especially the ones that threaten to overpower her. It's never been something she's very good at, and now she doesn't even bother. She wants Henry to know she's angry. To see how he's betrayed her.

Tricked her into betraying her people.

"What would you have done, if I'd told you everything?" Henry asks.

"You know what I would have done," she says. "I would have stopped him."

"Killed him?"

"If I had to," Alice says, knowing in her core that it's true.

"I believe you," he says. "But what would you have learned from that? You won't always have all the information, Alice. Not in Endgame, not in life. You need to learn to act on the information you've been given. Tips, guesses, hunches. You need to know who you can trust, and be willing to act on their word. You need to take action that might seem distasteful to you, and trust that it serves a higher purpose."

"You want me to just follow orders, is that it?" she says snidely. "Last I checked, I was the Player, not you. Last I checked, you were *never* good enough to be a Player. Why would I follow anyone's orders, especially yours?"

She expects this to push him over the line, but instead the words seem to move him in another direction. He softens, if only slightly.

"You're not really angry at me," he says.

"Wanna bet?"

"You're angry at yourself. For letting all these people die."

"You—"

"No, Alice. *You*."

Something in her disintegrates. Because even if he's wrong, he's still right. Not him. Or not just him.

Her.

She switches off the TV, but she can't switch off her mind, her photographic memory calling up every body part, every tearstained face, every scream. These will remain in her head, forever. These will remain on her shoulders, forever.

"It was difficult for her at first too," he says, and Alice goes still.

He's talking about her mother.

He almost never talks about her mother.

"She had to learn to wall away her humanity," he says. "To Play coldly, rationally. It's not enough to know you can kill in the heat of action. You need to be able to kill because necessity dictates it, because *reason* dictates it, no matter how you might feel."

"You want me to kill off my humanity?" Alice says, incredulous.

"If that's what's necessary to win Endgame, then what's the point? How could the slice of humanity worth saving be the one that's least human?"

"If Endgame comes, you won't be Playing it to save your own life," her father points out, almost gently. "You'll be Playing to save your people. Maybe it's worth it to make yourself a little less human, if it means your people can live. Your mother thought so."

Alice can't bear to hear this anymore.

She can't bear to hear him urging her to shut off, to shut down, to make herself someone cold and heartless.

She can't bear to hear him claiming that her mother did exactly that.

She can't bear to think he might be right.

In the dream, she is alone.

Alone with cold earth and empty sky.

The Mothers and Fathers and Sisters and Brothers of the line have abandoned her, for she has abandoned them.

She listens for her people.

Listens for the earth.

Listens.

Listens.

But there is only silence.

This has happened before. A Player walking away from her duty. And so from her people.

A Player who will not Play.

Alice knows: there is no place for a soul like that among the Koori. No place in the eternal stream of ancestors, no place in past, present, or future.

To walk away from one is to walk away from all.

To exile oneself from the Koori and the land, from the heart and the breath of life.

To be alone.

She cannot live like this, in this abomination of silence.

Life cannot survive in a vacuum.

Alice cannot survive the emptiness left in her ancestors' wake.

She is Koori, and Koori are never alone.

To be alone is to be no longer Koori.

To lose them is to lose herself.

This dream, she knows, is her future.

One possible future.

But only if she chooses it.

She chooses her people. She chooses her duty, her obligation, her privilege.

She chooses her father.

And her mother.

She can't make up for what she's done—for what she's let this monster do.

But she can make sure he never gets the chance to do it again.

She can be cold and rational; she can weigh the risks of due process and a juried trial; she can decide, heartlessly, that, better late than never, Zeke Cable should die. At her hand.

In the dark before dawn, she leaves her father a note, assuring him that when she comes back, she'll be ready to begin her training in earnest.

To turn herself into whatever her people need her to be.

Even if it's a killer.

The prison is a couple hundred miles outside of Sydney. It is a maximum security facility, with several layers of security checkpoints and a fleet of armed guards. It is a cement fortress, impossible to break out of—or into.

Alice doesn't need to break in. They open the door wide and welcome her through the gates. Because all the technology and armory in the world can't compensate for human foolishness.

She's always looked older than her age, and her falsified documents are flawless. One checkpoint after another waves her through, just another government agent with top clearance come to speak to the high-priority prisoner. A young female one, and so easily overlooked. Easily underestimated.

She insists on being alone with the prisoner. His legs are chained together, and another chain wraps from his ankles to the wall. He is nailed in place like a rabid guard dog, but he's no danger to her. He's no fighter. She knows him well enough to know that.

Though she's been wrong before.

"Who are you?" he says sourly. "Another fed? I'll tell you what I told them. The only criminal here is the government. You're the oppressors. We're the slaves. All I did was deliver a wake-up call. Sacrifice to a higher cause. You all want to talk about killers and innocent victims, look in the mirror. Look at what your so-called civilization has done to the planet. To the people. Wake up, and see what you've wrought. Wake up, because there's more to come."

"That's more than enough. I'm not here to talk," she says, and lets down her hair, pulling out the long strand of wire that's been holding it in place. She stretches the garrote tight, giving Zeke Cable a chance to take in the razor-thin, gleaming wire she intends to wrap around his throat.

"Give me a break," he says. "You think you can scare me into naming names? Giving up all our plans? You all may be a bunch of criminals, but you're not stupid enough to try that."

"I don't know who you think you're talking to, mate, but I can promise you, I'm not stupid. And I'm not trying to scare you into anything." He must hear something in her voice, something that spells out serious business, because his face goes pale. He starts yelling, screaming for someone to come.

But the cell is soundproofed, and he can't reach far enough to press the switch that would summon the guards. She's wearing a low-frequency signal disrupter that will force the video surveillance into a stutter: Anyone watching will see only the same few seconds played over and over again in a loop. No one will see what happens next.

They are alone, and they will remain alone until the job is done.

"What are you," he whispers, "some kind of crazy vigilante?"

"There's nothing crazy about this," she says, though her heart doesn't seem to know it, thumping away like a lunatic pounding on its padded walls. "Killing you, after what you've done? To keep you from doing more? That's just logic. It's justice. An eye for an eye, mate. A life for a life."

"Bullshit, it's revenge," he spits out. "It's murder."

"You can't murder an animal. I'm putting you down, that's all. Like a wild dog." She doesn't know why she's bothering to argue with him. Why she's letting him postpone the inevitable.

"Then we're both animals," he says. "Look in the mirror, sweetie, we're the same. You're about to have blood on your hands too."

"There won't be any blood," she says, and advances on this man, this man she's watched at home and at work, with his child and with his wife, this man she's seen snore through the night and whistle through the day, this man she thought she knew but never knew at all.

This man who has carved a wound across his city that will take years to heal.

This man who deserves to die. So she tells herself, and she believes it.

This is justice.

Not vengeance. Not rage. Not sorrow or guilt or raw animal need.

He is the animal, she tells herself, trying to do as her mother would do, freeze out the heat of anger and need, wall away her self, retreat to something cool and calm. But there is nowhere to retreat to. Not from the screams of his victims—*their* victims. Only one thing will silence those. Only one thing will start to fix the thing they broke together. *I will put him down.*

She will.

She does.

She loops the wire around his neck.

She pulls it tight, cutting off his airway.

She listens to him gasp and wheeze.

She holds firm against his flails and spasms.

She feels the life leak out of his body; she feels him lose the will to live.

She feels herself lose something too.

She feels the pulse stop beating.

She feels the skin grow cool.

She has done this.

She has killed.

It was supposed to be easy, erasing this man, whoever he was and is and might have become, from the living world. It was supposed to feel right. To *be* right.

She turns the body to the wall. She presses the switch on the cell door to signal her readiness to leave, walks calmly down the corridor, submits herself to the security searches, readies herself for the possibility that she will be caught, that they will see through her to the thing inside, the thing that has killed.

Now, finally, too late, she feels cold.

Numb.

Now, finally, too late, her mind is clear, her blood ice.

And clearly, coldly, numbly, she hears her father's words echo in her ears.

Killing is one choice you can't take back.

Henry is waiting for her outside the gate.

"I didn't tell you to come," she says, through the car window.

"I know," he says. There's gray in his hair she's never noticed before. Lines creasing his forehead, hollows beneath his eyes. They've both gotten so much older than they used to be. "I came anyway. Get in."

She collapses into the passenger seat.

Says nothing.

Closes her eyes, wishes for the obliteration of sleep.

Hopes not to dream.

They drive for a long time, in silence. She opens her eyes only when the car eases to a stop. They have parked in a glade, a wonder of grass and trees and stream, all emerald greens and vivid sky blues. A delicate white footbridge crosses the stream. It feels like a storybook, and it's easy to imagine a troll crouching beneath the bridge, fairies peeping out from periwinkle blossoms.

She stumbles on the pebbled path, and he reaches out to steady her. She lets him. Even though they both know she doesn't need him; she's too strong to fall.

"Do you know where we are?" he asks.

Alice can't breathe. She nods.

She hasn't been here in nearly a decade. She hasn't been here since her mother died.

This is the place they would come, she and her father, when the hospital got too much for them. When they needed a moment to breathe, to forget central lines and IV drips, to listen to the wind and the water rather than the beeping of heart monitors and the siren song of a code blue. This hidden idyll, only a few miles from the hospital, was where they would come to return to the earth, if only for an hour or two. To root themselves in the land and try to believe there would be life after death—that they could lose their foundation and somehow still go on.

They stand on the bridge, side by side, staring down at the water. It's cloudier than Alice remembers.

"I did it," she tells Henry. "I killed him."

"I know."

"I thought it was what you wanted. What she would have wanted.
I thought I could do what you said, be cold. Like a machine. Do it
because it was the right thing to do."

"But . . ."

"But it doesn't feel right," she admits. "It didn't feel cold." She shivers,
cold now, cold always. She wonders if she will ever be warm. "I can't
do that again. I won't."

"No, I don't think you will."

"I mean, I can kill, if I need to. But only if I need to. Never again like . . .
that."

"I know."

Alice can feel the tears leaking out, and is ashamed. She is the Player.
Players don't cry. "I've made so many mistakes."

Henry puts his hand over hers. "I made the mistake."

"I can do this," she insists, suddenly terrified that he's regretting
all their choices, regretting pushing her as hard as he has. That
everything will be taken away from her. "I'm strong enough. I am."

"Of course you are," he says. "I'm the one who . . ." He shakes his
head. Sighs heavily. "You had to learn to kill. But this wasn't the way
to teach you. This wasn't the lesson you should have learned. None
of this was." He finally faces her, and squeezes her hand, so hard it
nearly hurts. "You didn't fail me, Alice, and you didn't fail your people.
I'm the only one who's failed here."

"No," she says, too quietly to hear. Then louder, because it's true, and
she needs him to know it. *"No."*

"Was this the right choice for you, this life?" he says. "Are you happy?"
They're both surprised when a small snort of laughter bubbles out
of her. "Not right now." She smears a sleeve across her nose. "But
usually? Yeah." She realizes the deep truth of it only as she says it out
loud. Playing was never a choice; it was a birthright. She would Play

because her mother Played. That was the plan from the beginning. That was the agreement between her and Henry. Playing was how they would keep her mother alive.

That was how it began.

But now?

She Plays because she is the Player.

Because she *wants* to be.

She has chosen. She keeps choosing, every day. Even when it hurts, even when it burns, this is the life she chooses. Not because it's the only life she's ever known.

Because it's the life she wants.

"It's been good, Henry. Training. Playing. It's all good. I'm good. I'm telling you, I can do this. I can be as good as she was."

"Alice, you can't be the Player your mother was," he says.

No words have ever hurt more.

But then he continues. "You can only be the Player *you* are. You can only be Alice. I was wrong to try to make you into something you're not. I don't know, maybe . . ." He hesitates, as if afraid to say it. "Maybe your mother was wrong herself. But you, Alice. You're not cold. You can't be, and you shouldn't be. All that crap about walling away your humanity? You know what that was?"

"Crap?" she guesses, laughing again. It makes her feel lighter; it makes her feel almost like herself again.

"You cling to that," he says fiercely. "Your humanity. Your humor. Your incredibly maddening stubborn streak. You cling to everything that makes you Alice. *That's* what will make you great."

She leans her head on his shoulder, remembering other days by this stream, when she only came up to his waist. When her father seemed the biggest, strongest person in her world, strong enough to save them both.

"*This* is what will make me great," she tells him.

Maybe things would be different, if her mother were here. Maybe she would be a different Player, or no Player at all. But she'll never know.

This is the life she has, this life with the two of them.

This is the Player she chooses to be, one who will do anything for her people and for this most important person, one who will make her own decisions and Play by her own rules, one who will temper ruthlessness with mercy, one who will make mistakes, and do what she can to fix them. One who will never let herself forget what it is to feel love or anger or pain.

One who will never forget what it is to feel human.

ENDGAME

THE TRAINING DIARIES

— VOLUME 2 —

DESCENDANT

LA TÈNE
AISLING

This is the story Aisling Kopp, Player of the 3rd line, does not know.
This is the story Aisling Kopp will never know, because the only one who could tell it is dead.
This is the story of her life and her line—the story of how she began and how the world will end.
This is the story of a hero and a traitor, neither of them certain which is which.
This is the story before the story.
Before Aisling.

The end:
Declan Kopp stands at the mouth of the cave, a 2,500-year-old sword in his hand. The heft of it calms him. The familiar grip reminds him of a time when the Falcata was rightfully his to wield, a simpler time, when he could lay its blade against flesh and enjoy the kill.
A time before Aisling was alive, a time before Lorelei was dead, a time when he was young and foolish and the sword was a symbol of all things just and good.
Now it's nothing but a symbol of the lines he's crossed.
The people he's betrayed.
The home he's left behind and the family to which he can never return.
The ancient sword, like the polished stone in his pocket, like the baby whimpering in the dark depths of the cave, is a precious stolen good.
Not his to take—but taken nonetheless.

That's what *they* would say, at least.

They: the High Council. The La Tène Player. His father.

Everyone who matters to him, or once did.

Once, he had so much in his life. Family, love, hope—the belief that his life's mission was just and his future was fated. Once, he had certainty.

Now he has only his stolen child, and her birthright.

He has the Falcata, whose razor-sharp blade has taken 3,890 lives and awaits its next kill.

And he has a few precious hours, or maybe minutes, before they come for him and try to reclaim what he's stolen—before he and the sword make their last stand.

The child's cries echo through the dark.

"Peace, Aisling," he calls to her. "Daddy's here. Daddy will protect you, I promise."

She's too young to understand—and too young to recognize the lie. He can't promise to protect her. Only to try.

He's given up everything, trying to save his daughter from her fate— but still it's not enough. The cave is surrounded. There's no way out. No way down the mountain, not for him. The final battle is coming, and he will not survive it. He knows that.

He's lured them here, knowing that.

They will pursue him wherever he goes. He finally understands: There is no safe place for him and his daughter, not in this world. He fought; he lost. Letting them follow him here is his last, final, desperate effort to make them see the truth.

If they see it—if he can *make* them see it—everything he's given up will be worth it. Even his life.

The child cries and cries.

Declan can't stand the sound of it.

He turns his back to the cave opening, even though he knows never to turn your back on the enemy.

He retreats into the dark, following the sound of his daughter's cries, and lifts the squirming child into his arms.

At his touch, she quiets. He kisses her forehead, makes soothing noises, inhales the scent of her soft red hair, wonders if she will remember him.

If she will ever know how she came to be here on this lonely mountain, or why.

If she will ever forgive him for what he's done, and the things he has wrought.

Aisling is still in his arms when they come for him.

Two of them, their headlamps sweeping across the dank cave walls.

He could hide in the shadows, for just a little longer, but there's no point. He's come here to face them.

To try, one last time, to show them the truth.

"We know you're in here, Declan." It's a young woman's voice—Molly, his niece, who he's known since she was born. The La Tène Player. He knows exactly how deadly she is; he trained her himself. "Show yourself."

Declan does as he's told, steps into the beam of light. Aisling squints and, recognizing Molly and the gray-haired man by her side, giggles and waves.

"We don't want to hurt you," Declan's father says, lifting a rifle to his shoulder. "Just give us the child."

The beginning:

Sometimes, Declan thinks, it began the day his inbox pinged with the strange anonymous message. *You've been lied to,* it said, no more than that, and he felt only a mild twinge of curiosity before sending it to the trash. Thinking spammers got more inventive every day. Thinking he was too clever to believe anyone's lies.

Maybe it began the day his curiosity got the better of him, and he finally responded to one of the strange messages.

Or the day he stood in dark woods, met the eyes of a cloaked stranger who told him everything he'd ever believed in was a lie. *Don't you ever want to know why you fight, what you fight for?* the woman asked, before melting back into the shadows, and for the first time, Declan did.

Maybe, he sometimes thinks, it began long before, on the day he first took his father's rifle into his scrawny young arms, aimed at a paper target, pulled the trigger. "You will make a fine Player," his father said, ruffling the fire-red hair that marked him as a Kopp. "You'll make me proud."

But maybe it didn't really begin until he was a father himself. Until he understood what it meant to love unconditionally, with his whole self, to know he would give his life for his daughter. Until the High Council decreed that his infant daughter would be the Player once she came of age. Then he knew the time for waiting, for questioning, was over.

It was the time to act.

He managed to keep it together until the end of the High Council's meeting, knowing there was no point in arguing. He's aware of what they think of him: that he's bitter and washed up, that he was warped by his tenure as a Player, by the fact that Endgame never happened. Some of them—his father among them—think he's mad. So he smiled and nodded as if he were happy they wanted to turn his daughter into their puppet, an agent of needless death.

Then he hailed a taxi he couldn't afford and held his breath as it sped down the Brooklyn-Queens Expressway, until the towers of Downtown Brooklyn came into sight and with them the dingy brownstone where his wife was waiting.

Now here he is, standing before the door of his apartment, taking a deep breath and preparing to change their lives forever. Thinking, *How did I get here?*

But he knows exactly how he got here.

And he knows what has to happen next.

Declan bursts into the apartment and finally lets his panic off the leash. "Pack everything!" he booms, into the tiny bedroom, where his money and passports are stashed, and his wife and little Aisling are sound asleep.

"Declan?" Lorelei blinks groggily on the bed, baby napping on her chest. She sleeps whenever the baby sleeps, which is never enough for either of them. "Quiet, hon. You'll wake her."

"We've got to go," Declan says, in a quieter voice. He's ripping through their tiny closet, throwing shirts and dresses haphazardly into a suitcase. "Now."

"Go? Go where? It's nearly midnight." Gently, Lorelei settles Aisling into her crib. She goes to her husband, stands behind him, and wraps her arms around his waist, lets him feel her slow, steady breathing, the rhythm of her heartbeat. "Take a breath, Declan."

Declan breathes.

"Now, tell me what happened."

Declan turns to face Lorelei, the love of his life, the outsider who, for love of him, adopted his traditions and his people as her own. She did it because he asked her to—and now, because of that, because of *him*, their daughter is in danger.

This is all his fault, he thinks, panic blooming again.

"Declan." She can always tell when he's spinning out of control.

She's always been the only one who can stop him.

She fixes her gaze on him, and, for just a moment, he lets himself get lost in her sea-gray eyes.

"It's going to be okay," she says, in soft, measured tones.

He knows he's no longer the man she fell in love with, the man she married.

That man was full of righteous conviction, strong and proud; that man had been raised to believe he could save the world.

"Whatever it is this time, we can handle it," she says, pressing a smooth palm to his stubbled cheek.

She married that Declan—and got saddled with this one instead, till death do they part. Erratic, paranoid, afraid of shadows, consumed by guilt. Shamed. Obsessed. Broken.

"Now, tell me what happened," she says, once his breathing finally draws even with hers and his panic temporarily abates.

When he met her, he thought Lorelei was the miracle of his life. Now he knows that the true miracle is that she still loves him, even now. But that might change when he answers her question. When she understands what loving him means for Aisling.

"The High Council has named the next generation's Player," Declan says. He takes his wife's hand in his own, holds tight. "They've named our Aisling."

She doesn't gasp.

She doesn't scream.

She doesn't yank her hand away and castigate him for drawing her into his nightmare.

She only nods and says, "Okay. So what does that mean?"

"What does it mean?" He's raging again. He needs to make her understand. "It means we have to get out of here, now. Disappear—go somewhere they can never find us."

"Isn't that a little dramatic, Declan?"

"Lor, are you hearing me? They want her to be the *Player*. They want to turn her into a soldier, brainwash her into this Endgame madness, just as they did me."

"I'm not saying I want that either," she says. "But can't we just say no?"

Declan sighs. Were it only that easy. "It's not like this is a game of tag and they decided she's *it*," he says. "This isn't a game you can just decide not to play."

The High Council doesn't ask; the High Council commands.

Declan knew it was a possibility, of course. The Player has always been a Kopp, for as long as anyone can remember. But there are so many of them now, little Kopp children running around Queens, so many cousins he can't remember all their names. What were the odds they would choose Aisling? They thought Declan an apostate, a madman— what were the odds they would name his daughter the Player?

"We don't like it any more than you do," the High Council's leader told him at the meeting. "But the stones have spoken."

"Screw the stones!" he shouted.

The High Council looked scandalized, all of them but his father, who simply looked tired. Pop was the first to give up on him, the first to accept that Declan had turned his back on his people. Or at least that was how Pop saw it. The move to Brooklyn from Queens, the railing against Endgame, the marriage to an outsider, the trips all over the world in search of answers to questions he wasn't supposed to ask—Pop thinks Declan has rejected his family, his line, his sacred duties. Pop doesn't understand, none of them do, that Declan loves his family and his people fiercely. He's too old to be their Player, but he still sees himself as their warrior, charged with their protection. That's why he fights them so hard: not because he's a traitor, but because he's *loyal*.

"The High Council has made its decision," Pop said. "We journeyed to Stonehenge and asked our question. The stones gave us their answer, and the answer is Aisling."

A gaggle of old men measuring angles of light and lengths of shadow, their protractors consigning Declan's daughter to a useless life of blood. He wanted to scream, to overturn the table, to seize the Falcata from its place of honor on the council wall and slash off their heads—but none of that would help Aisling. So instead he pretended to accept it, and came home to do what needed to be done.

"If they want her to Play, she'll Play," Declan tells Lorelei. "Whatever we want, whatever she wants, they won't care. They'll turn her into a killer. They'll make her help the gods with their genocide. And if she dies, they'll shrug and pretend to care, and then they'll throw another poor child to the wolves."

What he doesn't tell Lorelei, has never told Lorelei, is what being the Player really means: how much blood has been spilled, even without Endgame. So much death, all of it justified as "necessary to protect the line," necessary to prepare for Endgame. Declan has killed 23 people, and he remembers every single one of their faces. Just as vividly, he remembers the face of the current Player when

Declan helped her make her first kill—the face of a 13-year-old who has learned what she's capable of, who's drawn blood and murdered her childhood and is equal parts terrified and proud. These are the faces he sees in his dreams every night; this is the fate—guilt, sorrow, regret, obsession—he wants to spare his daughter. Terrible to imagine that she too will someday be tortured by the faces of those she's killed. Even worse to imagine that she won't be.

"Declan, that's your family you're talking about," Lorelei says. She loves his family, always has; she has none of her own. "Surely, if we just tell them how we feel, they'll understand—"

He shakes his head.

He met Lorelei when they were both 22 years old. She was freshly out of college; he was adjusting to post-Player life, trying to decide what to do with himself for the next 50 years. He told her stories of his life before they met, but he spared her most of the gory details. He didn't want her to see that side of him, the soldier who would do whatever was necessary to survive. He regrets that now.

"Fine, Declan," she says. "If you say that this is a problem, then I trust you—but why is it a problem we need to solve *now*? Aisling is still a baby—that gives us more than twelve years to figure this out."

"No. No!" As soon as the stones choose their Player, the training begins. Everything begins. They'll mold Aisling into what they want her to be—and they will always be watching.

"We can't risk waiting," he says. "We've got a small window of opportunity here, *maybe*. They won't expect us to make a move this quickly. That's our only chance."

"So what are we supposed to do, Declan?" She's starting to sound irritated. "You want me to quit my job, abandon our family, take off with you for god-knows-where? Where will we go? How will we support ourselves? How long do we have to stay away? Have you thought any of this through?"

"We'll figure it out as we go," he says. Another thing Lorelei doesn't know: he has plenty of money, enough to support them for the rest of their lives. When he disavowed Endgame, he also disavowed the money he'd been gifted for serving his line all those years as the Player. Blood money, he thought. He and Lorelei have been raising their daughter in near poverty, but that was by choice, not necessity. Declan's choice, one of many he made without telling his wife. He regrets that now. He regrets so much. "We always figure it out."

She shakes her head. "Pop was right," she says. "I've let this all go too far. I've let you get carried away."

"You talked to Pop about me? About this?"

"He's *worried* about you, Declan. He thought maybe you needed some time away, a rest—"

"I know what he thinks," Declan snaps. His father wants to send him back to the old country, for what he calls rehabilitation. But Declan has heard stories of the isolated camp in the Alps where faithless members of the line are sent. None of them ever come back. "He thinks I've lost my mind."

"You're not exactly sounding like a beacon of sanity right now, honey."

"Endgame is a lie, Lorelei. You know that."

"I know you believe that."

With those words, he knows he's lost her.

"Can we take a little time?" she asks. "Sleep on it, maybe talk more in the morning?"

Declan gazes at her, this woman to whom he's sworn his lifelong love. The woman he fell in love with the first time he saw her, hunched over a book in an uptown branch of the New York Public Library, strands of hair curling over her face. "Of course we can," he tells her. "We can talk about it as much as you want. You're right, we shouldn't make a rash decision. We won't do anything until we both agree it's the right thing to do."

"You promise?"

He kisses her, takes her in his arms, and holds on like she's a buoy in rough seas, the only thing that can keep him from drowning. "I promise," he tells her.

Then he waits for her to fall back asleep, and kidnaps their daughter.

He tells himself it can't be kidnapping, because Aisling belongs to him as much as she belongs to her mother.

But he knows better.

Declan drives all night with Aisling sleeping in the backseat. They can't leave the country yet, not until he puts together a fake passport for the baby. But he can at least put as much distance as possible between himself and his family. He hears the Amber Alert on the radio, but by that time he's ditched the car for a hot-wired Pontiac and is halfway to North Carolina. When he's too exhausted to keep his eyes open, he checks them into a motel, paying in cash. He's taken $5,000 from the safe at the back of the closet, which should get them through the first few hurdles of the journey. Declan has accounts in banks all over the world, accounts that Lorelei doesn't know about, and he supposes he should feel proud of himself that he's so prepared. But he's not proud, only profoundly sad that he's so good at keeping secrets from the woman he loves. This is exactly the life he doesn't want for Aisling.

He never wants her to learn not to trust.

He plays with Aisling on the dingy motel carpet while the press conference plays on TV in the background. Lorelei has wasted no time calling the cops on him. He can't blame her.

He's glad of it, actually, because he knows the High Council would prefer to conduct their search in secret. Having police bumbling around and getting in their way will only help Declan.

Still, he can't stand to hear the pain in Lorelei's voice.

"Please, Declan, bring her home," she says, before a crowd of eager reporters. Aisling looks up at the sound of her mother's voice, reaching eagerly for the TV screen. "We can figure this out together, if you just bring her home."

He wonders what she's told the police. Probably that her husband's gone off his rocker.

He hasn't given up on her yet. Now that she knows he's serious, maybe she can still be convinced.

Declan gathers Aisling to his chest, trying to soothe her to sleep. He lets his eyes close, and he dreams of Lorelei's tears.

His training taught him to get by on only a few hours of sleep, so it's not long before they're on the road again. Declan has a contact in West Virginia who's more than happy to make the baby a new passport, for the right price. While he's waiting for it to be ready, he and Aisling duck into a drugstore. He buys a pink stuffed bunny nearly as big as her head for her and a cheap burner phone for himself. It's a risk, but it's one he has to take.

He dials Lorelei's number.

"Declan." She breathes his name into the phone, as if she's afraid to scare him away. "Declan, what have you done?"

"I'm sorry." He swallows hard, fights back the tears, presses his lips to Aisling's forehead, reminding himself why he's doing this, why he must. "I'm so sorry."

"Is she okay?" Lorelei asks. "Please, just tell me that."

"She's fine. Of course she's fine. You know I would never let anyone hurt her."

"I don't know anything anymore."

"I can't come home, Lorelei. I can't bring her back. It's too dangerous."

"Then tell me where you are."

"So you can send the cops for me? Or Pop?"

"So I can come to you," Lorelei says. "I know you, Declan. If you want to take Aisling away, hide her where no one will ever find her, you can do it. So you win, okay? I can't be away from her. Tell me where you are, and I'll come with you. Wherever you want to go, whatever you need to do. I'll go. I'll do it. Just tell me. Trust me."

Her voice is full of pain—and love.

"What do you think?" Declan whispers to Aisling, ruffling her red hair. "Can we trust Mommy?"

At the word, Aisling bursts into tears. It's the only answer he needs.

"Okay," Declan tells Lorelei, hoping he's not making the biggest mistake of his life. "Get a pen and paper, and I'll tell you where to find us."

He trusts his wife.

But he also knows his wife.

"Stay quiet, little girl," he murmurs to Aisling as he nestles her carrier beneath a tree. She sucks at her pacifier and, he hopes, dreams of happier days. Declan has stationed them on an overlook that gives him a perfect sight line into the valley. Down there, in a deserted stretch of field in the heart of the Ozarks, Lorelei will come for her daughter. He lies flat on his stomach, camouflaged by the weeds, and raises the binoculars.

He's been careful.

He chose a place he knows like the back of his hand, an open field easily surveilled from the surrounding hillside.

This oasis of wilderness is special to him; it's where Le Fond first made face-to-face contact with him. *Le Fond* is his own name for the network of shadow warriors, a small joke with himself: *La Tène* means "the shallows," so he thinks of these strange messages from the dark as "the deep." With few exceptions, they exist for him as whispers, anonymous texts, faces hidden by cloaks and masks.

The young woman who met him here wouldn't reveal her name or background, wouldn't explain how she'd come to know about Endgame or why she'd chosen Declan to recruit. "We watch all the Players," she said. "We saw something in you."

At the time, he'd taken it as an insult. Had Le Fond seen some fault in him that he didn't even know was there, some evidence that his faith was weak, that he would be willing to betray his cause?

It's only slowly, as he follows the bread-crumb trail around the world, that he begins to see. As he searches through artifacts, discovers long-lost documents by long-dead Players of the La Tène line, as he follows their questioning and their clues back and back through the ages, as he finds, finally, the secret cave with its astonishing paintings, he understands. What Le Fond saw in him wasn't weakness; it was strength—the strength of loyalty and conviction that would drive him straight back to Queens, send him marching into the High Council chambers, desperate to share what he learned. To open their eyes to the truth: that Endgame is a cruel joke of the gods, that the Player's true role is to kick-start the apocalypse, that this is an endless cycle that the lines can only end by choosing not to Play. That the power is in their hands, if only they decide to use it.

It didn't occur to him that he'd be laughed out of the room.

Or that when they stopped laughing, they would strip him of his duties in the line and brand him as a heretic.

It's not just what they want to do to Aisling that scares him.

It's the worry that, fearing his influence, they'll never let her see him again.

This patch of overgrown wilderness has lodged itself into his heart; this was where his eyes were first opened. Maybe, he thinks, it will be a lucky spot, and he can open Lorelei's eyes too.

He holds the binoculars steady.

He waits.

And he sighs with disappointment, but not surprise, when Lorelei arrives at the coordinates—flanked by his father and the La Tène Player. She's betrayed him, just as he knew she would, and he can't even hold it against her.

She's doing what she believes is best for her daughter.

He loves her all the more for that.

Declan's set up a listening relay, a bug in the meadow so he can hear what's said down in the valley and speak if need be. He can hear his wife's confusion.

"Where is he?" she says, panic in her voice. "He said he'd be here. I don't understand. He wouldn't lie to me. Not about this."

"Oh, he's here somewhere," Pop says, gazing into the hills. His eyes seem to alight on Declan's hiding spot, and though Declan knows it's impossible, he can't shake the feeling that his father sees straight through the brush, is glaring straight at him.

"You are, aren't you?" Pop says. "I know you, son. You're watching us. Listening to us. Don't blame Lorelei for wanting what's best for you. We all want what's best for you."

"Declan, if you can hear me . . ." Lorelei sounds hesitant, like she's starting to wonder whether Pop has gone as crazy as his son. "Stop hiding and come deal with this like a grown-up. If you'll just be reasonable—"

She gasps as the Player seizes her. A gun materializes in the Player's hand, its muzzle pressed to Lorelei's head.

Declan stops breathing.

Molly is only 17 years old, and she's known Lorelei since she was a child. Lorelei once babysat for her, and Molly in turn has babysat for Aisling. Molly and Lorelei have gone shopping together; they've ridden the carousel in Central Park together; they've sipped frozen hot chocolate and dunked churros into caramel sauce; they've watched terrible movies on rainy days; they've been the best kind of family to each other. And Declan has no doubt that if Molly thought it was necessary, she would pull the trigger without hesitation.

"You know I'll do it, Declan," Molly says calmly. The listening device is sensitive: he can hear Lorelei's rapid and frightened breathing. "You're the one who taught me how to be ruthless."

Declan trained her to shoot. Declan was with her for her first kill. He steadied her, whispered in her ear all the lies he once believed, about how Playing called for blood, how killing could be righteous when in service to the line and the game. He created her, as his father had created him. Thousands of years of cruel lies, all come down to this: A killer he made. A woman he loves. A daughter he's sworn to protect. A gun.

"I'm sorry, Declan," his father says. Declan's heart breaks at the sound of his voice, so disappointed—so hard. "You've left us no choice."

"You want her to live, show yourself," Molly adds in a hard voice. "Now."

"Please," Lorelei murmurs. "Please, Molly, don't."

He spent so many years learning how to shut down his feelings, to do what needs to be done. But now, when it matters most, his love and fear threaten to overwhelm him.

He tries to clear his head. Aisling and Lorelei need him focused. They *need* him.

He swaddles the pink bunny in Aisling's blanket and presses it to his chest. He kisses his daughter good-bye. "I'll be back," he says, but he doesn't promise. He tries never to make promises he can't keep.

"Don't hurt her," he says into his comm. Then, just in case, shouts it as loud as he can, his voice booming across the green. "We're coming!" Then he descends into the valley, taking a circuitous, untraceable route down.

"Give me the child," Pop says as soon as he comes into view.

Just seeing his father makes Declan nearly lose his grip on his emotions again. For so many years, Declan has excused the man's obstinance, telling himself that his father is trying to do the right thing. That Pop believes his stubbornness is in service to a higher cause, and that even wrong, there is virtue in loyalty and steadfastness, in Pop's commitment to his people and their beliefs. But no more. Here is the man who raised him, swore to love him—the man who is willing to put Lorelei's life at risk, to sacrifice his beloved granddaughter, all for a *lie*. "No."

"You'd risk your wife for this insane delusion of yours?"

"Endgame is a *lie*," Declan says, fury rising. How many times has he tried to force his father to face the truth, and how many times has his father refused to listen? "If you would just hear me for once—"

"I've listened to enough of your bullshit!" Pop snaps. "We all have, and I can't let you humiliate yourself anymore."

"You mean humiliate *you*—"

"I mean disgrace your family and your line and yourself!"

Lorelei is murmuring something, soft and urgent, trying to convince them all to calm down, to lay down their arms, but Declan and his father are too focused on each other, too angry, both of them too determined to finally win this argument they've been waging for years, both of them so certain, both of them so hurt, both of them so lost without each other, neither of them hearing Molly when she snaps, "Enough!" and makes a move to reach for Declan's bundled blanket and Lorelei won't let her lay hands on the child and fights free of her grip and there's a struggle and a shout and then instincts kick in, a mother lunging for her child, a Player fighting for her line, and a trigger is pulled and a shot echoes, and only then do Declan and his father fall silent, and see.

Lorelei, on the ground.

Lorelei, bleeding.

Lorelei, eyes open to the sky, unseeing.

Lorelei, gone.

Molly drops to her side, screaming. "I didn't mean to," she says, over and over again. "It wasn't supposed to go like that."

Declan lets the blanket drop from his arms. The bunny rolls in the grass, lands a few feet away from the pool of blood.

Pop looks back and forth between his son and his daughter-in-law, between the living and the dead, frozen in between. "Son," he says. "I'm—"

But Declan will never know what he is: Sorry. Not sorry. Tired of blood. Thirsty for more.

Declan no longer cares.

Declan cares for nothing now but his daughter.

He turns his back on his father. His Player. His lovely, raven-haired miracle bleeding into the grass.

He runs.

* * *

148

Declan doesn't know how to tell Aisling what happened to her mother. Not now, when she's too young to understand—and not later, when she will have questions that he can't answer. Questions about the choices he's made, and the mistakes.

He doesn't know who to blame.

He can't help blaming himself.

He spirits Aisling away from the Ozarks and drives her into the heart of the Mississippi delta. Deep in the swampland, miles from civilization, an old woman lives in a shack, like a fairytale crone. She speaks with the thick accent of the old world, and wraps him and Aisling in gnarled arms when she finds him on the doorstep.

"I've been waiting for you," she says. Her name is Agatha, and she claims to have the Sight. Declan doesn't believe in such things, but there's a fire roaring in the hearth and stew boiling on the stove, and the couch is made up as a bed. He stumbles in gratefully, allowing Agatha to take the child from his arms.

He feels empty without her weight.

"It's happened, then?" Agatha says, her voice a rough croak. "They've designated her as a Player, and you took her away?"

"The Sight?" Declan says, skeptically.

"The evening news," Agatha says. "I extrapolated."

Agatha is La Tène, like him, which is why he is allowed to know her name, see her face. And like him, Agatha is an apostate, a traitor, a nonbeliever. He grew up hearing tales of her, a bogeyman invented to scare the children: ask too many questions, the wrong kind of questions, and you'll be sent into the wilderness, where Agatha the witch will find you and gobble you up. Agatha has been with Le Fond for longer than Declan has been alive.

She's lived in hiding for decades, because the La Tène have never stopped hunting for her and the ancient scriptures that she stole from the archive.

Agatha blazed the beginning of the trail that Declan has been following.

She discovered the first clues that Endgame wasn't what it seemed, in the words of their very own forebears—and as a reward she will live out the rest of her days in lonely exile.

She can be trusted.

"She's gone," Declan says. It hurts to speak the words aloud. "Lorelei. They killed her."

Agatha says nothing for a long moment. Her expression never changes. Then, though he hasn't asked yet: "Yes, you can leave the child here with me for as long as you need. Until it's safe. Do what you need to do."

What he needs to do.

Go north.

North as far as Canada, where he can slip across the New York border unseen, then south again as far as the city, his city, where he found the happiness he will never have again.

Dye his hair, turn telltale red into mousy brown.

Disguise his face with false nose and beard.

Return to Queens.

Watch his people from the crowds and the shadows. Watch his father.

Watch his Player.

Simmer with rage.

Burn.

Burn.

He could kill them, all of them, easily. They're not expecting him to return. They're not on guard. He could slip through Pop's window in the dark of night, slit his throat while the old man snores in his Barcalounger, *Honeymooners* reruns droning on the ancient TV. He could break into the deli across the street from Molly's apartment, aim his sniper rifle at her window, send a bullet into her head while she sips her morning tea. Or he could nestle an explosive in the brakes of Molly's mother's car, turn her into a ball of fire on the Queensboro Bridge. He could assassinate the High Council one by one. But first take out everyone they love, make them watch. Spatter them with blood.

An eye for an eye.

A loss for a loss.

Declan's blood is ice; his heart is a stone. He could do it. He could do anything.

But he holds himself back.

Not for the La Tène line or for the dying embers of family loyalty, not for the sake of his humanity.

They robbed him of that, his father, his trainers. They made him a killer, and it's only justice that they reap the benefits.

He holds back for Aisling.

Someday she will be old enough to know him.

He will be a man she deserves to love. He's come back here partly to prove to himself that he can be. That in the face of the greatest temptation, he can show restraint. That he's not simply a soldier and a killer.

Still, he burns.

And now they will burn.

They've posted guards in front of his old apartment; he knocks one out with an efficient choke hold and the other with a blow to the head, then lets himself in to retrieve what he needs: a bottle of Lorelei's perfume, so he can breathe her in when he needs to remember.

His journal, a record of every step of his journey from ignorance to acceptance, which he'd left behind in hopes that Pop and Lorelei might come to understand. A photo of Lorelei, so that Aisling will never forget her mother's face. Then he sets the incendiary device and watches his past bloom into flame.

Next stop: the High Council chamber. Hidden in the basement of what looks, from the outside, to be a dilapidated veterans' hall.

Declan disables the security system with a few simple clips of the wire cutters, picks the complicated locks on the chamber door, and lets himself in.

It's easy.

They gave him all the tools he needs to betray them.

The Falcata is hanging in its place of honor over the long council table. He takes it in his hands, presses his lips to the cool metal, a sign of respect for its deadly blade.

Sitting in an ancient brass bowl in the center of the table is a small, polished stone.

This is the mark of the Player. The symbol of responsibility and commitment to the line, of the promise made to the gods and to the coming apocalypse.

Once, his birthright.

Now, Molly's.

Soon, Aisling's, unless he can stop them.

He pockets the stone.

Then he places the second incendiary device.

Slips out into the night with the ancient sword, activates the device. Stands in the shadows, watching the heart of the La Tène line burn to the ground.

It's only a symbol. A message. Meant to remind them that he is out there, that he will destroy everything they have and everything they are if that's what it takes to stop them, to prevent Endgame, to save Aisling. Destroying what's precious to them doesn't make up for what he's lost. But it feels good.

When he returns to the delta, the shack is gone.

Razed to the ground.

No Agatha. No Aisling.

Declan turns his face to the sky and shrieks his pain to the heavens. His scream shreds the silence of the swamp. Birds scatter into the clouds. Coyotes sing back to him, and together they howl at the moon. Then, from the trees, another sound. Faint, but familiar.

A child's cry.

He follows the sound, his heart thumping, lips moving in time with the drumbeat of his pulse, *please, please, please.*

He finds them curled up together in the hollow of a fallen tree, Aisling tearstained and screaming, Agatha bleeding from too many wounds.

"I don't know how they found me," she whispers, as Declan frantically tries to staunch the blood. "But they don't know the swamp."

"Where are they?" Declan asks, panic flooding him. Has he just walked into an ambush?

"They looked for a while, then gave up," Agatha croaks. "Took their guns and their helicopters away. Outsmarted by old Agatha. Again." When she laughs, blood froths at her lips.

"You saved Aisling," Declan says in wonder.

"No more children should be sacrificed to this bloody game," she says, gasping at his touch. Her forehead burns.

"How long have you been hiding out here?"

"I held on until you came back."

"We've got to get you to a hospital."

He can't risk it, but for her, after what she's done, he will.

"No," she croaks. Then: "No point."

When he was the Player, Declan learned how to kill, but he also learned how to save. And he learned how to know when people are beyond the point of saving. How to recognize the absence of hope.

She wraps her fingers around his wrist. "Save her from this life," she says.

He nods. Promises. "Tell me what I can do for you," he says. "Anything."

"Save me too," she says, her gaze feverish but fierce. "Make the pain stop. Please."

He uses the Falcata, because she is a hero and deserves an honorable blade.

An honorable death.

Declan runs; the La Tène give chase. The line has spent a millennium sowing a global network of allies and informants—there is nowhere beyond their reach, nowhere to hide. He creates a labyrinth of dummy accounts, uses cash whenever possible, invents several fictional personae and sends them off on planes and trains to the ends of the earth. He lays careful bread-crumb trails leading to dead, and sometimes deadly, ends; he sets traps, drawing on his own networks and on mercenaries whose loyalty he can afford to leave in his wake, faceless men and women who alert him whenever the La Tène catch his scent and close in.

As they always do.

Sometimes he and Aisling are gone long before they show up, leaving behind hotel rooms scoured of prints, dingy apartments stuffed with a stranger's belongings. Sometimes the two of them only just make it. He's a former Player; he knows never to set up camp without formulating an escape plan, and so everywhere they squat, whether it's for hours or weeks, he devises a hiding place for Aisling, somewhere she will be safe if he has to fight their way out.

Most of the La Tène won't dare attack if he has the baby in his arms— she's too precious to them. But Molly, a Player herself, doesn't see any Player's—or future Player's—life as sacred, and she's all too confident in her own aim. She comes at him no matter who might get caught in the crossfire.

They have been on the run for two months when they slip across the French border and make their way to Paris. Declan finds them a small garret on the Left Bank, a few blocks from the Seine, and as weeks pass uneventfully, he begins to relax. Aisling falls in love with the city, or at least her small corner of it—they spend hours every day in the large children's playground in the Jardin du Luxembourg. She becomes snobbish about croissants, only favoring the ones from the boulangerie down the street, and has already started chatting with the pigeons in her own pidgin French. Declan wonders whether it's possible that they have found a new home.

They're sitting in Place Dauphine, dipping croissants in a steaming mug of hot chocolate, when it happens. Nothing major, nothing he can put his finger on, just a flicker of motion in the corner of his eye that sets his heart racing.

As Aisling nibbles on the soggy croissant, and Declan keeps a smile fixed on his face, he scans the plaza—and gasps.

There it is, in the northern corner of the square, nearly hidden behind a rack of secondhand books, that familiar head of black hair.

Molly.

Swiftly but casually, Declan straps Aisling into the pouch on his chest that he uses when they need to make a quick getaway, and stands from his chair. If he can just get her safely out of the square and into a crowd—

Aisling screams as something whistles past her ear.

Then, suddenly, there's a hail of tranquilizer darts and a puff of tear gas and the square erupts into chaos.

Declan runs.

He holds tight to Aisling and takes off toward the Seine, vaulting onto the Pont Neuf and kicking his nearest pursuer over the rail, sending him tumbling into the murky river. He pushes through crowds on the Quai des Grands Augustins, racing for Notre Dame and its swarm of oblivious tourists. Past bridges and bouquinistes, knocking over carts and crepe trucks, anything that will stall them in their chase, across the Petit Pont, until finally the gray, gargoyled edifice looms over them and Declan melts into the crowd, hundreds of parents holding squirming babies to their chests, just like him. He allows himself a heartbeat of relief, but this is only a temporary escape. He lets the throng push him across the square, then slips into one of the apartment lobbies with an entry code he's memorized for just such an emergency. He waits in the lobby as the hours pass and the shadows deepen, Aisling miraculously calm in his arms, as if she understands exactly what's going on and trusts him to deal with it. He wishes he trusted himself that much. There's relief in this escape—but not much of it, because Molly is still out there, somewhere. Maybe Molly will always be out there.

When night falls, he decides it's time to risk it—they slip out of the building, and his enemies are nowhere to be found. The search has moved on, for now, leaving Declan space to flee the country and seek out yet another new home.

He knows better this time than to imagine that he'll find anywhere they can stay for long. No matter how far they go, no matter how safe it seems, he's always expecting Molly to find them.

And she always does.

It happens again in Mexico, this time an ambush in the plaza outside San Miguel de Allende's Parroquia, and he loses them in that pink monstrosity, holding a mask to Aisling's face as the tear gas drifts over them and they make for a back exit leading to the Cuna de Allende and, beyond it, freedom.

He always has an escape plan, and he always needs to use it.

Dangriga, Belize; Mzuzu, Malawi; Stockholm, Sweden; Bến Tre, Vietnam. Six months pass, then a year, and still there is no safe haven for them, no home, no rest, and no end—not unless the impossible happens, and the La Tène give up.

Or he does.

"This is no way for you to live," Declan tells his daughter. "Your mother would hate this. And hate me for it."

They're sitting on the eastern bank of the Rhine River. Aisling plays happily in the mud along the shore. She's just starting to walk now, and can say a small handful of words. Soon she'll be old enough to ask questions Declan can't answer.

"You see that giant rock, Aisling?" He points across the river, to the jagged stone jutting hundreds of feet into the air.

She claps her hands. "Mountain!"

Declan brushes her hair away from her face. It's a tangled nest of red curls. He should be taking better care of it. He should be taking better care of everything.

"Sort of a mountain," he agrees. "Do you know what its name is?"

Aisling shakes her head.

"It's called the Lorelei," he tells her.

Aisling shouts happily, "Mama!"

He's taught her well.

He shows her Lorelei's picture every night, tells her stories of the mother she's already started to forget. Lorelei has been dead for one year, three months, and four days. Aisling doesn't cry about her mama anymore, or ask for her. Declan doesn't know whether this is tragedy or relief.

"Yes, your mama was named after this Lorelei," he says. It's not precisely true. The German poet Heinrich Heine wrote a poem about the Lorelei, and her parents named her after that.

"Ich weiß nicht, was soll es bedeuten, Daß ich so traurig bin," he recites for his daughter now, as he so often recited for his wife. He loved this about Lorelei, that she was born inside a poem. She didn't speak German, but he does, of course—he speaks almost every language— and she liked to hear the words in their original language, in his voice. He translates for Aisling, now: "'I don't know what it should mean that I am so sad.'"

But he does know what it means.

He knows why he's brought her here, to this deserted spot near Saint Goarshausen, where he feels like his wife is watching over them both. He and Lorelei came here on their honeymoon—she wanted to show him her rock. *It's not every woman who has her own mountain,* she told him then.

They were so happy.

"We can't keep running forever," he says. He's talking to himself; he's talking to Lorelei. He takes Aisling into his arms. She squirms for a moment, then settles happily onto his lap. "We can't keep living like this. *You* can't keep living like this."

He came here so he could find the strength to admit it.

He was the Player; he was trained to give everything to the fight. To believe he could win until his dying breath.

But running isn't winning. Even if they could run from the line forever, that's no way for Aisling to grow up.

That's no way to carry out the promise he made to himself, that he would do everything he could to stop Endgame, to persuade his line that they've made a terrible mistake.

He's done with running away.

He's going to do what he's been trained to do, and *fight*.

Maybe he will lose.

Probably he will lose.

But either way, Aisling will have a place to grow up, people who love her, a home. Either way, Lorelei will be avenged and Declan will know he's done everything he can to make things right.

"That's it, Aisling. No more running." The thick clouds blow open for a moment, and a splash of sun lights up the Lorelei. "Now we make our last stand."

The climb is more difficult than Declan remembers. Of course, the last time he was here, he didn't have a small toddler strapped to his chest. The last time he was here: it was six years ago, the culmination of many months of searching. For clues, for artifacts, for answers.

"None of this is ours to know," Pop told him, when Declan explained why he was traveling the globe, why he was so desperate to track down the evidence of his forebears, the Players of the La Tène line stretching back for hundreds and thousands of years.

"How can it not be?" he asked Pop. "We're supposed to give our lives up to a cause we don't even understand? What sense does that make?"

"It made perfect sense to you until last year," Pop said, irritable. They'd had the conversation one too many times. "What changed?"

"Nothing," Declan said, because he'd promised Le Fond never to breathe a word of them. "I just started asking questions, that's all. That's not a crime."

"Be careful," Pop warned him. And when Declan said that there was no need to be careful, that he could climb a 1,500-meter mountain in his sleep, Pop said, "That's not what I'm talking about."

Six years ago, Declan summited a peak in the Italian Alps, high above the *Lago Beluiso*, and picked his way into the darkness of an ancient cave. He aimed his headlamp at a wall covered in primitive paintings. They looked as old as time itself.

There was the painting of 12 humans standing amongst tall stones—Stonehenge, he'd realized almost immediately. The sacred place.

That understanding had come easily. The others had taken time. Days of fasting and meditation to clear his head, hollow it out so he would hear the gods speak.

What did it all mean, the picture of the strange creature descending to Earth with a stolen star? The six men and six women screaming into the skies? The woman in the boat, so alone on a desolate sea?

He stared at the images until he was half mad with hunger and solitude, and only then did truth cut through the fog. He saw what he was meant to see.

He saw Endgame for what it really was: the vicious cycle, the evil joke. The end of days.

Now he returns with his child. He returns to wait for someone to come for him, to kill him and take her away. Six years ago, he returned to Queens bursting with his nightmare truth—and no one would hear it. His father refused to listen. The High Council commanded his silence.

Now they will come for him, to this place where he found those unwanted answers.

Maybe they will finally listen.

Maybe they will see what he saw.

It would be worth it, giving up his life, giving up his daughter, if there's even a chance that he can make them hear the truth.

He hopes it won't come to that. But if it does, he's prepared.

He lights a fire, he roasts some meat, he feeds Aisling and himself, he sings his daughter to sleep, and he waits.

He waits for two days and two nights.

Then they come for him.

"We know you're in here, Declan." Molly shouts. "Show yourself."

Declan holds on to Aisling as he steps into the light. She giggles and waves at her older cousin and her grandfather. It warms him, that she still recognizes her family. It means she hasn't forgotten everything yet. Some part of her must still remember her mother.

"We don't want to hurt you," Declan's father says; he takes aim with the rifle. "Just give us the child."

"You won't shoot me while I'm holding her," Declan says, hopes. "You won't risk it."

"It's over," Pop says. "Give us Aisling. Come *home* with us. We'll work this out."

"There's nothing to work out," Declan says. "Look around you—simply open your eyes and *see*. Why do you think I brought you here?"

Pop sighs heavily. "I don't know why you do anything you do, Declan."

"We have to break the cycle, pop. We *have* to. We can stop this now. Look at the paintings, Pop." Declan shines his flashlight at the cave wall. "You see those twelve figures, those have got to be Players, and I'm certain that the figure in the center—"

"You will stop this nonsense or I will shoot you where you stand," his father snaps.

So that's it. Even now he won't listen. He won't *see*. Declan's given his father all the chances he can. "I tried," he says, then slips a hand into his pocket and presses a small switch.

The cave mouth explodes in a hail of shattered stone. Molly dives out of the way, lightning fast, but Pop's body is no longer as quick as his instincts. He takes a rock to the head and goes down.

Somewhere, in the back of Declan's mind, where he's still capable of rational thought, he feels sorry to see it.

There's no time for regret, not as long as Molly's still alive. She's fast, but she's still been caught off guard—as soon as he sets off the device, Declan is in motion before Molly has regained her footing. Declan leaps over his father's body and launches himself toward her, swinging the Falcata at her neck. Molly dodges the blow, comes at him low and hard with the knife, slashing at his knees, trying to knock him off balance so she can get a clear shot at his jugular. He stabs the sword through her foot.

First blood.

She shrieks with rage and lashes out with the blade. Metal bites into his flesh—cheek, shoulder, side, collarbone, but all of them flesh wounds, because he is always one step ahead of her, knows what she's going to do before she does, because, of course, he trained her.

He *was* her, once. He understands how she thinks—but she will never understand him. What it's like to fight for your child, and the memory of your wife.

He is motion; he is fire; he is a being of light and fury. Everything he's taught her not to be. He taught her control and dispassion. He taught her to be cold and rational. To think through every strike, to form a strategy and follow through.

She's no match for the wild creature he's become.

No match for the Falcata, which whistles through the dark, then stops short, hitting flesh, hitting bone.

There's a soft moan, and then Molly drops to the ground.

"I didn't mean to kill her," Molly says, blood pouring from a gaping wound on her abdomen, bubbling at her lips as she tries to speak.

"I loved her." Declan tells himself that there's no joy in this, no vengeance. There's only necessity, safety for him and his daughter. There's only a 17-year-old girl that he once loved, lying in the dirt. Then she says, "It's your fault that she's dead, you know. *You* killed her." And he brings down the sword again, this time to her throat. She will never speak again.

"You've killed the Player."

It's his father's voice.

Declan turns around, slowly. His father stands behind him, bloody and unsteady. He holds Aisling in one arm.

It's over.

"I'll never understand how it came to this," Pop says. Aisling has wrapped her chubby arms around her grandfather's neck. She burrows her face into his shoulder.

Propped on his other shoulder is the rifle.

"Is there another way?" Pop asks. "Please tell me there's another way."

The other way is surrender. Declan could raise his hands, palms out, agree to return to Queens with his father. Allow his Pop to raise Aisling in his own image, turn her into a warrior. Try his best to be a voice of sanity, keep asking unwanted questions, forcing their faces into disturbing truths, bide his time until Aisling is ready to listen.

Except that he's killed Molly; he's killed the Player. Even if Pop can forgive that, the High Council won't.

Even if they could, Declan couldn't forgive himself.

For losing Lorelei, for losing Aisling, for losing everything.

Declan can't stand by and watch as they turn his daughter against him.

"I'll never stop trying," Declan says honestly. "Not as long as I'm alive. There is no other way."

Declan's father nods. He knows when his son is speaking the truth. He strokes Aisling's hair and levels the rifle.

"Promise me something?" Declan asks.

"If I can."

"Tell her about me?"

"Of course."

"No," Declan says. "Not that easy. Not your version of me. Not just the parts you approve of. Tell her what happened here. What I tried to do for her, what I believed—whether you agree with it or not."

Pop doesn't say yes or no, so Declan presses on.

"There's a small notebook, tucked into her carrier. It's my journal. Everything I've learned about Endgame over the last few years,

everything I've been trying to tell you. It's in there. Even if you refuse
to look at it—someday, let her make her own choice. I need her to
understand why her parents left her alone."

"She'll never be alone, son. I promise you that."

"She deserves to make her own choices someday, Pop. She deserves
answers."

"She'll get them," he says. "When she's old enough. When she's ready. I
can promise you that."

"Okay, then. Do what you have to do. I'm ready." Declan drops his head.
He thinks about the day Pop taught him how to fire that rifle, and
how much he wanted to please his father and strike the bull's-eye. He
thinks about the first night he kissed Lorelei, his fingers threaded in her
long, black hair, the street falling still around them, the stars shining
impossibly bright, such a rare thing in New York. He thinks about
Aisling, the sweet, clean smell of her scalp, the pressure of her little
fingers curling around his thumb, the musical chime of her laughter, the
delight she takes in squirrels and birds, chasing them through the trees.
"I'm so sorry," Pop says, but Declan barely hears him; he's wholly lost
in his vision of Aisling—as she is, and as she will be. He can see her
clearly as if he's seeing through time: tall and proud, her mother's
fierce eyes and her father's fiery hair, an Aisling old enough to fight
and wonder and fall in love, an Aisling he will never meet, and as his
father pulls the trigger, he says good-bye to this Aisling of his mind's
eye, says *I'm sorry* and *I love you* and *someday you'll understand*,
and he can almost hear her voice, lilting and sure like her mother's,
promising him that yes, someday she *will* understand, someday she
will pick up his fight, and she will be the one to win it.

Declan smiles at this, and is still smiling when the bullet comes home.

Declan's father is alone with the bodies.

Alone with the bodies, and his granddaughter. Though she is crying,
she is warm and breathing and alive, so he focuses on her, not the
pooling blood, the tragic waste. There's nothing he can do about the

past; he focuses on the future.

He finds the journal where Declan said it would be. A small, black leather notebook, crammed with his son's familiar sloppy handwriting.

He takes a lighter from his pocket, flicks three times until flame sprouts, then touches fire to page.

Aisling stops crying. She stares in wonder as the pages char and turn to ash: Declan's delusions and madness, banished from this world for good.

Declan's father hopes he's doing the right thing.

He has to be.

"Come on, sweetheart. Let's get out of here." He bundles up his granddaughter and then himself, preparing for the long walk back to civilization. He'll send a team in for the bodies—outsiders, not members of the line. No La Tène will ever return to this cave of horrors, not if he can help it. He will have the bodies brought back to Queens for a hero's burial. Declan, after all, was a hero once. That's the Declan he'll tell Aisling about someday. A father she can be proud of. A father she deserves. "There's nothing here for us anymore."

He carries her past the bodies, out of the dark cave, into the light. He will take her home, raise her and love her as his own, train her to fight and to win. He will tell her lies, stories that it will be easy for her to hear, and he will live every day in fear that she will catch a scent of the truth, follow in her father's mad footsteps, that he will lose his granddaughter as he has lost his son.

Maybe, someday, he will even tell her the truth, and she will be his judge.

He treks back down the summit, head lowered against the freezing wind, protecting Aisling from the chill as best he can. Behind them, the cave settles back into ancient quietude. The strange paintings wait, as they have always waited, to deliver their silent message. Someday, perhaps, someone will return to hear it.

* * *

This is the story Aisling's grandfather will never tell her, though many times he wonders if he should.

This is the story of how everything could have changed. How maybe it still can.

Maybe, now, it's Aisling's time: to try again.

She will trace her father's footsteps back to the place where his life ended and her new life began; she will follow his answers to questions of her own. She will, if she has the wisdom and the courage, defy what she has been taught—defy the mission given her in infancy, and forge one of her own.

And she will, just maybe, find a way to fulfill her father's dream that she determine her own fate, and her grandfather's dream that she save her people.

A way to succeed where her father failed.

A way to break the cycle.

This is the story of Aisling Kopp's past.

Her future—and that of all humanity—has yet to be written.

HARRAPAN

SHARI

Breathe in.
Breathe out.
Focus.
Be.

Shari Jha sits cross-legged in the corner of the schoolyard, eyes closed, hands pressed together at heart center.

At least, her body is in the schoolyard.

Her mind floats. She drifts through the dense fog overhanging the multicolored roofs of Gangtok, rises above it, skims across the Himalayan peaks, soars up into the empty, endless blue.

"Can't believe *she's* going to be our Player."

"Sitting there like a lump every day."

"Shh, she'll hear you!"

"*Taato na chaaro.* Don't be an idiot. She can't hear anything when she's like this."

She does hear, of course. Every word, every snicker. When she turns inward like this, lets her mind unspool from her body, her senses only grow sharper.

She will not dignify them with her attention.

They don't matter.

Nothing matters but maintaining her focus.

Proving to herself that she can find her inner calm, no matter how dire—or irritating—circumstances may be.

Breathe in.

Breathe out.

"What's your problem with her, anyway?"

"She's a snob."

"Not to mention a wimp."

"How's she supposed to save our line when all she does is sit around and meditate?"

"*I* heard she hasn't even killed anyone yet."

"*I* heard they tried to make her, and she cried."

Someone snorts. "We're all doomed."

"It's not like she's the Player *yet*."

"You guys, I still say she can hear us."

"She's out of it—look, I'll prove it."

Something hits her cheek, cracks sticky and foul. A raw egg, by the smell of it.

Thrown, by the voice of it, by Aman Dhital, her second cousin, who's been an obnoxious little worm since birth.

Shari doesn't open her eyes. She doesn't let their words disturb her, or the globs of yolk dripping down her face. She doesn't let her mind lose its purchase on peace and calm, up there in the clouds.

But she does dig her hands into the earth, choose a solid, smooth stone one inch in diameter, and fire it with perfect accuracy at the center of Aman's forehead.

There's an indignant squeal of pain, then a storm of footsteps as the boys take flight.

Breathe in.

Breathe out.

Smile.

Someday, Shari will be the Player.

This has been true for as long as she can remember. It is the first true thing she knew about herself, along with her name and the rosewater smell of her mother's skin. "You will be our Player, *meri jaan,*" her mother would whisper, wrapping her in soft blankets and rocking her to sleep. "You will make us proud."

The Makers decreed it, when she was still a bulge in her mother's belly, still half dream. The Harrapan elders read the signs, in the chai leaves and the stars, and they knew Shari would be one of the chosen.

In two years, when the current Player lapses, she will be the Player of the 55th line, the Harrapan Player, as were Helena and Pravheet and Jovinderpihainu and Lavilninder before her. At 13, she became old enough to be eligible for Endgame, but there can be only one Player at a time. Shari will not take over the role until the current Player turns 19. She is 14 now, and for the next two years, she will train, she will wait, she will live in this strange limbo, pretending at a normal life and waiting for her destiny to begin.

This is her honor; this is her burden; this is her life.

It is a lonely one. Shari would never admit this out loud—and if she did, who could believe her? With seven brothers and 13 sisters, most of them all living in the same house, with her aunts and uncles, with her father's many wives, with cousins scattered all through Gangtok, with the telltale Jha features reflected back to her wherever she looks, with a life so crowded that solitude is nearly impossible, how can she be lonely?

And yet.

Family is family; they love her without knowing her. As for beyond her family, there are those who know her as a future Player and keep their distance through fear or respect. There are girls at school who dress and speak like Shari, whisper eagerly about her every move, but never get close; there are boys who disapprove of the kind of Player she intends to be, who want a warrior, not a thinker, who mistake her silence and stillness for frailty. Then there are those who don't know what she is—only an inner cadre of Harrapan know of Endgame, the Player, the Harrapan stronghold in the Valley of Eternal Life, and they are all sworn to secrecy. These strangers, who live in her city and go to her school but don't know this most basic fact about her— they don't see her at all. To them, she is only Shari Jha, the solitary girl with sad eyes who rarely speaks.

The knowledge of Endgame is considered so powerful, so dangerous, that it's safer to keep it limited to a trusted few. The others know only that there are things they *don't* know, and that they are better off. Sometimes, Shari wonders what it might be like to be among the ignorant, to imagine that her world would continue on without end. Sometimes, she envies them.

Shari knows what it is to have a friend, but only through watching others: She watches her little brothers and sisters laugh easily with the children they bring home from school, fighting with sticks or chasing peacocks. She sees her older siblings strut proudly through the marketplace with their throngs of friends; she sees them fall in love, go starry-eyed and weak-kneed, court and marry and build a home.

She thinks: *Not for me, not now.*

She thinks: *Maybe someday, when I have lapsed.*

She does not think: *If only . . .* or *I wish . . .*

Shari has trained her mind to follow her every command. It does not stray without her permission, and she does not permit it foolish hopes or imagined lives.

She focuses on her training, physical and mental. She does her daily calisthenics, studies her books, hones her memory, meditates, waits. Then, one day, a voice breaks into her meditative fog. This voice is different—neither hostile nor curious. It doesn't interrupt her focus but instead, somehow, adds to it, as if the voice is speaking from within.

Also different from the other voices, which whisper and giggle and wonder about her. This voice speaks *to* her.

"I don't know how you do it," he says, his voice pleasantly reedy, like the sound of wind humming through the birch trees. He has a strange accent, not the Nepali-inflected English of her homeland, but not quite foreign either. It shifts and flows as he speaks, as if each word and syllable is deciding for itself to whom it belongs. "Thirty seconds and I'm already bored."

Shari can tune out anything.

But for reasons that escape her, she doesn't want to tune out this. She opens her eyes.

An unfamiliar boy smiles back at her, his grin rakish and inviting, like he's eagerly waiting for her to ask what's so funny, so he can let her in on the joke. He's a couple of years older than her, and though she knows everyone in this school—everyone in this city, it sometimes seems—she doesn't know him.

"Didn't mean to interrupt you," he says, running a hand through unruly black hair. Maybe he intends to smooth it, but he has the opposite effect, and Shari has the strange impulse to reach over and flatten his cowlick. A blush reddens his umber cheeks. "Well, actually, I did. So I guess . . . mission accomplished?"

"Can I help you?" Shari asks. She speaks formally, though without hostility.

The boy shrugs. "You always look so peaceful over here, figured I would try it too, but . . ." He casts an amused glance down at his knee, which is jiggling against the ground. "Guess I'm not really built for peaceful."

"It can take practice," Shari says, smiling as she remembers the first time her grandfather taught her to turn inward, how she managed to clear her mind for about 30 seconds before she heard Tarki screeching and was already halfway across the yard in chase of the peacock before she remembered she was supposed to stay quiet and still.

"What's so funny?" the boy asks.

She doesn't answer personal questions as a general policy. But something about this boy tempts her to make exceptions. "I didn't really learn to meditate until I realized I should practice in a room where I couldn't hear our pet peacock."

His eyes widened. "You have a pet peacock?"

"Well, he's not technically our pet, but . . ." How to explain the wild peacock that has made his home in her backyard? "He's chosen us, I suppose."

"You're full of wonders, Shari Jha," he says, and before she can ask how he knows her name, he adds, "and you have a very nice smile."

Shari's not used to compliments. At least, compliments that aren't about her coordination or dedication or mental acuity. She stares at the ground, waits for the moment to pass.

"You're wondering how I know who you are," he says.

"If I were wondering something, I would ask."

"So I guess you're not wondering who I am?"

She says nothing.

"There's that smile again," he says, like he's won something. Then he holds out his hand. "I'm Jamal Chopra. New kid. Grade ten. And I know who you are, because everyone seems to know who you are, but no one will tell me why."

"Is that why you came over here?" she asks. "To discover why I'm so noteworthy?"

"Well, yeah."

"And?"

"And . . . I'm still mulling it over."

"I think I should be offended by that," Shari says.

"Something tells me my opinion of you is very low on your priority list."

"That's assuming you've made the list," she says, and realizes she's having fun.

"So, if I wanted to continue my research—"

"Into the source of my exceptionalness?"

"Indeed. Might you be persuaded to join me for a chai after school?"

Shari tenses. "I, uh, I don't do that."

"You don't drink tea?"

She can feel a blush rising in her cheeks. "No, I don't . . . you know. Go out. With boys."

It's not like her to stammer. But then, none of this is like her.

"Never?" he says. "Not one single date?"

"Never."

It's not actually a rule for the Player designate, more of an unspoken tradition—she's not supposed to have anything in her life that could distract her from her purpose. It's never mattered much before.

He laughs. "Then it's a good thing I wasn't asking you on a date."

"Oh." Now her cheeks are on fire. She tells herself that it doesn't matter what this stranger thinks of her, that she's beyond such trivial things, that she's spent years making herself a placid surface, hard as diamond but smooth as glass. All of this is true, and yet she still wants to drill a hole in the earth and sink into it. "I'm sorry, I didn't mean to presume; I simply—"

"Chill out," he says, an Americanism that doesn't sound so foreign in his strange accent. She doesn't like to be told to calm down—she doesn't like to be told *anything*. She is Shari Jha, solely in charge of herself. But the timbre of his voice has its intended effect: she chills. "I could use someone to give me the lay of the land. Haven't had a good chai since I got here, so if you know where to go, that's a start."

"Do I know where to go to get a good chai?" Shari echoes. "You've asked the right question, Jamal Chopra, new kid of grade ten. Pay attention, because I'm about to change your life."

Shari watches him carefully as he takes his first sip. She likes this boy well enough, but if he can't appreciate a steaming mug of Rayamajhi chai, he's not worth much.

There are some who claim the best chai in Gangtok will be found at Golden Tips, while others swear by the café in Pagdandi Books, but as far as Shari is concerned, these people don't know what they're talking about. The third best chai in all of Gangtok is the tea that Jovinderpihainu's wife used to make, a recipe lost with her death. The second best chai is made by Shari's own mother, served with a ginger and lemongrass mixture sprinkled across the top. But the best chai in the city—in all the world, in Shari's opinion, at least in the 36 countries she's visited—is the mouthwatering blend served in Sri Rayamajhi's tiny café off Nehru Road. It doesn't look like much:

The door, squeezed between an old bookshop and a car repair shop, is barely visible from the street and layered with rust. The four tables inside all wobble on crooked legs, and Shari once fell through the seat of one of the rickety chairs. The air is thick with dust, the ceiling crumbling plaster. Sri Rayamajhi is ancient, and as mean as he is wrinkled. He treats Shari with respect, because of her position—but his version of respect is barely concealed contempt. She doesn't mind; as long as his chai continues to taste of nirvana, the old man can scowl at her as fiercely as he'd like.

"Well?" she says, when Jamal places the mug back on the table and closes his eyes. He sighs deeply.

Finally he opens his eyes. "This makes it all worthwhile," he says.

"What?"

"Moving, *again*. Moving halfway across the world to some random mountain in some random country where I don't know anyone. Inviting myself out to tea with a very intimidating girl. All of it, worth it for this." He takes another sip. She forgets her own tea, so absorbed is she by his expression of pure joy.

She's never brought anyone here before, not even her siblings. The tea shop is her private solace, somewhere she can come to be alone with her thoughts and her chai without having to worry about who she is or who's watching. It's as much a home to her as her parents' house, and she thought it might feel strange to bring Jamal here—*wrong*, even—but being with him is, in a way, like being alone.

"So, what's the story at school?" Jamal asks, once he's taken sufficient pleasure from his drink.

"What do you mean? It's a school like any other," Shari says.

He shakes his head. "I don't think so. I've been to"—he counts on his fingers, lips moving silently through a list—"eleven different schools, and I've never seen one quite like this. Sure, there are always groups, cliques, that kind of thing, but here? It's like there's a line drawn down the middle of the student body that no one ever talks about. Like you're all inhabiting the same building, but you're completely different schools, if that makes sense."

Shari understands exactly what he means: this is the invisible line between the Harrapan who know about Endgame and all the rest of the line. She's just surprised that he noticed. The division is subtle, something that even new teachers take a few months to notice.

"When you move around as much as I have, you learn to suss things out pretty quickly," Jamal says, anticipating her question.

She seizes the opportunity to change the subject. "Why have you moved so often?"

"My father's business," he says. "International finance—lots of Very Important Opportunities with Very Important People, you know how it is. Or at least that's how he said it was. You ask me, I think he just always wanted to be somewhere else. It always felt like he was running away from something." Jamal shrugs like he doesn't care, but Shari knows how to read people—she can see it as an act. "Maybe that's stupid. Occam's razor, right? He was probably just running away from us, and too polite to ask us to stop following him."

There's a bruise here that Shari doesn't want to press, not yet. "Tell me about it," she says. "The world. The places you've seen."

Most people she knows have never left Gangtok. Shari listens eagerly as he tells her of the sights he's seen: the spires of Notre Dame, the Great Pyramid at Giza, the view of Victoria Harbour from the Peak in Hong Kong. He assumes, of course, that she's never seen these wonders for herself, and she lets him. It doesn't feel like lying, because everything looks different through his eyes. Yes, she's been to London, but only to break into the British Museum and steal back a handful of Harrapan artifacts that were stolen by British colonizers centuries before. She's seen the Mojave Desert, but only through a feverish haze of thirst and hunger, when she was left there on her own for several weeks without food or water. She learned how to survive, and how to retreat from desolate solitude into the secret caverns of her inner mind, but not how to appreciate the beauty of bare rock and sheer cliffs burning orange in the setting sun.

By the time he finishes listing his many homes, their cups have emptied. Without having to be asked, Sri Rayamajhi bangs two fresh cups before them with a clatter. Shari presses her palms to the sides of her mug, soaking in the heat.

"And now you've come to India. How long before you have to leave?" She tries to make it sound like she doesn't particularly care, because there's no logical reason she should.

"My mother says this time's for good," he says.

"But what about international business, Very Important People, your father—"

"My father's dead."

"Oh." She curses herself for overstepping. Now he will politely excuse himself and disappear, so as not to have to answer painful personal questions. It's what she would do. "I'm so sorry."

"You didn't kill him," he says. "Unless you're a heart attack wearing a very good costume?"

It's not like before. He's not acting, not pretending away pain. He's signaling her that this is not forbidden territory—that she's allowed to ask more questions.

"So why have you come here?"

"My father was born here," he says. "Lived here until he was a teenager, then took off—in the middle of the night, to hear him tell it—and swore never to come back again. We don't know much about his family, but I guess I've always thought . . ."

"Yes?"

He looks down.

"I've always thought that if he was running from something, it must be something here. And maybe that's what my mom thinks too. She's from Mumbai, but she wanted to come here. To feel closer to him, she said, but I think she's expecting to find some kind of answers."

"Why are you telling me all this?" Shari says, honestly confused. She's a stranger to him, who's given him no reason to assume she can be trusted. The more truth you reveal about yourself, the more vulnerability you offer a potential enemy—this is something that's been impressed on her from childhood. But here he is, spreading himself wide open for her, like a kitten exposing its soft belly.

"I don't know," he says, sounding somewhat confused himself. "I've never told anyone that. But . . . you asked."

"You didn't have to answer."

"Isn't that what friends do?"

And so they are friends.

Her first friend.

Her best friend.

She shows him Gangtok, not just the city's obvious attractions—the Rumtek Monastery, Ganesh Tok, Tsomgo Lake—but the Gangtok she loves. The scents of the marketplace on a Sunday morning, cinnamon, curry, sandalwood; the sensation of biting into a steaming Tibetan momo, fresh from the vendor's pot. The narrow alleyways that twist and turn, climbing up and up into the clouds. The shifting views from the cable car—the rainbow of houses bright in the afternoon light, the way the hillside seems to catch fire as the sun sets. She takes him to her favorite viewing overlook, and they watch Mount Kanchenjunga's snowy peak poke through the dissipating fog.

He tells her everything: About his childhood, growing up with his mysterious and often absent father, his dissatisfied mother. About how it felt to come home and see his mother's expression gone hollow, to know before she told him that his father was finally gone. He tells her about his favorite bands, and through him she discovers a love of music she never knew she had, music from across the globe and through the decades: the Mountain Goats, Titica, Rilo Kiley, Julieta Venegas, Pompeya, the Hold Steady, Thelonious Monk, Renaissance chanting. They share earbuds and listen over and over to Tom Waits's "Alice," which becomes their favorite song, something about it feeling like the voice of great Kanchenjunga itself.

She tells him nothing and everything, all at once.

All the important facts of her life, the list of truths that make up Shari Jha, she keeps to herself. She doesn't tell him that she will be the Player, or what that might mean. She doesn't tell him that she knows six variants of martial arts and can kill a man twice her size with her bare hands, though she's never chosen to do so. She doesn't tell him how she spends the afternoons when she's not with him, long hours in the gym honing her fighting skills or in the library deciphering the mysteries of the past, nor does she reveal where she goes on those days or weeks she disappears on a training mission—and he doesn't press her for answers, because he understands her enough to know that there are answers she'd rather not give. She doesn't tell him that she's asked around about the Chopra family, about who his father might have been and what he could have been running from, and has gleaned that the man was Harrapan, knew enough to know about Endgame. He was one of the chosen few ushered into the inner circle, sworn to the sacred responsibility of supporting the Player however she might need—and had most likely, shamefully, run scared from his duty and his gods and the end of the world.

But the things she *does* tell him . . . they feel more important, somehow, because they are the private, secret things that no one knows.

What it is to be lonely.

How it feels to have her future decided for her by her family. The alignment of the stars at her conception and birth.

How she sometimes slips away from school in the middle of the day and sneaks into a movie theater, losing herself in the noise and color of someone else's life.

She teaches him yoga and helps him practice his rudimentary Nepali; he teaches her to appreciate sushi and makes her laugh.

She advises him on girls, how they think, how they might be thinking of him; he teaches her, by example, how to flirt.

It's true that she doesn't date, and she lets him believe that this is because her family is a traditional kind, that someday they will make her a match. She lets him assume that *this* is the circumscribed fate she alludes to when she says, wistfully, that sometimes it might be nice to decide for herself what the shape of her life would be. There are many families in the city who intend arranged marriages for their children, and no reason for him to believe the Jha are not among them. No reason to tell Jamal that she doesn't date because she sees no point in it, not with the deadline looming two years hence. Once she takes her place as the Player, there will be no time for love or courtship, no space in her life or heart for anything but her training, her mission. She suspects that even friendship will have to fall by the wayside, which makes these days with Jamal all the more precious.

She tells herself that's all it is.

Friendship.

There are, of course, many families in Gangtok who have embraced the more modern version of courting, and their school is filled with girls willing to date—all of them, it seems, more than willing to date Jamal.

Shari likes watching him flirt in the schoolyard. She still uses the time to meditate in quiet corners, but often, now, she will interrupt her session to check on his progress with one girl or another. She knows him well enough that she can tell what he's talking about just from the way he stands or waves his arms. He moves one way when he's excited by a new band, another when he's complimenting a girl's clothing, yet another when he's complaining about a teacher. She enjoys playing these games with herself, as she enjoys watching him flirt, because she can always catch the distinctions between the way he acts with these girls and the way he is when the two of them are alone together. These girls don't know him, but Shari does, and that makes her feel like the two of them are sharing a silent secret.

Still, even if she doesn't mind him flirting, she doesn't like it when the girls flirt back.

They meet frequently in the tea shop, or for long walks through the city, and he asks her for advice: Should he ask Kaili or Sita to the movies? Does Samana like him too much; does Menka like him at all? Why does Kamala always lean in his direction and twirl her long black hair but refuse to accept his gifts or let him walk her home?

"She thinks you're a flirt," Shari points out. The monsoon season is abating, and the sun has finally lost its shyness, poking out from beneath the clouds. They are picnicking on a hillside, in the shadow of Mount Kanchenjunga, tinny music playing from the speaker of Jamal's phone.

"Why ever would she think that?" Jamal asks, sounding indignant.

"You've been in Gangtok for, what, three months now?"

"About."

"And you've kissed how many girls?"

"A gentleman never tells."

"I suspect Kamala has decided you're no gentleman," Shari teases.

Jamal pops a samosa in his mouth, moaning with the taste of it. This is one of Shari's favorite things about him, how little it takes to make him happy. He loves food especially, and unreservedly, and she loves watching him eat.

"Then I suppose she's smarter than she looks," he says.

She gives him a light shove. "Be nice."

"I can be nice or I can be honest," Jamal says. "And I know you prefer the latter. It's what I like about you."

Shari swallows. If he knew how dishonest she was with him, how much she never told . . .

"Then tell me honestly," she says. "Why is it that you bounce from one girl to the other so quickly. Is there no one in all of Gangtok good enough for Jamal Chopra? Or do you simply have an attention deficit?"

"Very funny."

"No, I'm seriously asking. Don't you want something more, sometimes?" She has long imagined the life she will have, someday, when she's lapsed, the husband who will love her, the children who will cling to her, the life filled with embraces and laughter. It seems

179

like such an impossibly long time to wait, and it mystifies her that someone like Jamal, who could have so much *right now*, denies himself.

"You're seriously asking?" Jamal has been lounging backward, like a sunbather, but now he sits upright, fixes her with a quizzical look. "Seriously?"

"Yes, seriously. Is that so difficult to believe?"

"Well, frankly, yes," he says. "I assumed it was obvious."

"What was?"

"Shari, don't you know?" There's a helpless note in his voice, almost pleading. "Don't you know why I distract myself with these other girls, why none of them can matter?"

She shakes her head.

But even as she's doing so, she does know.

Something in her, the voice of prudence and responsibility, says, *No.* Says, *Remember, this can't happen.*

This cannot be yours.

"It's you," Jamal says. "There's no one but you," and Shari silences the part of her that knows better, listens only to the wind in the trees and their favorite song, their "Alice" on the breeze, and the melody of his surprised laughter when she twines their fingers together and closes the distance between them.

They keep it a secret, the thing between them.

The love between them.

That's what it is, of course; Shari can't deny that. This is no flirtation, no casual thing that can be shrugged off, tucked into the margins of her life, abandoned without a backward look once her tenure as a Player begins.

She hides it carefully from her trainers, most of them aunts or uncles who love her almost as much as they love the line—almost, but not quite. Their job, their life, is devoted to making sure that Shari is the best Player she can be, that she has the best chance possible of winning Endgame. And she knows that their vision of the Player's life doesn't include love.

So she lies to them.

She lies to them, and she lies to Jamal.

"What do you do all that time, hiding away at home?" he asks her finally, after an intense weekend of training takes her away from him for 48 hours straight, and—much as she hates it—she lies. "What are you going to do after high school?" he asks her, assuming that, like everyone else at school, she has a choice in the manner, and she lies. "Why do they act like that around you?" he asks, about the boys who whisper about her in corners or the girls who emulate her every move or the people in town who give her extra helpings of kebabas or fried plantains or a free scarf that she's made the mistake of admiring aloud, and she lies.

"What do you think my father was running from?" he asks. "What is it about this place that drove him away?"

She lies.

He loves her, he tells her he loves her, but how can he love her when he doesn't know who she really is?

Shari thinks that maybe it's *because* he doesn't know that he can see her clearly; he's not blinded by her position or her destiny. With him she's not Shari Who Will Be the Player. She is simply Shari. She has always kept a piece of herself separate from her job, from Endgame, a sliver of soul untouched by the demands of the Harrapan, owned only by herself, and this is the piece she gives to Jamal.

So she tells herself, when she's feeling especially guilty.

She could tell him the truth, let him peer behind the veil of secrecy and see the world's true workings. He is, after all, Harrapan, and besides that, he is Jamal, and can be trusted—it would violate nothing to take him into her confidence. As the Player designate, she has full discretion. She's allowed to tell him everything.

But then he would know she's lied to him, and he would know too much of the truth, and every time she steels herself to risk it, he touches her cheek or kisses her lips or runs soft fingers through her hair, and she stills her tongue, because she can't lose him.

She's the strongest Harrapan woman of her generation, but losing him is a blow she could not survive.

Someday, she promises herself. Then fate takes the decision out of her hands.

The earthquake strikes at 2:32 p.m. and scores a 4.7 on the Richter scale. Seven people die, 32 more are injured, and a block of housing burns to the ground. This is what Shari finds out later.

In the moment, nothing is so clear. The moment is chaos and screaming and terror and instinct.

One second she and Jamal are holding hands in a cable car, dangling hundreds of meters over the Gangtok hillside, naming the animals they see in the clouds. Elephant. Horse. Llama. Shari has just picked out a fluffy white monkey when the car begins to sway violently. Far, far below, the earth has awakened and given a mighty shudder.

There's an earsplitting screech as the cable car comes to a stop. Then it lurches alarmingly and plunges several meters. The cable catches, but the thick cords are twisting and fraying. The passengers are thrown from their seats. They panic; they scream.

Only Shari stays calm. She peers through the window, quickly understanding the situation: The earthquake has destabilized the posts suspending the cable car. The cable is still supporting the weight of the car, but she can see the tension pulling at it, knows it will only be a matter of time before the posts give, or the cable snaps, and the car plunges hundreds of meters into the hillside.

They have to get out of here.

Shari has to get them out of here.

The cable car sways lazily over the hill. The 11 passengers are all crying or screaming, all but Jamal, who has his arms around Shari as if to protect her.

"Everyone, stay calm!" she announces to the passengers. "We will be fine. I will get us out of this." None of the passengers in this car are Harrapan; they do not know her, or what she can do. But there is authority in her voice, enough that they fall silent and listen.

"Can you climb onto my back and hang on?" she asks the one child in the car, a small girl of six or seven. The girl nods solemnly, and Shari kneels down and lets her hoist herself up.

"What are you going to do?" the girl's mother asks, voice trembling. Jamal's eyes are wide, confused. "Shari . . . what?"

Shari gauges the thickness of the cable, the distance to the end, the weight of the car, the swaying of the line, does some quick calculations, and says what she hopes will be the truth. "You have to trust me. I can save you all, but you have to stay very still and very calm in the meantime. Wait for me to come back."

"Come back from where?" the mother asks, and Jamal, suddenly understanding, cries for her to stop, but Shari ignores both of them. There's no time to waste. With the girl clinging to her shoulders, she climbs—very carefully, very gently—through the cable car window and takes hold of the line. They dangle from the cable, hundreds of meters above the ground. One handhold at a time, she carries herself and the girl toward safety. The girl's weight is nothing. Her cries are distracting, so Shari retreats into that calm place at the center of her mind. She will not think about how far below the ground is, or how many lives depend on this working. Emergency crews will take too long to arrive—Shari is the only hope these people have—but she doesn't think about that either. She thinks only about her grip, one handhold and then another, moving steadily toward the top of the cable line, as if this were training, as if this were easy—and so it is. She deposits the girl on solid ground, warns her to stay still and wait.

Thirty meters from the cable car to solid ground.

Thirty meters back again.

Shari takes off her socks, wraps them around her palms to protect her skin, and lets herself slide along the cable, like it's a zip line, catching herself just before she slams into the car. Jamal is gaping at her in shock. They all are, except the girl's mother, who has her eyes closed. Tears stream down her cheeks.

Shari takes her next.

Then an old man too weak to hang on by himself, so she rigs a rope and ties him to her back.

Then another woman.

One by one, she ferries them up the cable, deposits them on the ground, praying to the Makers that there will be enough time, because she must save the most able-bodied for last, and Jamal is the most able-bodied of all, and every time she climbs up the cable and the distance opens between them, she imagines what will happen if the cable snaps and the boy she loves falls and breaks.

The cable holds.

The passengers hold on.

Until, finally, there are only the two of them left, Jamal and Shari. He doesn't want to, doesn't think it's right, but sees that there is no other way—climbs on, hangs on, lets her tow him the 100 meters to safety, whispering only, "You're like a superhero," once, midway up.

At the top, he kisses her, holds her in his arms while the passengers lavish her with gratitude, but he says nothing more, only, "I have to go make sure my mother is okay," and then, with a squeeze of her hand, he's gone.

In the wake of the earthquake, the city buzzes with gossip. Many speak about the cable car, and the mysterious girl who saved its passengers and then slipped away before she could be identified and rewarded.

Shari says nothing to anyone about it. She goes straight home, makes sure that her house is intact and her family safe, and then she waits.

That night, Jamal comes to her.

They sit in her yard beneath the stars, Tarki wandering through the grass, flashing his feathers as if to distract them from what is to come, but there can be no more delaying.

"So, what *was* that back there?" Jamal asks, finally. "Are you Wonder Woman? Batman?"

She forces a laugh.

And then, finally, she tells him the truth.

"This is going to sound insane," she begins. "But you have to trust me."

"I will always trust you," he says. "And nothing you tell me could be more insane than what you did today. That was . . ." He shakes his head. "That was incredible. *You* were incredible. And I mean that literally, like beyond the credible. Beyond belief."

She sighs. He has no idea how far his credibility will need to stretch if he's to believe what she has to tell him.

"The story, my story, starts thousands of years ago," she says. "When our Harrapan civilization began. When the beings came from the stars."

"Come on, no jokes, this is serious," Jamal complains.

She quiets him with a look. Then tells him the whole story. The Makers. Endgame. The oath sworn by generations of Harrapan. The Player.

When she finishes, there's a long silence.

"Did you hit your head or something?" he finally asks.

"No."

"You're just screwing with me, then."

"No."

"So you're telling me, seriously, that you're part of an ancient bloodline—"

"We," she says. "You are Harrapan too. I will be your Player too."

"Okay, that *we* are part of an ancient bloodline that someday soon will be wiped out, along with the rest of humanity, when aliens come back and pit a bunch of teenagers against each other in some perverse global cage match, and you've spent your entire life training to be one of them? And in less than two years you're going to be this Player thing, and then you'll have to give up everything in your life to work and train and maybe get yourself killed by a bunch of murderous teenagers, or maybe some masochistic aliens, if it comes to that?"

"That's not precisely how I'd put it," Shari says, "but yes."

"No," he says. "No! This is the twenty-first century, and you're a smart girl; you can't possibly believe this crap."

"I do," she says. "As do my parents, and my entire family, and many of the families you've come to know well. As, I believe, your father did. I've asked around. He was afraid of Endgame. Had he stayed, he would have been asked to devote himself to preparing for the final battle . . . to helping me. He wanted a more normal life, beyond the shadow of apocalypse, and thought if he ran away, he could find it. Even if it shamed his family. Even if it meant leaving everything he knew and loved behind."

Jamal stiffens. He nearly leaps to his feet. "Don't do that," he says. "Don't bring him into this lunacy."

"I'm sorry," she says. "But that's true. All of this is true."

"If it *were* true," he says slowly, "if that were possible, which it one hundred percent isn't, it would mean you've been lying to me, about everything."

"Not everything."

He laughs harshly. "Right, not everything. Just everything that matters. My father. You. Us. Is that what you're saying? Is that what you're asking me to believe?"

She lowers her head, wishing down to her core that she could say no. "Yes."

"I have to go," Jamal says.

"Please don't. Stay. Let's talk about this. I can answer your questions. I can make you understand—"

"No," he says. "Enough for tonight. Enough lies. Enough truth. *Enough.*"

She calls to him as he strides past her, out of the yard, into the street. "Jamal, please, what happens now—are you coming back?"

He won't look at her, won't even pause. "I don't know."

He's right after all: that's more than enough truth for one night.

Three days pass.

Three days, three nights, no Jamal. He doesn't come to school. He doesn't answer his phone. He doesn't come to her home, and when she goes to his, he won't see her.

Shari didn't know it was possible to be so afraid.

She's faced bandits and jaguars, scaled cliffs, and endured pitiless desert sun, but nothing has terrified her the way this does.

Before Jamal, she could accept being alone—she knew no other way. But after Jamal?

No.

There is no after Jamal.

He has filled an emptiness in her; they did that for each other. He is her soul mate, her other half, the completion of the sentence that is Shari Jha. Without him, there are only jagged edges and silence.

On the fourth day, the phone rings, and his voice sounds strange, closed off. For the first time since they've met, he is walling himself off from her, wearing a mask.

"Please, will you meet me at the tea shop at four this afternoon?" he asks her, so agonizingly polite, as if he is speaking to her grandmother, that a fault line in her heart splits open, because this must be it, the end.

"Of course," she says, then adds, "I'm sorry," but he has already hung up.

"You seem distracted today, child," Pravheet says as he aims a sharp kick at Shari's kneecap. She darts out of the way just in time, a beat too slow. Pravheet is right: she's been slow all morning. Pravheet, the most respected living former Player, is not her official trainer, but sometimes they spar together. She likes to test herself against someone at his level, and she likes to talk to someone who understands the peculiarities of her life; Pravheet likes to give her advice. But he can't advise her about what to do when she sees Jamal this afternoon, because he doesn't even know about Jamal—none of them do.

She whirls on her heel and kicks her heel into Pravheet's face, but he is already somewhere else—behind her, pinning her arms behind her back.

Shari goes limp in defeat, and Pravheet lets go. "I'm sorry," she says. "I suppose my mind is elsewhere."

"You're supposed to be beyond such problems," Pravheet points out.

"I know," she says, ashamed.

"Shari, why do you look away from me?"

She is staring at the floor, trying not to cry. She is soon to be the Player, after all—she is far beyond the weakness of tears.

"Shari," he says again, quietly insistent.

Shari looks up to meet his fierce gaze, steadying her breath and calming her nerves. She draws strength from the look in his eyes, which suggests he knows more than he's saying, and understands.

"You don't have to worry," Shari tells him. "I'm distracted, yes, but I'm dealing with it. After today, there shouldn't be a problem. There will be nothing left"—she won't let her voice catch on the words—"nothing left to distract me from what matters."

Pravheet takes her hands in his. They are large and calloused and strong, and make her feel very small. "Shari, you know that no two Players are alike, do you not?"

"You've told me many times," Shari tells him. Pravheet is the only one of her trainers who has been sympathetic to her desire not to kill, at least not until it becomes absolutely necessary. Pravheet himself swore never to kill again, after he lapsed. He defended her choice to the other Harrapan, and has always encouraged her to stand up for what she believes, to Play the way she feels she should.

"There are some Players who feel they need to purge their lives of everything beyond the game," Pravheet says.

"Of course," Shari agrees. "Absolute focus." That's what she's always been taught, and, until recently, it's what she has always practiced.

"But you have to find your own way." Pravheet gives her a strange, kind smile. "Do you see what I'm getting at?"

"Honestly? I'm not sure."

His smile widens. "Don't worry. You will be."

She shows up early; Jamal is already seated and waiting for her. He has ordered her a mug of chai, prepared just as she likes, with milk and three spoons of sugar.

Shari has spent the last two hours meditating. She's ready for whatever Jamal has to tell her.

The session with Pravheet has convinced her that she will be better off without Jamal. This relationship has been a distraction from her training, from her duty.

The fact that she actually let herself think she couldn't live without him? That was melodrama and weakness that should have been beneath her.

There's only one thing she can't live without, and that's her responsibility to the Harrapan line.

She reminds herself of this unshakable truth, then sits down.

"So," Jamal says.

"So."

They watch each other.

Even now, under these circumstances, it's good to see him. Her eyes have been thirsty; now, in the long silence, they drink.

She likes to imagine he is doing the same.

"I believe you," he says.

"Okay."

"About all of it. The things from the stars, the game, the Player, your weird secret superhero life, the thousand-year conspiracy, my . . . my dad, all of it."

She sips her tea. "I said okay."

"You don't want to say anything else?"

"Like what?"

"I don't know, don't you want to ask me why I believe you? Or what I think? Or what I want to do?"

She sighs. If he thinks he can sucker her into breaking up with *herself*, then he doesn't know her at all. "What do you want from me, Jamal? I told you what was true; I told you why I lied to you before; I told you I was sorry. I told you I loved you. I told you everything I had to tell. I came here because you said you had something to tell me."

He shifts uncomfortably in his seat. Shari readies herself. This is it.

"Not tell you, exactly," he says. Then he puts a small cardboard box on the table and removes its lid. The thing inside sparkles. "Ask you, really."

Shari reaches for the box, takes out the sparkly thing.

"What . . . what is this?" It's a stupid question; it's obvious what the thing is: a ring.

"It's not real," he admits. "I mean, it's not exactly from a gumball machine, but . . . close enough. Best I could do on short notice."

"Is this what I think this is?"

"Marry me," he says. "Please?"

It's the last thing she expected, and without thinking, she bursts into laughter.

Jamal grins. "Not exactly the answer I was hoping for."

"Is this a joke?" she says. "*Marry* you? Why?"

"Why not?"

"Now, *that's* romantic."

"Give me a break, it's not like I've done this before," Jamal says.

"That's comforting, at least." She could banter with him like this all day; she could banter with him like this for the rest of her life.

And with that thought, her laughter vanishes, because she realizes: This is real. Jamal is asking her to marry him.

And everything in her wants to say yes.

Jamal's mood shifts back to serious right along with her. "I know it sounds crazy, but I've thought it through. I know what I want, and it's *you*, Shari. It's always been you, even before I met you. How's that for romantic? I always thought that kind of thing was cheesy garbage, the sort of thing you said to get girls to like you, but it's actually true. I want you now, I want you forever, and I don't want to wait. Especially now that I know about this Player thing—if you're going to be running around the world risking your life, I want you to have a reason to survive. To come back."

"Not wanting to die isn't reason enough?" she says, but the joke falls flat.

Jamal's not laughing anymore. "I know what you're going to say," he says. "That we should wait until we're older. Until you're not the Player anymore, and you're ready to start the rest of your life. But why shouldn't the rest of your life start now? Why shouldn't you be a Player with a husband, with a *family*—"

"You mean . . . ?"

"Yeah, I mean kids," he says. "I mean, if you think you want that?"

"Of course I do," she says, and it's true, even if it has always seemed impossibly out of reach. The Harrapan often marry young. Many of her siblings married when they were 14 or 15, and had children quickly after. But Shari's never considered the possibility of that kind of life. For her, a husband, children, they're all part of some unimaginable future, after she lapses, and something else she suddenly realizes: there's a part of her that doesn't believe in a life after. Her time as a Player is like Mount Kanchenjunga—a towering reality that's always been there, looming over her life. Too large to see beyond.

"I can't stand the idea of you sacrificing yourself for the Harrapan, or for this stupid game, or for anything," Jamal says. "I want you to have something to live for."

"I live for myself and my people," she points out. "That's always been enough."

"Don't you want more? Don't you want . . ." He rests his hands on the table, palms up, and she appreciates that he doesn't reach for her. He waits for her to lay her hands on his. She does. They're warm, and she can feel his pulse beating at his wrist. "Don't you want me?"

What she wants is to fling herself across the table and into his arms.

She wants to slip on the ring and never take it off.

She wants Jamal, but she also wants to be the Player that her people deserve, and she doesn't see how she can have both.

"I have to think," Shari says. "I need some time. Is that okay?"

"Of course it's okay. But can I ask one more thing?"

She squeezes his hands, holds tight. "Anything."

"Don't do all your thinking alone?" He smiles. She missed that smile. She wants to wrap herself up in its warmth and fall asleep. "I missed you."

They spend the rest of the evening together. They spend every minute they can find with each other, and it's as if nothing has changed.

Except that he knows the truth about her now. And he loves her anyway.

A week passes, and another, and Jamal doesn't pressure her for an answer. She can't give him one. The answer she wants to give doesn't make any sense, and the answer that makes sense is the opposite of what she wants. So she meditates, and asks the Makers what to do, and breathes, and waits for clarity.

It comes to her in a dream.

She dreams of a child.

A toddler with dark hair and bright eyes—Shari's eyes.

The little girl has Shari's hair, Shari's laugh, and Jamal's smile.

She stands in a field of golden grass, her head tipped back and her arms open wide, as if to embrace the sky.

Mama, she says, in a voice like a flute. It makes Shari's heart flutter.

Mama, I'm waiting for you.

"Why?" Jamal says, after he's managed to stop kissing her, after he's slipped the ring onto her finger, after he's swung her off her feet and through the air and thanked the gods for his fortune. "What made you so sure all of a sudden?"

It was the dream, and it wasn't.

It was the little girl, their daughter—Shari knows as surely as she's known everything that the girl is out there somewhere, waiting to be born—but not just their daughter.

It was Pravheet's prescient reminder that every Player must forge her own path.

It was Jamal. It has always been Jamal.

"I love you," Shari says. "I simply decided that was enough."

Other than the decision itself, there's nothing simple about it. They marry in secret, so no one can stop them. Jamal continues to live with his mother, Shari with her parents, even after they've been joined in holy matrimony. She wears her ring on a chain around her neck, keeping it beneath her clothes, close to her heart. They steal time with each other in grassy knolls and the backseat of Jamal's rusting Honda, which barely runs but has wonderfully soft leather seats. Shari continues to train, to wait for the current Player to lapse, to study and meditate and let her elders believe her life is empty of anything but thoughts of Endgame.

Jamal, at least, stops flirting.

They keep the secret between them until the marriage becomes something no one can question, until they've passed a point of no return—until Shari finds out she's pregnant.

"You did *what*?"

"Are you out of your *mind*?"

"How *could* you?"

The questions are fired at her like artillery, each angrier than the last. Shari and Jamal called the Harrapan elders to her family's house to hear the news. Her parents sit quietly beside her as the room explodes. They don't agree with her choice, but they will not argue with her now that it's been made.

The others have no such compunction.

"This is extremely irregular," says Jovinderpihainu, the eldest among them.

"Shari has always been irregular," says Pravheet, giving her a wink so she knows it's meant as a compliment.

"I know it's irregular," Shari says. "But it's happening. There's nothing to be done about it now." She will have the baby two months before she's due to become the Player. There has never, at least in recorded Harrapan history, been a Player with a husband and child. It is unheard of, perhaps unthinkable.

There are some who think it unacceptable.

"I can think of something," Peetee says angrily. "We can find someone else to be our Player. Because you've proved you don't care enough to do it." There's a roar of support for this sentiment.

"She's proved no such thing," Helena snaps, and the room falls silent. Even Shari is shocked.

Helena was a Player herself, more than 40 years ago. She is the second most respected of the last two centuries, and she has never had much respect for Shari. It was Helena who called Shari a coward for not wanting to learn to kill, Helena who time and again has questioned Shari's readiness and commitment to the cause. She is a fearsome woman, still strong enough at 64 to fend off almost any enemy single-handed—if anyone would dare attack her.

She also, Shari now remembers, married her husband at midnight on the day she lapsed. Shari has always known this, but never gave much thought to what it implies: that Helena was once young and in love, that she spent her years as a Player waiting for her time to come, waiting until she could finally put her duties aside and give herself to Boort.

"We are a line that values tradition, but we need not be imprisoned by it," Helena says. "Simply because a thing has never happened before, does that mean it *may* never happen? Simply because a woman has a family, does that mean she cannot serve her people, fulfill her obligation to the greater good?"

"Doesn't mean she *can* either," Peetee mutters.

"The Makers chose Shari for a reason," Pravheet reminds the assembled Harrapan. "Perhaps this was the reason. Perhaps this was all meant to be."

Jamal has stayed silent throughout the meeting, tensing when Shari came under attack but keeping his mouth shut. Now he rises. "Meant to be, not meant to be?" He waves the question away. "This is what is. What *will* be."

Shari rises to her feet beside her husband, who, for the first time, seems less like the boy she knows and more like a man who will be father to her child. "My husband speaks true," she says. "I asked you here not to gain your permission, but to tell you what will come. Thank you for listening."

She takes Jamal's hand, and together they stride out of the common room and back into the private bedchambers of the house, without looking back.

"So, that went well," Jamal says wryly, once they're alone.

Shari is about to answer when a swell of nausea surges over her. She drops Jamal's hand, runs for the nearest bathroom, and slams herself inside just in time to heave up her breakfast. She sits on the cold tile, head hanging over the toilet, sweat dripping down her face, and breathes, waiting for the nausea to pass.

This is morning sickness, yes.

But this is also defiance—of her people and her traditions, and perhaps her common sense.

This, Shari thinks, is how it feels to know there's no turning back.

There's a soft knock at the door. "I'm fine, Jamal," she says, pressing a palm to the door, like she can draw his strength right through it. "I'll be out in a moment."

It's not Jamal.

"I said you *could* do it," Helena's sharp voice says. "I didn't say it would be easy. Don't disappoint me."

No part of it is easy. Not the morning sickness (which lasts well into the afternoon and twilight), not the swollen ankles or the sore feet, not the compressed bladder or the heartburn, not the fatigue, not the headaches, not the acne, not the way that she's come to think of the baby—this thing she's looked forward to for so long—as a rapidly growing parasite that is colonizing her body from the inside out. Shari has always thought of herself as a Player of the mind, not the body, but for more than a decade she's maintained rigorous control over both. She's worked hard to transform her body into a graceful and powerful machine, all coordination and ropy muscle. Now, after only a few months, all her efforts have been erased. Her balance is gone, her limbs clumsy; her lungs heave and her heart pounds after only a few flights of stairs. She once heard her sister-in-law say that being pregnant made her feel like a hippopotamus, but Shari now thinks that's an understatement. She feels like an elephant. A whale. Maybe even a brontosaurus, some lumbering prehistoric creature out of sync with the modern world. She feels ancient and impossible—and many nights, lying in bed, cramping with the kicks of the thing inside her, listening to Jamal sleep peacefully and hating him for it, she wonders if she'll feel this way forever.

If she's made a terrible mistake.

Jamal senses her hesitation, her regrets, and resents her for it, and they've started fighting—tentatively at first, two people afraid of hurting what they love most, but then full-throated, no-holds-barred screaming matches. He accuses her of loving Endgame more than she loves their family; she accuses him of dismissing everything she holds sacred, of not knowing her at all. She accuses him—though only in secret, in her mind, because this is a line she fears to cross—of suckering her into making the worst decision of her life.

Then she argues with herself, and remembers that she loves Jamal, and that she loves their child, or will, and the joy that feeling brings her is worth lumbering around like an elephant.

At night, in bed, Jamal tells her stories of what their lives will be like soon, and strokes her hair, and she pretends to be strong and doesn't admit that she is afraid.

Maybe, she sometimes thinks, she was wrong and everyone else was right. How could she have been so arrogant to think that she could be both the Player and a mother? She loves Jamal, she loves her line, she loves her duty—but what's to say love is enough? What's to say the love of one won't destroy the others?

As the days skid downhill toward her delivery date, it's as if she can feel a clock ticking from her swollen stomach.

She wakes one night to a stab of fear, alarm bells ringing in her mind, a nightmare already fading but the urgency of it still sharp: explosions in the sky, blood on the ground, and Shari, too clumsy and slow and big to do anything but watch.

"I can't do this," she whispers, and then gasps as there's another stab—it's not fear after all, it's pain, and the mattress beneath her is wet with her broken water and the baby is writhing and kicking and this is labor.

This is happening—whether she can do it or not.

The pain splits her wide open.

The pain screams through her, a wild sound of monsters tearing each other to shreds.

The pain is a creature of its own, devouring her.

The pain is an ocean, tossing her on its waves.

Somewhere, in the foggy distance, is her mother's soothing voice, the urgent pressure of Jamal's hand, but these things seem irrelevant, almost imagined; there is nothing real but her body and the baby and the pain that fuses them together into one.

Shari retreats into herself, as she's been taught to do, finds the eye of calm at the heart of the pain.

Finds clarity.

Finds *strength*.

There is pain like never before, and the tidal wave crashes down on her with such force that the old Shari might have broken, but this new Shari, strong and sure and ready, bears it and endures . . . and then? An absence. An emptiness. A wave washing out to sea. A hollow inside, where once she was full.

A soft weight in her arms.

A baby's cry.

A new life.

Jamal brushes her hair back from her sweaty forehead. Shari holds the child.

Her daughter.

Shari smiles down at her child and finally understands how very wrong she was to doubt this. To imagine that she should, that she could, deny herself this moment—that she could not Play and love all at once. That she had to choose.

There is no choice.

There is no weighing of priorities, no danger of distractions, no question of which matters more, Endgame or her family, her duty or her love.

There is only this child. There is only love in her.

Playing, fighting, preserving tradition, protecting the line, all of that is a *part* of loving her, all of that will be better for loving her, because as Shari fights for the Harrapan and for herself and Jamal, she fights for her daughter. When Endgame comes, if it comes for her, she will triumph over the other Players. She must. Because what they will want, she will *need*.

Shari will Play for this small, precious girl; Shari will do anything and everything to save her world.

"What do we name her?" Jamal asks, and Shari loves him more than she ever has, because look what they have created together. It seems impossible that they have found each other, but impossible to imagine a world where they didn't. She remembers the first time he confessed himself to her, the first time she took him in her arms, and how strange it was for something to feel so right, so fated, understanding now that it was fate, guiding them here. To her.

They will name her Alice.

And she will save the world.

NABATAEAN
MACCABEE

When the phone rings, Maccabee Adlai is dreaming of soft hands
massaging cold skin, nails scraping across flesh, lips parting in a
pleasurable gasp of pain. Satin sheets shimmer in the warm glow of
candlelight, and beyond the window ocean waves lap at a tropical
shore.

He wakes with a sigh to the phone's shrill ring, his girlfriend's snores,
and the cheap, scratchy cotton that passes for bedding around here.
Part of him is inclined to silence the phone and slip back into the
warm embrace of the dream. If it were anyone else on the other end of
the line, he would.

But he knows that ring.

His caller will not be silenced.

Maccabee feigns a yawn and groans, just in case the girl is awake
after all and observing him. The average 16-year-old boy would take
seconds, maybe minutes, to ease into alertness at four a.m., especially
one who'd only fallen asleep a couple of hours before, after consuming
a bathtub's worth of gin (or at least appearing to). And his mission
here depends on seeming like a normal teenage boy.

The yawn is fake, but the groan is real. Maccabee is anything but
average, and there's little he hates more than feigning it.

He slips out of bed, snatches the phone, and silently retreats to the
tiny closet he shares with his roommate. Maccabee has been stuck in
this hellhole of a boarding school for six months, and he still hasn't
adjusted to its indignities. It isn't just the thin, overstarched sheets or

the limp, bland meals masquerading as food. It's the rooms the size of prison cells and the privacy they deny him, the communal bathrooms filled with the stink and stains of oafish adolescents. It's the need to pretend that the homework isn't beneath him, that the teachers aren't borderline illiterate, that he cares about grades or football scores or who is screwing who and why. The Baden Akademie is meant to be an elite educational institution, its student body drawn exclusively from the 1 percent. It claims to afford every advantage to the children of the rich and powerful, who will one day grow up to be masters of the universe. For Maccabee, that's motivation enough to endure its daily tedium. He just didn't realize it would all be so depressingly *ordinary*. He's tired of pretending to be anything but himself: Exceptional.

"What is it?" he whispers into the phone as quietly as he can. His roommate imbibed enough vodka and Klonopin last night to knock himself out for a week, and his girlfriend once slept through not only a fire alarm but an actual *fire*, but Maccabee doesn't believe in taking chances.

"Kalla bhajat niboot scree." It's a woman's voice, speaking in a language nearly as old as time itself. Only 10 people on the planet understand these words, and Maccabee is one of them. Direct translation is impossible: they're an expression of trust and security, alerting him that she can speak frankly, asking if he can do the same.

"No, Ekaterina. There is no privacy here," he reminds her.

She grunts, plainly annoyed. He enjoys her irritation—after all, it's her fault he's here.

"No matter," she says. "We need to set up a meet. I need something of you."

"When?" He won't allow himself to sound eager. She hates that.

"I land in Zurich on Tuesday."

Two days from now and, conveniently, visitation week. Wealthy, neglectful relatives will be flying in from all over the world, the rules relaxed in their honor.

"I'll reserve us an eight p.m. table at Der Kunstkochen," he says, before she can insist on some disgusting hole-in-the-wall with rancid beef. He knows her ways too well, and he understands that sometimes circumstances call for discretion. But sometimes—as when Maccabee has endured six months of dining hall cuisine—circumstances call for Zurich's finest restaurant, for caviar, champagne, and a perfectly fried filet of wild sea bass paired with black olives and shallots.

"I don't know," she says, but he can hear the hesitation in her voice. After all, Ekaterina is the one who taught him to appreciate the finer things in life. She's the one who, before sending him to this godforsaken city, told him of the Kunstkochen and its caramel soufflé with the apple tatin heart.

"Eight p.m.," she says, the temptation of impeccably prepared pastry too much for even her iron will to withstand. "Don't be late."

"I look forward to it," he says, then hopes he hasn't said too much.

"Indeed, my—" She stops herself abruptly. She always calls him "my Player," but she can't do so on an unsecured line. No one here can know Maccabee's true role in the future of humanity, that he is the Nabataean champion, pledged to save his ancient race from extinction. And so she swallows the word, replaces it with one she never uses. "My son."

She cuts the line.

"Love you too, Mom," he says sarcastically, into the dead air. *Love.* It's not a word he would ever dare say where she could hear him, or would ever want to. That kind of sorry playacting is for his inferiors. They cling to family, to their pathetic ideas about how mothers should care for their sons and how sons should cling to their mothers, because it's all they have. Maccabee has Ekaterina, who's taught him to be strong, to raise himself. She's given him so much more than so-called motherly love. She's given him a destiny, a place in history. Only ordinary people have ordinary mothers, Maccabee reminds himself.

He slips the phone beneath his pillow and climbs back into bed.

His girlfriend's eyes drift open. "Who was that?"

"Business," he says.

She laughs unhappily. "You're funny," she says, but he knows what she's thinking. That it was another girl on the phone. That the rumors about Maccabee, how he takes what he wants from a girl and casts her aside, are true. That this boy who claims to love her is taking secret four a.m. phone calls from someone else. Maccabee lets her think it. Having a girlfriend in this place is useful in more ways than one, but it doesn't matter who the girl is. When this one gets too tiresome, there will always be another.

In the meantime . . .

"Since you're awake," he says, "I should point out we have two hours before you have to sneak back to your room."

"However will we fill the time?" she says playfully, then tucks her long, blond hair over her shoulder and exposes a long stretch of neck.

He closes his eyes, thinking of Tuesday night, wondering at the need for the meeting and what will come of it, whether change is on the horizon, if Ekaterina will be proud of all he's done here, and then he presses his lips to bare skin and wraps his arms around a narrow waist and, for the time being, thinks no more.

Sometimes this place has its advantages.

Maccabee arrives at the restaurant early. Ekaterina, of course, is earlier. She has never allowed him the upper hand, even for a second.

"Mother," he says, unbuttoning his blazer, then sitting down across the table from her.

"Ekaterina," she corrects him.

"Yes, of course. Ekaterina. I trust your flight over was smooth."

"We aren't here for small talk, my Player," she snaps.

"Of course," he says again. He has been wondering whether perhaps there is no important mission; perhaps it's just been long enough that she wanted to see him, made an excuse.

But he should have known better.

A waiter silently materializes at their table, handing Maccabee a wine list. "Will you have something to drink, sir?"

Maccabee suppresses a smile and orders two glasses of their most expensive wine. Six feet five, more than 200 pounds of raw muscle, with a fine dusting of stubble across his tan chin, he looks at least a decade older than his age. It comes in handy. He catches the waiter glancing back and forth between him and his mother, brow subtly furrowed, and knows what the man assumes. That this is an intimate rendezvous, that this woman must be *very* wealthy to entice such a handsome younger man.

They make quite a mismatched pair, Maccabee and Ekaterina.

Like the restaurant, with its fine china and antique chandeliers, its tuxedoed waiters moving in elegant sync, Maccabee oozes wealth and good breeding. He speaks fluent German with a perfect Swiss accent (one of 13 languages he can speak like a native). His nails are manicured and buffed, his bespoke suit worth thousands and his A. Lange & Söhne watch worth exponentially more. He makes himself the center of every room he steps into.

Ekaterina taught him how.

She taught him everything: how to dress like a gentleman, to speak like he owns the world, to infuse his chilly smile with warmth when required, to charm the most beautiful of women into giving him what he wants, to woo and entice and persuade, to carry himself like a man of power with enough conviction that it becomes the truth.

Not that anyone would guess it to look at her.

In her youth, Ekaterina possessed legendary beauty and knew how to use it. She wielded her appearance as a weapon—hardly the only one in her arsenal, but often the most dangerous. But Ekaterina has no vanity. Invisibility carries a power of its own, she taught Maccabee. Especially for a woman of her age: Men *want* to underestimate her, to ignore her. She helps them do so, wearing frumpy dresses two decades out of fashion and two sizes too big, spraying her hair into a tangled and graying nest, letting her caterpillar eyebrows creep across her face. Tonight she is wearing a fanny pack.

She looks like nothing so much as a hapless tourist who stumbled

upon this Michelin-starred restaurant while in search of a
McDonald's. And this, Maccabee knows, is exactly the way she likes it.
"You still share a room with Jason Porter?" his mother asks. Their
shared native language is Polish, but she speaks in the ancient
Nabataean dialect, a long-dead language closely related to Aramaic.
They are the only two on the continent who speak it.

This place is not your home, she told him about Warsaw, as soon as he
was old enough to understand.

This language is not your language.

These people are not your people.

He was three years old when she told him of their Nabataean heritage,
four years old when she told him of Endgame and promised that she
would make him the Player.

Nine years later, the promise came true.

Maccabee has spent years studying the Players of the other lines—his
competition. He knows most of them have been chosen for the honor
through prophecy or competition. Children pitted against children
in demonstrations of brute force, children trusted with the fate of
their people because some alignment of the stars or the tea leaves
suggested it would be so.

It is, in Maccabee's opinion, foolish. Worse than foolish: naïve.
Moronic. Fatal. To leave such a crucial choice to fate or accident?
To imagine that because an eight-year-old could win a wrestling
competition or a baby happened to be born in the shadow of Mercury
in retrograde, they were worthy of Playing the ultimate game? Anyone
stupid enough to believe that deserves to perish, as all those lines
inevitably will.

The Nabataeans know better. The game is strategy; life is strategy. The
honor of Endgame falls only to those savvy enough to accrue power,
ruthless enough to use it. Ekaterina is both, and she has created her
son in her own image.

Maccabee doesn't know how many strings she had to pull, how
many people she had to blackmail, how many millions she had to

spend. What he knows is that he is the result of her life's dream. He is the reason she sought out a Nabataean man with the body of an Olympian and the brain of an Einstein, bore his child, then disposed of him so he couldn't interfere. Maccabee is what Ekaterina made him, and he cannot remember a time when he hasn't shared her dream of the future. He Plays for her as much as he does for his line.

"You know I would have alerted you to a change in condition."

She nods. "Good. The Porter boy's mother arrived in Zurich this morning and is staying at the Schlosshotel im Altstadt. I need you to gain access to her room and retrieve a thumb drive. She carries it in a bottle of aspirin."

"Might I ask why?"

"You know better than that," she says.

He does.

His mother has no official job and never has. The line is, ostensibly, ruled by a council of three, elected every five years. But these are merely figureheads, puppets; those who know anything know that Ekaterina pulls the strings, even though she's not officially a council member. No one begrudges her, or if they do, they don't live long enough to act on it—she's proved she wants only what's best for the line. She accrues financial and political power for their people, in any way she can, and embedded Maccabee at the Akademie foreseeing exactly this kind of opportunity. Children, she has explained to Maccabee many times, make their parents significantly vulnerable. Most children, at least. Most parents.

"I'll need you to do it in such a way as to guarantee she doesn't raise a fuss when she discovers it's missing," Ekaterina adds. "That's essential."

"Do you have a suggestion?"

"Do what you do best," she says. "What I raised you to do."

They both know what that means.

He raises his glass. "Consider it done."

* * *

Here is what everyone knows about Serena Porter, his roommate's mother: She is the first female CEO of Intellex, the world's third largest tech company. She's famous for her efficient management style and ability to turn million-dollar acquisitions into billion-dollar stock surges; she's infamous for her ability to juggle work and family, the leadership of a Fortune 500 company with the nurturing of a husband and two children. (Personally, Maccabee finds this rather less impressive and substantially less interesting than the billions of dollars in profit.) She's written two books about her time-management strategies and parenting advice and is about to launch both a magazine and lifestyle reality show about working mothers.

Here is what Maccabee knows, from prowling through his roommate's emails and from paying attention: Serena Porter shipped her two kids off to boarding school as soon as they were old enough to read. The daughter is in rehab and the son, Maccabee's roommate, is a semi-illiterate, fully alcoholic meathead who's been expelled from schools in four different countries. The husband is having ongoing affairs with both the former nanny and Serena's current secretary; he and Serena live in separate wings of the Porter estate and see each other only for photo ops.

Here is what Maccabee can tell about Serena as soon as he spots her across the hotel bar, sipping halfheartedly at her single malt Scotch: She's lonely.

This will be a piece of cake.

Maccabee and Jason are polite strangers. They rarely speak, never interfere in each other's business. But Maccabee has a tap on Jason's phone and knows exactly where and when the boy plans to meet his mother. He knows Jason's schedule inside and out, and knows that after hockey practice and before dinner he will stop back in the room to slurp a shot of vodka. Maccabee dissolves a handful of valium in the bottle of Belvedere, and then waits.

Soon Jason is passed out and drooling on their floor—he's woken up that way plenty of times before, and will think nothing of it.

Maccabee slips into his favorite charcoal-gray suit and slips a pale blue silk handkerchief into his pocket. He slicks back his thick, wavy hair and grins at himself in the mirror.

Irresistible.

He finds a place at the hotel bar, sipping ginger ale from a crystal tumbler—he can't afford to cloud his head with alcohol, but the soda looks enough like whiskey to pass. He makes idle small talk with the bartender, admires the mahogany bar and its array of top-shelf liquors, pretends to be engaged by important business on his tablet. And all the while, he watches her.

Serena Porter sips her Scotch, checks her watch, checks her phone, stares into space for a few moments as if forcing herself to be still, sips her drink again, then gives in, checks her watch, and on and on. Her expression never changes, but Maccabee is an expert student of body language. He can see it in her tight grip on the glass, the tremble of her finger on the phone, the firm set of her lips: She knows her son isn't coming.

She half expected it.

Maccabee bides his time, waiting for the perfect moment. After she's accepted that the evening is a lost cause—before she gives up on the night and retreats to her room for more lonely hours in front of a computer screen. In between, there's a sweet spot, when she will long for him without even knowing he exists.

He waits for it.

A sip of Scotch, she checks her watch, and then—she puts her phone away. This is defeat.

Maccabee makes his move.

"Send the lady at the end of the bar a glass of the 55-year-old Macallan, on me," he tells the bartender. Priced at $600 a glass in Serena's home currency, the drink will show he means business. First-class business. "Tell her it's better than the swill she's drinking." He watches as his command is carried out, sees Serena's thoughts flicker across her face as clearly as if they were spelled out for him in cartoon bubbles. She should not engage; she should go back to the room, answer her emails, leave a stern voice mail for her son, go to sleep.

She picks up the glass of Scotch and slides into the seat beside him. "What makes you so sure I'm drinking swill?" she says.

He smiles, though not too broadly. A woman like Serena will want a bit of a challenge. "Everything is swill, compared to this. Trust me."

"You have me confused with another kind of woman," she says.

"You don't trust people?"

"Certainly not strangers."

"Certainly not anyone, I'm guessing."

That earns him a cool smile of reappraisal. She won't want a pretty face with an empty head; that's not her type. Even for an ill-conceived one-night rendezvous, she's the kind to want an equal. He can lower himself just enough to make it appear he is one.

She sips the Macallan. And, though she tries to hold it in, a small sigh of pleasure escapes her lips.

"A gentleman never says *I told you so*," he says.

She turns to face him, boldly meeting his gaze for the first time. She looks good for her age—good for any age. Her long, black hair falls in soft, refined waves. It reminds him of pictures he's seen of his mother, before he was born and she let herself gray. "You, on the other hand . . ." He laughs. "I did tell you so."

She nods to the bartender, orders a second glass of the Macallan. "And put it on my tab. His too."

"*Ja*, Frau Porter."

"I can afford my own drinks," Serena tells Maccabee.

"And mine too, apparently. So much the better. I like a woman who will keep me in the style to which I've grown accustomed."

"Ah, I'm keeping you, am I?"

"Would you throw a poor stray like me back on the street?" He bats his eyelashes mockingly.

"Are you flirting with me, young man? You must be young enough to be my—"

"Son?" he suggests.

She snorts. "I was going to say younger brother. How old do you think I am, anyway?"

"I'm not as dumb as I look, and I'm certainly not going to answer that. How old do you think *I* am?"

She appraises him. "Old enough to have very good taste in watches, Scotch, and women. Too young for me."

"And yet." He smiles.

"And yet."

They continue on in this vein, tension simmering between them, shallow cleverness pinging back and forth, until he sees the loosening of her expression, knows she's ready to go deeper.

He asks what's brought her to this part of the world, and how it is she's sitting alone in a bar, drinking her sorrows away. "Surely no one would be so foolish as to stand you up."

"What is it about a woman drinking alone that's so difficult for people to believe in?" she says. "Do I need an excuse to be here? Do I need to be waiting for someone?"

"You don't need anything, I suspect."

"Exactly." Then she sighs. "I'm waiting for my son."

"He's late?"

"He's drunk," she says flatly. "Probably passed out in some girl's dorm room."

"I'm sorry."

"Me too."

"Enough about me," she says. "Too much about me. Tell me about you."

In his 16 years, Maccabee has invented so many life stories, he's nearly lost track of the real one. He tells her he's an artist—he knows she cares little for art. He exploded onto the scene in his early twenties, just out of art school, he tells her, and is now in Europe to be feted at the upcoming Art Basel. His pieces, he implies, sell for millions and are housed in museums all over the world. He's been on the road for several months and is looking forward to getting back to his studio in Jordan. He longs for his homeland when he's away: the red rock desert, the sweeping open spaces, the scent of garlic and thyme wafting on the air, sizzling dishes of mansaf, kubbeh, and wara aynab spread on his mother's woven tablecloth. He tells her of how his sculptures are inspired by the stone city of Petra, its ancient fortresses carved into rock, as if they grew from the mountains themselves.

The lies come effortlessly, especially that last.

Petra is the only place that has ever felt like home.

Maccabee was born in Warsaw, Poland, as was his mother, and his mother's mother. But Petra is the Nabataeans' ancestral home. Tourists may flock to its unearthed temples and archaeological digs, but only Maccabee and his people know of its miles of caves, deep beneath the earth. It was here, thousands of years ago, that the Nabataeans mined gold for their gods. It was here, through centuries of dutiful labor, that they earned their place in Endgame, earned their chance at salvation. And it was here that, three years ago, Maccabee knelt on barren ground and spoke the ancient Nabataean oath that would seal his destiny. His mother may have secured him the role as Player through manipulation and blackmail, but in that sacred place there was only truth. Maccabee swore to do battle for his line, and mingled his blood with Petra's ancient soil. A part of him will always live in that darkness beneath the Rose City, and it's the part of him that always yearns to go home.

"You have people there waiting for you?" she asks. "Missing you?"

"No wife, if that's what you're wondering," he says. "No girlfriend either."

"Family?" she says.

"No one of note."

"How sad," she says, and sounds like she means it.

Maccabee knows a vulnerability when he sees it. He nods. "I never knew my father," he says. "And my mother . . . she's dead." He feels disloyal saying the words, but this is simply a part like any other. Ekaterina would want him to play it to the hilt.

"I'm sorry," Serena says. "Was she a good mother?"

He lets a careful note of regret slip into his voice. "I wish I could say yes."

"So do I," she says, and sighs softly. "But it's harder than it looks."

He puts his hand over hers. They lean toward each other, and for a moment he can feel it, the current running between them wild and dangerous. She feels it too; she must.

Then she stiffens and pulls her hand away.

"I've let this go on longer than I should, Maccabee. You should get home. You'll miss your curfew."

He doesn't let his eyes widen. He doesn't let his jaws tighten. He doesn't even let his heartbeat rise. He allows himself no somatic signs of shock.

It takes all the effort he has.

She shakes her head, laughing harshly. "Did you really think I wouldn't have my people investigate every student at my son's school? *Especially* his roommate. Maccabee Adlai, born in Poland—excellent description of Jordan, by the way, that was an especially nice touch—father unknown, mother investment banker. Very much alive. Unremarkable academic record, impressively clean disciplinary one, at least compared to my son. Hobbies include swimming laps and breaking girls' hearts. Do I have it about right?"

He relaxes, just a millimeter. She doesn't know quite as much as she thinks she does, at least. But she knows enough to be a problem for his mission.

His mind spins.

He hears his mother's voice.

Find her vulnerability.

Use it.

"Just about," he admits. "So if you know who I really am, what are we doing here?"

"You first," she says.

He's flying blind. But he has excellent instincts. He can turn this around. Get back in control. "I'm a bit of a fan," he says, and has enough control over his somatic responses to force a blush. "I'm intending to go into business, and your leadership of Intellex has been truly inspiring, especially your—"

"That's crap," she says sharply. "Try again."

She's giving him a second chance; he senses he won't get a third.

"I felt sorry for you," he says. The words pop out without thinking. Her eye twitches, and he knows he's struck gold.

His people have always been good at that.

"*You* felt sorry for *me*," she says.

He nods.

She looks like she's considering exactly how swiftly and how flat to crush him beneath her heel.

"Funny," she says, without any humor in her voice. "Because here I was feeling sorry for you."

"You're right: Jason's wasted," Maccabee says, ignoring that. "He's always wasted, but I thought he'd keep it together for you. When he didn't, I thought about you sitting here by yourself waiting for him, and . . ." He shrugged. "I figured you could use some company."

"So you decided to pretend you were a decade older and hit on me?" Serena shook her head. "I think you're the one who wanted some company, Maccabee. I think it's parent visitation week and your parents aren't here. I think you're too tough to admit that bothers you."

"So you thought you'd indulge the poor motherless child?"

"It passed the time," she says.

"Time's up," he tells her, and stands.

She puts her hand over his.

Yes.

"Stay," she says.

"Why?"

"I thought maybe . . ." She hesitates and, for the first time that night, looks uncertain of herself. "Will you tell me about my son?"

They talk long into the night. Maccabee tells her about her son, answering all her questions with the truth. What Jason drinks, who he sleeps with, how much he pays the geek down the hall to do his homework, where he actually goes (Ibiza beaches, Thai discos, Amsterdam brothels) when he claims to be visiting colleges. Maccabee owes nothing to the roommate, and besides, he likes this about Serena, how desperately she wants to know, how honestly she judges her own ignorance.

"I should know all of this already," she says, more than once. "What kind of mother doesn't know?"

"You have more important things to think about," he points out. "Jason's a big boy. He can screw up all on his own."

She doesn't believe him, he can tell. But he can also tell she likes to hear it.

When they run out of sordid details about Jason's life, she begins to ask him about his own, and Maccabee finds himself telling her the truth, or at least a version of it. No, he can't stand the food; yes, he thinks several of the teachers are subpar; his favorite courses are physics and philosophy, his least favorite art. All the tedious, mundane details of his tedious, mundane life, and Serena acts genuinely interested, complimenting him on his facility with languages and arguing with him for nearly an hour over his philosophy teacher's interpretation of Kant.

"Tell me about your childhood," she says.

His childhood: He remembers, dimly, cold afternoons in Warsaw, drinking a steaming cup of hot chocolate from the Wedel café, then padding through the snow in Łazienki Park. He remembers his mother's gloved hand folding around his mitten, holding him tight and pulling him upright when he stumbled, but this must be a false memory, because his mother is not the hand-holding type.

He remembers the day she told him of his destiny, and all the days that followed: the weapons training, the series of strict instructors who taught him ancient Aramaic and knife throwing and electrical engineering and the beautiful variety of ways to kill a man. Poisoning. Strangling. Stabbing. Neck breaking. Shooting. Smothering. Maccabee is a master of them all.

His childhood is a series of firsts. The first time he kills a living creature: a fawn in a snowy field, shot dead by his arrow. The first time he kills a living human being: one of his mother's business rivals, all too ready to underestimate the 10-year-old sitting beside him on a park bench, hypodermic needle secreted beneath his sleeve. The first time he kills someone he knows: the very instructor who taught him so many ways to kill, because, his mother says, "What better test of your skills could there be," and anyway, "It's the safest way to ensure he won't talk."

His childhood is a blur of cities, New York and Mumbai and Hong Kong and Buenos Aires, so many houses and penthouses and villas and not one of them an actual home. His childhood is a series of good-byes, because his mother is always leaving him, again and again, for one piece of important business or another; his childhood is a stretch of long absences, punctuated by the joy of her return, the glow of her attention for as long as he can hold it.

His childhood is a triumph, because he passes the tests set for him by his Nabataean elders with flying colors. Because it all plays out as his mother promised: he is taken to the secret caverns below Petra's ruins; he is sworn to serve his people; he is given the great honor of saving his line. Because his mother stands by watching, and afterward she calls him "my Player" and shakes his hand and he knows he has done well.

His childhood is no childhood at all, but a series of tasks and missions. He works hard to exceed expectations.

"It was nothing special," he tells Serena, shrugging. "We moved around a lot."

"That must have been hard for you," she says.

"I'm pretty tough."

"Children shouldn't have to be tough," she says.

"I was no ordinary child."

She smiles. "I suspect that's the most truthful thing you've said tonight."

It takes hours, but eventually she's comfortable enough, or tipsy enough, to answer his questions about her, to confess the truth of her broken marriage and her fears that she's ruined her children's life. Her shameful secret, that she resents her children for not loving her the way she loves them; the depressing truth of motherhood, that love persists unconditionally, no matter how irrational. That sometimes she wishes she could stop caring, and she wonders whether her children wish that too.

They talk through one bartender shift and then another, until finally the woman behind the bar lays down their bill, her polite way of suggesting they leave. Maccabee reaches for it, but Serena snatches it out of his grasp.

He's about to argue when the bartender says, "Oh, go ahead, let your mother pay. It makes her happy, trust me."

Maccabee and Serena both laugh at that; he lets her pay.

It's funny, Maccabee thinks, how this woman assumes they're mother and son, when no one ever guesses that about him and his own mother.

It should be funny, at least.

They walk out of the bar and into the hotel lobby. Serena has good taste in lodging: no old world opulence here. The Schlosshotel is all bare surfaces and clean lines, the simple elegance that only the truly wealthy can afford. The hotel has no need to advertise its luxury; luxury is assumed. Serena fits in here well, and it's another thing Maccabee likes about her. She's comfortable enough with her power that she doesn't need to advertise it; like Maccabee, she knows how to wear a mask.

"It was nice to meet you, Maccabee," she gives him her hand to shake. "It was a lovely evening."

He turns it flat, raises it to his mouth and presses his lips to her fingers. "Enchanting," he says, and smiles to show he's both joking and not.

"It was nice," she said. "Having a little company."

"I don't have to go yet. You don't have to be alone tonight. If you don't want to."

"Very funny," she says.

"I'm just suggesting a nightcap. Not anything untoward. Unless you want something untoward."

"You're my son's age—you're my son's *roommate*."

"You're lonely. So am I. But I'm a little less lonely, tonight. Is that such a bad thing? Is it so wrong to want that to last a little longer?"

"What people would think . . ."

"Who cares about people?" he says. "I care about us. About you."

"You don't even know me," she points out.

He cocks his head, as if to say, *Oh, really?*

"Maybe I care about you too," she admits. "Maybe that's why you have to leave now."

He simply stands there, watching her. Lets her watch him, his broad shoulders and his thick biceps, his warm eyes and dimpled chin.

"Maccabee . . ."

He waits.

Meets her gaze, lets the silence sit between them.

It's important to let things take their course.

Let her think she's in charge.

Wait her out.

The lobby is deserted, except for a lone busboy and the man behind the check-in desk, crisp in his starched white suit, as if it were nine a.m. rather than three in the morning.

Working at one of the finest hotels in Europe, they're well practiced in the art of not seeing. So they carefully avert their eyes as Serena

Porter leans toward the handsome boy young enough to be her son. He holds himself very still: it's important, for a woman like her, to believe she's in control. That she make the first move.

He closes his eyes. Feels her breath, a warm mist of cinnamon and whiskey.

Soft lips brush against his forehead. He can sense her hesitation—and her need.

She burns with it.

She burns for him.

He whispers her name, quiet as a sigh, and then her lips are pressed to his, gently at first, then urgently, the kiss a question, a desire: *More. Please.*

The hotel staff continue to do their best not to see.

No one watches Serena take his hand and lead him onto the elevator.

No one sees what happens when the doors slide shut and close them in.

She's a sound sleeper. He extricates himself and climbs noiselessly out of bed. There's a black leather bag sitting on the corner of the bathroom sink, and he finds the thumb drive exactly where Ekaterina said it would be, tucked into a bottle of aspirin. He retrieves his pants from the rumpled pile of clothes by the bed, folds them neatly, and slips the drive into the pocket. It's that easy. Then he retrieves the spy cam he positioned on the nightstand earlier, and puts that into the pocket too. He doesn't need to check the footage: he's good at gauging angles, sight lines. He got everything he needs, a little extra insurance. Ekaterina will love it.

Maccabee climbs back into bed. Serena stirs, her eyes opening.

"I dreamed you left," she says, groggily.

"Not yet," he assures her, and takes her in his arms.

She nuzzles her head into his shoulder, breathes a luxurious sigh. Their fingers weave together. "That's some ring," she says, her thumb rubbing the thick brass ring on his pinkie.

The ring is embedded with stone cut from the mountains of Petra. He wears it always, to remind him of his duty and his home.

"Someone gave it to you," she says. It's not a question, but he answers anyway.

"My mother."

"I'm sure she loves you," Serena murmurs, drifting back into sleep. "She wants to do better by you. All mothers do."

Maccabee holds her tight, imagining how it must feel to be held, to feel safe and protected.

"You're a good mother," he whispers into the dark, but Serena is already asleep.

This time, Ekaterina chose the restaurant. And, just as he feared, it's a dive. Grim and gritty, the aluminum table streaked with fluids, the source of which he chooses not to contemplate. They're tucked into a booth in the back, ignored by the handful of bedraggled customers, most of whom are hunched over cooling cups of coffee and look as if they've been there for weeks. Ekaterina is tucking into a steaming plate of bratwurst; Maccabee sticks with water. Even that might not be safe, judging from the filthy condition of the glass.

Sometimes he thinks his mother drags him to these dumps to punish him. For what, he can't imagine. Never has he disobeyed or disappointed her.

Never has he even seriously considered it.

"Well?" she says.

He places the thumb drive in her open palm.

She nods. "Any trouble?"

There's been plenty of trouble—a demerit and a lecture for skipping his curfew, a breakup with the tedious and tediously suspicious girlfriend, who wouldn't stop whining about wanting to meet his mother, a Latin test that, in his exhaustion, he forgot not to let himself ace—but none of it was the kind of trouble she means, or anything she'd want to hear about. And she certainly wouldn't want to hear about the note he left by Serena's pillow, just before he slipped silently out of her room. *You look beautiful when you sleep,* the note said, and it was true.

He shakes his head.

She doesn't congratulate him on a job well done, or thank him for his efforts.

He's performed up to expectations, and Ekaterina doesn't thank people for doing their duty.

In his pocket is another thumb drive, the one with the incriminating video, the little something extra.

"What are you going to do with it? Whatever's on that drive?" he asks her.

Ekaterina betrays no surprise, but Maccabee knows her well enough to see it in her eyes. "Why do you ask?"

"How badly are you planning to hurt her with it?" he asks.

Her eyes narrow. "Does it matter?"

"I'm just curious," he says.

Serena's no fool. She'll deduce who took the thumb drive—she's in no position to report the theft, given the way it happened, but she'll know. Whatever happens next will be on him.

"Why are you asking me this?" she says, her voice starting to rise.

Again, they're speaking in their ancient dialect, protecting themselves from eavesdroppers. Maccabee has a sudden, inexplicable urge to switch into Polish, the language of his childhood. He was not the kind of boy who threw tantrums—excess of emotion was forbidden in their home—but he fantasized about it sometimes, watching other children on the streets of Warsaw, their faces red and fists clenched, tears streaming as they screamed at their mothers, *No, I won't, you can't make me!* He studied those children intently, wondering how they dared protest, and wondering why their mothers allowed it—why some of their mothers would scream back, faces equally red, finger wagging and threats pouring out, while other mothers would take their children in their arms, hold tight until the wailing quieted.

When he was very young, he would lie in bed at night, imagining, practicing, sometimes even whispering the words to himself in the darkness: *No, Mother. I won't.*

He never got up the nerve to say it to her face. And by the time he was five years old, the urge had passed for good.

"Don't tell me you're having an attack of *conscience*," she says, as if it's a dirty word. "Surely I've raised you better than that."

"Of course you did," he says quickly.

"No, don't lie to me." Her thick eyebrows are knit together, her voice tight with fury. "I know when you're lying—I'm your mother."

She wields the fact like a weapon.

"You *care* about this woman, what happens to her," Ekaterina sneers. "You should be concerned with what's best for the line, what's best for *us*, and instead you're focused on this stranger? As if she *matters*, as if her existence has any purpose beyond what she can do for us? That's not my son. That's not the son I've sacrificed everything for. Have I bet on the wrong horse, Maccabee? Tell me now, before it's too late."

Maccabee has never seen her like this.

She's trained him to master all fear, but he's never been so afraid. He's spent his life trying not to cross her, but even when he has, she's not been like this.

This is different, he realizes, because this isn't a question of disobedience. This is a question of *character*.

Is he the son she raised him to be? Or is he a stranger?

He's afraid of her, but even more, he's afraid of himself. Of how easy it would be to set fire to his life.

Just imagine if he said: *Yes, I care about this woman. No, I am not the son you raised. Yes, you've gambled and lost.* Imagine if she walked out of this crap restaurant and took everything with her. The money. The power. His destiny. She could pull the right strings, have him removed from his position, choose a new Player to mold and control.

She could leave him behind and never look back. He knows that.

If he says those words.

If he says anything but what she wants to hear, he will never see her again.

He takes the second thumb drive out of his pocket and lays it on the filthy table between them. "I was only asking for details because I wanted to know whether this would come in handy," he says.

"And what is that supposed to be?"

"A little extra insurance." He raises an eyebrow, and she smiles.

"Ah." She knows exactly what that means, and it pleases her. She makes both thumb drives disappear, then bows her head briefly. "I'm sorry for misjudging you, my Player. You've done well."

She's never apologized before.

She's never told him that he did well.

Maccabee tries not to think about the images on the drive, about what the camera captured in its unblinking eye, about what it will do to Serena, knowing the record exists, watching him on-screen betraying her with every touch. She is, after all, a stranger. Just a tool to be used to get what he wants, or what Ekaterina wants.

He focuses on Ekaterina instead, and how she is pleased.

She drops a handful of Swiss francs on the table and rises to her feet.

"Wait!" he says. "Where are you going?"

"Now that our business is concluded, I have a flight to catch."

"Oh."

"What is it, my Player?" she asks. "Is there something more I should know?"

He shakes his head, but she returns to her seat, peering intently at him.

She is his mother; she knows.

"It's only . . ." He hates the way his voice sounds, tentative and needy. "I suppose I thought that since you've come all the way here, we could spend some time together."

Ekaterina laughs in his face.

"What did you think this was?" she says. "Have you been impersonating one of these children long enough that you've forgotten

222

who you are? Who I am? Did you expect me to bow and scrape for your teachers and curtsy for the dean? Meet your *friends*? Come poke around your dorm room and check your underwear drawer for condoms? Have a nice mother-son *brunch* where we chat about your *homework*?" She doesn't sound angry this time, simply amused. "What do you *want*, Maccabee?"

What does he want?

Not that, he assures himself.

But also . . . not this.

She checks the time. "Well?" she says, impatiently. "I have a flight to catch, so if you have something to say to me, you might want to spit it out."

"I understand you have important business elsewhere," Maccabee says, an idea suddenly occurring to him. "And surely I can be of more help to you on that than I can be here. Take me with you!"

"Out of the question."

"But—"

"I know this isn't where you want to be, my Player, but you must trust me that right now: this is the best use of your time."

"I'm the Player, Ekaterina. The entire fate of the Nabataean line rests on my shoulders, and you've got me twiddling my thumbs and pretending I don't know how to do basic multivariable calculus? How can that be the best use of my time?"

"Either you trust me or you don't," she says. "And if it's the latter, better I know now."

"Of course I trust you, Ekaterina."

"Then trust that, for the moment, you're more useful to me here."

"Is that all I am to you? Useful?" The words are out before he realizes it, and then there's no taking it back.

He steels himself, but this time there's no anger.

Instead Ekaterina flags the waitress.

Maccabee can't help noticing that the woman only has seven teeth. It doesn't stop her from grinning widely when Ekaterina orders a slice of kremšnita, with two forks.

"You expect me to eat the food here?" Maccabee says, once the waitress has set down the vanilla and custard cream cake between them and scuttled back into the shadows. He notes a spot of brown crud on the fork's tines.

"Don't be so finicky," Ekaterina says cheerfully, digging in.

"I'm not finicky," he says hotly. He's eaten monkey brains, fish intestines, cockroaches dug from the ground and roasted live on a gasoline fire, when circumstances demanded; his training dictates that he do whatever necessary to survive. He can *endure* filth—that doesn't mean he prefers to.

But now, circumstances demand. He picks up the dirty fork and breaks off a piece of kremšnita. It's too runny and overwhelmingly sweet—but also somehow delicious. He takes another. "I thought you had important business," he tells Ekaterina.

"This is important," she says. "You asked me if that's all you are to me. *Useful.* You need an answer."

He spreads his arms wide: *Go ahead.*

He doesn't expect her to make a stirring speech of maternal love. It's not her way. But in the long pause that follows, he assumes she's mustering her strength to offer an uncharacteristic show of affection. She will tell him that *of course* he's not just a tool for her to use, a weapon for her to wield. Of course she values his usefulness to the cause, but he's so much more than that.

He's her son.

She loves him.

She loves him above and beyond whether he succeeds as the Player, whether he lives up to her expectations, whether he disobeys her or rebels against his future or simply makes one choice, any choice, of his own.

She loves him no matter what.

She's his mother, so he knows this must be true—but maybe now, after 16 years of waiting, he's finally going to hear her say it.

"I'm your mother, and I love you," Ekaterina says, "*because* you are useful to me. I made you—I created you from nothing, gave you life, and I did so to fulfill a specific purpose. I wanted a son who would be a Player. Who would bring glory and victory to our line. I love you for fulfilling that purpose. I love you for proving your worth to me, for carrying out my demands, for continuing to be good enough. But make no mistake, Maccabee, my love is conditional. That detestable greeting-card nonsense, unconditional motherly love? The ridiculous idea that simply because I carried you in my womb I should be bound to you for life, regardless of your performance? You and I are beyond that, my Player. That kind of foolishness is for the weak; that kind of love is only pity. I raised you to be strong, didn't I?"

Maccabee can only nod.

"I thought so," she says. "This is the greatest gift I can give you. A love that must be earned, *always* earned. A love contingent on your choices, your behavior. Serve my purposes, serve our line, and you will earn my love. Prove yourself useless, and you will prove yourself unworthy of a mother like me. Are you inclined to test me on that?"

He shakes his head.

"I thought not," she says. "I thought all this had been made clear long ago, but I can see the risk I've taken, leaving you here among the plebeians. Beware camouflage, Maccabee—never let yourself believe you are that which you pretend to be. Are we clear?"

Maccabee is clearer than he's ever been.

He has been weak; he has been confused. He has done exactly as she has said, and forgotten who he really is—who both of them really are. No more. He will allow himself no more weakness, no more pathetic indulgence of this sorry sitcom fantasy of family. He will be the Player his line needs him to be, ruthless and useful and alone.

He will be his mother's son.

She's given him no other choice.

"We are, Ekaterina."

She takes the final bite of kremšnita and brushes the crumbs off her lap, then stands up again.

"I'll contact you when I need you," she says.

"Understood," he says, and finally, it is. When she turns to leave, he lets her go.

One week later, Serena Porter is arrested on charges of embezzlement and racketeering. Federal agents storm into her office and handcuff her, load her into a police van like a common criminal. Maccabee watches it on the news, trying to get a glimpse of her expression, but the cameras never get close enough.

She claims to be innocent.

She claims that she's been set up.

She claims that someone must have gained access to her secret passwords, to her files, must have inserted the incriminating data. But she has no evidence to offer in her defense. In return for a light prison sentence, she makes a deal. Her husband files for divorce, spirits himself and several million of her dollars away to an island with no extradition treaty with the United States.

The rest of the money is confiscated by the government; Jason is withdrawn from school, and Maccabee finally has the room to himself.

Intellex files for bankruptcy and is acquired by its main competitor, which itself is owned by a shadowy holding company whose primary interests are controlled by the Nabataean line.

The job is done.

Maccabee forces himself not to wonder whether it will be hard for Serena, living behind bars in a prison-issued jumpsuit. Whether she'll enjoy the irony of it, that her schedule will finally be free enough to spend time with her children, to be the mother she always wanted to be—but she can only see them during visitation hours. He certainly won't think about the way Jason, the 'roided-up hockey-playing thug, burst into tears when news broke of his mother's arrest, and had to be sedated until he could be escorted off campus and flown home—coach.

None of this is relevant.

He's helped his line; he's helped his mother. He's been of use.

After the arrest, he receives an anonymous text, terse but clear: *You've done well.*

He knows who it's from—and he knows that this is her way of saying she loves him. That he's made her proud.

That's what matters. All that matters.

It's nice, having his own room. Especially now that he's acquired a new girl—it proves much easier to persuade her to do as he wants when there's no mouth-breathing meathead spying on them from the opposite bed. The girl is the daughter of a German diplomat, or at least that's what she believes—Maccabee is certain her father is a spy, and knows that could come in handy. She's a mousy girl, quiet and nervous and thrown off balance by the thought that someone like *him* might want someone like *her*. He's certain she'll be useful to him, and—despite her oversized nose and undersized cleavage—he'll keep her around as long as she is. He'll cultivate her, and offer her up to his mother as a gift, next time Ekaterina comes to town.

Charming her will be worth it.

Enduring more days and weeks in this exile will be worth it.

Anything will be worth it, if it means proving himself to his mother. He understands now that he can never stop proving himself, can never get lazy, can never relax, even for a second. That's the gift she's given *him*. That's how she's made him strong. She has ensured his endless dedication to serve his line, to prove his worth. To make her proud.

DONGHU
BAITSAKHAN

The polecat's neck fits perfectly in Baitsakhan's small palm. He squeezes—*gently*, he reminds himself. It wouldn't do to sever the spine. Not yet, at least. Baitsakhan presses the polecat against the hard-packed dirt, trying his best to hold the squealing animal still. It squeaks and wriggles, but that is no matter. It cannot escape. It's utterly under his control. When Baitsakhan unsheathes his dagger and, with a sure hand, brings the blade down on its tail, it can do nothing but scream.

Its screams sound almost human.

Baitsakhan finds this interesting.

Also interesting is the blood spilling from the creature, splashes of bright red against the dirt. The raw meat of the wound. The rotten-sweet smell of it. The way the keening noise trails off, turns to a whimper, then a hiss, then nothing. Baitsakhan notes all of this carefully.

Most of all, he notes the look in the polecat's eyes. Pain and terror. The same look the dog gave him when he sliced out its entrails. The same look his baby sister gave him when he pressed the sizzling cattle brand to her foot, hand over her mouth so she couldn't scream. It should, perhaps, amaze him that pain is such a powerful leveler, that it brings all creatures, large or small, to the same hellish ground.

But nothing amazes Baitsakhan.

Amazement is a word without meaning for him, like *sorrow*, like *love*. But *pain*? That, he understands.

Also *joy*.

Joy is what happens when he causes pain in others.

The polecat's blood flows and flows. If he liked, Baitsakhan could release his grip: the creature is too weak to escape. Or he could tighten his grip, a few millimeters, choke the air from its lungs, crush its throat, put the animal out of its misery. It would be merciful. But it would not be joyful.

Time passes, and the cat does not die. Good. The wound is not fatal—there will be time for more. Baitsakhan carves the polecat carefully, like his father dissects their evening meal. First the paws, then the flank, then, when he finally grows bored, the tender belly, letting the steaming innards drop to the ground with a soft plop. He waits impatiently for the creature to expire. Then he reaches into his box for another one.

It is his sixth birthday.

This is his present to himself.

One year later, the Trials begin.

The Donghu hold the Trials every six years. Those Donghu children, ages six to eight—fortunate enough to be born within the right window, to have the chance to serve their people—are brought to an arena 100 kilometers south of Ulaanbaatar. This is the law of the land, and those who violate it are severely punished. For three days and three nights, more than 100 children pit their skill and strength against each other, whether they want to or not.

Baitsakhan has been waiting for his Trials ever since he was a toddler. The children are pitted against one another in feats of strength and ferocity. They are not trained in fighting methods—or, at least, they're not meant to be. They are simply handed weapons and set against each other in the arena. No rules, no adult interference, only the young Donghu, pitted against each other like animals, fist to fist, knife to knife, two by two, until one emerges supreme.

That one, strongest and fittest, will be the Player of his generation.

Baitsakhan has spent his entire life in the barren depths of the steppe, and he has wide eyes for this strange village, with its closed-in spaces, its sturdy buildings digging their roots into the earth, its people. Such teeming hordes of people, the smell of them, the filth of them, clogging the air. Baitsakhan feels wrong here, like a caged animal. His people are migrants, following their crops and their herd, carrying their possessions and even their homes with them when they go, reveling in harsh nature and open sky.

His home is nowhere and everywhere. His home is gray sky and ashen ground, warrens of dark caves eating through cliffs, dunes of sand undulating into infinity.

Such emptiness offers so many wonderful places to hide. Baitsakhan can be alone whenever he needs, to do whatever he needs, safe from prying eyes.

He thanks the gods, now, that he doesn't live in a place like this, where foul people would always be watching.

Baitsakhan stands under the dome of the arena with his twin cousins, Bat and Bold, and their younger brother Esan, listening to them chatter about who will triumph. Within a week, one of the children here will prove himself superior to the rest, and this child will be named the next Player of the Donghu people. Baitsakhan does not join his cousins in their idle speculation; he has no need.

He gets what he wants; he takes what he wants. That has always been his way.

And he wants this.

To be the Player is to be powerful, and the more powerful he is, the more of the Earth's sorry creatures he will be able to hurt.

The Player who Plays Endgame will ensure the death of billions. It is a beautiful gift that the gods have promised their chosen people. That someday they will have the chance to purge the Earth of its inferior bloodlines. For millennia, the Donghu have waited patiently for the sacred promise to be met, for the time to come. For millennia, generations of Donghu Players have waited at the ready, preparing for genocide. Perhaps each of them thought: *I am worthy; the gift will come to me.* But none could have been as worthy as Baitsakhan.

As soon as he learned of Endgame, the Player, the promise of apocalypse, he knew: this was to be his fate.

The Player will eradicate his competition one by one, hunt the other Players to the end of the Earth, destroy them and their lines along with them. He will be walking death, visiting torment and devastation upon the world.

He has to be Baitsakhan.

The Trials begin, and Baitsakhan shows the judges what he can do. Every child enters the arena with the weapon of his choosing. Baitsakhan favors the curved saber. He likes the feel of metal cutting through flesh. He's taught himself how to fight, practicing with his cousins and watching the men of his camp come to blows after too much drink. Some fathers violate tradition and give their sons and daughters instruction on weaponry and battle. But Temür, a shepherd's son, chooses the halberd, and is obviously self-taught as well. His feet are clumsy and his blows uncertain. Baitsakhan knocks him out easily with an elbow to the head. Qarajin, an older girl who sleeps in the *ger* beside his, wields a straight blade. Baitsakhan takes his time with her, enjoying the noises she makes when his saber flicks against her skin. She is a bloodied mess by the time she rests her knife on the ground and bows before him, ceding defeat. Buka, Hulagu, Oghul-qaimish, Bat, and Bold, one by one, the children fall before him or back away in fear. Some he knows; some are strangers to him, brought hundreds of kilometers across the Gobi to compete, as the law demands. Many are strong and skilled, but all of them are, in their secret hearts, afraid of pain. Pain doesn't scare Baitsakhan; pain is his dearest friend.

His final competitor is an unexpected one: his cousin Esan, the youngest boy at the Trials. Barely six years old, he is only days past the qualifying age, and he has always seemed a useless boy. He is the kind adults like, bright-eyed and eager, with enough mischief in him to earn the respect of his peers. *That Esan will go far,* Baitsakhan has heard his parents say, with clansman pride.

Baitsakhan despises him.

Esan grins, an insouciant smile that betrays how little he cares about this, how little he needs it. He has cut his way through the competition on a lark, and his smile says, *Let us fight, cousin; then let us walk away friends.*

Baitsakhan bares his teeth.

He raises the saber, slashes at Esan. The younger boy dodges out of the way, then whirls around, swipes his own saber at Baitsakhan, nearly draws blood. He is fast. Baitsakhan will have to be faster. They dance around each other, blades sweeping out wide arcs in the dry summer air, clanging together as they dodge and parry. Baitsakhan moves on instinct, enjoying the feel of the saber—it's like he was born with it in his hand, born knowing what to do with its deadly blade. The Donghu watch from the sidelines, shouting gleefully when Baitsakhan first draws blood, and again when Esan's blade slices Baitsakhan's cheek. He glories in the sharp pain of it—even his own pain is a precious jewel, to be polished to a shine. This is what the fearful creatures around him fail to understand, and this is why he will always triumph.

They are two whirling animals, fierce and wild. Esan's foot lashes out, makes contact with the back of Baitsakhan's knees, knocks him hard to the ground. When Esan crouches to take his advantage, Baitsakhan swipes his feet from under him. Then they are rolling on the ground, Baitsakhan's grip tight on Esan's wrist, forcing his saber into the dirt, Esan driving a fist into Baitsakhan's gut and yanking his hair out of his scalp, the Donghu judges leaning in, trying fruitlessly to track the movements of the two young boys who now seem one impossible beast. And then—

Baitsakhan spots his opening. His knife flashes, blade meeting flesh. He has killed enough animals to know how to deal a fatal blow, and how to avoid it. He knows exactly how hard to bear down if he wants to draw enough blood to win, but only enough. If he wants to spare Esan his life, he can do so.

Or he can slice through Esan's jugular and spill the boy's life force from his veins.

Baitsakhan must decide in a heartbeat—but really, the decision was made for him, the day he was born. Baitsakhan is who he is.

There can be only one choice.

He strikes.

The tangle of limbs goes still. Blood pools. Baitsakhan rises to his feet. Esan does not.

Esan never will again.

In the stands, a woman's keening cry. This, Baitsakhan knows without looking up, will be Esan's mother. He knows other things too: that it is not intended for children to die in the Trials, but it is not unprecedented. Accidents happen.

No one will know the truth.

That the feel of the blade tearing open Esan's throat is something Baitsakhan will revisit in his dreams.

That killing this boy is the purest joy he's ever known, better than slaughtering cows and dogs, better than the bloody corpses that populate his dreams. He is already eager to do it again.

That he has found his true calling.

He reveals none of this. Instead he fakes sorrow. He is good at faking, and getting better every day. He apologizes to his aunt, and nods sadly when she acknowledges that it was a noble death, and that Baitsakhan will make an excellent Player. He allows his father to clap a hard hand on his shoulder, and pretends not to enjoy the extra helpings of dessert they give him every night that week. They are so eager to reassure him: *Life is a battle, and sometimes there are casualties.*

These are lessons every Donghu learns in time. Life on the steppe is hard, and death is a part of that life. Death served in battle, in the pursuit of glory, is a great honor. Few are forced to learn so young, and Baitsakhan allows his people to believe that their comfort has meaning for him.

Soon his training will begin. He has six years to learn how to Play and how to win—six years to learn how best to hurt and maim and kill. Until then, he will bide his time. He will seem sorry.

If he were capable of astonishment, he would be astonished at how easy it is. These creatures, like cows, just wanting to be led. He leads them to whatever conclusions he needs them to draw.

Only his mother seems to understand the truth. He may not understand emotion, but it proves useful to recognize it in others, and so he has studied. He sees the fear in her eyes when she looks at him, the caution in her movements, like she knows he is dangerous.

"Your aunt will always love Esan," she tells him one afternoon, while they are taking their tea. "She will survive his loss, but she will never forget it."

"I know that," Baitsakhan says, cramming another poppy-seed bun into his mouth. His aunt's pain is an ongoing pleasure. He has become a very solicitous nephew, stopping by her ger with meats and sweets nearly every evening. He likes to simply watch her face, her nearly imperceptible flinch whenever he says Esan's name.

"Yes," his mother says, in a strange voice. "I thought you did."

She rises from the table then, and begins tidying up the ger. Their home, like all the homes of their tribe, is a simple wood structure covered in felt—like a tent, it can be assembled and disassembled with ease, loaded onto the camels, and carried with them wherever they go. Inside, his mother has created a riot of opulence and color. The soft, polished red of the wooden supporting poles gives the interior a warm glow. The ground and gently curving walls are layered with a rainbow of tapestries. The ger sometimes feels like a living creature. It makes Baitsakhan feel dead inside, as if it long ago sucked out all his color and breath.

She tends to it like it is her child.

When he was very small, Baitsakhan's mother told him stories of other small children and the mothers who loved them. He wondered whether his mother loved him, what that would look like, and why he should care. These are things he no longer wonders about. *Love* is simply a word that tethers his mother to him, obligates her to feed and clothe him, which suits his convenience—for now.

But his mother sees him too clearly, Baitsakhan thinks.

Someday that will need to be dealt with.

To be the Player-elect is good.

As soon as the Trials are decided and Baitsakhan is named, his people respect the power he will someday wield. Baitsakhan is no longer required to tend the herd or feed scraps to the dogs. As the seasons change and the tribe migrates, Baitsakhan is not called upon to join the men who build the new gers, and he is not forced to join the other children when they help the women with their chores. Baitsakhan is spared these menial duties, because his only job is training for Endgame. When the time comes to ride, he is accorded the finest of horses. When the time comes to hunt, he is honored with the chance to take the death blow. He receives the choicest cuts of meat and the thickest leather shoes. His young cousins do whatever he tells them, and even his brother, Jalair, already married with a child of his own, has begun to obey his commands, treating him like a respected elder. Baitsakhan makes the twins hand over their sweets, and when he orders them to go for days without eating, they fast until they are half starved. Baitsakhan wonders if they are foolish enough to starve themselves to death, simply on his word.

They will do anything for him.

Just like everyone else.

Yes, to be the Player-elect is good—almost like being a king.

But to be the Player is better—almost like being a god.

Baitsakhan watches the current Player carefully, hating him from head to toe. Al-Ulagan wastes his opportunities. He could have anything he wanted from his people. He could torment them with his capricious whims. Instead he bows and scrapes like the lowest of men. He pretends to be a servant to his line, rather than its despot. It is disgusting. Every time he smiles, which is often, Baitsakhan imagines a fist powering through his teeth, knocking them down his throat. The thought of the blood pouring out and those hollow sockets left behind helps Baitsakhan smile back.

Someday Baitsakhan will be the Player, and he will do it better. But if he is going to reach this goal, he must obey his trainer, the sour, elderly man who is meant to mold him into a warrior. He is meant to do everything Surengan says, to be respectful and compliant, even though he is young and powerful and Surengan is old and decrepit. This too is disgusting.

Still, Baitsakhan is careful and disciplined—and he knows that Surengan has much to teach him about the infliction of pain. As the years pass, Surengan shows him many outstanding new ways to kill. Baitsakhan learns the body's weaknesses, the points of pressure that will cause even the strongest of men to shriek and wet themselves. He and Surengan explore the rich spectrum of pain, all the ways to break a human mind, force it to its limits and beyond so it can be bent to Baitsakhan's will. Where before, he took his pleasure with animals only in the dark where no one could see, now he is encouraged to practice his craft on the herd. There's no need for Surengan to know the extra efforts he takes, practicing his knife work. Whether he slaughters the goats efficiently or takes his time with it, eking out every last second of agonizing life, they end up just as dead.

Surengan tells him that the Players of other lines travel all over the globe, exposing themselves to the world's peoples. Not so for the Donghu Player. Baitsakhan learns their strange languages and mores, yes, but only for the advantage it will give him in the game. He stays close to home; he stays untainted by the so-called modern world. There is nothing of value in the land beyond the steppe, Surengan tells him, and Baitsakhan believes it.

Out there, somewhere, foolish people crowd together in cities of glass and neon, hiding their brute animal nature beneath the lie called civilization.

Out there, people are weak and confused. They have grown distant from their inner beast.

Out there, Surengan tells him, the Players of other bloodlines have been corrupted by modernity, weakened by the luxuries of the so-called modern world.

Here on the steppe, life is hard but honest. Here on the bare rock, under the pitiless sun, lies like civilization wither and die, like a tourist lost in the desert, corpse wrinkled up like a prune.

This, Surengan tells him, is why the Donghu will triumph in Endgame. The Donghu Player will have no mercy, no vulnerability, only purpose. The Donghu Player will be a creature of pure violence, tearing a swath of death through his opponents.

This lesson is one Baitsakhan eagerly heeds.

Surengan also teaches him much about the history of the Donghu Line, its glorious birth in the Gobi desert, where a lord of the sky created the first man and woman from clay. For 800 years, the Donghu ruled with the blessing of the gods, pillaging and tyrannizing tribes all across the steppe. Surengan tells him of the day of darkness in 150 BCE, when a Xiongnu prince slaughtered the Donghu leaders, and of the hundreds of generations since, desert warlords dreaming of their conquering past and the promised future, days to come in which they would triumph over humanity's inferior bloodlines and rule. Dreaming, above all, of Endgame.

Baitsakhan listens obediently to all of this but does not hear. He does his best to feign pride in his line, allegiance to the Donghu people; he promises Surengan that he understands what it means to be the Player, that it requires selflessness and self-sacrifice, and putting himself in service to a greater good.

Baitsakhan lies.

He cares nothing for his people, their past or their future.

He craves Endgame for its promise of blood, tidal waves of it unleashed on an unsuspecting Earth. He is an artist of death, and Endgame will be his greatest canvas. He will lie about his true purpose, he will disguise his true self, for as long as necessary. And when he is alone, he laughs at the gullibility of Surengan, at the sorry, misplaced pride of the Donghu people. He laughs at the idea that he would sacrifice himself for the greater good or anything else. Baitsakhan Plays only for Baitsakhan. He kills for the sake of killing. Pain is his only god, and he serves it well.

The antelope streaks across the steppe, leaps gracefully over the dry riverbed, runs and runs but cannot escape its bloody, imminent death. The men of the tribe chase behind it, spears raised, two of them letting fly.

One blade slices through the air, stabs the antelope through the heart, dropping it in a lifeless heap of meat and bone.

The other, released at the wrong moment and the wrong angle, takes a disastrous turn, buries its tip in the chest of one of the men.

As the man grunts with surprise and pain, then crumples into the dirt, Baitsakhan stops abruptly. He fingers his own spear, almost confused to find it still in his hand.

So many times, he has envisioned this moment, casually allowing his weapon to find its way into one of his own people—and not just any of his own, but this one, this man.

His father.

He has always thought it would be fun to kill one of his own, and now fate has done it for him.

Baitsakhan will simply have to take advantage of the unexpected opportunity, before time runs out. The men shout and wail; Baitsakhan's father bleeds and bleeds into the steppe. Baitsakhan kneels by his side.

"It is good that a son be with his father in the last moments," he hears a voice behind him say, and he can sense the other men of the tribe pulling back to a respectful distance, giving him the privacy he needs to say good-bye. Baitsakhan bows his head, rests a hand on his father's chest.

His father neither weeps or moans. He's always prided himself a strong man, one who will greet death stoically, as a friend.

We'll see, Baitsakhan thinks. Then he presses a fist into his father's wound.

The man spasms, limbs shuddering and mouth and tongue working like there's something he needs to say. No sound comes out, only bubbles of spit and blood, but Baitsakhan can imagine the message his father has for him.

No.

Stop.

Please.

He presses harder into the wound, then twists his hand sharply to maximize the agony. It would be better, he thinks, if there were more screaming. But he can see the pain in his father's eyes, and that will have to be good enough.

His experiments with animals have shown him that a body under enough strain will simply give up. Surengan has taught him that the same is true for humans. A heart will do whatever necessary to put its body out of its misery.

It is Surengan who has helped him understand the exact amount of strain and torment the human body can bear.

"Don't die, Father," Baitsakhan says, loudly, so the other men can hear. But his hands bear another message for the man, pressing and tearing at the gaping wound. *Die slowly,* they say, *slowly and painfully, but surely.*

Baitsakhan is given the honor of carrying the corpse back to camp. He anticipates his mother's expression when he lays the burden before her, the way she will shriek her grief to the heavens. Her pain, he thinks, will be nearly as entertaining as his father's death.

But she denies him the pleasure, merely kneeling beside the body, kissing its cold forehead, then meeting Baitsakhan's eyes.

"So it is done," she says coolly, her gaze blank. It's as if she knows exactly what he wants to see, and is denying him, simply out of spite. Most emotions are foreign to Baitsakhan, but he understands hate. He has never hated her more.

In the wake of his father's death, there are some who say to Baitsakhan, "Now you are a man." They watch him, expecting that his father's death will transform him in some way.

Baitsakhan wonders if they know something he does not, and so he watches himself, curious, waiting to feel.

He feels only relief.

With his father gone, there is one less person to keep track of his comings and goings, one less person to gauge his behavior, catch him in his lies.

There is one less person to keep an eye on his baby sister.

Baitsakhan has discovered that pain is most pleasurable when inflicted on those who are the weakest, and those who are the closest to him.

Little Arslan is both.

When she was first born, she was like an animal—poking and prodding her was like torturing a wild dog, if somewhat less enjoyable. For if he cut off his sister's finger, someone was sure to notice, and this was a risk Baitsakhan was unwilling to take. As the Player-elect, he is expected to be brutal but disciplined, cruel but honorable. Honor means nothing to Baitsakhan, but being the Player means everything, so he's smart enough to play by Surengan's rules. Even if he dreams of a day when he will no longer have to.

What Baitsakhan does with his sister, to his sister, must stay between the two of them.

The older she gets, the more fun she offers. He likes how she says his name, with such wounded confusion, as she did when he brushed her hair back from her neck and pressed a hot poker to her skin. She never tells on him, because he warns her not to. He is her brother, and she loves him; she thinks this is how brothers are supposed to be.

He liked the game of it, making her love him and fear him all at once, so that she would keep his secret.

"Are you sure?" she says to him, blinking big, trusting eyes and holding the cup of nails between her two tiny hands. He is 11 years old and she is five, old enough to know better.

"I'm sure," he tells her, and promises, "Nothing bad will happen."

He's her brother, and so she believes him. She tips the cup to her lips. Forces herself to swallow one small nail, and another. Baitsakhan grins, encouraging her, and soon she is giggling, because it's not so hard after all.

Because he is happy, and that makes her happy.

He's not exactly sure what the nails will do to her—that's what makes it such an interesting experiment. He expects them to tear up her intestines, to cause internal bleeding, to make her scream.

He doesn't expect them to kill her, but he's not displeased when they do.

The years of his training pass. Baitsakhan tires of pretending, playing at a so-called "humanity" he has no desire to possess.

He dreams of a day when he will no longer need to hide. When he can do as he pleases with impunity.

Until then, he keeps his true self hidden in the shadows.

He waits.

Baitsakhan spends little time in his ger with his mother. His older brother has a wife and family of his own; his sister and father are dead. It is only the two of them now, and the small, domed dwelling feels both too big and too small.

He dislikes the way she looks at him, peering from around corners when she thinks he isn't watching, the way her gaze rests on him when he pretends to sleep.

"I will always love you, whoever you grow up to be," she tells him, whenever he beds down in their ger.

His mother has faded over the years. As the ger has grown more crowded with color and decoration, she has hollowed herself out. Her husband's death struck one blow, her daughter's another, but Baitsakhan suspects her true exhaustion comes from enduring her youngest son's existence, day in and day out. And that pleases him. She rarely speaks, never smiles. Her gaze is flat, her lips so often pressed together in a thin straight line that Baitsakhan often forgets she's lost most of her teeth.

She is aging poorly, his mother, and he enjoys watching it.

"Sweet dreams," she always tells him when he closes his eyes.

He likes that, and sometimes believes she has the power to make it so. Because it's when he sleeps at home that he most often has the best kind of dreams, dreams of blood and corpses and a dead, scorched world layered in ash. He kills when he dreams; he kills when he wakes. This, he thinks, must be what people mean by the word *happy*.

Baitsakhan is nearly 13 years old. He can count the days until eligibility on his fingers and toes. He need only wait half a moon, and he can be the Player.

But *can* is different from *will*.

Al-Ulagan has three more years before he ages out. Baitsakhan is expected to wait those three years, doing as he is told, pretending to be someone he is not.

This is intolerable.

"I am stronger than him, Master," he tells Surengan. As always, the word *master* curdles on his tongue. Baitsakhan has no master. "Faster than him. Most certainly smarter than him."

"And yet he is the Player and you are not," Surengan says.

"Exactly!" Baitsakhan pounds his fist into rock. They are climbing a desert cliff. The old man is still strong enough to hoist himself up a steep incline. But sometimes Baitsakhan wonders what would happen if his trainer lost his grip, dropped hundreds of feet to the ground with a satisfying crunch. Who would be left to order him around then?

Surengan sighs. Baitsakhan knows his trainer dislikes him, and is pleased by it. "Again and again, I have tried to teach you patience." Baitsakhan wants to laugh. If Surengan only knew how patient Baitsakhan has been. All these years, all these interminable lectures, and still Surengan lives.

What better testament to Baitsakhan's patience can there be?

"The patient Player is the dead Player," Baitsakhan says. "When Endgame begins, the slow will be the first to fall. The meek and the merciful are doomed. *You* taught me that."

"Indeed, young one," Surengan says. "And when your time comes, you will be able to act without hesitating. Because you will have taken the time to learn."

Baitsakhan snorts.

"Respect," Surengan reminds him.

Baitsakhan again thinks how easy it would be to knock the old man from his perch. Surengan is his great-uncle, one of many in the tribe. While his grandfather, Suhkbatar, is considered to be the wisest of the elders, Surengan is by far the more powerful, and the more meddlesome. Baitsakhan knows he is supposed to feel something about this, as he is supposed to feel loyalty to all those who share his Donghu blood. *Family. Loyalty.* Such strange concepts. This is why Bat and Bold follow him wherever he goes, begging for his favor. This is why Jalair struts through the camp with pride, letting his brother's power go to his head, as if Baitsakhan's achievements have anything to do with him. Baitsakhan understands so much about blood, but he will never understand this.

Surengan and Baitsakhan summit the cliff with ease. They ride their horses back to camp.

"Pack your belongings, young one," Surengan says. "Tonight we take a journey."

"To where?"

Surengan shakes his head.

"Why?"

Again the old man shakes his wrinkled head.

Baitsakhan glowers, but he does as he is told.

Patience, he tells himself.

The word tastes of rotting goat.

They hike aimlessly across the steppe. Surengan has forbidden them horses or camels. Walking, he says, will make their minds clear.

He says the same thing about the pain of the wind on their faces, the way the chill air burns their throats. Surengan says that there are many who believe that because the Gobi is a desert, it must be hot. This is the kind of willful foolishness that makes men so easy to kill.

They march into the wilderness for many hours, never stopping, never speaking. The sun rises and falls. The moon chases in its wake. The stars poke crisp holes in the canvas of sky.

Finally Surengan points at a rocky outcropping. "Here," he says. "We will make camp."

Baitsakhan looks sharply at him. Surengan has always cautioned him against stopping to rest in the wide open, especially in this region, where bandits roam the steppe. It is unwise to leave oneself open to ambush.

"We passed a cave, not long ago," Baitsakhan says. "We can go back."

"We sleep here tonight," Surengan says, settling to the ground. "You may build a fire, if you would like."

Baitsakhan likes none of this.

But he does like the sounds he hears in the night as he lies awake, waiting for the sun. He hears the sound of hoofs and whispers, and knows that trouble has indeed come to find them. He could awaken Surengan now. It would be nothing for the two of them to fight off the ambush, send the bandits racing for their lives.

But Baitsakhan does not want that. Not after the day he's had.

He wants blood. And so he lies still, his favorite knife in his hand, waiting.

Waiting for them to creep closer, unsheathe their knives.

Waiting for them to come near enough that there will be no escape. Waiting for his moment—and then it is time.

He is a whirl of motion, a cyclone of death. His knife flashes in the moonlight. He attacks in silence, slitting open their bellies before they have a chance to scream. There are five of them, and two survive long enough to attempt to fight back, but Baitsakhan makes quick work of it, chopping off their hands at the wrist. These two he leaves alive, writhing on the ground, and he gets to work. He hears Surengan calling his name. It was apparently too much to hope that one of the bandits managed to slit his throat. Baitsakhan ignores his trainer. Let the old man wait for once; Baitsakhan has waited long enough.

It is immense fun, carving up the first man, listening to the terrified whimpers of the other. The second kill proves even more satisfying, because this man knows what's in store for him, or thinks he does. Baitsakhan has discovered that humans are remarkably bad at anticipating pain.

The words *carve out your eyeballs* have no meaning in the imagination.

Some things must be experienced to be truly understood.

It's only when the five bodies have all gone still and Baitsakhan kneels in a pool of their mingled blood that he remembers Surengan.

The old man clears his throat.

"You put us in danger, old man," Baitsakhan snaps. "You're welcome."

"Sit, young one."

Surengan is a shadow in the night. Baitsakhan lowers himself down to the dirt. "Sitting," he says snidely. He is in no mood for a lecture.

"I saw what you did to these men," Surengan says.

"Yes, I killed them. I don't know about you, but that's what I do when someone's attacking me."

"It was unnecessary, what you did to them," Surengan says. "It was overly harsh."

"Harsh?" Baitsakhan laughs. "I've seen you slice off a woman's fingers one by one. I've seen you gut a man from throat to belly."

"I have done these things, yes," Surengan says. "But I have not enjoyed them."

"Yeah? Me neither."

Surengan shakes his head. "I've been watching you, young one. You think you can disguise what you are, but I see you. Perhaps I've tried not to see, but no more."

"And what is it you see, old man?"

"I see the joy you take in killing."

"As you taught me, uncle."

"You're young," Surengan says. "You've misunderstood so much, and perhaps this is my fault. We are Donghu, child. We live in a brutal world, and to survive, we lead brutal lives. This has always been our way, and our ways are good."

Baitsakhan yawns.

"We are brutal by necessity," Surengan says. "We kill when we need to, and we do not shy from what must be done. We live as soldiers, because our lives are war. But soldiers must have honor. Soldiers must despise the kill. You, Baitsakhan, you kill without honor. You kill without reluctance."

"What kind of Player would I be with reluctance?"

"You will be no Player at all, if you cannot learn this lesson."

This stops him short.

"I will be the Player," he insists. "The Trials decreed it."

Surengan shakes his head. "Something else you have misunderstood, young one. The Trials select the one worthy of training. But to be a Player? You must pass through me."

"You're telling me that if you think I'm not good enough—"

"Yes, Baitsakhan. What I say shall pass."

"I've done everything you wanted me to do," Baitsakhan says. He hears it in his voice, the weakness, the desperation, and despises himself for it. "I've proven myself again and again."

"You are strong and you are smart," Surengan allows. "Perhaps the strongest and smartest Player the Donghu have produced in a long time. You are steel, but steel must be tempered."

"This was a test," Baitsakhan realizes. "You brought me out here because you knew this would happen. You want me to fail."

Surengan shakes his head. "I want you to learn. This is all I've wanted for you. And now you must learn that actions have consequences. Make different choices, Baitsakhan, or I will be forced to make one of my own."

Baitsakhan drops his head. "Master, I don't know what to say."

"Say you will heed me."

"But what if I can't? What if . . . I fail?"

"You have never failed at anything you've set yourself to, Baitsakhan. Set yourself to this. You must find your respect for life, for all life, especially that which you take away."

"And you will help me?" Baitsakhan asks. His voice quavers.

Surengan approaches, stoops before him, takes Baitsakhan's arms in his aged hands. Gently, he pulls his student to his feet. Baitsakhan is tall enough to meet him, eye to eye. "I will help you, if you are willing to be helped," Surengan says.

This man is the one person in the world who has power over him. The one person who can take away the thing Baitsakhan most wants. Baitsakhan cannot let that happen.

Will not.

And so he wraps his hand around Surengan's in a tight grip and makes his solemn promise. That this will be a new beginning. That from tonight, Baitsakhan will be a new man.

This is a promise Baitsakhan fully intends to honor.

Which is why, as soon as Surengan lets go his hand—so arrogant, so sure of himself, so pathetically certain that his young charge will heed his warnings, despite all he's seen and all he should know— Baitsakhan stabs him in the gut.

Bat and Bold are target shooting along the cliff's edge when he returns.

He returns on horseback, a magnificent chestnut stallion that he has claimed from the dead bandits. Only a fool like Surengan would choose to walk across the steppe when he could ride. And Baitsakhan will suffer no more fools.

"Baitsakhan!" Bat shouts, shooting an arrow into the sky to celebrate his cousin's approach.

The arrow arcs toward the clouds, then falls back into gravity's grasp, speeding toward the earth—and toward Bold, who stands directly in its path. Alerted by the whistle of air, he ducks out of the way just in time, then smacks the back of his brother's head. "Dolt! You nearly killed me."

"Slow and stupid deserves to die," Bat says, thumping his fist against Bold's shoulder.

"I see only one stupid face here, and it looks a lot like yours."

"That's what makes you my identical twin, you horse's ass. Your face looks like mine. Only dumber."

This is the final straw. Bold slaps Bat across the cheek. Bat seizes Bold's fingers and bends them backward until Bold screams. Bold wraps his elbow around Bat's neck and squeezes, yanking his other hand free and grinding his fists into Bat's scalp. Bat yelps. Bold growls. Soon the two are on the ground, muttered curses mingling with hisses, spits, yowls, and, briefly, an argument about which of them should have been left out on the steppe to die in infancy.

Baitsakhan watches impassively. This idiocy, he knows, is how the brothers demonstrate and cement their love.

They are pathetic creatures, but they are fierce and they are loyal.

This could come in handy.

At the sound of his footsteps, the brothers look up from the dirt.

"You've returned quickly, cousin," Bat says, dropping his hands from around Bold's throat.

Bold gives his brother one last sharp kick in the shin, then rises to his feet. "And you've returned without Surengan," he observes. "What happened out there?"

Neither of them notes that he is covered with dried blood. Baitsakhan considers his options.

"If I asked something of you, would you do it?" Baitsakhan says.

"Of course," Bat says quickly.

"Whatever you need," Bold says.

"*Anything* I ask?"

The twins nod. "You're our Player," Bat says.

"And our blood," Bold says.

"Our brother," Bat says. "The only one we have."

The brothers have never held Esan's death against him. In fact, like their mother, they have only loved him more since that bloody day. It is as if by killing Esan, Baitsakhan claimed his cousin's place.

"You would swear this to me?" Baitsakhan asks. "Your obedience? Your loyalty?"

The twins nod again, solemnly this time. The gravity of the moment has penetrated their thick heads.

"We would give our lives for you, Baitsakhan," Bat says.

"It would be our honor," Bold agrees.

"Swear it on your blood," Baitsakhan says, producing a dagger. He marks a sharp slash across each of their palms, then his own. Flesh presses together. Blood mingles. Vows are spoken. Pledges offered, lives sworn. Bat and Bold are his, in blood and spirit.

"Now," Baitsakhan says, "ask me again what happened in the desert, and I will tell you a story."

This is the tragic story Baitsakhan tells the rest of his tribe, when he returns to the camp with Bat and Bold:

Deep in the unforgiving desert, he and Surengan were set upon by bandits. They came in the night, silent and under cover of darkness. They came with knives drawn and hearts of stone, and before Baitsakhan could wield his weapon, Surengan was butchered where he lay. Baitsakhan took his vengeance, cut out their hearts and took off their heads, but it was cold justice, because Surengan was dead.

"I buried him where he lay," Baitsakhan tells his tribesmen. "The gods were cruel this day."

"You do him honor," Baitsakhan was told by the men of his tribe. "You have become the warrior he always knew you to be."

That much is true.

The night after he returns, Al-Ulagan summons Baitsakhan to his ger.

To be summoned: this is nearly more than Baitsakhan can bear.

He reminds himself of the virtues of patience. He waits in silence as Al-Ulagan blathers on about Surengan, who trained them both, who was a fine and noble man, whose spirit will look on in pride and satisfaction as the two of them carry on his teachings. "We are like brothers, you and I," Al-Ulagan says. "I know you have lost Surengan, and I know the pain that must cause, but you still have me. We have three years until you take up my mantle, and in those three years, I would be honored to teach you everything I know. Allow me to be your master, and I will gratefully offer what wisdom I can."

Allow me to be your master.

The words burn.

Baitsakhan bows his head. His fingers twitch at his dagger, so eager, so impatient. But he cannot leave his line without an eligible Player.

The people would never stand for it.

Twelve days until he reaches the age of eligibility.

Twelve suns and 12 moons, and then he will be his own master.

He will master all.

He will wait.

The camp is silent and still, the sky gray with predawn light.

Baitsakhan is, today, 13 years old.

Eligible for Endgame.

Tired of waiting.

For 12 days, he has watched the Donghu carefully, marked those who might see what Surengan saw, who might have the temerity to fight back. He has drawn up a list of 13 names.

He likes the symmetry of this. Thirteen names, 13 years. On the day he is about to become the Player of the thirteenth line.

There are other ways to go about this, of course. Other, less bloody ways, but those hold no appeal for Baitsakhan. Although he has no understanding of what it means to feel, to love or to fear, he's studied the men and women around him for many years now. He understands that *they* feel, and he understands what makes them do so.

He has paid special attention to the emotion they call *fear*, and he knows how best to instill it.

Bat and Bold stand watch for him as he slips into the first man's ger. Bayar, his father's second cousin, who once challenged Baitsakhan's right to a flank of meat from a fresh kill. Bayar lies on his fat stomach, snores rumbling with every breath.

"Why?" Bat and Bold asked him, when he told them of his plan.

He could have said: *Because if I'm going to seize control, I need to take out my enemies, and my potential enemies, and all those they love. I need to slaughter enough people that those who survive know it's only because I let them.* This was rudimentary strategy, the art of war and domination.

Let your plans be dark and impenetrable as night, said Sun Tzu's *Art of War.* Surengan had made him memorize the whole thing. *When you move, fall like a thunderbolt.*

Sun Tzu said, *The supreme art of war is to subdue the enemy without fighting,* and this is what Baitsakhan intends to do. He will murder a handful of his people, to save himself the trouble of fighting the rest of them; he will ensure they are too frightened to fight back.

All of this is true, in a sense, but it's not the whole truth, and Baitsakhan is doing this so he no longer has to lie.

"Because I want to," he told Bat and Bold instead. "Because I have always wanted to, and from now on, I'm going to do whatever I want." Now he wants to cut into the back of Bayar's fatty neck, slicing through his spine.

And so he does.

Bayar's eyes fly open. Paralyzed by his severed spine, he watches Baitsakhan slice the throats of his wife and three daughters. He is dead by the time Baitsakhan steps over these bodies and into the ger of Bayar's oldest son, now married with a family of his own. Baitsakhan stabs the son in the heart, wishing he had the luxury of lingering: This man once broke Baitsakhan's favorite bow. It was an accident, but still, debts must be repaid, and Baitsakhan would like to cut his eyes out and feed them to him one by one. There is no time. Instead, a quick death for Bayar's son, for Bayar's son's two young boys and his pockmarked wife.

Then Baitsakhan turns to the next name on his list.

He saves Al-Ulagan for last. This one is special to him.

When Al-Ulagan takes his last breath, Baitsakhan will finally meet his destiny. He will be the Player. He will be the master of all he surveys. He will be one step closer to Endgame, to the apocalypse of his dreams.

Al-Ulagan is the only one capable of stopping him, the fierce warrior who carries the hopes of his people on his strong shoulders.

And yet here lies Al-Ulagan, asleep. Helpless as a baby.

First Baitsakhan will cut the Player's vocal cords, so that he cannot scream.

It wouldn't do, making unseemly noise, summoning others to interrupt their private gathering before he's ready.

Baitsakhan has been waiting a long time to meet the Player man to man, knife to flesh.

He intends to take his time.

Sunrise is greeted by wails of shock and grief.

Fifty-two bodies.

An ocean of blood.

The Donghu Player: dead.

Baitsakhan sounds the alarm, summons his people to assembly. They look to him with hope and rage. He is their Player. He will know what to do.

"You are wondering who could have done this," he says, and pauses. He can still turn back. Lie, blame the massacre on a neighboring tribe, lead his people into a bloodbath of vengeance. It could be fun. But he is tired of hiding who he is and what he wants.

No more.

"*I* have done it," Baitsakhan tells his people. "I have killed your Player, as I killed my own trainer, the great and mighty Surengan. I have killed your brothers and your sisters, your cousins and your wives, and I have done it on a whim, because they displeased me. Because I *wanted* to. And that is all you need to know. I am your Player, and that means you will do as I say, you will do what I want. This will be the new Donghu way. I have removed all those I believed might object to this. If there are more of you, please speak up now"—he pulls out his blood-stained knife—"so we might discuss."

No one speaks.

No one moves.

"If you are ready to swear loyalty to me, you may drop to your knees and do so," Baitsakhan says.

Bat and Bold immediately fall to their knees. Baitsakhan's brother follows suit, averting his eyes.

The rest of the crowd is still.

"*Now,*" he says, and, slowly but surely, they drop to their knees before him, until only his mother is left on her feet. They stare at each other across the bowed heads of their clansmen. Baitsakhan senses she is sending him some kind of silent message, but he doesn't know what it could be.

Then she nods her head deliberately, and lowers herself to her knees. She keeps her eyes on him, though, and it is Baitsakhan who finally looks away.

Instead he surveys his people, his servants. His slaves. He's almost disappointed that they obeyed so easily. He wouldn't have minded more bloodshed.

Then he remembers.

He can have as much blood as he wants. He is his own master now. There is no more need for trumped-up excuses to kill, no more hiding in the shadows to carve flesh where no one can see. No need for fake sorrow or regret. He can torture and kill with impunity now, if he likes, and they will obey him. Because they are his people. And he is their Player.

"It is an honor to serve," he tells them.

Let the games begin.

He commands his people to build him a new ger, one of his own, bigger and more lavish than any of the others. Not that Baitsakhan cares for such meaningless luxuries, but he understands the symbolism of power. He wants a home that will remind his people who is master and who is slave.

He wants a home that will not be his mother's ger, that will not make him feel like a child.

But the first night of this glorious era, he sleeps beneath her roof. He needs to know what she will do.

Many hours pass before she does anything. Baitsakhan lies still, feigns sleep. Waits.

The moon has nearly returned to the horizon before he hears his mother padding softly across the ground.

Baitsakhan keeps his eyes closed. Surengan has trained him well: He doesn't need sight to kill. He can track her movements by sound and smell. He can feel the minute displacement of air as she nears. He could cut her down where she stands, before she knows what has happened.

He does nothing, yet.

She stands over him, as if considering.

She is considering whether to kill him, Baitsakhan thinks. It's the rational thing to do. It's what he would do.

"I know you're not sleeping," his mother says softly.

Baitsakhan does not open his eyes, does not move.

"I held you in my arms and rocked you to sleep," she says. "Before that,

I held you in my womb. You fed of my blood. You breathed my air. You think I don't know what you look like when you're truly asleep? I know everything about you, my little Baitsakhan. I know you better than you know yourself."

"I doubt that, Mother."

"You think I'm going to kill you," she says.

Baitsakhan laughs. "No one can kill me. Least of all you."

"But you think I want to."

"Of course," he says.

"You murdered your sister."

It is the last thing he expects her to say—the first thing she's said that surprises him. Baitsakhan starts to wonder if his mother is maybe not so stupid as she seems.

"Of course I did," he says, masking his confusion. He smiles, thinking back to the noises the little girl made as the nails tore her intestines to shreds. "Do you want to know why?"

She laughs, softly. He's never before noticed, how their laughs sound alike. "I know why," she says. "I told you, I know you too well."

"What do you want?" he asks. It's too dark to see her face. He doesn't like this, the not knowing, and thinks perhaps it would be easier just to kill her now, be done with this.

"No," she says. "I don't think you will kill me. You will kill many, before this is finished, simply because you can. But not me."

"Why not?" he asks. He genuinely wants to know why she's so sure. Because he worries she may be right.

"Because I am your mother," she says. "Because I created you."

"And I'm supposed to what? Be grateful? *Love* you?" He snorts. But there is a strange feeling spreading through his body, a warmth. Perhaps, he thinks, this is what the thing called emotion feels like; perhaps this is what it feels like to be truly seen, truly known.

"You love only pain," she says. "You know how best to hurt. It is your greatest gift. And so you will keep me alive, to bear witness. To bear the most pain of all."

Only when she says it does he understand how right she is. He will never kill her.

Her silent agony sustains him, strengthens him, *feeds* him. And after all, isn't this what a mother is for?

"And you, Mother?" he asks. "What will *you* do?"

She falls to her knees beside him, as the tribesmen did earlier. Lowers her head. Offers him her hands, palms up, the sign of surrender.

"I will serve you," she says. "I will stand by you, with your brother and your cousins. We are your blood, and blood binds. I will protect you, my little Baitsakhan. I will love you."

"I'll never understand you," Baitsakhan says, and he means his mother, but not just her. He doesn't understand any of them, these *people*, with their strange fantasies about love and family, their determination to cling to illusion: That life is anything but blood and meat and bone. That some bodies matter more than others. That anything matters but survival and pleasure. He can predict them, and he can certainly defeat them, but he will never understand them, and feels tainted by the effort. He is lucky to be so pure, so clear-eyed.

"I know," his mother says, and lowers her face to his, kisses him gently on the forehead, like a benediction.

She was right about one thing, at least: He's never heard anyone speak with so much pain. She's radiating torment.

She's right about something else too. He won't kill her. He wants her beside him, now and always; he wants to bathe in her suffering. He wants her to see what he does next. Who he hurts, and how. He wants to show off for his mother, like any child. He wants to show her that she doesn't know him as well as she thinks, that she can't even conceive of his unquenchable thirst for pain. He wants to, and so he will.

This is going to be fun.

ENDGAME

THE TRAINING DIARIES

— VOLUME 3 —

EXISTENCE

OLMEC
JAGO

Jago falls in love with her at first sight. It's like some cheesy movie cliché—it's like *every* cheesy movie cliché. Their eyes meet across a crowded room. His heart skips a beat. Fireworks explode. The earth shakes. He hears music, smells flowers, sizzles with a lightning bolt of love.

The girl is lithe and lovely, whirling to the techno salsa beat as if her body is made of music. Hair like blond silk whips through the air; slender arms twirl overhead. A radiant smile lights up the room, and Jago's heart.

Then the strobe lights flash and go dark, the song changes, dancers flood the club floor, and she disappears behind a sea of bodies. Jago forgets her in a heartbeat.

It's like that for him: love, girls, beauty. He loves to love, falls hard and fast, gets distracted just as quickly. Sometimes it takes a month, sometimes a week, sometimes, like tonight, only a few minutes. Nothing pleases him more than parading through the streets of Juliaca with a beautiful girl on his arm, lying beside a warm body on the shores of Lago Titicaca, stroking an exquisite face in the moonlight. And because he is Jago Tlaloc, every girl in the city is happy to be loved by him—because to be loved by Jago is to be showered with expensive gifts, to be admired and envied, to be on the arm of the scion of the most powerful organized-crime syndicate in Peru. He knows they love him only for his money and power, and he forgives it. To be loved by Jago is to be forgiven all sins.

To be loved by Jago is to be left by Jago, but ask any girl in Juliaca and she'll tell you: it's worth it.

He hasn't come to the club tonight looking for love. He came to dance, to sweat away the week, to forget himself in a storm of noise and motion. To lose himself in a crowd. Thrashing at the heart of the dance floor, pressed body to body with the crush of strangers, this is the only way Jago can be anonymous, a stranger to himself. He's spent the last several days doing odd jobs for his family, paying visits to those who thought to cross the mighty Tlalocs . . . and making them understand the consequences of their poor choices. Reminding them where their loyalties should lie.

The Tlaloc syndicate, of course, employs plenty of muscle—but some acts demand stronger reminders. Some unfortunate souls demand a visit from Jago himself, heir to the family business, Player of the Olmec line. Not everyone knows he's the Player, of course, like so many eldest Tlaloc sons and daughters before him, or that if Endgame ever comes, he will bear the weight of all their lives. They don't know they should be grateful to him.

But they know to fear him—and that's enough.

Jago does what he has to do, hurts who he has to hurt. But sometimes, after, he needs to drink and dance and forget.

So he's not looking for love, any more than he's looking for trouble. Both find him.

Her scream is nearly inaudible over the music and the noise of the crowd, but he's spent years honing his senses.

There are three of them, muscled thugs in their midtwenties. They have the girl pinned in a dark corner, are laughing at her obvious fear. One of them pokes at her shoulder. Another threads his fingers through her blond hair, smoothing it over her face.

This is when Jago inserts himself into the situation. Three of them, one of him, and he is only 16.

But he is a Tlaloc—and a Player.

He is built like a mountain and could kill all three of them without breaking a sweat.

Instead he says, from behind them, "I think you'd all prefer to find a different club tonight, wouldn't you?"

The men whirl about, ready to laugh, ready to fight—then they see his face.

They see the scar that cuts from his left eye down to his neck, souvenir of a childhood knife fight. He pulls back his lips in the gruesome imitation of a smile, and they see his teeth, gold-capped incisors studded with diamonds.

"*Feo,*" the biggest of the men breathes, and when he speaks Jago's nickname, there's terror on his tongue.

They know that scar; they know that smile; they know to back away quickly, with shallow bows of respect and apology, to leave this club and never be seen here again.

Jago waves them off with satisfaction, and only then does he turn to the girl.

She's not hiding behind her curtain of hair or blinking back tears, not pressing herself into the shadows to make herself invisible, not shaken or stirred. She watches him intently, with fierce curiosity, and there's something strange about her expression, something compelling, and it takes him a moment to understand what it is. Then it hits him.

She doesn't know who he is.

She doesn't know anything.

Jago closes his lips over his teeth; he claps a hand over his scar, and hopes the club is dark enough to smooth his pockmarked face. He wants to hide everything ugly about himself.

Something is happening to him.

Something he can't name.

Not love, it can't be that, he thinks, because he's felt love, knows it well, in all its fleeting and shallow glory.

"Those men were afraid of you," she says in English, her voice full of wonder.

He nods.

"Should *I* be afraid of you?" It comes out like a dare.

"Probably." He wants to smile. He wants to laugh. But he doesn't want to frighten her. For the first time in a long time, he doesn't want to look like Jago Tlaloc. Maybe he doesn't want to *be* Jago Tlaloc, not with this girl, not tonight.

"Good thing this is my summer of bad decisions," she says, and laughs. "Dance with me?"

He takes her hand, and for a moment he can't breathe.

"What's your name?" she asks him, as they step onto the dance floor. He touches his hand to his ear, cocks his head, as if to say, *Too loud, can't hear you.* Then he leads her into the dancing throng. Tomorrow he will be Jago Tlaloc, scion, monster, savior. Tonight he will be just another body in the dark.

"You're really not going to tell me your name?" she says as he walks her back to her dorm. She's a British high school girl, on a summer study-abroad program in Peru, though she knows no Spanish. She's from a place called Cornwall, and is a ballet dancer, or was, she says; she's not sure which one. She's been all over the world, she says, but has never seen anything, and though that doesn't make any sense, Jago almost understands it.

He's been everywhere too, traveled to every continent, sometimes on family business, sometimes for Player training, always for something ugly and brutal, always for a purpose, never simply to *see*.

She tells him many things, as they walk hand in hand through the empty Juliaca night, not about her life but about her dreams of a new one, how she wants passion and poetry and awe, she wants new experiences and wild adventures and terrifying risks and world-conquering triumphs.

"And love," she adds, looking at him steadily. Her grip on his hand is warm and firm, unashamed. "I want earth-shattering, fireworks-exploding, heartbreaking love. Have you ever had that?"

Jago shrugs. "I've had girlfriends, if that's what you mean."

"No, I don't mean 'girlfriends.'" She imitates not just his accent, but the deliberately casual way he tossed off the word. "I mean a soul mate, a person who feels like your other half. A love that changes your life—that swallows it. A Pablo Neruda kind of love."

"So you loved a man named Pablo?" he asks, confused.

She laughs gently, and links her arm through his. "I see we have some work to do."

"I don't know if I believe in that kind of love. A kind that could swallow my life, as you say." He doesn't know why he's admitting this to her. Everything he knows about girls tells him this is the precise wrong thing to say. But there's something about this one that makes him want to be honest. "My life is too crowded for such a love, I think."

"Crowded with what?"

"Duty, for one," he says. "Family." He can't tell her that he's sworn his life to a single, all-important goal. That as long as Endgame looms on the horizon, he can never love anything as much as he loves the Olmec people. Even if it weren't unthinkable, it would be forbidden.

"Duty?" She laughs again, a familiar song he wishes would go on forever. "You talk like you're ancient." Then she shakes her head. "Not me. I wasted too long on duty. I know what's out there. What's possible. And I'm going to have it."

She sounds so much younger than him, but also, somehow, older—because she talks as if time is running out, as if she wants all these things *now*, here, in this summer, in this city. Tonight.

She stops abruptly beneath a streetlight and takes both of his hands in hers. "Do you want to know a secret?"

He nods.

"This is it. This summer. Everything changes. Everything I used to be, that's over. I'm breaking free."

"Of what?"

"Everything holding me back. All the people telling me what I have to do, who I have to be. All the obligations. All that *duty*. Haven't you ever wanted to do that? Just shake it all off? Run for the hills? Scream into the night?"

"I—"

She tips back her head and hollers, *"Freeeeeee!"* The streetlight gives her a glow, like an aura, and Jago is almost afraid to blink—as if he's imagined her, as if she might disappear.

Everything changes, she said, and he feels it, a buzz in the air, his skin bristling with electric charge. Everything changes tonight.

Tonight, for the first time, he can imagine wanting what she says. Freedom. Escape. Wild adventure with this strange, wild girl, the two of them flinging themselves into a great unknown.

She won't tell him her name until he offers his.

Even after they kiss under the streetlight beside her dorm, even after she presses her body to his and lets him feel her heat, her need.

"Who *are* you?" he says in wonder, when they break, and he means, *What are you?* What kind of strange, enchanting, beautiful creature could make him feel this way, like she's the first girl he's ever touched, the first girl he's ever wanted?

"You first," she says.

He doesn't want to offer his real name—this is the twenty-first century; the first thing she'll do when she goes inside is Google him and his family, and she'll discover all the things he doesn't want her to know, the rumors and allegations that inevitably swirl around a crime syndicate even when the government declines to prosecute, or care.

"Most people call me Feo," he says, offering his nickname instead.

It has always felt right to him, as if naming his secret, fundamental truth.

"Feo?" She wrinkles her nose. "Does that mean something?"

Jago laughs. "You really don't know any Spanish at all, do you?"

"Tell me what it means."

Her combination of stubborn ferocity with wide-eyed innocence is addictive and irresistible. He can see it in her eyes: this girl is fearless. "Guess."

She appraises him carefully, narrows her eyes, smiles. "Mountain."

He shakes his head.

She presses a finger to his lips, slips it through, taps one of his capped incisors. "Golden boy," she guesses. "Diamond head."

"Not even close."

"Tell me," she says, and kisses his neck.

"No."

"Tell me." She kisses the tip of his nose.

"No . . ."

"Tell me." She kisses his palm, the inside of his wrist, works her way up his forearm, and he knows this girl will be trouble—this girl will take whatever she wants from him, and he has much to lose.

"*Feo,*" he says, giving in. "'Ugly.'"

She flinches. "Who would call you that?"

He shrugs, smiles to show he doesn't care, that it's all a good joke to him. "Who wouldn't?"

She grazes her fingertips down the length of his scar. "I wouldn't," she says softly.

He's embarrassed, suddenly, not of the nickname, but of the fact that he allows it, and for an impossible moment feels a flicker of rage toward this girl, that she can make him burn with shame. One moment, one spark of anger; then it's gone as if it never existed.

"Your name is so much better, I suppose?"

"It's Alicia." She rises up on her toes, gives him a quick peck on the lips, suddenly demure. "Think you can remember that for next time?"

"Next time?"

She retreats, carefully eases open the door to her girls' dorm—it's hours beyond her curfew, but she seems unconcerned, says she's snuck out before, and anyway, what can they do to her, these overcautious nursemaids? He loves the way she talks.

"You know where to find me," she says, before she disappears into the citadel. "Just make sure you've come up with a better name by the time you come back."

The following night, Jago takes her to dinner at Los Gatos, an exclusive bastion of candlelit elegance where the waiters keep a bottle of their finest champagne on ice for him, just in case he happens by. He orders every appetizer on the menu and four entrées, so they can have a taste of everything, and once they've sipped their champagne, he summons the waiter and requests a bottle of their most expensive wine.

As they drink the rich red, Jago puts a small velvet box on the white tablecloth. Alicia opens it up to find a small sapphire dangling from a delicate gold chain.

"Oh," she says, then closes the box and digs into her meal.

It's not exactly the reaction he was hoping for.

"You don't like it? I thought it would bring out your eyes."

"It's gorgeous," she says. "But, it's so . . ."

"What?"

"Well, it looks crazy expensive, and we just met, so that's kind of weird, don't you think?"

"I think it's beautiful, and you're beautiful, so it seems like a perfect match."

She shakes her head. "Well, um, okay. But I don't really wear much jewelry. It would be wasted on me. So . . ."

It's not like it was at the nightclub, or in the moonlight. It's not easy between them, and he doesn't know why. He excuses himself to the bathroom, and on his way slips some money into the palm of the maître d' and makes a whispered request.

When he returns to the table, a violinist comes over to join them and begins a mournful rendition of a childhood lullaby. Jago waves over an old woman shuffling past the tables with an armful of roses, and buys a dozen, gives her a tip ten times their value. He offers them to Alicia—she takes them but doesn't smile.

"I'm sorry, but . . ." She stops, turns to the violinist, and says, "That's lovely, but I've got a bit of a headache, so . . ."

The violinist looks to Jago, who nods his assent, and the musician backs away, looking abashed, surely afraid he's displeased the monster of Juliaca.

"I'm sorry," Jago says quickly. He can feel the night slipping away from him, and if he doesn't understand what he's done, how is he supposed to fix it? He speaks eleven languages fluently, knows nineteen ways to kill a man with his bare hands, holds this city in the palm of his hands . . . yet somehow, he's powerless to make this one girl smile. "I didn't realize you had a headache."

"I don't, I just . . ."

"Is it a law, in England, not to finish your sentences?" he snaps—then instantly regrets the flare of temper. He's simply not used to this kind of frustration.

She grins. "Aha! *There* you are."

"What? Of course here I am."

"No, I mean, *you*. Like, the real you, not this cheesy romance bullshit. The you from last night."

"Excuse me, cheesy romance bullshit?"

"Flowers, candlelight, champagne, violin music? A necklace, for a girl you've just met? I don't know what kind of girls you usually date, but . . ."

He dates girls who like "cheesy romance bullshit" and the rewards that come with it. These are the kinds of girls who want to date a Tlaloc—at least a Tlaloc who looks like him. These are the girls who won't ask hard questions or make demands he prefers not to fulfill.

"And what kind of girl are *you*, Alicia? What would you prefer to do?"

"How about *talk*?" she says. "You could tell me about yourself."

He shrugs. "There's nothing to tell."

"You go to school?"

"Sure," he lies. "Who doesn't? Junior year's a bitch."

"SATs, picking colleges, all that, right?" she says.

He nods like he knows what she's talking about. Jago's life doesn't resemble that of the teenagers he sees on TV. He's been homeschooled for his entire life, taught by tutors and physical trainers behind the walls of his family's gated estate, trained not for a life of college and banal employment but for duty, sacrifice, courage, and, eventually, rule.

"I'm thinking about, uh, law school," he says, wondering if that will impress her.

"Bullshit."

"Excuse me?"

She stands up. "Do you think I haven't figured out who you are, *Feo*? You must think I'm pretty stupid. And I don't date people who think I'm stupid."

"Wait! Please!"

Jago stops. Composes himself. All over the restaurant, heads are turning. He can't afford to be seen like this, begging. Tlalocs do not beg. When he speaks again, it's with imperious scorn. "What is it you *think* you know about me?"

"I know you're Jago Tlaloc, that you're part of some kind of mob family, and you're the heir to it all. I know this whole city's scared of you." Her voice softens, almost imperceptibly. "And I know you're a terrible dancer." She shrugs. "That's about it. I came here tonight because I wanted to know more—not because I want expensive champagne and jewelry. You can't *buy* me, Jago. Not with a fancy dinner, and definitely not with a bunch of crap lies about your life. That's not who I am. I didn't think that was who you were."

"It's not," he protests.

"Then prove it," she says. "Show me who Jago Tlaloc is. The real one. The one I fell for the first time I saw him."

"You . . . you did?" He doesn't understand. No one could fall for him, just from looking at him. His face is not designed to melt hearts; it's designed to freeze them.

"Of course I did," she says. "I told you: I'm not stupid."

They ditch the restaurant. Jago takes Alicia to his favorite street
vendor, an old man who grills up anticuchos and picarones just
north of the city center. She tries a bite of everything, and the way her
eyes light up at her first taste of choclo con queso makes the whole
night worthwhile. They sit on the edge of a crumbling brick wall
overlooking a vacant lot and stuff themselves, licking the grease off
their fingers and kissing it off each other's lips, passing back and forth
a frothing bottle of Pilsen Callao, and all the while, they talk.

Jago tells Alicia about his life, his *real* life. He doesn't speak of being
the Olmec Player, of course—that secret is as sacred as the oath he
swore to protect and serve his line. But he tells her what it's like to be
a Tlaloc, to grow up in privilege surrounded by poverty. To be loved
and loathed in equal measure, to never know whether the people
around you are freely giving of themselves or obeying out of fear. Jago
has his parents and his siblings; he has José, Tiempo, and Chango,
three boys he grew up with who he can trust to the ends of the earth.
But beyond that, he has minions, underlings, hangers-on, colleagues,
enemies.

Sometimes, Jago admits, his enemies feel like the truest thing in his
life. At least he always knows where they stand; at least he knows the
passion they feel for him is real.

Jago tells Alicia about working his way up, learning the ropes of the
family business when he was just a child. Going out on protection
runs, defending territory . . . He lets her believe that he would wait in
the car, because to explain that he was a black belt in several martial
arts by the time he was eight and spent far more childhood hours
with guns, knives, and bombs than he did with cartoons and teddy
bears—that would raise questions he can't answer.

But he doesn't lie to her.

When she asks if he's broken the law, he says yes.

When she asks if he's hurt someone, even killed someone, he
hesitates . . . then says yes.

She doesn't run away.

He tells her he doesn't like it, hurting people—that he does it because it's necessary. And she touches his scar again with those soft, careful fingers and says, "I believe you."

When she asks if he's ever imagined a different life for himself, turning away from what his family wants for him, choosing his own path, he doesn't hesitate. "That's not an option for me," he says. Being a Tlaloc, being a criminal, being the Player, these things are inextricable for him, and none are *choices*, any more than breathing, or living. It's a joy for him, serving his family and his people, living up to their expectations. To be the Olmec Player, to be the Tlaloc heir, these things define him, no matter how ugly or difficult they may sometimes be. "And even if it were . . . it's not all pain and crime. My family does good things for Juliaca. We've built hospitals; we have several charity foundations. We make sure none of our people starve. We give to the poor. We only steal from—"

"The rich?" She laughs. "Okay, Robin Hood. You're a hero of the people. I get it."

If you only knew, he thinks, wishing that he could tell her the whole story, explain that he's sworn to protect his people against an attack from the sky, against the end of the world, that he would sacrifice himself for the survival of the Olmec line—that he has already sacrificed so much.

And then he remembers that she is not Olmec. That if Endgame comes, he will not be fighting for her.

"I am who I am," he says quietly. "Who my people, my family, need me to be. That's all I can be. You wouldn't understand." He watches TV, he knows what life is like for people like her, who live sequestered from their own poor, who have infinite choices and no greater worries than alarm clocks and acne.

She threads her fingers through his, holds tight. "You'd be surprised." She tells him that she's been taking ballet lessons since she learned how to walk—that her mother is a former prima ballerina who had to

270

retire when she got pregnant, and who has never quite forgiven Alicia for ending her career. "She's never forgiven me for being more talented than her either," Alicia says, without modesty or bitterness, and Jago likes her all the more for it.

For thirteen years, Alicia has done almost nothing but dance. "Morning, afternoon, night," she says. "I was homeschooled for a while; then I got into the academy, where classes are a joke—everyone knows nothing matters but dancing."

"I bet you're a beautiful ballerina," he says.

"I was," she says, again without modesty. He notes the tense.

It's hard not to stare at the unfathomably long line of her neck, the graceful way her arms arc and wave as she makes her point. Every move is graceful, efficient, almost as if she were a fighter, like him. And maybe they're not so different after all. The hard work, the oppressive training schedule, the tunnel vision for a life oriented around a single goal . . . he recognizes all of them, and wonders whether this is the magnetic field that draws them together, this singularity of purpose.

"I've been to Paris, Tokyo, Buenos Aires, Cape Town—name a city, and I've danced there," she says. "Danced, and nothing else. No sights, no culture, certainly no local foods. Nothing that would get in the way of the training regimen. No distractions whatsoever." She peers at him through lowered lashes. "Definitely no boys."

"It can't be as bad as all that," he says. "You're here."

"Exactly. Because I quit."

"What? You said dancing was your life."

"It *was* my life, and what kind of life is that?" She steals the rest of his anticuchos, gulping them down with relish. "I couldn't handle it anymore. I just did one plié too many, you know?"

He shakes his head. Tries to imagine walking away from his life, from any of it. Declaring independence from everything he's ever known. There's such a thing as too much freedom, he thinks. Freedom from everything can leave you with nothing.

"My father was cool about it, but my mother?" She shakes her head. "*Freaked. Out.* I finally convinced them to send me down here for six weeks, kind of a trial separation from ballet, you know? I'm supposed to be 'thinking about my options.'" She curls her fingers around the words, and it's clear that she hopes to do very little thinking while in Peru. "I've basically missed out on the first sixteen years of life, Jago. I plan to make up for it, starting now."

"That's a lot to catch up on in six weeks."

"I'm very efficient," she says. "It only took me four days to find you, didn't it? And about ten minutes to catch you?"

She's so sure of herself—so sure of the two of them, even though they've spent less than a few hours in each other's presence. "You think you caught me, huh?" he teases her. "I may be more slippery than you expect."

She puts her arms around him, pulls herself onto his lap. "Just try to get away," she whispers in his ear. "I dare you."

Summer school isn't like real school, especially in Juliaca. Alicia has plenty of friends to cover for her, and the teachers and guardians at the study-abroad program don't require much covering. There's no one to care if she spends all her time with Jago.

So she does.

It's different than it's been with other girls: she doesn't want him to buy her anything; she doesn't care about his power, or the things he can make people do. She likes to hear the details; she finds it fascinating, the contours of power, the things he knows, the strings he can pull. She likes to hear about corrupt officials—who gets paid off and how much—about how you can learn to attune yourself to the smell of weakness and cowardice, about how to sniff out an Achilles' heel, and exploit it.

She likes it, but he doesn't like telling her, because he can see the judgment in her eyes, hear it in her voice. She's fascinated . . . but she's also repulsed. "I just think there's something better out there

272

for you," she says, whenever he talks about his family and what they do, or what they expect of him. Or, sometimes, "The police really just look the other way? No matter how many laws get broken? How many people get hurt?"

She always phrases it that way. Not "when *you* break the law." Not "when *you* hurt people." She thinks he's different from the rest of his family, different from this entire city, perhaps, and he knows he should resent that.

She makes him ashamed of the things he's always been most proud of, and he should probably resent that too.

But it's not resentment, the thing that burns in him when he looks in her eyes, when he speaks her name.

It's a thing that has no name, that's too big and powerful for words. But if he had to pick a word, it would be *love*.

He likes her because she doesn't want anything from him, because she doesn't want him for his power or his money or his family name. But the bigger feeling, the one that wakes him up in the middle of the night, sweating and gasping from a nightmare in which he's lost her—the all-consuming feeling that, as she once put it, has swallowed his life—that's not because of what she wants. It's because of what she sees.

She looks at him and sees a person he didn't know he could be. Not Feo, not the Player, not the heir to the Tlaloc fortune. She sees *Jago*, the boy she loves, and this boy feels both like a stranger and like the truest version of himself he has ever known. He loves her because she sees not simply what *is*, but what is possible.

She asks to hear the stories of his scars. She wants to know who's hurt him, she says.

"You should see the other guy," he said the first time she asked, but she didn't laugh, and he knows she understands the meaning behind his words.

"It's not like I *enjoy* it," he added quickly. "I don't hurt people for *fun*."

"I would never think that. It's just . . ." She kissed the scar on his face.

"I don't care what you've done in the past, Jago. What you've done doesn't have to define you. What your parents want doesn't have to define you. Who are you *now*? Who do you want to be?"

"You say that like I get to pick."

"You think this ugly life is all you can have, Jago, but you're wrong."

He wishes he could tell her the truth. That his aunts and uncles train him for more than the family business. That the reason he spends so many hours in the gym or at the firing range, the reason he speaks so many languages and knows how to make a computer do whatever he asks of it, isn't simply for commerce and brute force. For all his life, being a Tlaloc and being the Player have seemed two parts of the same whole. Yes, he divides his time between training for Endgame and helping the syndicate. Yes, sometimes he wields his weapons in defense of the Olmec people and sometimes to preserve his family's turf. But he's been taught that these are the same: that Playing is a sacred family duty. That in return for their centuries of Playing, for the sons and daughters they've sacrificed to the cause, the Tlaloc family deserves compensation—they deserve respect and power.

But now, he wonders.

Perhaps he's mistaken two duties for one. His family, his business, his bloodline . . . is it possible these are extricable after all, that commitment to one doesn't necessitate commitment to all?

Alicia doesn't like what she knows of his duty, because she thinks it's about intimidation and corruption, greed and crime.

If she knew who he was beneath that, the solemn oath he's sworn, the harsh gods he serves, she might think differently.

Or, he considers, she might not. Endgame is still about violence—war and blood. Alicia has no love for such things, and doesn't want them for him, in any form. She wants to make his life beautiful.

She introduces him to Tchaikovsky and Prokofiev and Stravinsky, to the love poems of Pablo Neruda and the folktales of nineteenth-century Russia, all beautiful things she's learned to love through ballet. He asks her, "How can you say ballet has blinded you

274

to the world when you've seen so much?" and she says, "I want more."
He plays Mudra for her, and Almas Inmortales and Sanguinaria and
Hand of Doom, all his favorite metal bands.

"Ugly," she pronounces the music, her word for anything she doesn't
like.

But for love of him she listens, watches carefully the look on his face
as he turns up the volume and thrashes to the beat of the noise. It
is ugly, and full of rage, and this is what he likes about it. This is the
music that plays in his head and heart; this is the sound of his life.

"There's no room for bullshit in this music," she muses. "Nowhere to
hide."

"Exactly."

She gets it; she kisses him, and though he is supposed to have left
for the gym twenty minutes ago, though he's already missed his last
three weight-training sessions, he kisses her back, and knows he's not
going anywhere, not anytime soon.

So what if he's neglecting some of his duties? Alicia's only in Peru until
the end of the summer. Everything else can wait for three more weeks.
Even Endgame. He hopes.

No one approves.

"Look who's coming—it's the invisible man!" Tiempo crows, as Jago
joins his friends for a game of dudo, which he hasn't done since he met
Alicia. She's taking an exam in her Spanish class—he spent all night
helping her study, but still, he misses her for the two hours she's not at
his side.

"We thought you disappeared on us, *Feo*," Chango says, shaking his
cup of dice. Everyone in Juliaca plays dudo, from the little kids on
the street to Jago's great-grandmother. Jago has been playing it with
his buddies ever since they were young enough to be betting with
chocolate coins. Now they use real ones, and Jago almost always
cleans up.

Once in a while, he suspects his friends of letting him win. They've known each other for more than a decade, yes, but he's still a Tlaloc; their parents work for his. He tries not to think about it.

"Finally ditch *la gringa*?" José teases.

Jago scowls at them. "Don't call her that."

José holds out a cup of dice for Jago. "You blind? That's what she is, Feo."

"She's Alicia," Jago says. "And I'm not ditching her."

"She probably ditched him," Chango says. "Or she's getting ready to."

Jago has been looking forward to this afternoon, imagining that he would tell his friends how everything looks different now, how the world has changed—but now that the moment is here, he doesn't know what he was thinking.

Chango, Tiempo, and José have fought with him—they would die for him—but they're not interested in hearing about his feelings.

"How come you never bring her around, Jago? She embarrass you?" José asks.

Chango elbows him. "*We* embarrass him." Chango has always been the smartest of the three.

"No way is that true," Tiempo says. He, on the other hand, has always been the most loyal. "Tell him that's not true, Feo."

"That's not true, Chango."

"So you're keeping her your dirty little secret because . . . ?"

"If you ever found a girl who could stand your ugly face, you'd know why Feo wants to keep her to herself," Tiempo says. "See, little boy, when a man and a woman *really* like each other—"

Chango rears back. "Shut your mouth, *cojudo*, or I'll ram these dice down your throat."

Tiempo only laughs. This is how they talk to one another, this is how they have always talked to one another, and Jago never saw anything wrong with it, until now.

Or, not *wrong*, perhaps; just *less than*. They know one another so well, love one another so much—why can they only communicate in jokes and insults?

"So what does Mama Tlaloc think of your gringa—sorry, *Alicia*?" José asks.

Jago shifts uncomfortably. "She doesn't know about her."

Now they're all laughing. "Your mother knows everything, amigo," Tiempo reminds him. "She just takes her time. Remember when we broke her bathroom window and blamed it on the gardener? And she pretended to buy our story?"

Jago doesn't like to think about that. What his friends don't know is that before his mother fired the gardener, she had him beaten bloody. *His pain is on your shoulders,* she told Jago. *This is what happens when you're too cowardly to tell the truth.*

"She bided her time," José remembers, shaking his head in admiration. "Waits six months, then—"

Chango slaps his hand against the pavement. "*Bam.* The Tlaloc hammer comes down. At the worst possible moment. She makes us all cry in front of the Laredo sisters."

José smiles, sighs. "Ah, the Laredo sisters . . ." He tuts his finger at Jago. "What I remember most about the Laredo sisters is that you kept both for yourself. Always so greedy, Feo."

"My point," Tiempo says loudly, "is that you can bet everything that your mama already knows about your gringa, and you might want to deal with it before she does."

"Or get rid of the problem," Chango says, with what could almost be genuine concern. "You know how these tourists work, Feo. You've dated enough of them."

"You've *dumped* enough of them," José puts in, laughing.

"She's slumming it," Tiempo insists. "This is her vacation, but it's *your* life. Don't be so blind you do something you'll regret."

The only thing Jago regrets is joining his friends today, imagining that they could be happy for him, that they could accept that he's no longer the person he used to be. He's different now.

Or at least he wants to be.

* * *

He takes her to the desert.

He takes her to see the Nazca lines, those ancient glyphs that, for more than a thousand years, have spoken their ancient truth to the sky. He shows her the lines from above, hovering in a Tlaloc helicopter that he pilots himself; then they land and hike to the lines themselves, so she can feel the ancient dirt beneath her feet.

He doesn't tell her that the lines scraped into the earth are messages from the Sky, that they symbolize an oath between an ancient people and their gods.

He doesn't tell her that he once stood on this sacred ground and pledged his life to his line, and to a game that might end the world. That he slipped a knife across his palm, let the blood drip into the ancient lines, became one with his past and his future.

These things are forbidden.

Bringing her here now, when the tourists have faded away and they can breathe in the silence of a starry night, is the closest he can come to revealing his secret. He says it without words: *This place is my heart. This ground beneath us, this sky above us, these messages from the dead—this place is my soul.*

They lie on a blanket side by side, their hands linked, their eyes on the stars.

"Do you think there's anyone up there?" she asks him.

"Do you?"

"Are we talking about God or little green men?"

"It was your question," he points out.

She sighs. "I think . . . all those millions of stars, all those planets, we probably can't be alone. But I kind of hope we are."

This isn't the answer he expected. "Why?"

She turns onto her side to face him, and he rolls toward her.

"I don't like the idea of someone up there watching," she says.

"Judging, or whatever. I like the idea that we get to choose for ourselves what it all means. Who we're going to be. And I guess . . ."

"What?"

"I . . . I don't really know how to say it. I never talk like this. Or I never did before." She touches his face, so gently. "You turn me into someone new, Jago. Every day, you make me a stranger to myself."

"That doesn't sound like a good thing."

"It's the best thing," she tells him, and then, for a time, there's silence, as her lips meet his and they find a wordless way to speak.

It's not until they're nodding off to sleep beneath the stars, her delicate body folded into his sturdy arms, that she finishes her earlier thought. "I guess I don't want to believe in UFOs or in, you know, some kind of higher power, because I think it's beautiful that we're the only ones. Billions of stars, and only us to see them. Like a single spark in the darkness, you know?"

He squeezes her, gently but tightly, to say, *yes*, he does know. And he wishes she were right.

"You never answered. What do *you* think?" she asks. Her breath is warm on his neck. Her head lies on his chest, and he wonders if she can hear his heart beat.

It's strange—this is the place where he became the Player. It's saturated with memories and blood. But he's never felt less like Jago Tlaloc, Player of the Olmec line. He feels like just a boy, lying beside a girl. He feels like nothing matters here but the two of them, their even breathing, their beating hearts, their warm bodies, their dreams, and their love.

She asks him questions no one has ever bothered to ask.

She trusts him to be gentle, to be kind, to be so many things he never knew he could be.

She thinks him beautiful, and here in the dark, he can almost believe it's possible.

"I don't know if we really are alone," he lies. Then he says something true, the kind of thing Jago Tlaloc, Player of the Olmec, would never admit. "But that's how being with you makes me feel. Alone in the universe. Only the two of us."

"A spark in the night," she whispers.

"A bonfire."

Jago takes his friends' advice about one thing: He tells his mother
about Alicia. She pretends to be surprised.

"Invite the girl over for dinner," she says, and it is not a request.

He obeys.

He always obeys his mother.

Jago picks her up in one of the family's bulletproof Blazers. Alicia
draws in a sharp breath as they approach the first of the guard
towers, then seems to hold it for the entire long, winding drive up to
the hacienda. He tries to see it through her eyes, this castle on a hill,
and wonders if she's judging him for living like a king despite the
teeming swarm of poverty below. The Tlalocs do a great deal for the
poor of Juliaca, but they could do more—they could always do more.

"This is *amazing*," Alicia breathes, as they pull up in front of the
beautifully manicured grounds and he opens her door. There's
something new in her eyes when she looks at him, and he realizes
she never thought of him growing up in a place like this. He's told
her so much about the Tlaloc power—less so about the money that
enables and derives from it. Other than that disastrous first date, he's
refrained from giving her lavish gifts or taking her out for expensive
meals. Alicia isn't that kind of girl.

But there's a radiant smile on her face that he hasn't seen before.

"What?" he asks.

She shakes her head. "I just . . . I didn't know."

Dinner is exactly the disaster he expects it to be, although Alicia has
no idea. Jago's mother, Hayu Marca, is expert at appearing sweet and
nurturing—but beneath these layers of maternal fluff is impenetrable
steel. This is what strangers never seem to see.

Alicia is intimidated by his father, Guitarrero Tlaloc, who she
assumes is the head of the family. Jago's mother, on the other hand,
greets her at the edge of the property and immediately envelops her
in a warm hug, and afterward Alicia whispers to Jago, "I don't know
what you were so worried about; she's lovely."

Jago murmurs a noncommittal response.

The kitchen staff has gone all out, preparing an opulent spread of lomo saltado, aji de gallina, pollo a la brasa—the best Peru has to offer. Alicia eats heartily, and doesn't bat an eye at the roasted guinea pig served whole, on a spit. She takes a small bite and pronounces it "interesting." This is her highest compliment.

"Jago says you're a dancer." His mother's English is flawless. Like Alicia, she refuses to call him Feo, but not because she thinks the nickname doesn't fit. Naming a son is a mother's prerogative, she always says. She's not about to abdicate that responsibility to the streets.

"*Was* a dancer," Alicia corrects her.

Jago's father raises an eyebrow. "You quit?"

"I think there might be something better out there for me. Or at least, I just want the chance to find out."

"And what do your parents think of all this?" Jago's mother asks pointedly.

Alicia shrugs. "They're parents. They like what they know. You know?"

"Mmm." Jago's mother frowns.

"But in the end, they want me to be happy," Alicia adds, perhaps sensing things are going awry. "I mean, isn't that what you want for Jago? For him to find whatever makes him happy?"

"What makes Jago happy is fulfilling his duties," Jago's father says.

"There's got to be more than that," Alicia argues. "I know you have a lot of family traditions here, but don't you want him to find his own way?"

Jago takes her hand under the table and squeezes gently, hoping she will understand the message: *Stop, please.*

She does, and the subject abruptly shifts to the movies, and the difference between Hollywood and South American heartthrobs, something Jago's younger sister and mother can both discuss at length, and Alicia does an excellent job pretending to care.

He knows it's too late; the damage has been done. He waits through dessert, through after-dinner drinks, through his mother's extended good-bye rituals, the compliments and hair stroking and promises traded, to keep in touch, to be family, to love each other because they both love Jago. He can tell from Alicia's radiant smile that she thinks she's aced her test, and she kisses him good night in full view of both his parents, promising to meet him for breakfast first thing in the morning. Then she climbs into the bulletproof car with the red talon slashing across its shiny black paint. Jago's men will see her safely home.

They've already arranged to meet long before breakfast—Jago will slip out later and rescue her from her dorm, "like my very own Prince Charming rescuing me from a tower," she likes to say.

But for now, she leaves—and leaves him alone with his parents.

"No," his mother says, reclining into her favorite leather armchair. "I don't like this one." This house is several generations old, but when his parents got married, his mother redecorated it from floor to ceiling. She chose furnishings and tapestries that would look ancient, as if they'd always been there—as if this were *her* ancestral home. The bloodred eagle claw that serves as a family crest is emblazoned on the archway over the door, and etched into each of the stone tiles beneath her feet. This estate is her domain, now. She may have married into the family, but sometimes Jago thinks his mother is more of a Tlaloc than any of them.

"*I* like her, Mamá. That seems somewhat more relevant."

His father, as usual, remains silent on questions of love.

"She's going to put ideas in your head," his mother says.

"How do you know *I'm* not going to put ideas in *her* head?"

"Oh, Jago." His mother leans forward and clasps his hands. "You think you're such a strong man, but you're still a soft boy. You're weak, here." She taps his chest. "You always have been."

"What are you worried about, Mamá? That I'll be happy?"

"This is a girl who doesn't understand anything about your life or your responsibilities, Jago. If it were simply a distraction, if you were merely slacking off . . ." She stops him before he can object. "Yes, I know all about the training you've missed, and I don't care. Boys will be boys, and all that. I want you to have your fun, Jago. But you can't go thinking it's anything more. This girl, she doesn't fit into your life—not now, not ever. And you can't afford to start thinking that the two of you are the same. What you do . . . you can't just quit because you get bored."

"Don't you think I know that?" he snaps.

He's thought about it plenty, what it would take to walk away, how much he would have to want it and how much he would be giving up.

"Watch your tone, Jago."

"Alicia isn't just some girl, Mother. She's not a distraction, but she's also not a bad influence. She's . . . Alicia. She's amazing. And you would see that, if you weren't so judgmental."

He's the only person who dares talk to her this way, and often she likes it. Not tonight.

"I could forbid you from seeing her," his mother muses, as if weighing the idea.

"Don't do that," he warns her. "Don't make me choose."

Her eyebrows shoot sky-high. "Oh?"

He can't look at her.

"I see," she says. "Then I suppose I'll simply have to live with it, won't I?"

She stands up with great dignity, turns her back on him, and strides out of the room. He's won, he thinks. But he doesn't feel that way. Maybe because she's right about one thing. Alicia *has* put ideas in his head, made him wonder whether violence and duty are his destiny, or only one choice among many.

He could be the Player without being a criminal, he thinks. He could choose a different life without renouncing his obligations. Isn't that possible? He could walk away from the family business, be a poet or a musician or some anonymous man selling fried meat in an alleyway . . . couldn't he? The Tlaloc family's rule over Puno has been inextricably linked with Endgame and the Players for as long as any of the Olmec can remember, but just because something once was, must it always be?

He could even walk away from Endgame altogether, renounce his status as the Player, hand the sacred duty over to someone else. He could be free of all the training, of having the fate of his line rest on every choice he makes.

Jago remembers the first time he truly felt like the Player. He was 13 years old, just months past swearing the oath, binding himself to this life and this duty. He had been on training missions before, of course, but this one was different. This wasn't simply some exercise put to him by his uncles, an attempt to hone his skills. This was real. Meaningful.

He had scaled a skyscraper in Buenos Aires, disabled an alarm system, slipped past a security force armed with machine guns, cracked a safe owned by the richest man in Argentina, and taken an ancient Olmec knife that this man's ancestors had stolen from Jago's people long ago.

There have been so many missions since then that Jago barely remembers this one. He left some bodies behind, he remembers that. There was a bit of a mess on the way out—an alarm, an explosion, a hasty escape down the Rio de la Plata—but mostly, it's a blur.

What he has never forgotten, what he will *never* forget, is how it felt to arrive home with the ceremonial knife in hand. How his uncle, a former Player himself, kissed his forehead, and said, "You have done well for your people."

Jago had won victories for his family before; he had been fighting for Tlaloc honor in the streets since he was six years old. But this was different. This wasn't for the Tlalocs; this was for the Olmec. This was noble; this was *right*.

That day, Jago didn't feel like the monster of Juliaca, the ugly, scarred Feo who takes whatever he wants, whose face makes his people cower in fear.

Jago felt like a hero.

He could never give that up. Without Endgame, he's nothing. He's nobody.

But maybe he wouldn't have to give it up. Maybe he could have Alicia, and the beautiful life she wants for both of them, and still be a hero. Even thinking this way, even imagining, is a betrayal. That's how his mother would see it, at least, and she would never let him speak to Alicia again. His mother loves him; he knows that. But her love is the opposite of Alicia's: It comes with conditions. It comes with expectations. She loves her son, who is the heir to the family business, who is the Player, who is strong and ruthless and powerful. She couldn't fathom the idea of a son who was none of those things, who was simply Jago, her boy. For his mother, love and power are inextricable. If he ever gave up the one, he would lose the other. He knows that.

But it doesn't matter, he reminds himself. These are just idle thoughts, not acts, and thoughts are safe. No one can peer inside his head. His mother will never have to know.

But thoughts do have consequences.

Even the *act* of thinking can have consequences.

This is one of the first lessons Jago learned as a child, as he mastered rudimentary hand-to-hand combat. Instinct is always faster than conscious thought, and in a combat situation almost always more accurate. When thinking drowns out instinct, when it makes you second-guess yourself or hesitate to do what must be done, that's when it can be most deadly.

Jago should have known that; he should have known better.

But on that Friday afternoon, one week before Alicia is due to leave him behind, as he tracks his prey to a flophouse on the edge of the city and corners them in a seedy room rented by the hour, he's not thinking about his childhood lessons.

He's thinking about what Alicia said to him that morning: "Let's run away together, just the two of us. Let's see the world."

Does she mean it?

Would she do it?

Would he?

He's been tasked with hunting down two men, former employees foolish enough to steal from the Tlalocs and think they could get away with it. This is a crime that comes with a standard punishment: death.

He doesn't want to be here, in this dark, crumbling motel with its fetid stink and suspicious stains. He doesn't want to be creeping through a rat-infested hallway, locking the silencer onto his gun, preparing to assassinate two men who have stolen from a family so wealthy it barely noticed the loss—two men whose greatest crime is stupidity. Tiempo and Chango wanted to come along, but Jago insisted on going alone.

It's one against two, maybe. But the one is a Player.

The two don't know it yet, but they're doomed.

Jago creeps up to the door. The manager, after a small bribe made its way into his pocket, gave him the room number and a tip: the lock is broken. There's nothing standing in Jago's way.

You think this ugly life is all you can have, but you're wrong, he can almost hear Alicia saying as he eases open the door.

One of the men, Julio, is sprawled on the bed facedown, snoring. Alejandro is shaving, with his back to the door. Two bullets, one in each head, easy in, easy out—that's what he's been trained to do.

What you've done doesn't have to define you. What your parents want doesn't have to define you. She's said it so many times. She wants so much for him.

Jago takes aim. Alejandro first, because at the sound of the shot it will take Julio a second to shake off sleep and get his bearings, and by the time he does, he'll be dead.

I don't care what you've done in the past. Who are you now? Who do you want to be?

His finger tightens on the trigger, as it has many times before. This is a simple calculation; these men are enemies of the family, of the line. *You can choose.*

For the first time in his life, Jago hesitates.

Then fires.

Alejandro screams as the bullet blows off his ear. Jago has perfect aim. He knows how to kill—or how to wound. As Julio leaps out of bed, Jago pulls the trigger again, firing a second shot through Alejandro's other ear, another through his hand, a third and fourth through each of his feet. A final shot to his gut, an inch above the intestines. By the time Julio has reached his weapon, Alejandro is writhing on the floor, screaming and bleeding, and Jago's gun is aimed at Julio's forehead. Julio drops his weapon, raises his hands in the air.

"Take your friend, leave this city, and never return," Jago says. "And tell everyone that the punishment for crossing the Tlalocs is swift and painful."

Julio nods quickly, repeatedly, murmuring, "*Sí, sí,* whatever you say, Feo, anything, please," and—with Jago's permission—kneels at Alejandro's side, trying his best to staunch the bleeding.

Jago wonders whether Julio will get the wounded man help, or simply abandon him. If the latter, it will be a very painful death. But it will not be on Jago's shoulders.

This is what mercy looks like, he thinks, backing away from the men and out the door, down the hall, home to Alicia's embrace. This is what mercy *feels* like.

He won't tell Alicia.

It's not good enough for her.

Not yet.

On the day everything changes, Alicia's last day in the country, Jago thinks he has never been so miserable and so happy at the same time. They have driven to the eastern beach to watch the sun set over Lake Titicaca. "Nice metaphor for our relationship," Alicia says, with something adjacent to bitterness. She still wants him to run away with her. He says, day after day, he can't . . . he might . . . he shouldn't . . . he doesn't know . . . he needs more time.

They're running out of time.

She could go back home; they could email and text and do whatever it is normal teenagers do when an ocean gets in between them, but nothing about them is normal, and Jago fears that once she leaves, he'll never see her again. She'll run away without him—or she'll go home, return to the dance studio and the life her parents want for her, forget she ever flirted with being a different kind of girl. They have this one last day together, and then either he leaves behind everything he's ever known and loved, betrays his duty and generations upon generations of Tlaloc Players, shames his family, breaks his sacred oath, gives up all the certainties of his life and steps into the unknown—or he loses the only girl he's ever loved, and all hope of a beautiful life.

Leaving is impossible. But so is the thought of losing her.

She hopes against hope he'll change his mind and go with her; he hopes against hope she'll decide to stay.

In the meantime, they try not to think of the future; he holds her hand, and, quietly, they watch the sun sink in the sky. Waves lap at the shore. The sky is streaked with gold. Clouds glow an angry pink. "It's like fire," Alicia murmurs. "Like the sky is on fire."

Jago looks beyond her, to the east, where the sky is a flat, peaceful blue, cool and calm. This is what loving Alicia feels like: firestorm and tranquillity, all at once. He feels wild when he's with her, his skin sparking, his brain spinning, his heart leaping with possibility—but at his center is something so quiet and sure. A peace he's never known without her, and fears he will never know again.

They're both looking at the sky, not at the waves, not at the sand, not at each other, and certainly not at the empty road that winds along the strip of beach. Not even when an engine roars in the distance and a car approaches do they turn; Jago is determined that this moment be perfect, that for once they be alone in their pocket universe, no obligations to anyone but each other. His heart is beating so loud it drowns out his instincts.

And so he doesn't see the car slow, the window roll down, the tip of a Kalashnikov poke through. He doesn't, until it's too late, see Julio's face at the wheel, the face of the man he spared.

When he does see it, he throws himself at Alicia, but even the speed of the Player is no match for a bullet, and the bullet has already been fired, and Alicia is already screaming, already falling; Alicia is in his arms, bleeding and pale and fading away.

Julio guns the engine and speeds off.

This is what mercy looks like.

This is what mercy looks like: a pool of blood, seeping into sand. Pale skin, limp body, tearstained cheeks. A balled-up T-shirt pressed to the wound, bleeding through.

"Please," Jago says, and he's talking to the man on the other end of the phone, a man who works for his family, who fixes problems, whatever they may be—and he's talking to Alicia, who won't stop bleeding. Jago knows first aid, he knows how to dress a wound, how to triage, how to think clearly in a crisis—and also knows how little he can do, alone on this strip of sand. Maybe he should put her in the car, drive to a hospital himself, but the car is nearly a mile walk down the beach, and he doesn't want to move her unless he has to. Help will come, he tells himself. Help will come in time.

He lays her on her back, lets her weight seal the makeshift bandage to the wound, holds her hand, hopes.

"Jago," she whispers. "I can't."

"Tough luck," he says. "You have to. Hang on. Someone's coming."

"No, I can't . . ." She draws in a rasping breath.

"You don't have to talk," he says. For her, he tries to keep his voice steady, fearless. He is Jago Tlaloc—he's supposed to be immune to fear.

She coughs blood. He wipes it away, gently as he can. Her skin is hot to the touch.

"Who were they?" she asks him. "Why did they?"

"I don't know," he lies again.

But she's always able to see through his bullshit. Even now. "It's because of you," she says. There's more strength in her voice now. There's fire. "This is because of *you*."

"It doesn't matter," he assures her, and that's the worst lie of all, because what could matter more?

"Someone *shot* me," she says in wonder. "I got *shot*. What the hell?" She's laughing, suddenly, and he worries that this is delirium, that this is the beginning of the end, and the road is still empty; help is nowhere in sight.

"I'll kill him for you," Jago promises. "I'll track him down, I'll take him apart, piece by piece. I'll make him *hurt*."

"Oh God," she gasps. *"You."*

"What?"

"You . . . are just like them. Fucking monsters."

He thought it couldn't hurt any more than it already does. But this is worse. "No, Alicia—"

"You kill him, and then what? His family kills you? Is that where it stops? Does it ever stop? Or does it just keep going, pain and blood and blood and pain and pain and *pain* . . ."

She's so pale. Her voice is thin and thready, the words floating away from her, like they belong to someone else. He tells himself that she's feverish, in shock, that she doesn't mean what she's saying, that it doesn't matter what she says, as long as she's all right.

"Shhh. I know it hurts," he whispers. "I know."

"But it doesn't." She looks at him in childlike wonder, then coughs up another soft spray of blood. "It doesn't hurt, Jago. I can't . . . I can't feel it. My legs. I can't feel anything. . . ."

He stops breathing.

"Jago?"

Steady, he reminds himself. *Calm.* "That's normal," he lies. "Don't worry." He brushes her hair back from her sweaty face.

"Normal? This is normal?" She's laughing again, laughing and crying and shaking, shuddering, her hand squeezing his as if of its own accord, all of her trembling. Except her legs—those are still. "What if I can't dance again? What if I can't . . . No. *No. You.* Get away from me."

"I'm not going anywhere, Alicia."

"You destroy everything. You make everything ugly, like you. I wish I never—"

"Don't say that, Alicia." She's always seen the truth in him, the possibility. If all she sees is a monster . . . "Please." If he were the monster she says he is, wouldn't her words anger him? Wouldn't he push her aside, tell her that she entered freely into this life, fooled herself into believing it couldn't touch her, fooled *him* into believing that he had a choice?

He isn't angry; he doesn't push her aside. He wants to hold on to her forever, if she will only let him. "Please, Alicia, tell me you know I love you. That I will never let anyone hurt you again. That I can fix this. Please."

She doesn't say it.

She doesn't say anything.

"Alicia?"

Her eyes are closed. Her face is as gray as the sunless sky. Sirens blare in the distance, so slow, so useless. Jago holds on to her, willing her to wake up, even if she wants to call him a monster, yell at him to let go. He never will.

She survives.

He knows this because he bribes a doctor to tell him.

She'll recover; she'll walk. It's a medical miracle, the doctor says, and nothing more than that.

No one wants to tell him anything, not officially, because he's not family.

And she won't tell him herself, because when she wakes up, she refuses to see him. He could insist, of course. No one, certainly not the doctors working in the hospital's brand-new state-of-the-art Tlaloc Memorial Wing, would dare tell Jago Tlaloc where he can and cannot go.

But he won't violate her wishes, and she wishes to never see him again.

That's what the kind nurse says, after he's spent three days in a row in the waiting room, hoping she'll change her mind.

"Go home," the nurse suggests. "Get some rest. Get a hug from your mama. The girl will come around."

Jago does go home; Alicia doesn't come around.

Instead, she sends a letter.

Dear Feo, she writes, and that's when he knows what kind of letter this will be. He's *Feo* to her now. An ugly beast, and this is no fairy tale. There will be no third-act transformation. He is the monster, and she's lucky to have escaped with her life.

The doctors say I'll make a full recovery. Please don't blame yourself. This isn't your fault; it's mine. You are who you are; your life is what it is. I never should have tried to turn you into someone else. I never should have let you believe this was anything more than a vacation for me—I guess I let myself believe it too. But when this happened . . . I know what I want now. Who I am. I've given my entire life to dancing, and I'm not going to turn my back on that. It's my dream. My destiny, I guess you'd say. It took almost losing it to figure that out. I went a little crazy for a while, thinking it was so easy to just wish yourself into a different life. I'm going home, Feo. Thank you for helping me understand that I belong there. Just like you belong here. I'm sorry for ever suggesting otherwise.

Best wishes,

Alicia

Jago doesn't understand. Has he done this to her? Broken her, convinced her to give up her dreams?

He's the one who put her in harm's way, by failing to live up to his responsibilities. If he'd only done his job, killed Alejandro and Julio, not fallen prey to this stupid delusion of kindness and mercy, then Alicia would have been safe.

His job, his entire life, is to protect his people. Maybe this is his punishment for imagining he could escape that, or want to.

Or maybe she means it, and this was, as she said, simply a *vacation* for her, a break from her cozy life.

Either way, this was inevitable. His mother was right: They're too different. They're too dangerous for each other. Alicia made him soft . . . and the consequences of that have made her heartbreakingly hard.

You are who you are, she wrote.

Best wishes, she wrote.

He doesn't know which one hurts more.

Jago locks himself in his room for two days and two nights. He gives himself over completely to his anguish, letting it sweep over him, wash him out to sea; he drowns in it, drowns in memories of her. Jago has been taught how to withstand pain, how to retreat to a place in his mind where he doesn't feel it, but he lets himself feel all of this: pain, guilt, betrayal, fury. He lets the fire rage inside of him, lets it burn everything away—and then, when he's hollow and clean, burn itself out.

When he's ready, when it's done, he sets fire to the letter, drops it into the trash bin, and watches the flames consume what's left of her.

He emerges from his room a different man.

A man who's learned his lesson. Not to dream, not to wonder, not to love. Not to think he deserves anything more than what he has—not to think he's anything but a monster. *Feo,* outside and in.

This is good. This is as it should be.

He will not forget himself again. He will not be tempted by mercy or beauty. He will not show weakness. He will find Julio, and punish him, as he will punish all enemies of the Tlaloc and the Olmec. But he won't do it for Alicia, who ran away from him. He vows he will never again put some girl, some stranger from a foreign line, ahead of his own friends and family. He will never stop loving her; he will never forget her. But she is his past, and his past doesn't have to define him. She taught him that.

A new future starts today. And from today on, he will act only for his line. He will care only for his own. They're the only ones who can understand what he is, and love it.

They're the only ones he can trust.

Hayu Marca Tlaloc steps out of the SUV and ventures into the abandoned alley, her high heels clicking against the cobblestones. She looks down in disgust, carefully stepping over a pile of drying dog shit. She'll have to throw the shoes out when she gets home.

A small sacrifice to the cause.

At her side, she carries a small briefcase, filled with US$100,000.

Julio's eyes light up when he sees it.

"You did a good job," she tells him.

He bows his head. *"Gracias, Señora Tlaloc."*

"But I'm surprised you're not halfway to Brazil by now—my son's sure to come looking for you, and I promise, he's not very happy."

He doesn't dare meet her eyes. "I came for my payment."

"Ah, yes. Your payment. Well worth it, I have to say."

Her plan has worked out better than she could have imagined. Poor Jago will be heartbroken for a bit, she knows, but he'll get over it. Every man needs a few dents in his heart—it's how he learns to be hard. He'll blame himself, of course, but he'll forgive himself too. Men always do. It will be easier for him, believing that the girl made a full recovery, and Hayu has paid the doctors and nursing staff enough to ensure no one will ever say anything different.

As long as he never sees *la gringa* again, all will be well.

And *la gringa* has been taken care of.

"If you ever try to contact my son again, I will kill you," Hayu told her in the hospital room. "Do you understand me?"

"I love him," the girl said, as if that were allowed, and Hayu nearly smothered her with a pillow. "I said all these hateful things to him, and I have to tell him—"

"You will *never* speak to him. I don't like to repeat myself, so I don't want to have to say this again. Are we clear?"

The girl nodded.

"I'm sending you back home, but be sure: even there, I'll have people watching you. For the rest of your life, I'll be watching. I have that much power. And as for mercy . . . I'm expending all of it right here. This is the only chance you'll have. Do you believe me?"

The girl nodded again, tears streaming down her face.

She was alone in a foreign country with a flimsy grasp of the native language and a bullet hole in her spine. She'd just been told she would never walk again. She'd lost all will to fight.

Once reality sank in, she would blame Jago. Hayu may have forged the letter to Jago, but she truly believes it's what *la gringa* will want to say to him, once she understands the cold facts of her new life. The brilliant dancer, confined to a wheelchair for the rest of her days, and all because she made the mistake of loving the wrong boy. She will most certainly come to hate Jago, Hayu thinks. Almost as much as she'll hate herself.

Maybe that's why Hayu takes the risk of letting her live.

Transgressions like hers must be punished.

"Of course, my son can never know about this," she tells Julio now. "Understood?"

He nods. "*Claro, señora.* Of course."

"You know I don't like to take risks of any kind."

"I have heard that about you, *sí.*"

"So you'll understand, then, why I have to do this." Hayu slides a very small revolver from her purse and shoots him in the head.

Julio drops to the ground, a neat hole at the center of his forehead. Someone will find the body in a day or two, but the police won't investigate very hard—not a man like that, in a neighborhood like this.

Not that it matters. The police are in her pocket. All of Juliaca is in her pocket. And now her son is there again too, right where he belongs. She slips the gun back into her purse and clacks her way back to the SUV, noting with displeasure that the pigeons have crapped all over the windshield. Hayu shakes her head. She abhors coming down into this part of the city, almost as much as she abhors the violence that inevitably comes with it.

The things we do for love, she thinks ironically, then sighs and starts the long drive back to the hacienda. She's eager to get home. Her son is the Player. He is the most powerful man in Juliaca. And he needs her. He will always need her.

Whether he knows it or not.

SHANG
AN

When the air horn blasts in his ear at dawn, An Liu is already awake.
He has been awake since four a.m., waiting for the day to start.

He has been waiting for this day for six long years.

"Happy birthday, An Liu," his father says, as An springs out of bed
and speeds through his waking rituals, the cleansing and tidying
demanded of him by his father. If his bed is left rumpled, if his ears
are left clogged with wax or his cowlick is left sticking up, there will
be consequences. His father believes all messes should be punished.
An hasn't made a mess in years. He no longer remembers how.

"Have you chosen?" his father asks.

An nods yes.

He will not speak until necessary.

His father believes in efficiency. Sloppiness of all kinds will be
punished, and this includes excess words.

"What will it be?" his father asks.

An's birthday is the one day of the year when he gets to choose. On his
fifth birthday, he chose knives, and the blade carved five sharp lines
of blood into his back. For his sixth birthday, six lashes with the whip;
for his seventh, a blowtorch applied to seven points along his arms
and legs.

Every year, he chooses carefully, picking the worst pain he can think
of. His father has taught him that this is how to be a man. A man
wants to be tested; a man wants to be hurt. The body is molten steel;
pain hardens it into place.

Six years have passed since his training began. Today he is 10 years old; today he is steel, he is ready.

"I choose the brand."

His father smiles: He has chosen well. "Good."

The kitchen smells of persimmon, and his stomach is stuffed full of his mother's shì zi bīng. The little sweet buns stuffed with black sesame paste are his favorite, and for his fourth birthday, he is allowed to eat as many as he wants.

"Anything for my little Liu on his big birthday," his mother says, squeezing him into a hug so tight it makes his full belly hurt, but he says nothing, because he likes it too much, hiding in her embrace. It is safe here, behind her sturdy arms, pressed against her soft chest. An is afraid of so much: thunderstorms, large birds, small spaces, dark shadows, even butterflies. He is even afraid of his uncles, who tease him in their booming voices and say that he will never make his way in the world if he insists on being such a little worm. But in his mother's arms, he is not afraid. She will always protect him.

This is what he believes, as he believes the world is bounded by the park at one end of his street and the bridge at the other, as he believes the only people who matter are his uncles and his mother. His uncles are stern but fair; his mother is everything. He believes the world is full of justice and generosity, because that is all he has been allowed to see.

He believes that he is special, because that is what his mother tells him. He believes that his father is dead, because his mother tells him that too.

"His brothers wanted to help raise you, because they are good men," she tells him.

They are good men, and he thinks his father must have been too. Maybe the best of men.

But after lunch, the door opens, and a tall shadow falls across the floor. A booming voice shouts his mother's name. An runs into the living room and hides under a table.

He is also afraid of strangers.

In the kitchen, there are raised voices, the sounds of adults arguing. An curls into a ball. The stranger calls his name, but he doesn't move.

"What's wrong with him?" the man says.

"Nothing," his mother says. "Liu, come here; there's someone who wants to meet you." She doesn't sound quite right, not like his mother, strong and fierce. He wishes his uncles were home. They are big, scary men and would send the stranger away, make everything right again.

"Is he stupid?" the man asks.

"Of course not."

"Then why can't he obey a simple order?"

"He's not used to—"

"An Liu!" the man barks, and then a hand closes around his arm and drags him out from his hiding place, onto his feet. The hand lets him go, and An Liu is relieved for a moment—then the hand rears back and cracks him hard across the face.

He bursts into tears.

"Mother?" he whimpers, and holds his arms out to her, because he is hurt and scared and it is her job to protect him. But his mother stands beside the mean man, her eyes on the carpet. She doesn't move.

"You will look at me," the man says.

An blinks back tears, takes a hesitant step toward his mother.

The man slaps him again, so hard it makes his vision go blurry. There's a soft, insistent buzzing in his ears.

"I said, look at me. Not her. Me. And stop crying, if you know what's good for you."

An looks at him. The man is built like a tree, tall and thick, his face craggy, his eyes a beady black.

"Do you know who I am?"

An shakes his head, trying very hard to hold back his tears. He's afraid of what will happen if he can't stop them from streaming down his face.

"I'm your father," the man says. "You may rejoice, because I've come home to make a man of you. And I see I'm just in time."

An sits on the edge of the bench, his posture rigid. His gaze is fixed on the long branding iron. Its tip, carved into the shape of the Chinese character for *strength*, glows orange as his father turns it slowly over the flame, heating it to 400 degrees Celsius.

The color changes with the heat; his father has taught him that. A black iron will singe; a red iron will destroy. His father pulls the long rod off the flame, waits for the bright orange to fade to the color of ash, the proper color for a permanent mark.

An prepares himself. He breathes slowly, turns inward. Pain is an old friend, its habits familiar and well-worn.

"Turn," his father said.

An bares his naked back to the iron. His father presses it to the soft skin at the base of An's neck.

The iron sizzles.

The noxious smell of burning flesh fills the air.

Inside his head, silent and safe from his father's scorn, An screams and screams.

Three seconds.

Two seconds.

Pain pain pain pain pain pain pain pain pain pain pain pain pain pain pain pain pain pain.

One second.

Release.

"That's one," his father says, then returns the branding iron to the fire to heat it back to the proper temperature. Soon they will begin again.

An Liu is supposed to have longevity noodles and cake for his birthday dinner.

He gets no dinner at all.

Instead, the man who calls himself An's father takes him down to the basement. An is afraid of the basement and the things that might live in its musty dark: spiders, rats, roaches, monsters. He kicks and screams and cries, until the man picks him up and hurls him down the stairs.

In a tangled heap, in the dark, dazed and in pain, An finally falls silent.

The man, the father, clomps down the stairs and towers over him.

"I'm going to give you the facts of life," he says to An, and then tells him a series of amazing things.

That An's people are descendants of an ancient civilization, once ruled by strange gods from above. That when these gods returned to their home in the sky, they promised they would someday come back to end the world, sparing only that bloodline most worthy of survival. That every generation, one Player is chosen, and that that Player must be special and strong, for if the gods return, that Player will Play for the Shang, and all hope will rest on his shoulders.

That the oracle bones have just been cast, and of all the Shang boys in all the world, they named An Liu. When he turns 13, he will be his generation's Player.

An understands little of this. The words flutter past him like moths, flitting away as he reaches for one after another.

"I made a mistake. I'm not too proud to admit that. I assumed you would be as worthless as your mother. I should have known my blood would breed true. Now that I know what you are, what you're fated to become, I will repair what's been broken in my absence. I will make you strong. The Shang have tasked me with this."

The father unbuckles his heavy leather belt and takes it into his hands.

"Why?" An cries, as the man starts whipping him with the belt.

"Pain is its own answer," the man says, as the belt rises and falls, and the pain overtakes An, and finally, mercifully, the world goes black.

When he wakes, he is in a narrow, hard cot. The walls around him are bare, and too close. He recognizes the space: the basement closet, rarely used, smelling of mold. His sheets are stiff with dried blood.

"This is where you will sleep now," his father tells him.

An hurts all over.

"Mother?" he says.

"Your mother is gone."

This doesn't make any sense to An Liu. He's never spent a day or night

*without his mother. How could she be gone, when they are a part of each
other?*

*"She's disgusted by you," his father says. "She sees how soft you are,
how weak, and she left you to me. If you do as I say and learn to make
yourself hard and strong, then perhaps she will come back."*

"When?"

"Not for a very long time," his father says.

*"But when?" An says, and flinches, thinking his father will strike him for
asking the question again, but he must know.*

"When you're older. When you're a man."

*"When I'm ten?" An asks, grasping for an unfathomably old age. This is
what a very long time means to him. By then he will be all grown up.*

"If I say yes, will you stop asking about her?"

An nods yes.

*"Then yes, when you are ten. If you do as you're told; if you're good
enough."*

An swears he will be good enough.

*When the pain fades so that he can creep out of bed, he tiptoes up the
stairs to his mother's room. It is totally bare. Her belongings are gone.
All that remains of her are the blue scraps of the last dress she sewed
herself. An scoops up a handful of the sky-blue cloth and buries his nose
in it.*

It smells like her.

*He tucks the fabric into his shirt. If this is all he has left of her, he will
treasure it.*

"An Liu!" his father shouts.

*An scurries toward the sound of his father's voice. He will do whatever
he's told, obey any command he's given. He will find a way to please this
man, and when he finally does, he will have his mother back.*

After his flesh has stopped sizzling and he's able to slip a light shirt
over his bandaged skin, An Liu's day proceeds as usual.

He stays in the basement, his home within the home, and works his body, training with all the traditional Shang weapons that he wields like an expert: spears, poleaxes, dagger-axes. Then he works his mind, studying the engineering blueprints and circuit diagrams that, once committed to memory, will allow him to disable any security system and dismantle any explosive the world has been able to invent.

It's not that he likes it down here—*like* is one of the words that has lost all meaning for An Liu, along with *choose* and *pleasure* and *happy*. But he feels comfortable in this dank place. The scratching of insect legs against the stone wall makes him feel he is surrounded by friends.

He takes his dinner at the table beside his father and his uncles. They chat politely with one another, but no one speaks to him, as is his father's decree. They feast on bowls of yáng ròu pào mó, shredding the tender bread into strips that will absorb the soup, slurping until their bowls are clean. An Liu eats his customary rice and broth.

No one says anything about his mother.

True to his word, he has not asked about her in six years. But he has not forgotten.

He knows that an answer given to a child is not a promise—and that the only promise his father ever made him was that there would be pain and, beyond that, more pain. But there is a part of him that chooses to believe that today is the day. That the moment he has been waiting for is real, that he has proven his worth and his strength, and so his mother will finally return.

Except that the day passes, and then the evening, and soon An has completed his nighttime rituals and received his daily dose of pain— easily accomplished, tonight, with a hand pressed to the fresh brand marks.

His father is not a man inclined to explanations. But gradually, over the years, An Liu has come to understand the man's philosophy of strength and weakness.

Weakness derives from fear, and all fear is fear of pain.

Thus it is only the man with no fear of pain who has no weakness;

as An Liu learns to inure himself to pain, he will relinquish all fear, and he will grow strong. The theory has borne out. The body and its tortures hold no secrets for An Liu. There is nothing he will not risk, for there is nothing he cannot endure. As for that other kind of pain, the pain of losing that which he loves the most? An Liu's father has taken care of that too. He's stripped An Liu's life of everything and everyone that could be loved. There is nothing left to lose but his life, and that would be a mercy. There is nothing left to fear.

This, his father says, is how the Shang mold a Player true of spirit, capable of victory. This is his father's claim, but An Liu has come to understand many things over the years: he has learned to read his father's expressions, and he can see the joy on the man's face when skin tears and burns.

Other men may fear pain; An Liu's father feeds on it.

Perhaps this is why he says nothing about An Liu's mother—perhaps he can see the desire burning in his son's eyes, and enjoys watching as the hours pass and the fire burns itself out.

"Bed," his father commands, as he does every night at precisely 10 p.m.

This time, the first time since the day his father arrived, An does not obey. He stands up and faces his father, who is the only thing left in the world that can frighten him. An is no longer the boy he once was, no longer the soft and weak worm that his father first met. He is still a boy, yes. Still smaller than average for his age and thin as a reed, with soft features that offer the illusion of innocence. But his arms are muscled, his legs powerful; his mind is sharp, his will unbreakable.

"Where is my mother?" he says.

"Excuse me?" His father looks surprised. It has been a long time since An has spoken anything but the direct response to a question.

"You said she would return when I was ten years old, and today I am ten. Where is she?"

For the first time in An Liu's memory, his father starts to laugh. "Did I tell you that? When could I possibly have told you that?"

An's hands are curling into fists. He doesn't like to be laughed at. Especially in front of his uncles, who watch from the kitchen with avid interest. An Liu is surprising them tonight; he's surprising himself.

"The day she left," An reminds him. "You told me if I worked very hard and made a man of myself, she would come back. When I turned ten."

"You? A man?" His father snorts. "You, little worm? I suppose you think you're worthy to be the Player now too?"

"Yes, Father. I do." An Liu has three more years before he will be old enough to take on the mantle officially, but he feels ready right now, to fight for the life of his people as he's been groomed to do.

"Then you're dumber than you look."

This is An's cue: to scurry away before he earns a punishment. Always before, he has done this. But always before, he had a purpose. He had this day to look forward to; he had hope.

Now he has nothing.

"I want you to bring my mother back," An says. He's older and wiser now than he once was; he understood long ago that his mother wouldn't have left voluntarily. Her absence or presence is under his father's control, just like everything else. In this home, his father is the only god. "It's time."

"Are you suggesting that your life is missing something? That this life your uncles and I have given you isn't good enough?"

An summons all the courage he has. "Yes."

"Then I suppose I've failed, and you're just as disgustingly weak as you ever were," his father says. "We'll have to redouble our efforts." He turns to An's uncles. "Brothers, join me in giving An Liu his final birthday gift."

An Liu knows the uncles will do as he says—they always do. Unlike his father, they take no joy in cruelty, but they believe in doing what needs to be done. When he was younger, he struggled to understand them, how they could have allowed his father into their lives, how they could have turned on the boy they once claimed to love. Before that, they had not been gentle, but neither had they been cruel. Once, An Liu cared about this change, wondered whether, secretly, they hated his father as much as he did, whether they were equally afraid. But An Liu has learned how to stop caring. He sees his uncles clearly now, not for what they once were, but what they now are: the enemy. The men form a ring around An and raise their fists. Now it's An who laughs. He will not cower away from them; he will not hide or fear what is to come.

He will fight like a man.

He will fight like a man with nothing left to lose.

"You've taught me well, Father," he says, raising his own fists. "I have no fear left."

He doesn't wait for them to make the first move. Instead he swings a punch at his father, and the crunch of his father's nose against his knuckles is the sweetest sound he's ever heard.

His father shrieks with rage. As An fights his uncles, whirling and ducking and holding his own, one well-trained 10-year-old against four grown men, his father takes up the branding iron from its home by the fireplace. He slashes it through the air and strikes An solidly across the chest, knocking him to the floor. His head smacks hard against the concrete. Thunder and lightning explode at once, and he is consumed by the noise and the light and the pain.

Then all is still.

An Liu is somewhere else.

Far away, in the black.

Untouchable. Untouched.

He feels nothing, sees nothing, cannot know that even after his eyes close and he goes limp, his father continues to beat him, teaching him a lesson he will never learn, because he is gone.

His uncles are tasked with curing him of his fears.

When he is five years old, the uncle who was once his favorite nails him into a coffin and buries him in the ground.

An screams in the dark. He kicks at the pine walls closing him in, tries to catch his breath, feels like he will lose his mind if he doesn't get space get air get free get out get out get out.

He does not get out.

His voice goes hoarse; his mind goes blank.

He lies still, in the dark, whimpers, waits.

Somewhere above, up in the light, he hears his uncles' voices raised in argument. He clings to the sound, evidence that a world still exists.

"This is not right, Hua. You know that. He's only a boy."

"A boy who will be the Player someday, and you know that makes all the difference."

"The things we're teaching him . . . what kind of Player will he be?"

"To harden a Player's spirit, to teach him the shape of pain, you know this is the Shang way. He learns pain now, or he learns death later. This is how we help him survive."

"No, Hua. Not like this. Pain tempered with love, with mercy, with wisdom. That is the Shang way. This is . . . I don't know what this is."

"This is how our brother sees fit to train his son, Chen. It's a father's right to train his Player. This is also the Shang way. And if things go too far, at least we will be here."

"Too far? He's got the boy in a coffin—"

"Keep talking like this, it might be you in a coffin. You know that best of all."

The argument ends there.

Endless time passes. An Liu cries.

"Peace, Little Liu." His uncle Chen, from above, pain in his voice. "Patience."

He cries out for Uncle Chen, who once fed him sweets when his mother wasn't looking and told him stories about dragon slayers and princesses when he had trouble falling asleep. He says, "Uncle, don't you love me anymore?"

There is a silence, and then a low voice. "This is love."

And so An Liu learns: Pain is love. Fear is love. Violence is love.

Life is love, so An Liu learns to hate it.

He learns other things too: how to shoot all manner of guns, how to speak the languages of the modern world and those long dead, how to use a computer to explore and dominate, how to manipulate code and circuitry to make machines do exactly as he wishes, and this is his favorite language to speak, because the machines are the only things that obey him. Inside the computer, he has ultimate control; inside the computer, he is God, and his father doesn't exist.

Xi'an, China, is filled with wonders. It was an imperial capital for 1,000 years, the seat of 13 dynasties, ruled over by 73 emperors. It is surrounded by the world's largest city wall and home to remnants of glorious civilizations past: the Big Wild Goose Pagoda, the army of terra-cotta warriors, the sacred mountain Huàshān—An Liu sees none of it, knows none of it.

He is not allowed out of the house. He is rarely, and only with supervision, allowed out of the basement.

An's Liu's world is dark and small, peopled only by his father and his uncles.

His time is structured and scheduled. Like everything else in his life, it is not his own.

It belongs to the Shang, his father tells him. His life belongs to the Shang.

"You will Play and you will win," his father often shouts, when whipping An for minor failures. It becomes a mantra, drilled into An's subconscious, something he knows about himself as surely as he knows his name.

He will Play.

He will win.

He will be the savior of the Shang people, rescue them from extinction when Endgame comes. He knows this; he simply doesn't know why he should have to do such a thing, why the Shang would ask it of him.

He doesn't understand how he can be the only one who dreams of escape from this life. Who are these fools, that they would choose to survive?

For fifteen days, An Liu is unconscious, drowning in the black.

His body lies in a hospital bed, strung with wires and tubes. Monitors beep irregularly as his pulse bounces, his heart soldiers on. One tube delivers fluids; another carries them away. A machine breathes for him. His head is shaved, wrapped in bandages. Skull fragments have been carefully extracted from his brain. Gray matter has been pared away, damaged bits sliced off and dropped into a metal bin. Pieces of An Liu, of who he used to be, now medical waste, put out with the trash. A steel plate replaces the chunk of skull that was lost. The brain swells against its casing, the coma persists, and the doctors have little left to do but wait.

He will wake, or he will not.

He will be the same, or he will not.

Time will tell.

These are hard truths the doctors are prepared to tell his loved ones—but An Liu is alone in the secure private facility, abandoned to expert care. The doctors receive their payment, and know who to contact when the time comes, when there is an answer, one way or another.

In the meantime, no one sits by An's side. No one holds his limp hand. The nurses gossip over his still head, about their bosses and their love lives, and sometimes one will put a soft hand on his forehead and wish him well.

He is just a child, they say to each other. Broken, probably beyond repair. He shouldn't be alone.

His eyes twitch behind his lids, and they wonder if, in his state, he can dream.

He dreams of a different life.

He dreams of a different An Liu, one who has a mother, not a father.

He dreams of a 10th birthday full of cake and presents and love, a mother's radiant face and gentle kiss. He dreams that he goes to school, has friends, sleeps in a room with a window and posters on the wall.

He dreams of warmth and joy and human touch.

He dreams himself into a fantasy world, and when the images dissolve in a shower of blinding light, when he blinks himself back to reality, a stranger aiming a flashlight at his pupils, a voice asking if he knows who he is or where, a stabbing pain in his head unlike anything he's ever known, he wishes only to return to the dream or, even better, to the mercy of death that lay just beyond it.

After, things are *blinkblink* different.

An Liu is *shiver-SHIVER* different.

The world jumps and jitters, will not *blink-shiver-blink* sit still. His tongue is clumsy in his mouth; his limbs are numb blocks of wood. And when he *blink* tries *shiver* to *blink* focus, to *shivershiver* stand, to *BLINKblink* read, his mind jitters, his body rebels; he tics and shudders and eventually *blinkblinkblinkblinkblinkblinkblinkblink blinkblinkblinkblinkblinkblinkblinkblinkblinkblinkblinkblinkblinkblink blinkblinkblinkblinkblinkblinkblinkblinkblinkblinkblinkblinkblinkblink blinkblinkblinkBLINK* loses himself to frustrated rage.

Anger makes it worse.

Everything makes it worse.

An has spent six years learning to control his body and mind—the only two things in his life he has any control over at all—and just like that, it's all gone. He's been a prisoner in his father's house, but now he will be a prisoner in *SHIVER* his own body.

His doctors tell him to be patient.

His father, who visits only once, tells him to be a man.

The *blinkblinkSHIVER* tics are *blink* much *SHIVERshivershiverBLINK* worse when his father is there.

"D-d-d-d-d-id y-y-ou you you dooooooo this-s-s-s t-t-t-to m-m-me?

ME ME ME?" An asks, cursing his halting and stuttering tongue. Losing patience, his father walks out before An manages to finish the sentence. Maybe this is for the best, but An *blinkblink* doesn't care. He's not afraid of *SHIVER* his father anymore.

He's not afraid of anything. Except living *blinkblink* like this.

For three *blinkblink* months he lives in a secure private rehab facility. He *SHIVER* learns to walk again, one jerking step at a time. He practices with a speech pathologist until *blink-shiver-blink* he can force his tongue to make the right letters again. He retrains *SHIVERblink* his brain to retrieve the words he needs to express his anger.

It's *blink-blink-blink* slow.

Thoughts flutter away from him; words escape him.

An Liu could once *shiverBLINK* multiply matrices and solve quantum wave functions in his head. Now his *blink* studies *blink* are *blink* simpler.

He looks at pictures, tries to remember the words that go with them.

This is a clock.

This is a dog.

This is a . . .

"A-a-a-a-a-a-apple!" he finally screams, and throws the fruit across the room in frustration. It goes only a couple feet.

His body is as weak as his mind.

What they did to him, what they took from him: it is irreplaceable. What is left behind: a steel plate, a Swiss-cheese brain. A fragmented memory of his father's angry shouts and a rod slamming down, again and again. Pain, in his body, in his head, throbbing pains, stabbing pains, aching pains—and the perpetual fog in his brain from the medicines intended to take it away. And, *shiver* forever *blink* with *shiver* him, tics and stutters, stutters and tics.

"K-k-k-k-ill memememe," he asks his physical therapists.

"P-p-p-l-l-l-ease."

He hates them for refusing, as he hates his body for rebelling, as he hates his uncles and his father for leaving him in this state.

Hate. That's another thing he's been left with.

His hate is the purest thing he's ever felt, untempered by fear or hope. Someday, maybe, he will be *blinkblinkblinkblink* strong enough to use it.

An's mind heals faster than his body, but he begins to return to himself. He is slower and weaker than before, but he gets stronger every day. The tics and stutters *shiver* remain.

They will, the doctors say, likely always *BLINK* remain.

He *shiverSHIVERshiver* will never be what he was. Never as strong, never as coordinated. Nothing will ever be *blinkblinkblink* so easy for him again.

An Liu laughs bitterly when the doctors tell him that.

As if *blinkBLINKshiver* his life has ever been easy.

He goes home.

If he were of another line, if he were not *blinkblinkblink* Shang, then perhaps his people would *SHIVER* choose a different champion. They would deem him *BLINK* unworthy. Choose someone new to be their Player. Someone *SHIVERblinkSHIVERblink* whole. They would *BLINK* set *BLINK* An *BLINK* free.

Not the Shang.

The Shang believe in the oracle bones. The oracle bones were cast years ago, and they name An Liu as *BLINK* the next Player.

There is no question.

There is no escape.

If An Liu is *blinkBLINK* damaged, then it was meant to be. If An Liu's father deemed it *blinkblink* necessary to damage him, then it was *SHIVERblink* meant to be.

He will Play however he is able to Play.

He will Play no matter what.

He will not be given a choice.

He's not ready yet to resume his physical training. So his father and his uncles leave him alone to his basement and his computers. Maybe they think he's *shiverBLINK* no use to them in this state.

Maybe they *blink-blink-shiver* see something new in him, and they are afraid.

An doesn't care, as long as they leave him alone.

Hour after hour, he sits in the dark, in front of his computer, fingers *shiverBLINK* flying across the keyboard. On screen, in the bits and bytes, there are no tics. No stuttering. He calls himself LaMort377. *La mort,* French for "death"—he likes it because, out loud, it sounds the same as the French word for "love." There's nothing to tie the username to him except the number: the Shang people are the 377th bloodline. But no one would be able to piece that together, trace it back to him. This is a secret he shares only with himself.

Online, An can be whoever he wants to be. Do whatever he wants to do. He wants to destroy, and when the impulse seizes him, he does.

He hacks electricity grids. Banks. Air-traffic-control systems. He makes mischief of any kind that suits him. Some days he crashes stocks, other days *blinkBLINK* planes.

Every day, he searches for his mother.

Government databases. Social networks. Corporate mailing lists. Media archives. Anywhere and everywhere, he looks for evidence of his mother, something to lead him to her. Something, even, to prove she ever existed.

There is nothing.

There are no walls in An Liu's cyberspace. No locks he can't *blinkSHIVERblink* crack at will. No shred of information hidden from him—but his mother is a ghost.

He learns plenty about this father, answers to questions he never before thought to ask. An Bai grew up in Beijing, child of wealthy banker parents. His name, Bai, means "person of purity," and An Liu thinks this is well chosen. His father is impossibly pure, untainted by mercy, doubt, or love. When he was 16 years old, his parents died in a fire, leaving him everything: their penthouse in Beijing, the family estate in Xi'an, and four brothers who depended on him for everything. He controlled the money, and so he controlled them.

As he *blinkblink* continues to control them.

The more An Liu learns about humans, the more he comes to despise the human race.

Machines are better. Machines are rational, trustworthy, easily controlled. Everything in cyberspace is smooth and comprehensible— everything except for the fact that An Liu's mother is invisible, unfindable, even by someone with An Liu's unlimited powers.

This, An Liu cannot comprehend.

And there's something else: someone is *blinkSHIVERblink* watching him. There's no concrete evidence at first, just a sense he has, that someone is tracking his digital footprint. It should be impossible; he moves untraceably through the cyber world. He's a ghost in the machine, and yet . . .

And yet there are traces of another. Tiny bread crumbs left behind, almost as if this shadow wants An to notice him, as if the predator yearns to become the prey.

Then, one day, the impossible happens: despite the security protocols on An Liu's system, despite layers and layers of unbreakable firewalls, despite some of the best encryption in the world, the stranger breaks through, and a message in English pops up on An's screen, uninvited, unwelcome.

It blinks red, waiting for a response.

12GOLDENGATE12: GREETINGS AND SALUTATIONS, FRIEND. WANT TO PLAY?

An doesn't want to *blinkSHIVER* "play," whatever that means. He doesn't *blinkblink* want to be noticed, or watched, or tracked. He certainly *shiverBLINK* doesn't want a friend.

But 12goldengate12 is persistent.

12GOLDENGATE12: I'M NOT YOUR ENEMY.

An ignores him that day and the next.

12GOLDENGATE12: I CAN BE YOUR ENEMY, IF YOU'D RATHER.

He tries to trace his IP, find this annoying bug and squash it, but 12goldengate12 is the best he's ever seen, as good, almost, as An himself. The signal is bounced across 12 satellites, ping-ponging back and forth across the world—An is, finally, able trace its origin to the west coast of North America, but that tells him nothing he couldn't have guessed from the username itself.

It doesn't tell him how to find and eliminate this pest.

Or what the pest might want from him.

And *blinkblinkblink* as the days pass, An finds himself getting curious. His uncles and his father haven't spoken to him in weeks. They deliver his food to him in silence. It's a relief, this temporary respite from pain and torture—but it's a strange silence to live in. Sometimes An wonders if he's gone invisible. If he *blink* died *blink* after all, and is *shiver* doomed *BLINK* to haunt his father for all his days.

It's easy to imagine he doesn't exist—except that 12goldengate12 knows An Liu is there, and wants an answer.

After one week, An finally gives it to him.

LAMORT377: WHO ARE YOU AND WHAT DO YOU WANT?

12GOLDENGATE12: A FRIEND

12GOLDENGATE12: I COULD BE A FRIEND, AT LEAST

12GOLDENGATE12: DO YOU WANT A FRIEND?

This is a question An Liu has never asked himself.

LAMORT377: WHY WOULD YOU WANT TO BE MY FRIEND?

12GOLDENGATE12: DUDE I'VE BEEN WATCHING YOUR WORK. IT'S SOME NEXT LEVEL SHIT. NOT MANY PEOPLE OUT THERE CAN KEEP UP WITH ME. BUT YOU'RE ALMOST THERE. I CAN TELL YOU'RE LOOKING FOR SOMEONE, THOUGHT YOU MIGHT WANT SOME HELP.

It disconcerts An to think that the stranger has traced his steps well enough to figure out that he's searching for someone. What else does this interloper know? And how dangerous is it to have him out there, knowing it?

On the other hand, he appreciates that the stranger is impressed with him. Even if he's clearly not impressed enough.

LAMORT377: YOU'RE SUGGESTING YOU'RE BETTER THAN ME? THAT I COULD LEARN FROM YOU?

12GOLDENGATE12: FOR A GENIUS YOU'RE KIND OF SLOW. YEAH, DUDE, I'M SUGGESTING THAT. I'M THE BEST. SO I MUST BE BETTER THAN YOU. THAT'S JUST LOGIC

LAMORT377: PROVE IT

With that, An Liu shuts down his system. The stranger is galling, enraging—but *blinkblinkSHIVER* this is the first *shiver* tic-*blink*-free conversation he's had with someone since he woke up from the coma. The stranger has *shivershiver* no idea who An Liu is or that he is *blinkblinkblinkblinkblink* damaged. An Liu's father would certainly disapprove of An making contact with anyone, much less continuing it. He would *shiver* likely forbid it, if he *shiverBLINK* could—but An Liu surpassed his father's computing skills years ago. In this digital space, An Liu is free to do as he pleases. And perhaps the stranger simply wants to play. So An will give him a game.

Surely there's no harm in that.

They do battle. An Liu builds up his defenses, and again and again 12goldengate12 hacks his way through. When they get bored of this back-and-forth, they move on to other targets, racing to see who can be the first to burrow into the UN's mainframe or tamper with Interpol's digital archives.

12goldengate12 prefers stealing information to abusing it; he calls himself a force for good, and An Liu overlooks the priggishness because, for the first time in memory, he's having fun. An Liu is good, but he *blink* has to *shiverblink* admit that, every once in a while, 12goldengate12 is better.

Somehow, without realizing it, they slide from war into collaboration. Though they know nothing about each other, they *understand* each other—the hacker's language is universal, and their minds share the same contours, leap to the same wild conclusions. There's relief in finding another so like him, devoted to such a singular purpose.

Sometimes, hours passing without his notice, hunched over his keyboard in the dark as, somewhere beyond the basement, the sun rises and sets and rises again, he feels joy. They swap chunks of poached code and share security keys to some of the world's most secure systems. Together, they tackle Mossad, which neither has ever managed to crack on his own—working together, it's a breeze.

12GOLDENGATE12: NOTHING CAN STAND IN OUR WAY! LET THE WORLD BOW BEFORE US

An Liu has never *BLINKBLINKBLINK* been an *us* before.

In the world beyond the basement, An's father and his uncles wait for him to recover enough to resume his training. They *blink-shiver* grow impatient. Every week, An's father descends the stairs and gives his son a *blinkblinkblinkblinkblink* test. Sometimes this means hand-to-hand combat. Sometimes it is a pain challenge, hot coals or a nail driven into flesh, to help An's inner resilience return. The more disgusted An Liu's father grows, the more tics An *SHIVERblink* gets, and the more tics An *BLINKshiver* gets, the more disgusted his father becomes. Soon there are no tests at all, simply *blink-shiver-blinkBLINK* punishments.

An Liu endures.

12GOLDENGATE12: WHERE YOU BEEN?

LAMORT377: BUSY

12GOLDENGATE12: DAD AGAIN, YEAH? PARENTS SUCK, MAN

An Liu has told the stranger that his father is a *blinkBLINK* disciplinarian, that sometimes it's difficult to live up to expectations. Nothing more than that.

LAMORT377: WHAT DO YOU KNOW?

12GOLDENGATE12: I KNOW I DON'T LET ANYONE BOSS ME AROUND

12GOLDENGATE12: NOT ANYMORE

LAMORT377: WHAT'D YOU DO, KILL MOM AND DAD?

12GOLDENGATE12: HAHAHAHA

LAMORT377: ☺

12GOLDENGATE12: YOU DON'T KNOW HOW BAD IT CAN GET. I HAD TO GET OUT OF THERE, YOU KNOW? NOT SO GREAT ON THE STREET EITHER, THOUGH. NO COMPUTERS ON THE STREET. LUCKY I FOUND THIS PLACE

LAMORT377: WHAT PLACE?

12GOLDENGATE12: BUNCH OF KIDS LIKE US, SORT OF A COMMUNE THING, WITHOUT ANY OF THE HIPPY DIPPY SHIT. JUST HACKING, YOU KNOW? YOU SHOULD COME, YOU'D LOVE IT

LAMORT377: HOW DO YOU KNOW I'M A KID?

12GOLDENGATE12: COME ON, NO ONE OVER THE AGE OF 20 CAN DO WHAT WE DO

An Liu indulges the fantasy for the moment. Securing himself a plane ticket to California would be as easy as breathing. He could sneak out of the house while his father and his uncles slept, flee this place and this life. No more Playing, no more tests, no more *blinkblink* punishments.

But then what?

Maybe, if this were *blink-shiver* before.

If he were the *SHIVERshiver* boy he was.

Not now. Not when he's like this, with no *blinkblinkblinkblinkblinkblink* control. He *blink* spasms; he *blink* hurts. It's safer here, in his *BLINKshiver* basement, in the dark where no one can *shivershivershiver* see him. His damage. Now that An has a friend, he can't afford to lose him.

LAMORT377: A BUNCH OF GUYS ALL LIVING IN SOME SHACK TOGETHER? DOESN'T SOUND LIKE MY THING

12GOLDENGATE12: WHAT MAKES YOU THING I'M A GUY?

That stops him cold. It's never occurred to him that he could be talking to a *girl*. An Liu's hands freeze over the keyboard. He hasn't talked to a girl since . . .

He's never talked to a girl.

Never talked to any female, except for his mother.

And it's been so long.

12GOLDENGATE12: OH, DON'T FREAK OUT, DUDE. WHAT IS IT WITH NERDS, IT'S LIKE XX IS KRYPTONITE

318

LAMORT377: WHAT'S KRYPTONITE?

12GOLDENGATE12: LOL

12GOLDENGATE12: WE STILL FRIENDS?

LAMORT377: YOU KNOW IT

12GOLDENGATE12: PROVE IT.

LAMORT377: HOW?

12GOLDENGATE12: I TOLD YOU SOMETHING ABOUT ME. YOU TELL ME SOMETHING ABOUT YOU. SOMETHING TRUE

An Liu hesitates, but only for a moment. Then he takes a *blinkSHIVERblink* deep breath.

LAMORT377: I'M LOOKING FOR MY MOTHER

12GOLDENGATE12: HUH

12GOLDENGATE12: YOU FOUND HER YET?

He regrets it already. His father has *blinkblinkblink* taught him that weaknesses exist for exploitation. And now 12goldengate12 knows An's greatest weakness of all. What was he *blinkSHIVER* thinking?

12GOLDENGATE12: MAYBE I CAN HELP

12GOLDENGATE12: TELL ME HER NAME

12GOLDENGATE12: COME ON, YOU CHICKEN?

12GOLDENGATE12: YOU SHOW ME YOURS, I'LL SHOW YOU MINE . . .

12GOLDENGATE12: HELLO?

12GOLDENGATE12: SHIT, COME ON

12GOLDENGATE12: DID I LOSE YOU? DON'T BE LIKE THAT

12GOLDENGATE12: PLEASE?

LAMORT377: DON'T ASK ME ABOUT THIS AGAIN

They don't talk about it again. 12goldengate12 doesn't risk asking any more questions about An and his life. Instead, she tells An about herself. About how much she hates her parents and what it was like to walk away from them. About how she was convinced she deserved better for herself, and finally ventured to find it.

An is *blinkblinkblink* stunned by all of it.

To *BLINK* want better.

To imagine *deserving* better.

These are things that have never occurred to him.

Life is what life is; that's what he's always *SHIVERblink* assumed.

That's what he's been taught.

Sometimes life is hard.

Always life is pain.

Never is it happy, and how could happy be something one is
blink-shiver entitled to ask for?

An Liu has *blinkSHIVER* asked for only one thing in his life, and the
consequences will *blinkblinkblinkblinkblinkblinkblinkblinkblink* be
with him forever.

He certainly didn't ask for 12goldengate12's help, and has no intention
of doing so.

But 12goldengate12 doesn't wait to be asked.

12GOLDENGATE12: I HAVE SOMETHING TO CONFESS

12GOLDENGATE12: I FIGURED OUT WHO YOU ARE. YOUR NAME. AND I DID SOME
DIGGING. I THINK I FOUND YOUR MOTHER FOR YOU. SENDING YOU THE FILES NOW

12GOLDENGATE12: I'M SORRY

The files are a collection of photographs, videos, and police files that,
pieced together, tell a clear story:

An anonymous corpse on a morgue slab.

A coroner's report of a bullet wound in the forehead.

A ballistics report tracing ownership of the gun back to a prominent
and apparently well-connected Xi'an businessman who has his name
blacked out in all files.

A pauper's grave.

An Liu *blink* understands; he realizes now he should have understood
long ago.

Of course his mother is dead.

Of course his father killed her.

Of course.

* * *

blinkblinkblinkblinkblinkblinkblinkblinkblinkblinkblinkblink
blinkblinkblinkblinkblinkblinkblinkblinkblinkblinkblinkblink
blinkblinkblinkblinkblinkblinkblinkblinkblinkblinkblinkblink
blinkblinkblinkblinkblinkblinkblinkblinkblinkblinkblinkblink
blinkblinkblinkblinkblinkblinkblinkblinkblinkblinkblinkblink
blinkblinkblinkblinkblinkblinkblinkblinkblinkblinkblinkblink
blinkblinkblinkblinkblinkblinkblinkblinkblinkblinkblinkblink
blinkblinkblinkblinkblinkblinkSHIVERblinkblinkblinkblinkblink
blinkblinkblinkblinkblinkblinkblinkblinkblinkblinkblinkblink
blinkblinkblinkblinkblinkblinkblinkblinkblinkblinkblinkblink
blinkblinkblinkblinkblinkblinkblinkblinkblinkblinkblinkblink
blinkblinkblinkblinkblinkblinkblinkblinkblinkblinkblinkblink
blinkblinkblinkblinkblinkblinkblinkblinkblinkblinkblinkblink
blinkblinkblinkblinkblinkblinkblinkblinkblinkblinkblinkblink

The first time his father locks him in the box of rats, An is five years old and thinks he will die.

He wants to die.

Death would be better than this oppressive darkness, the scritch-scratch of tiny claws against his skin, the whisper-soft brush of fur, the screech and squeal of the rodents as they scamper up and down his body, biting and biting and biting, and An screams himself hoarse and prays to lose his mind and still the rats run and scratch and nuzzle and bite.

He lies very still.

In his hand, he clutches a scrap of his mother's dress. He takes it with him everywhere, sleeps with it under his pillow at night, breathes it in when he wakes, though it no longer smells like her.

He holds tight to it now, holds tight to her, imagines her here with him in the dark, smoothing his hair, whispering in his ear, promising him that she will save him, she will love him, she will come back for him.

He just needs to be patient.

He just needs to hold on.

When he comes back to himself, he knows what he has to do.

First, he finds a needle. He drains a pen of its red ink. Then slowly, painstakingly, working around his *blink-shiver* tics, he tattoos a bloodred tear beneath his left eye. So he will always remember this day, always remember what has been taken from him.

Then he kills the messenger.

It's unacceptable that there be someone out there who knows who he is and what he has lost. That cannot *blinkSHIVER* stand.

It was his mistake, exposing *shiver-shiver-blink* his weakness. But 12goldengate12 is the one who will bear the consequences.

An knows enough about her to find her. A commune of hackers at the heart of San Francisco—that level of computing puts out a signal as bright as the sun. He doesn't need to know her name to destroy her. He just needs to know her geographical coordinates the next time she's online.

12GOLDENGATE12: HOW MANY TIMES DO I HAVE TO SAY SORRY.

12GOLDENGATE12: I THOUGHT I WAS HELPING

LAMORT377: IT'S OKAY

12GOLDENGATE12: THERE YOU ARE! THOUGHT I LOST YOU. SRSLY, DUDE, DIDN'T MEAN TO OVERSTEP

LAMORT377: YOU'LL MAKE IT UP TO ME

12GOLDENGATE12: HOW?

An needs only to *blink* hack into the nearest *shiver* drone and *blinkblinkblinkblink* command it to drop its *blink-shiver-blink* payload. It's that easy.

Shiver.

12goldengate12 was a friend, and so An Liu gifted her with a merciful death.

The others will not be so lucky.

His father has taught him pain; his uncles have taught him patience. He has watched them *BLINK* play their parts, pretend respect, obey orders, bide their time.

Now An Liu does the same.

He takes his time; he wants to do this right.

There are *shiver-blink* things he needs to know. Things about the Shang, about Endgame, about being the Player that he has *SHIVER* never bothered to ask. The Shang elders believe in the ancient ways—but they live in the modern world. They cannot hide from An Liu's cyber-reach.

He learns of the council, how it *blinkblink* leaves Player training in the hands of family. How the father of a Player has *SHIVER-blink* ultimate control.

It has always been the way.

His 11th birthday passes without note. An feels as if a century has passed since the last one. That boy from a year ago was whole; that boy thought he could take on his father in a fair fight.

The boy An has become knows better.

He won't make the same mistake again.

He won't make any mistakes again. He proceeds carefully. He studies the lives of Players past. No Player has ever been stripped of his title—no matter his crime.

Once the oracle bones speak, fate cannot be changed.

An Liu will be the Shang Player.

No matter what he *SHIVERblinkSHIVER* does.

He learns that pain is, indeed, the Shang way, but not his father's kind of pain. This is *blink* new. The elders would, perhaps, not approve. But neither will they *shiver-blink* interfere.

That makes them guilty, An Liu thinks. As guilty as anyone.

But he will deal with that later. He will deal with all of them. He has nothing but time.

Time and fury.

Upstairs, his father and his uncles sleep peacefully through one night after another, dreaming, perhaps, of new torments to impose on their Player, the boy they've turned into a monster. They think he still needs to be trained; they don't know that he's *blinkblink* learned his final lesson.

He's learned that there is no hope. No escape. No return to a happier past, no flight into a better future.

There is only *blinkSHIVER* destruction and pain.

Only *SHIVERSHIVERSHIVERblink* the thing he's become.

The thing they made him.

La Mort 377.

Walking death. He will bring it to his father and his uncles—and when the time comes, he will bring it to his entire line. His entire species. Someday, finally, an end to misery and the delusions of life. An end to everything.

There are many ways to kill. An considers a bullet, since this is what took his mother away. But bullets are too fast, too merciful.

An wants it to *blinkblinkblink* hurt.

He considers his bare hands, but this is too risky. To win a fight to the death, you must have the will to live.

Does he have that? Truly?

An no longer knows.

blink

He has the urge to kill. This is good enough.

He considers sparing his uncles.

He remembers whispers overheard, snatches of conversation, evidence, perhaps, that they *SHIVER* are not bad men. That *blinkblink* they think they have no choice. His father is a killer; he knows that now. His uncles *shiverBLINK* have always known.

Maybe they were afraid for their lives.

So they sacrificed his.

This, perhaps, An Liu could have forgiven.

His mother's sacrifice? He cannot.

He comes to a decision. He makes a plan. He waits one week, then another, until he is *blink-shiver* sure. Until he is ready.

At night, he turns his face to the sky. "I-i-i-i-i-s thiiiis r-r-r-ight?" he

asks his mother, because he does this for her. "I-i-i-i-is thiiiis what
y-y-y-you w-w-want?" *BLINK*

His mother never answers, because, of course, they've taken her away
from him.

In the end, that's answer enough.

An slips into the kitchen and crumbles a bottle of sleeping pills into a
bottle of rice whiskey. He knows his father and uncles drink heartily
from it every night.

A day passes. He waits. As dinner comes, he listens at the door, hears
their merriment, the clink of glasses, the yawns and the thumps as
they stumble off dazedly to bed. Then An creeps up his stairs and
enters the first bedroom he comes to, where his youngest uncle, the
one who used to be his favorite, snores loudly. An douses him with the
whiskey—and lights a match.

He slips out of the room as the fire catches, is already halfway to the
next bedroom before his uncle begins to scream.

One by one, he lights his uncles on fire, until the house fills with
agonized cries and the smell of burning flesh.

His father slumbers on.

An pours the whiskey.

Whispers a silent prayer to his mother.

Lights the match.

This time, he doesn't leave the room, not yet. This time, he watches the
flesh singe and burn. He waits for the pain to cut through the drugs
and rouse his father from sleep; he listens, joy in his heart, to his
father's screams. Their eyes meet, and in those fathomless black pools,
An Liu sees pure terror, and An smiles.

His heart pings with something familiar, something he hasn't felt for a
very long time. This, he finally understands, is how it feels to be happy.
"Y-y-y-you—" An stops. *Blinks.* The moment is too much for his clumsy
tongue.

So he says what he needs to say in the silence of his mind.

You have reaped what you have sown.

He smiles, heart bursting with joy, watching his father burn and burn, until the flames leap from bed to floor to walls, and An Liu knows that if he lingers any longer, the fire will consume him along with his family.

He escapes the inferno, leaves his father and his uncles to their flaming death, watches the house burn to the ground, then slips away into the night.

Not because he craves any more time in this *blinkSHIVER* hell called life.

But because he *blink* has *blink* more to *blink* do.

He will go to the *blinkBLINK* Shang elders and tell them of this *SHIVERblink* tragedy. Perhaps they will suspect the truth.

But they will do nothing about it.

An Liu is *blinkSHIVER* fated to be their Player. With his father *BLINKBLINKBLINK* dead, he is in control. His *blinkblink* training is *SHIVER* complete. He is *blinkblink* soon to ascend. They will *SHIVERblink* leave him alone, as they have before.

This is the Shang way. All they care is that he Play, and he will not *blink* let them down.

He's been given a sacred duty, and he *shiverBLINK* will stay alive until he can complete it.

Until *blinkblinkblink* Endgame comes, and he can offer his gift to the Shang and all the bloodlines of earth.

He will *blinkSHIVERblink* bring them death, as he's brought his father death, as his father brought his mother death.

He will bring an end to everything.

And then, when the earth is dark and cold and empty, when all is burned to ash, he will *blinkblinkblinkblinkblink* finally be at peace.

His mother wakes him with a soft kiss on the forehead.

"Happy birthday, Little Liu," she says, tickling his feet until he laughs himself fully out of sleep. "Do you remember how old you are today?"

An holds up four fingers.

"That's my little man!"

"Am I a big man today, Mother?"

"Not yet, sweet," she says. "Don't be in such a hurry to grow up. You have plenty of time."

"What will happen then?" An asks.

"When?"

"When I grow up. When I am a big man."

"Oh." She smiles, sits down on the bed, and pulls him onto her lap. "I'm going to tell you a secret, Little Liu. Are you ready?"

An nods eagerly. He loves secrets.

"When you grow up?" She tickles him again, and he tries to wiggle away, but she's holding on too tight. He hopes she will never let go. "Little An Liu, when you grow up, you're going to change the world."

AKSUMITE
HILAL

Hilal is searching for peace.

He sifts through the dark recesses of his mind, seeking an oasis of calm.

The effort is in vain.

He longs for the still inner quiet that has sustained him for so many years. In times of chaos, pain, fear, he has always had this escape: to a silence deep inside. A placid water, smooth as glass.

But today, as yesterday, as the day before, he is troubled. Chased by memories.

He sits on the concrete floor of his hut, back pressed to the wall. Sunbeams filter through the thatched roof, painting prisms of light across his ebony skin. The hut hums with electricity, it contains half the computing power in Ethiopia, but today Hilal has no interest in the bits of data whirring through its veins.

This small compound in the Kingdom of Aksum is Hilal's home, and has been since he was six years old. But it doesn't feel much like home anymore.

One year ago, he was sent away from this place by his spiritual master. Eben ibn Mohammed al-Julan had sent Hilal out into the world many times before, for purposes of training or education. Sometimes, there is no clear mission, simply the instructions: Watch. Listen. Learn. *The true Player must be a citizen of the world,* Eben likes to say, and so Hilal has sampled cultures across the globe.

But this trip was different, for it was meant to last a year.

"How can I leave for so long?" Hilal said. "These are my people. And I am their Player. If Endgame begins—"

"If Endgame begins, I will summon you home. There are things you must learn that I cannot teach you, Hilal."

This seemed impossible to Hilal; surely, if it was worth knowing, his master could teach it.

"It will be good for you to live among people for a time," Master Eben said. "And it will be good for them, to live with a man such as you." He smiled gently. "We can't simply wait around for Endgame to arrive, can we?"

"We must spend each day saving the world as best we can," Hilal said dutifully. This was one of the first lessons his master ever taught him. And so he traveled halfway across the continent and took up residence in a village of strangers. He traded in days of study and weapons training for long hours of educating children, tending to the sick, cooking for the elderly, helping with the construction of a new sewage system. They knew nothing of him when he arrived. Hilal ibn Isa al-Salt was a mystery to them, and not a particularly interesting one. They didn't know or care that he was the great-grandson of Ezana or the grandson of Gebre Mesquel Lalibela, nor that he was the Aksumite Player, sworn to save his bloodline when Endgame comes, nor that he was in lifelong pursuit of a being called Ea, the soulless leader of the Brotherhood of the Snake. They didn't know about Endgame itself. They knew only that he was a stranger in their homeland, that he came bearing food and medicine and an ancient truth. And, gradually, they came to trust him, even love him, as he began to love them in return. He taught them what he could about the workings of the human soul—and learned, in turn, what it meant to be part of village life. Celebrating its small triumphs and mourning its losses, trading cheerful gossip and mediating petty grudges—Hilal became one of them. Or, at least, so it seemed.

They came to trust him, and when disease swept through the village like a firestorm, leaping from family to family and leaving only corpses behind, they thought Hilal might save them.

Instead, he abandoned them.

"Remember," his master told him, when he reported the situation, "your life is more precious than they know. Guard it well. Come home."

The village was full of brave men and women risking infection and death to take care of the ones they loved—but Hilal, who'd been raised to have no fear for his own life, to devote himself to the good of others, behaved like a coward. Snuck away in the dark of night. He was forbidden from risking himself; he was meant to believe that his life was more important than theirs.

So he fled from infection, from tainted blood and stacked corpses; he fled home.

That was two weeks ago. Fourteen days readjusting to the rhythms and comforts of home.

Trying to forget the village he left behind. The faces of mothers clutching babies to their chests, of children kicking soccer balls across barren fields, of strong men bearing heavy loads, providing for their families. So many people, and Hilal loved them all, and now he can only wonder what has become of them.

Whether any of them are left.

As a Player, he has pledged himself to saving the souls of all men, but saving individual men and women, and their children? That is beyond his parameters.

Still, he would have liked to try.

Every night, in his dreams, he tries again.

The door creaks open.

Hilal flies to his feet, takes a defensive stance, battle ready.

But it is no enemy. Hilal's face relaxes into a smile. He has been meditating in isolation for two weeks, and if his solitude is to be broken, this is the man to break it. "Greetings, Master," he says in eager welcome.

"You are the Player now," Eben ibn Mohammed al-Julan corrects him. "I am the master no more."

Hilal bows his head to acknowledge the claim, but will never agree to it. Eben has been his master and spiritual guide since he was a very small child—it was Eben who selected him, of all the children scrambling through the fields of his village, to train for this sacred role. Eben, a former Player, saw something shining from Hilal, knew somehow, even then, that Hilal had been anointed by the Lord. Master Eben took Hilal into his own home, taught him how to speak, how to think, how to fight, and, most importantly, how to follow a righteous path, how to serve and spread the ancient truth.

Someday, Hilal assumes, *he* will be the one to venture across the countryside, searching children's faces for the spark of the divine. This is how it has always been done: the Players of the past choosing those of the future. He has asked Eben many times what it was that the master saw—how he is meant to recognize the sign of a future Player, how he will know he has chosen wisely. Eben will only ever say, *When the time comes, you will know. The future Player will make himself known to you, as you made yourself known to me.*

Hilal wonders whether he will ever have Master Eben's wisdom— whether he will be able to train a new generation of Players as Eben trained him. It seems to him that Eben will forever be the master, Hilal the willing student.

"You seem troubled," Eben says, always able to read the truth in Hilal's face.

"I am having difficulty putting my memories of the year to rest," Hilal admits. "I feel like a traitor to all the people I've left behind."

"Those are not your people," Eben reminds him, "any more or less than all men of Earth are your people. Their mission is not your mission."

Hilal reminds himself that Eben knows best, and that Hilal's responsibilities to the Aksumite line and its future take precedence above all else. A hundred miles from here, a child is training with a master of his own, preparing to take on the role of Player when Hilal ages out, but he is not old enough yet—not ready. Were Hilal to die, the Aksumites would be left without a champion, and that cannot be. He had no choice but to save himself. He knows that.

Still.

Not since childhood has Hilal spent so much time amongst humanity, and though he did his best to remain removed—to remember that he was there to serve the villagers, not to become one of them—he was not entirely able to succeed.

Eben discourages personal relationships, individual bonds, anything that might distract Hilal from his commitment to the Aksumites as a whole.

God loves all his children equally, Eben likes to say, *and so must we.*

Hilal tries.

"I have come with a new task for you." Eben smiles gently, as if he has guessed at everything Hilal works so hard to hide. "Perhaps it will help you turn your attention away from the past."

"Anything, Master."

"We have located the Book of Ouazebas."

Hilal's eyes widen. "But I thought that was lost in the destruction of the Bayt al-Hikma?"

Bayt al-Hikma, the House of Wisdom, once a crown jewel of the Islamic Empire and the largest library in the world, has been in ruins for nearly 800 years. Hilal believed the majority of its works—among them a sacred Aksumite manuscript from the 4th century AD—were lost forever. According to legend, the Book of Ouazebas tells the story of an early Aksumite king's battle with the Brotherhood of the Snake. Some say it contains the secret of finding and defeating the brotherhood's ancient evil leader, Ea, once and for all. Few have harbored hope of finding the manuscript intact.

"The book has resurfaced in Egypt," Eben says. "It was found in an archaeological dig several months ago and has since found its way to the Museum of Antiquities in Cairo. As you can imagine, we've done our best to negotiate for its return to its native land, but the

Egyptian authorities refuse."

"You want me to retrieve it for you," Hilal guesses.

"For all of us," Eben says. "This could be what we've been waiting for. The answer to centuries of fruitless searching, the weapon we need in our final war. You, Hilal, could save us."

Hilal sloughs off the guilt and regret that has been weighing him down for the last two weeks. He stands tall and proud. "I am ready, Master. Tell me what you need me to do."

All things being equal, Hilal prefers walking to any other form of transportation. He prefers to wear loose, flowing robes that conform to the motion of his body and flap in the breeze; he prefers sandals with a single strip that expose his feet to the sand and the elements. He likes to feel the ground beneath him and the people around him, to move through the world as the ancients did, at one with the Earth and its creatures.

But walking to Cairo would take more than a month, and his master doesn't want to wait.

So Hilal takes a truck across the Sudanese border, then hops a rickety charter plane to Cairo, and does it all in the constrictive costume of a modern-day teenager. He wears jeans and closed-toe black sneakers and a garish T-shirt emblazoned with some nonsensical Japanese. "You need to fit in," Eben told him.

"They will stare anyway," Hilal pointed out. "They always do."

He says it not with arrogance or false modesty, but as a simple truth. Hilal, with his dark skin smooth and fathomless as marble, his azure eyes, his high cheekbones and ivory smile, is beautiful—almost inhumanly so. He knows this because he's been told, many a time, and because of the way strangers stare at him, sometimes with awe, sometimes with desire. It's not a thing to be vain about or ashamed of, simply a quality he's been endowed with, and he would be a fool to take exceptional pride in it. But he would be a bigger fool not to use it, when it can be used.

Fortunately, the men on this plane—businessmen, from the look of it, convinced of the great import of their petty deals—have better things to do than wonder about the tall, almost regal seventeen-year-old sharing their airspace. Hilal dons headphones for the duration of the voyage and bounces along to an imaginary beat, pretending to be lost in his own head.

Humans, he's noticed, are all too willing to believe that they're invisible. And it's only when they think no one is looking that they reveal their true selves. So Hilal sees the nervous primping of the elderly man in the bow tie and understands that he's on his way to a romantic rendezvous, while the furtive young man with the mustache and the briefcase he never lets out of his grip makes all too obvious his criminal intent. He sees that two other men are both employer and employee and father and son, that the father loathes and distrusts his offspring, while the son hopes and perhaps plots to soon have his father out of the way. He sees which of the men is a secret smoker, which is an alcoholic, which is satisfied with his life, and which hopes soon to end it.

They don't bother to see him at all.

The plane touches down in Cairo as the sun is setting, and his taxi battles brutal rush-hour traffic as it inches toward the museum. Hilal shifts impatiently on the leather seat—of course, if the museum is closed by the time he gets there, it won't be a problem; he'll find his own way inside. But he prefers to walk in through the front door: it's more dignified.

The setting sun glints off skyscrapers; overhead, the sky burns, and Hilal draws his patience from the moon, which bides its time, waiting for night's canopy to descend and the stars to show their faces.

The taxi screeches to a stop, and Hilal gives the driver twice the requested fare.

Here is the Museum of Antiquities, its white archway blazing bright against an orange facade, its classical Western architecture giving all the appearances of a European museum—belied only by the towering palm trees bracketing it on either side and the Egyptian flag flapping at its entrance.

The museum, Hilal knows, has been instrumental in the cause of returning stolen artifacts to their land of origin, chasing Egyptian antiquities halfway across the world, statues and jewels from tombs excavated centuries before, bought and sold and hoarded in private collections—bringing them back home.

Were he quicker to anger, Hilal might be enraged by the hypocrisy of it, the nerve of these curators and government officials who stake their own national claim while dismissing the Aksumites out of hand. But Hilal only smiles gently at the irony. It is another thing he's noticed about people, including his own: they have one set of rules for themselves, another for the rest of the world. And all rules are allowed to be broken, for convenience's sake.

In the new era, the era Hilal dreams of and works toward, there will be only one rule for the whole of mankind: the golden rule, and this is what Hilal tries to live by.

This is all that binds him, which is why it bothers him not at all to break Egyptian law and smuggle a priceless artifact out of the country. Laws like those are, literally, made to be broken.

Hilal purchases an entry to the museum and lets himself be absorbed by the crowds. He ignores the exhibits and instead surveys security measures, the cameras lodged in corners, the alarm system trip wires snaking along the wall, the glass cabinets with their feeble locks protecting the most valuable of valuables. So many blind spots, beyond the reach of both human and mechanical eyes. The museum's security is riddled with gaps he can exploit. It's almost as if they *want* their goods stolen. Even the Aksumite manuscript, worth more than all the other artifacts in this building put together, is housed in a room protected only by a flimsy alarm system and a glass case. As the clock ticks toward closing time, Hilal drifts through the crowd ogling the Aksumite exhibit, noting both the foolish security measures and the bored expressions on the tourists' faces. They have come to

Cairo to see elaborate statues and golden tombs, not some musty old manuscript in a language no one can understand. They don't know the value of what they're looking at, and they don't deserve to see it—as the museum doesn't deserve to hoard it. Hilal sees that the liberation of this manuscript is a righteous act.

And he sees that it will be child's play.

Hilal melts into the shadows, slips past a yellow rope into a corridor meant only for museum personnel—a corridor without any cameras. As if employees are to be trusted more than strangers; the assumption is kind, if foolish. The door to the basement is sealed with a padlock—not a problem. Hilal's backpack has several hidden compartments, packed with tools for any eventuality. He sprays the lock with compressed difluoroethane, which freezes the steel in seconds and turns it brittle enough to shatter under the pressure of a small hammer. He lets himself into the service stairwell and descends into the basement, where he waits out the time until closing.

Above him, somewhere, the sounds of tourists oohing and aahing, children whining, parents snapping, guards patrolling, and then, slowly, all noise fades away, the lights dim, and the museum goes still. Hilal ventures out of his hiding hole. He slides through the shadows and the security blind spots and makes his way toward the special exhibit area, where the Aksumite manuscript awaits him under glass. He has spent years honing his senses and his instincts, and has developed an animal's sixth sense of danger—he can feel the presence of the security guards in his bones. One pads across the floor above him; one snores in the corridor to his east. They should be easy enough to avoid—and, if not avoided, dispensed with.

All things being equal, he prefers not to hurt anyone.

But he will do what he has to do.

The overhead lights are off, but the displays remain illuminated. Hilal passes marble statues and golden busts, ancient weapons and divine engravings. He tiptoes through rooms crowded with stucco scribes and wooden priests. So many of the faces he recognizes from his studies—there is Akhenaton; there is Queen Nefertiti; there is the gold mask of Tutankhamen; there is the head of Hathor as a cow. Then, finally, in a small room of its own at the far end of the western wing, is the Book of Ouazebas, lit from below, seeming to glow in its glass case. The book looks different, now that it's alone—almost as if it were waiting for the tourists to leave before it came to life. The lock is alarmed, but this doesn't concern Hilal: he has no intention of breaking the lock.

Instead he pulls a slim blade from his pack, sharp enough to cut glass, and slices a square in the case just big enough for the manuscript to fit through. He reaches in and takes hold of the book of his people. He imagines it warming in his grip, as if it knows him, knows he will be its vehicle, the one to carry it home.

Very carefully, Hilal wraps the book in a soft, holy cloth he's brought with him, then tucks the sacred package into his bag. He slings the pack over his shoulder and makes his way toward the front door. One pair of wire clippers, one swift snip of the trip wire is all it takes to disable the alarm on the entrance and push the door open—it's not even locked from the inside.

Hilal knows it's a little foolish, almost arrogant, perhaps, leaving like this, in full view of anyone who might be watching. But he's laid claim to what rightfully belongs to his people; he doesn't want to slither away like a snake. He *is* arrogant, or at least proud, and he chooses to stride through the front entrance, leaving as he came in, without fear or shame.

As he is pushing through the door, a guard catches sight of him, shouts for him to halt. Hilal could slip away—no doubt he is faster than this burly man armed only with an ancient walkie-talkie. Instead he does as he is told, and stops in place.

"What are you doing here?" the man barks angrily. "The museum is closed."

Hilal offers the guard a peaceable smile, his grip on his backpack tightening imperceptibly. "Boring class field trip, you know?" he says in flawless Arabic. "I decided to take a nap on one of those fancy pharaoh beds you've got here, and when I woke up, the place was all dark. Spooky, right?"

The security guard peers suspiciously at him, but Hilal only blinks sleepily, affecting the apathy and ignorance of a schoolboy. The guard sees only what Hilal wants him to see: a bored teenager, delinquent in his studies, uninterested in anything but his music and his T-shirt collection.

The guard laughs. "Can't say I blame you, kid. Done it myself, on occasion. But don't let it happen again, you hear?"

"I have no plans of ever coming back," Hilal says honestly.

"Can't say I blame you for that either," the guard says again, and shakes Hilal's hand before sending him on his way.

That easily, the mission is accomplished: Hilal carries the priceless manuscript down the stairs, off the museum grounds, and into the Cairo night.

He's in the mood to walk, and he gives in to temptation, strolling down the palm-lined street, inhaling the smells and sounds of city life, even at this hour, a teeming chaos he so rarely has a chance to experience. He walks down Meret Basha, thinking he will pick up some falafel for himself in Tahrir Square and then get a taxi to the airport.

This is his first mistake.

Hilal has spent his life in cloistered study. He knows innumerable languages of man and machine; he has memorized his own Bible and several others; with the machetes he carries in his pack, he could slice up a battalion of men without breaking a sweat. In so many ways, he is wise beyond his years. But when it comes to the rhythm of city life, he is a child, innocent and easily distracted, led astray by bright colors and the wild music of humanity en masse, a stranger in a very strange land.

He assumes the noise and vibrancy he sees around him are normal; he assumes the shouts and cheers he hears in the distance are simply the heartbeat of Cairo, the everyday thunder and lightning of urban life. It's only when he approaches the square, discovers the pulsing horde of protesters, waving flags, thrusting handmade posters in the air, chanting slogans, that he realizes what he's stumbled into—and by the time he does, the amoeba-like crowd has absorbed him.

The poster-board signs allege government offenses, call for resignations; fists punch at the sky, voices call out for justice, for power, for freedom. The protesters are young and old, men and women, some in full hijab, some in modern gear, all of them vibrating with ecstatic rage. The square is lit with army spotlights, and men in uniform push through the mass of bodies, trying to restrain and subdue the protesters. Clouds of tear gas bloom over the crowd.

Hilal has to get out of here.

He can't afford to tangle with the authorities, not with the precious, illicit cargo he carries. He threads through the crowd, aiming for the eastern edge of the square, trying to avoid contact or notice, and is almost through, when he sees her.

A girl about his age, in nearly identical uniform, except that her black T-shirt reads, in English, *Live free or die.* She is smiling radiantly— even as the soldier looms over her and slams his elbow into her face. Even as she staggers backward, blood spattering from her nose.

"Stop that!" Hilal shouts, before he thinks better of it.

The soldier is raising a nightstick overhead, is slamming it down toward the girl, but before he can hit her again, Hilal has plucked the weapon from the man's hand, has wrapped it around his neck, squeezing just tight enough to cut off his airflow.

The soldier drops to the ground beside the girl, and a ripple runs through the crowd. Beneath the noise of protest, Hilal hears the drumbeat of boot steps making its way toward him. More soldiers, more trouble.

Exactly what he can't afford.

He scoops up the girl, who weighs almost nothing in his strong arms.

There's a whisper at his ear. "Bring her this way. Hurry!"

He turns, and two slim figures, one in a hoodie, the other in full veil, beckon. The boy in the hoodie rushes to the girl's side, staunches her bloody nose. The veiled protester starts clearing a pathway through the crowd. Hilal is no fool, and knows better than to trust a stranger's urgent entreaty. But as a clear corridor melts open before them, he decides his best course of action is to carry the girl's limp body through. He's more than capable of handling whatever lies in store for him on the other side, and he's not about to leave the girl behind, easy prey for the soldiers or the angry crowd.

"Hurry," the boy urges again, and Hilal follows them through the protest, cradling the girl in his arms like a small child.

"I'll take her now," the boy says, as the protest fades away behind them and they emerge onto a quiet street. He holds out his arms, but Hilal shakes his head. He's taken responsibility for this girl; he will let her go only when he's certain she's safe.

"I will see her safely home," he tells the two strangers.

"Safe?" the girl snorts behind her veil. "What country are you living in? And you really think we're going to tell you where we live?"

"Be nice, Dalila," the boy says. "He helped us out back there. We can trust him."

"He helped himself out with that soldier, then helped himself to Rabiah. Use your head, Akil. You want to trust him just because he's pretty?"

"You seem to be assuming I want your trust," Hilal says. "Or that I would be so foolish as to trust you. I simply want to see the girl to safety and be on my way."

"What do you care about her?" Dalila asks gruffly.

"I care about the safety of all people," Hilal says. "Hers happens to be the one I can most immediately safeguard."

"Forget what country are you from; what *planet* are you from?" Dalila says, and Hilal doesn't need to see her face to know her eyes are rolling.

"I don't care if he's from Jupiter," Akil snaps. "I care about getting us off the streets and making sure Rabiah's okay. You want to keep her safe?" he asks Hilal. "Then you follow us. Now."

Hilal tells himself that a momentary delay is actually a good thing—it will be better to stay off the streets tonight, find his way across the border come morning, once the protests have died down and he can carefully navigate their aftermath. Tonight there will be soldiers patrolling the streets and the borders; the nation will be on high alert, and Hilal can't afford to be noticed.

Better, for the mission, to wait.

He's not about to let himself be distracted, or allow these strangers or their cause to interfere with his own.

The girl, warm and stirring in his arms, is no one special; he will simply help her as he would help any living creature in pain or need, and then he will go home.

The strangers turn down one dark alley after another, carving an impossibly labyrinthine path through the Cairo night.

Hilal follows.

There are seven of them, all students at the university, all members of a liberal political group recently outlawed by the government. They use this place, a filthy apartment in a building on the edge of the slums, a building that looks abandoned and condemned, as their planning headquarters and safe house. It stinks of coriander and sweat.

Rabiah is their leader—and a prime instigator of the night's protest. She lies now on a threadbare couch, a hot towel on her forehead, barking orders at the others; the night's protest hasn't yet ended, and already they're making plans for another.

They've offered Hilal a bed—really, a spot on the floor and a thin blanket—for the night. In gratitude, Rabiah says, for helping the cause.

That's how she phrases it. Not "helping me," but "helping the cause."

As if they are the same.

"And what *is* your cause?" Hilal asks. He lets just enough of an accent slip into his voice to let them assume he is from elsewhere.

Conversation ceases, and they look at him like he's a fool.

"Don't you read the newspaper?" Akil asks. He doesn't stray far from Rabiah's side, and from the way he looks at her, brushes against her every chance he gets, Hilal can tell the boy is in love. From the way Rabiah looks at him—or, rather, looks through him—Hilal can tell she has no idea. And perhaps wouldn't care if she did.

"Don't you live?" Rabiah asks. "Don't you breathe?"

Hilal lives and breathes in cloistered isolation: even his missionary time has been intensely focused on the local, not the global. He has an encyclopedic knowledge of the ancient world, the strengths and frailties of the human body, the detailed myths and traditions of divinity across the globe, and those international events that might signify Endgame-related action: conflict between the bloodlines or a message from the stars. His knowledge of petty national politics is somewhat . . . lacking.

"Today is the anniversary of the revolution," Dalila explains. She has removed her veil, revealing a soft, rounded face and large, friendly brown eyes that belie the edge in her voice. "One year passes, and another, and nothing changes."

"Nothing will ever change, unless enough of us raise our voices to insist on it," Rabiah says. She's lying down, an ugly purple bruise blooming across her face, yet somehow she still radiates strength.

The others join in, spilling out their grudges against the government, their dreams of a new Egypt, a true democracy governed by rule of law. An end to oppression, an end to corruption, Rabiah tells him, eyes blazing. Freedom of speech. Fair wages. Antidiscrimination laws.

"Equality for women," Dalila says.

"Equality for everyone," adds Farid, a boy with a sharp gaze and a neatly trimmed beard. He slips an arm around the waist of the young man next to him, and they smile at each other.

"And you believe you can accomplish all these things with a night of protests?" Hilal asks. He realizes he has little grasp of politics, but this seems far-fetched.

"One night?" Rabiah laughs. "This is only the beginning, my naïve friend. This isn't a night; this is a *movement*. And we will move mountains."

"It sounds like a noble effort," Hilal says. "I wish you good fortune."

"It's not about luck," Rabiah says. "It's about hard work. So how about it?"

"Excuse me?"

"How about joining us?" she says. "You know how to fight, that's obvious, and you're no coward. You're well-spoken, you're attractive—"

Dalila coughs. "Understatement of the year."

The others laugh, but not Rabiah. "Exactly. You're ridiculously handsome, Hilal, and people are shallow. They respond to that. We could use you. We're having a rally tomorrow afternoon outside the university; you could—"

"No, thank you." Hilal tucks his bag into his chest, reassuring himself that the manuscript is still safe inside. He has to get the book back to Ethiopia, back to Eben. Right now, that can be his only priority. "I wish you luck with your fight, but I must return home to mine."

"You have something more important to do than change the world?"

"I prefer to effect change without fighting," Hilal says.

"No such thing."

"I disagree." Hilal is polite but firm. There is obfuscation here, because of course he *is* a fighter; he trains and prepares for the ultimate fight. But that is a higher battle, a battle *for* humanity rather than amongst it. He believes in the spirit of what he's saying—it is the spirit that has animated his life of service. "Choosing sides, waging a battle, these can be distractions. Who is helped, *today*, by your shaking fists and shouted slogans? While you demand justice for the poor, who will feed and clothe them?"

Rabiah snorts. "Ah . . . you're one of those."

"Give him a break," Akil urges her.

"No, I won't give him a break. He's everything that's wrong with this world." Rabiah looks Hilal up and down. "Let me guess, you're some kind of religious do-gooder."

"I do attempt to do good," Hilal allows.

"Missionary?" she guesses. "Think you can bring the Lord to a bunch of heathens?"

"I don't think in categories like that," Hilal protests. "I share the ancient truth, as I see it, yes. And I also share food and clothing and medicine. I *help* people."

"You help yourself feel better," Rabiah says. "That's it. If you really wanted to help people, you'd change the system that deprives them of food and clothing and medicine. You'd take a stand, fight for something. Instead of feeding the poor, you'd work to end hunger."

"You make complicated things sound simple," Hilal says, "but that doesn't make them so."

"Okay, then you tell me," Rabiah challenges him. "All those people you've supposedly helped, are they any better off now than they were before? You gave them a few meals, some medicine, but *structurally*? *Politically?* Is *anything* different? Did you change anything, or just say a few prayers and go on your way?"

Hilal doesn't want to argue with her anymore.

Hilal can't argue with her.

This girl is infuriating, but he respects her passion and admires her certainty. He feels a kinship with her, senses that, beneath the surface, they are more similar than she knows, both committed to saving their people, to creating a new world. He almost envies her, despite the apparent futility of her fight, because her battle is *now*. *We must spend each day saving the world,* Eben always says, but he also says, *You must save* yourself *for the final battle,* and these two directives are, for Hilal, increasingly difficult to reconcile.

Sometimes he tires of waiting.

"You're hearing me, aren't you?" Rabiah says, with the smile of someone who knows exactly how good she is at making people listen. "I'm getting through."

"Thank you for your hospitality," he tells her. She will think he's afraid to listen to any more of her talk, that he doubts his commitment to his own argument. Perhaps she will be right. "I must sleep now, in preparation for my journey. As I say, I wish you good fortune in your endeavors."

Despite her goading, he will say no more, and finally Rabiah gives up. Akil shows him a back room where he can stretch out and get some sleep. He uses his bag as a pillow.

"Don't mind her," Akil says. "She's on fire with this stuff. She can't see anything but the cause. She can't see that other people might . . . care about more than just one thing. That sometimes people are as important as systems." He frowns, casting his gaze into the distance, as if watching something approach that gives him great sorrow. "Sometimes I don't think she understands people at all."

"She sees the bigger picture," Hilal says. "Sometimes that's necessary."

Akil leaves him to sleep, but when Hilal closes his eyes, sleep won't come. He thinks about his own bigger picture, about Endgame and the Makers and the oath sworn by generations of Aksumites before him, that they will defend the ancient truth and protect their line at all costs.

He thinks about the village he's left behind, and the people there he was unable to help. How, even had he offered them a cure for their plague, it would not have rescued them from poverty; it would not have changed their system, or their futures. He thinks about how he has recused himself from intervening in the petty human squabbles of politics and governance, and that perhaps Rabiah is right, that this is naïve.

That this is wrong.

He listens to the soft murmur of voices from just beyond the door, these powerless students plotting to take on a nation—not sitting around, waiting for the war to come to them, waiting for their destiny to arrive at their doorstep, but making their own moment in history. Choosing *now*.

Hilal serves a higher cause, he reminds himself, and should be grateful for that.

But this night, in this restless darkness, he envies Rabiah and her friends and their hopeless fight.

He's almost sorry that, come the dawn, he will have to leave.

When the screaming begins, Hilal thinks he's dreaming it.

His dreams these days are full of horrors, screaming and gunfire and flames.

But this is no dream. This is the safe house filled with danger, soldiers knocking down doorways and guns drawn and these fierce protesters cowering in closets and beneath furniture. These are fighters with no idea how to fight.

Before he's fully shaken off sleep, Hilal is on his feet, a machete in each hand. They are his favorite weapons, deadly blades that feel like extensions of his limbs—of his very soul. The word *hate* is inscribed along the blade in his left hand. On the other, the word *love*.

Hilal detests violence.

But he is very, very good at it.

He streaks into the common room, where four soldiers have cuffed the students and are pushing them into a line against the wall.

Akil stands beside the soldiers, free. Abashed. Hilal, who sees into people so easily and sometimes too well, understands the situation immediately. Akil has betrayed them.

"I'll ask you once to set down your arms," Hilal tells the soldiers, politely but firmly. "I invite you to leave this place. Now." The soldiers whirl on him, but Hilal is already in motion, machetes slashing through the air. Gunfire echoes through the apartment, tears holes through the cheap plaster, but Hilal dances away from the bullets, ducks and spins and cuts down one soldier, slicing him from shoulder to hip. As he lashes a foot into the soft gut of a second, he slashes a bloody wound into the shoulder of the third, then spins, leaps over both of them, and lands hard on the fourth, knocking him to the floor. He doesn't want to kill these men, but he will if he has to.

"Retreat!" they're crying to one another, as Hilal knocks one weapon after another out of their hands, kicking the guns across the room, disarming and disabling all but the first soldier, the one with the gaping wound in his chest.

Hilal thinks him too bloody and beaten to be a threat, and so makes his mistake: he turns his back on the man.

Doesn't see him stagger to his feet, grab Rabiah around the neck, and put his gun to her head.

"Drop the knives, or she dies."

"You think we're scared of you, pig?" Rabiah struggles in his grasp, undaunted by the steel muzzle against her temple. "You think you can stop us? There are too many of us to stop."

"You said you wouldn't hurt her," Akil bleats.

"Shut up." The soldier is backing away with Rabiah. Hilal calculates the variables: the distance to the closest gun, the distance between his machetes and the soldier, the distance between the muzzle of the gun and Rabiah's temple.

He sets the machetes by his feet.

He will not risk her life.

"This one's under arrest," the soldier says, as his fellows join him in the doorway and back out of the apartment. "We'll be back for the rest of you."

"You did this." Dalila is pointing at Akil. "You turned on us, didn't you? Told them what we were up to, where to find us?"

Akil is crumpled on the floor, broken. "They threatened me. My family. You don't understand."

"Bullshit," snaps Farid, the one with the beard. "She didn't want you, so you decided to punish her. And all of us. Simple as that."

347

Akil rises to his feet. "You're all fools if you think you can win this. We're not talking David and Goliath. This isn't some storybook with a happy ending. This is the government. The *army*. And us—a bunch of kids who don't even know how to fire a gun. You stay here and fight your stupid fight to the death, if that's what you want to do. What I want to do is stay alive."

Hilal watches Akil walk out. No one stops him.

Now Dalila turns to Hilal. "You—how did you do that?" she demands. "Take out all those soldiers?"

"I think what she means is thank you," Farid says.

"No, I mean who the hell are you?"

Hilal bows his head. "I am no one."

"I think you should go," Dalila says.

Farid whirls on her. "Are you kidding me? This guy is some kind of one-man army, and you want to throw him out? Hilal, tell us you've changed your mind, that you'll join us."

"I—"

"Are you mad?" Dalila shouts. "Now is not the time to be trusting strangers! After Akil?"

"Akil is a worm," Farid says. "This boy is . . . who knows what this boy is, but he's obviously on our side."

Soon the room is filled with the noise of bickering, all of them seized with an opinion about what to do next, how to root out other potential traitors, whether to give in or fight harder, shout louder, press on.

Hilal sees how essential Rabiah is to this movement, how her sure vision gave them cohesion; how they are lost without her.

"What will happen to Rabiah?" he asks, his voice slicing through the clamor.

They fall silent.

"They'll take her away to prison," Dalila says softly. "There will be no trial. Or, if there is, it will be only for show. And once they've got her locked away, the things they'll do to her—"

"We won't let that happen," Farid says, resolutely. "We'll get her out. We need her."

Their will is evident; Hilal believes they want to save their leader. He believes, even, that they will attempt it.

And no doubt get themselves killed in the process.

Hilal has already saved Rabiah's life once: by Aksumite tradition, this makes her his responsibility—spiritually, she is now of his line.

By dallying in Cairo another day, ascertaining where a certain political prisoner might be held, he's only doing what he must. So he tells himself.

He tells his master only that there have been unforeseen complications, and that he will return home, soon. As they speak on an unsecured line, Eben asks no follow-up questions. Perhaps this is for the best.

He pinpoints Rabiah's location with ease, bribing two soldiers with the American dollars he's brought with him for emergencies. From there, Hilal stakes out the prison complex. Tora Prison is in South Cairo. It is divided into seven blocks, and holds activists and murderers alike. It costs him another handful of dollars to determine that Rabiah has been thrown in with a group of long-term inmates, all protesters against the government, some of whom have languished behind bars for years. He learns that Rabiah is guilty, as all the protesters are guilty, of violating a law forbidding groups larger than 10 from gathering in public spaces—and that it's likely she will be made an example of. Her capture is a coup.

He learns that the prison is guarded by tanks and machine-gun outposts and electrified barbed-wire gates and is thought to be impenetrable. It's everything the antiquities museum wasn't—but he's come to this country with the tools and skills to break into any facility, no matter how secure. He's prepared.

Still . . . Hilal considers leaving the manuscript somewhere safe, beyond the prison grounds, just in case something unexpected happens, something beyond his control.

He considers forgetting this plan entirely and returning home.

This is surely what his master would want, and what Hilal has always been taught to do. Think of the big picture. Safeguard the whole of humanity. Stay out of other people's fights; save himself for the final war.

This is prudent; this is the Aksumite way.

Rabiah may be his moral obligation, but she is also a stranger to him, one who knew the potential consequences of her actions when she took them, one with a devoted legion of followers who have far more reason than Hilal to risk themselves for her safety.

But whenever Hilal thinks about leaving Cairo, he remembers the pain of leaving people behind. Of valuing his own life over the lives of others. He remembers the faces of his villagers, looking at him for succor, trusting him to be their champion.

Eben would say that he has his own battle to fight, but who's to say that this hypothetical future battle is any more important than Rabiah's, which is real, which is *now*?

You are, Eben would say, and maybe he would be right, because the misery of these people pales in comparison to the potential extermination of billions.

Hilal can't argue with the phantom voice of his master.

But he can silence it.

He can promise himself that this risk is low, that this cause is just, that he can assist Rabiah's cause without endangering his own.

That perhaps he can redeem the betrayals of his past by giving Rabiah and her people a future.

He tucks the ancient book safely into his pack—logically, it might be safer left behind, but he can't stand to let it out of his sight. The book calls to him, *wants* to be in his possession. And so it shall be. He tugs the pack onto his shoulders, and, when nightfall comes, circles the prison, finds the hole in its defenses, a shadowed sliver in sight of neither camera nor guard, and, applying adhesives to his hands and sneakers, scales the outer wall in 90 seconds flat.

On the other side of the wall, he pulls out his hand-carved wooden blowgun, peers through its laser sight, and fires a dart into the man's neck. The blow is nonlethal; Hilal prefers not to kill unless he has to. Within seconds, the neurotoxin has infiltrated the bloodstream, and the guard drops noiselessly to the ground. He will wake in a few hours with a blinding headache but no long-term ill effects, and no idea how close he's come to death.

Hilal proceeds.

He fires darts at several more guards, taking them out efficiently, one by one. For the two security cameras he's unable to avoid, he chooses a more low-tech solution, cracking the lenses with two well-aimed pebbles. He scales another wall, and disables the engine of a tank while the driver is distracted by her cell phone, yelling at her boyfriend about standing her up the night before. He makes his way deeper and deeper into the prison complex, aware with every step that he's putting more distance—more walls, more bullets—between himself and safety.

When he reaches the block where, according to his sources, Rabiah is being held, he surveys the two guards at the entrance, gauging his options. After a few minutes, one of them descends his guard tower and retreats into the shadows, unzipping his pants and relieving himself.

Hilal sneaks up behind him and wraps an arm around his throat, squeezing like a vise. Thirty seconds later the man is unconscious, and in thirty more seconds Hilal has zipped himself into the ill-fitting uniform and looped the man's pass card around his neck.

He drags the body farther into the shadows, tucking it behind a Dumpster, but its absence will surely be noticed, sooner rather than later. Time is of the essence. To buy himself more of it, Hilal deploys a small electromagnetic dampening device that will disrupt any electrical or wireless signals in the immediate vicinity, so that even if the remaining guards do notice something awry, it will take a little extra effort for them to sound the alarm. He designed the device himself—sometimes, he told his master, a man needs more than pebbles.

Keeping his head down, Hilal enters the prison block, using the pass card to unlock one bolted door after another. He encounters only a few guards along his way, and none of them take much note of the tall young man on a mission. From behind some of the cell doors, he hears screams of pain, pleas to *stop*, wordless howls that say the same thing, so many souls here needing rescue, but Hilal forces himself to keep going. He's been taught to choose his battles.

Rabiah's cell is exactly where it's supposed to be.

She's slumped on the filthy floor, head pressed to her knees, and doesn't bother to look up when he lets himself in. "I told you, I don't care what you do to me; I'm not turning on my people."

"I would never ask you to do that," Hilal says gently.

Rabiah looks up—and treats him to the most radiant smile Hilal has ever seen. It seems to warm the dingy cell, light the cold stone with a holy glow. This smile embodies the ancient truth that Hilal has struggled all his life to understand and share: that every human bears the touch of the divine.

"How are you here?" Rabiah says in wonder. "How is this possible?"

"I came for you," Hilal says simply. "Anything is possible, if desired strongly enough."

"That's not exactly an answer. But fine, forget the how—*why* are you here?" She lowers her voice to a whisper. "Are you crazy? What if they catch you?"

"Indeed," Hilal says. "So we must do this quickly."

"Great, give it to me."

"Give you what?"

"The message," Rabiah says. "Didn't they send along a message?"

"They who?" Hilal asks, now thoroughly confused.

"My people," she says. "Or is it that they want information? There's already a lot I can give you—the layout of the prison, the timing of the

352

guard shifts, the names of the other prisoners, I've been keeping track of it all, I knew they'd find a way to make contact, I just didn't think it would be—"

Hilal holds up his hands to stop the flow of words. They're gushing out of her like water from a burst pipe, and he tries to imagine what it must have been like for her here, hour after hour, forcing her words down and her lips shut, staying silent in the face of all inducement to talk. "No one sent a message. No one sent me," he explains. "I've come on my own, to get you out of here. But we must go quickly!"

"You've come to rescue me? You don't even know me."

"I know enough," Hilal says, because there's no time to explain his tangle of motivations, the awe he feels for her and her commitment to her cause, the layers of guilt that have nothing to do with her, the responsibility he's decided to take for her life, the concept of spiritual bloodlines, the war between his common sense and his need to stop standing on the sidelines and *act*, the way she is simultaneously alien to Hilal and utterly familiar. He too is a warrior; he too has devoted his life to a single cause with monastic intensity—but he has also trained himself in tolerance and equability, in holding fast to his inner peace when all about him is chaos, in keeping the world and its mess at a distance. Rabiah wallows in the mess, hungers for it, and, stranger though she is, Hilal reveres her a little for it.

Rabiah shakes her head. "No. If you knew the first thing about me, you'd know I won't go anywhere with you. I don't need to be rescued. I don't want to be rescued."

"I don't understand."

"Clearly." The smile is long gone, but if anything, she's glowing even more brightly, lit from within by her own certainty. "I've done nothing wrong, and I won't be a fugitive from my own home. I won't live in exile, or in hiding. I can make a difference *here*. People will know my story. Even if I can't speak, they will hear my voice."

"This makes no sense to me," Hilal says. He's learned things in his efforts to gain access to the prison; he's heard rumors of the things that are done here, in the name of justice. He's heard of people lost in this darkness who never find their way back to the light. He's heard their screams.

"Your people need you. What will they be without your leadership? How will your cause triumph without you there to fight for it?"

"I'll be fighting for it here, Hilal. And my people will continue on without me. The movement is bigger than any one voice. You haven't been with us long enough to see that, but stick around and you will, I promise."

"And while they fight on, what will you do? There's less dignity in martyrdom than you think. And more pain."

"Is that what your God would say?"

Hilal knows the power of a story—the power of a sacrifice. It can echo down through the ages; it can change the world. But it can also be senseless. Purposeless. No story is worth this girl's life.

Rabiah lurches to her feet and crosses the distance between them. She takes his hands in her own. Hilal's hands are his only pride—they're beautiful. Flawless. He massages them daily with oils and tinctures, files each nail down to a smooth crescent moon, protects them from scars and calluses. The pristine stretch of soft skin is broken only by a small cross branded into the heel of his right hand. Rabiah rubs her thumb over its sharp lines and meets his eyes.

"I have no intention of being a martyr, Hilal," she says. They are strangers, but in this moment he feels as if he's known her forever. As if, in some impossible way, they are one. "I intend to continue my fight. To make noise. Let them make an example of me—I intend to make an example of *myself.* I don't intend to die, but . . . Is there nothing you would risk everything for, Hilal? Is there nothing you would die for, if it came to that?"

It comes to Hilal as an epiphany, in the truest meaning of the word, comprehension blooming over him like a mushroom cloud.

This fight is her Endgame.

He has no choice but to let her Play.

Hilal was six years old when he said good-bye to his parents and his brothers and sisters and began his new life: Scholarship. Training. Devotion to the ancient truth. Everything else, everything lesser, pared away.

He was six years old when his master sat him down and told him the story of the Makers, who came from above to imbue humanity with a divine spark—and departed just as mysteriously and abruptly, leaving only a solemn promise to someday return.

He was too young then to understand what he was agreeing to, but old enough to know what a promise meant—other than leaving behind everything he knew and loved. A Player was not meant to have personal connections. The Aksumite Player, Master Eben said, must belong to all, and to none.

He must love humanity, but also be free of it.

Every year, on his birthday, his master once again told him the story of the Makers from above, and again asked him, "Do you pledge your life to this cause? To fighting for the survival of the Aksumite line when Endgame comes? To fighting, every day, for the soul of humanity?"

Every year, Hilal understood a little more, knew better what he was promising and what he was sacrificing, and every year, he bowed his head before his master and gave his solemn oath.

Every year, until his 13th year, when his master asked him the question for the last time. This was the year that Hilal came of age—he was no longer a child. This was the year he became a man and a Player, and his oath would bind him for the rest of his days.

They stood alone in the Church of the Covenant, and Hilal could feel the power of that most sacred object buried deep in the earth beneath them, the Ark of the Covenant, protected by the Aksumites for countless generations. To make a promise in the presence of the ark was to bind himself to divinity; this was a promise that would not, could not be broken.

Hilal had spent seven years preparing for that day. Studying and training, learning fully what it meant to be the Aksumite Player—he had endured great pain, and inflicted it on others. He knew that if Endgame came during his tenure, there would likely be pain beyond his wildest imaginings. There would be danger; there could be death. And yet he did not hesitate.

"I swear," he said, in the shadow of the cross, in the aura of the covenant. He felt no fear, only the ecstatic joy of giving himself up to a higher power. Giving himself to the ultimate. "I pledge myself to this fight. To Endgame."

Because he promised on that day, he will now return home to Ethiopia and to his master; he will complete his mission. Because Rabiah has made the same promise to her own people and her own fight, he must leave her behind to her fate, whatever it might be. And so he sneaks out of the prison as stealthily as he snuck in. No alarm is raised; no more harm comes to anyone.

Hilal walks away from Tora, and simply keeps walking. He walks through the night, one kilometer after another, and though the city lights block out the stars, he can sense their watchful presence. He breathes in the night air, feels the earth beneath him, and tries to focus his mind on the future rather than the past. When dawn breaks, he takes the last of his American dollars and offers them to the driver of the first Jeep he comes across.

The offer is accepted.

Hilal takes the wheel and drives south. Day and night, he drives, crossing the Sudanese border by ferry to Wadi Halfa, charming his way through immigration with his fake passport and a gentle smile, pressing farther south, through Dongola and Al Dabbah and Khartoum, across Dinder National Park, the tires swallowing broken pavement, the hum of engine and roar of wind driving all thoughts from his mind, the landscape gradually resolving itself into the familiar contours of home, until, finally, nearly four days and nights later, he reaches the Church of the Covenant, where his master waits. "I was beginning to worry for you," Eben tells him, cradling the Book of Ouazebas as if it is a living creature, precious and fragile. "Did you meet unexpected troubles?"

"Life is made up of the unexpected," Hilal says, repeating one of his master's favorite sayings. "This is its greatest gift."

Eben smiles. "Indeed. You have done well for us, my Player. And the journey seems to have done well for you. You seem more settled than you have been. I sense your heart is no longer elsewhere."

"My heart is here," Hilal agrees, feeling the truth of his master's words, and his own. "My life is here."

Hilal rededicates himself to his ancient texts and his modern weapons, his scholarship and his training; in Cairo, the protests continue. As she expected, Rabiah's people continue on in her absence, carrying out her plans. As he expected, they have no luck breaking her free, or perhaps they had as much luck as he did, and once again she refused rescue.

Martial law is declared; soldiers patrol the streets; university students and businessmen and religious leaders and families mass in Tahrir Square, night after night, raising their signs and their voices to the sky. The international community raises its own voice in support of the protest and its leaders, and Rabiah's name circles the globe, a symbol of oppression—and hope.

Hilal watches it all on TV.

Hilal watches a lot of things on TV now: news broadcasts from around the world, news of local political squabbles, of oppression and poverty and disease and war. These updates are irrelevant to Endgame, and to his ultimate goals, yet still he watches. He is attuned, suddenly, to a world beyond the world he has always known. He's spent a lifetime focusing on the ancient past and the imagined future; now Hilal pays new attention to the present. He sees the effects of environmental degradation, the tsunamis and earthquakes and agricultural plagues. He sees children forced into sweatshop labor and children forced into battle. He sees villages burned, tribes exterminated; he sees dissent silenced, leaders of opposition parties hauled off to prison or gunned down in the streets. He sees the world ending, not in a single apocalyptic blow from above, but gradually, incrementally, in a thousand ways at once.

He hears the voices crying in protest.

He doesn't allow himself to wish he could join them. He doesn't let himself wonder what he could contribute to these fights, if he didn't have one of his own. If anything, he is more committed than ever to Endgame, to his master, to the ancient truth. In that sense, nothing has changed.

But in another sense, everything has.

Hilal has never given much thought to his life after his Playing days are done. If anything, he has imagined he will follow in his master's footsteps. Eben was a Player, once, and now he helps others do the same. He lives alone; he meditates; he prays; he holds himself separate from humanity; he loves all equally and none particularly. It is a noble life, and it is enough for him, as it has been enough for Aksumite Players through the ages.

Hilal needs more.

He will Play. He will give this life everything he has. He will fulfill his promise to his higher purpose—until he comes of age and his Playing time is past. Then he will be free to choose for himself again, and now he makes a new promise: that when the time comes, he will choose the mess, the chaos, of life. He will stop watching from the sidelines, and will instead choose a side, choose a people, perhaps even choose a *person*: he will love and fight; he will risk himself for what he believes is right. He will turn his gaze from the promised perfected future to the flawed present.

He will always keep fighting for humanity—and someday, finally, he will join it.

CAHOKIAN
SARAH

For as long as she lives, Sarah Alopay will never forget the sound of her brother's screams.

They are muffled by the steel walls that close him in, but she can still hear them. Sarah stands on the other side of a six-inch steel-reinforced door, her palms pressed against the cold metal, tears streaking down her face. Samuel Orozco, her brother's pain trainer, sits rigidly in a folding chair beside her, eyes fixed on his stopwatch. Samuel does not approve of 14-year-old Sarah's presence here, but she insisted, and her parents agreed, and so Samuel had no choice but to allow it.

So much of Tate's training is a mystery to her.

She knows about Endgame, knows that her big brother is the Player, the fate of their Cahokian line resting on his shoulders. She knows that he goes off to mysterious places for days or weeks on end, returning with bruises and scars—and, no matter what, a tacky souvenir for his little sister. She knows Tate is strong and brave, and proud to serve his people, no matter what it takes.

She knows he has no fear of pain.

So Sarah fears for him.

When he disappears on his training missions, she lies awake at night, praying that he will return safe and whole. So when she learned of this mission—a journey no farther than the reinforced shed in their Omaha backyard, a journey deep into the self, to a dark, tranquil meditative corner of the mind that pain cannot touch—she wanted to be there with him, as close as she could get.

"It's just a few hundred bee stings," Tate said cheerfully, before Samuel locked him in with the angry hive. He tweaked her nose. "How bad can it be?"

Sarah knows that Tate has been taught to withstand pain. She's seen him carve a blade across his skin without flinching; she's seen him walk across hot coals and press an iron brand to his own flesh, searing a Cahokian bird sign into his bicep. All of that without a whimper.

So she is not expecting the screams.

"It's normal," Samuel murmurs, finally acknowledging her presence. "To be expected."

Samuel is one of 10 trainers who serve her brother, turning him into the best Player he can be. Samuel is neither the strongest nor the strangest, but he is by far the most terrifying. His eyes never quite focus, and his face is unnaturally still. He's a master of inner retreat, of ignoring pain, but Sarah suspects there's a part of him in constant agony. All that pain must go somewhere. Maybe that's why he seems to so delight in inflicting pain on her brother.

He looks at her like he wants to experiment on her, like he's curious to see how much *she* can withstand, and this frightens her most of all. Which is why she can't find the nerve to argue with him.

Why she doesn't say, *No, stop, please.*

Something's gone wrong.

Let my brother out.

Seconds pass. Minutes pass. Tate screams and screams. And when the buzzer finally sounds and the door swings open, when Samuel has gassed the bees into submission and Tate emerges, Sarah understands what she's done.

What she's let happen by letting her fear rule her.

The creature that stumbles out looks nothing like her brother. He is a swollen monster, every inch of exposed skin inflamed by angry red stings, his face unrecognizable, his screams choked off as he struggles to breathe.

"Tate!" Sarah cries, and the creature that is her brother seems to hear her, turns his face toward her, peers through eyes swollen nearly shut—then drops to the ground, breath rasping, limbs shuddering and thrashing. Samuel has his phone out, is saying something about an error, an emergency, crucial speed and windows closing, but Sarah isn't listening; she's kneeling by her brother's side; she's weeping; she's saying, "I'm sorry I'm sorry I'm sorry"; she's saying, "Tate, please." She's shaking him, begging him, but Tate doesn't move, doesn't wake. He only lies there, swollen and limp.

Still.

Tate isn't dead.

This is what Sarah reminds herself, in all those excruciating hours in hospital waiting rooms that follow. She sits on uncomfortable orange chairs, flanked by her parents, waiting to hear how badly Tate is hurt, whether he can be fixed, whether he can be made whole again, waiting through the epi push and the morphine haze and the induced coma and the raging infection and the first surgery and the second, all the time reminding herself, whatever happens next: *Tate isn't dead.* As she waits, Sarah clutches Babar Jr., the gray stuffed elephant her brother once brought her back from Kenya. It was four years ago, one of his first solo missions as the Player, and she had begged him not to leave. He was 14, then, and had been training for most of his life. He was big and strong and brave, but she didn't want him to go—not across the seas all by himself, not to a strange land where terrible things might happen, not anywhere. *Please stay,* she told him, crying even though she was 10 years old, too big to cry. She meant, *Please live.* But Tate had just tweaked her nose and promised to bring her back an elephant. She'd half thought he meant a real one.

He was, after all, her big brother; he was capable of miracles.

Now she's 14 herself, but she's not strong or brave. She is too big for crying and too big for stuffed animals. Still, she hunches forward in the waiting room seats and lets her tears spatter on Babar Jr.'s matted fur.

She thinks about Tate, how he always snatches the last slice of pizza and the last piece of cake, because, he likes to say, "It's the least you can do for the guy who's going to save the world."

How her friends' favorite new game is to hide in the bushes and watch Tate lifting weights, how they giggle and say things like, "Your brother is so handsome" and "Someday I'm going to grow up and marry him," and Sarah says, "Gross, shut up," but secretly, she is so proud.

She tries to ignore her parents' whispers, something about the Cahokian Council of Elders and what to tell them, what to do if Tate can't . . . if Tate doesn't . . . These are things nobody should be saying, least of all her parents.

Tate *will*.

Tate *is*.

Tate is alive and will stay that way, the doctors told them, that first day.

There was damage, permanent damage, how much they didn't know, but he would survive.

The trial of the bees is a Cahokian tradition. No one could have known that Tate would have a near-fatal allergic reaction, or that the infection from the stings on his eye would rage through his system, that the only safe treatment would be cutting it off at the root. Removing the eye.

Tate is unconscious for all of it, and Sarah uses this time to try to get comfortable with this new version of her brother, weakened and scarred, a sunken hollow where his left eye used to be. She wants to be able to look at him without flinching when he finally wakes. She wants to be able to smile and promise him it's not so bad.

The day they pull him out of the coma, her parents go in first. Sarah waits just outside the door.

Sometimes it feels like she's spent her whole life waiting on the wrong side of a door.

She can hear her parents' soft murmurs, and the angry cadence of Tate's voice as he tries to piece together what's happened to him.

He hurts, he says, and it's like a moan.

She's never before heard him admit to pain. Not her strong brother, who's not just her hero but the hero of her people.

His voice is too quiet for her to make out the words, but she can tell he's asked a question, and when her parents don't answer, he asks it again. Sarah creeps closer to the doorway, hears her father's response. "I'm sorry, but the council voted. With only one eye—"

Tate chokes out a response.

Her father shakes his head. "I know. I tried to convince them. But they were adamant. They've already chosen someone to take your place."

Sarah gasps. This is the first she's hearing of a vote. Of a decision. It's unthinkable, that the council would take this away from her brother. Being the Player is all he's ever wanted.

Her father rests a hand on Tate's shoulder, then pulls it back quickly, remembering how every touch must burn. "I'm sorry, son. I'm—"

Tate shouts, and this time, Sarah understands loud and clear. "Get out!" He yells it again, louder, and again and again until his parents follow his command and back away. A nurse rushes past Sarah, flying toward Tate to calm him down before his blood pressure goes too high. She injects something into his IV, and he goes quiet and still again.

The next time he wakes up, he refuses to see them. He refuses to see anybody.

He tells his doctors he doesn't want to live.

That there's no point.

He's not dead, Sarah tells herself, over and over again. Even if he's no longer going to be the Player, he will still be Tate. He will find a way to be himself again. He will let her see him, let her love him. At least, she thinks, the worst is behind them. He'll have to understand that, eventually—that it's better for all of them that Endgame is gone from their lives, that they can just be a family again, two parents and two kids, happy and normal.

That night, Sarah's parents come to her room, saying they have something to tell her. Their faces are grave; her heart seizes. "Is it Tate?" she asks. "Did something else happen?"

"It's not Tate," her mother says. "It's you."

"What about me?"

"The council voted," her father says. "They've chosen their next Player."

"So what?" Sarah spits out. She hates the council, hates the next Player, whoever it will be, hates everything involving Endgame and the trainers and the creatures from the sky, all of whom have conspired to steal her brother away. She wants nothing to do with any of it, ever again. "What do I care who it is?"

Her mother fights her way to a sad smile. "Sarah, it's *you*."

Sarah can't remember a time in her life when she didn't know about the end of the world. The council selected Tate when he was four years old. No one knows why; the workings of the council are a privileged secret. Only the six Cahokian elders with the key to the council's underground bunker know what transpires in the meetings, and that knowledge is taken to the grave. They arrived on Simon and Olowa's doorstep, told them their son had a special destiny, and Simon and Olowa agreed on the four-year-old's behalf. There is no punishment for saying no to such an offer, but in the long history of the Cahokian people, only a handful ever have. To serve Endgame is the greatest of privileges.

Tate began his training immediately. He has always dreamed of saving the world.

Sarah was born less than one month later.

She wonders, lately, about the timing of that. Did they worry even then that Playing might rob them of their precious son, whether Endgame came soon or not? Did they want a backup?

That's how she thinks of herself now: a backup.

Several nights after the council makes its decision, when Sarah is still trying to decide whether to accept, she creeps down the hallway and stops in front of Tate's bedroom door. It's his first night home, and he went to bed without dinner. His eye, or the thing that used to be his eye, hurt, he said. Everything hurt.

Sarah knocks softly.

"Go away, little sis."

He's only started calling her that since the bees. She can hear the sneer in it.

"Can I come in?" she asks. "I have to talk to you."

"You can talk from there. In here you'd have to *look* at me. I'll spare you that nightmare, little sis."

Tate was always handsome, never vain. Girls have been throwing themselves at him since he was 12 years old. The doctors say that once the swelling goes down and the scars fade, his face will be almost like it once was. The doctors say that once they can fit him with a fake eye, most people won't even notice. They can forget any of this ever happened. Tate doesn't believe them. Sarah doesn't either.

"The council wants—"

"I know what the council wants," he growls. "Why haven't you given them an answer yet?"

"I . . ." Sarah swallows back a sob. Players shouldn't cry. They should be strong. She wonders, if she says yes, whether someone will teach her how to do that. "You're supposed to be the Player, Tate. It's supposed to be you."

"No duh."

It's something he used to say to her when she was little and she had excitedly reported some obvious fact of life to him that was news to her. He never used to say it so meanly.

"Will you hate me, if I do it?" Sarah asks.

"Probably," he says.

Only when he says it, when she feels her heart drop, does she realize how much she *wants* this. That maybe she wasn't supposed to be the Player, maybe she's just the backup choice—but maybe that doesn't matter. The council picked *her*, Sarah Alopay. Little sis saves the world. She likes the sound of it. More than she thought she would.

"Oh," Sarah says.

There's a long silence between them. She presses her palm to the door, and wonders if she should tell him—that if she'd spoken up sooner, yelled and screamed until the trainer let him out, maybe none of this would be happening. That she's a coward, and he's paid the price.

"But I'll hate you even more if you don't do it," Tate says. "It's your call."

Last month, for French homework, Sarah had to make a list of the things she liked best. She was bored by the assignment, bored by the class, which like all her subjects, comes easily to her. And she certainly wasn't going to reveal her true personal preferences to her French teacher, who has a unibrow and smells like foot. So she dashed off a list that was a lie, filled with whatever French words popped most quickly into her head: *le gâteau* and *les chiens* and *ma famille*. But that night, in her journal, she made a list for herself.

Things I Like:
my BFF
my brother
my parents, sometimes, when they're not being JERKS
soccer
algebra
being smart
Saturday afternoons
scary movies
Christopher
Christopher
CHRISTOPHER

Christopher is her boyfriend, and has been for nearly one year. He is handsome and funny and acts like a boyfriend out of a romantic movie, the kind who brings you flowers and candy and tugs at the

corners of your lips when you think you're too sad to smile. Sarah
is only 14, which she knows is probably too young to love anyone,
except that Romeo and Juliet were also 14, and that makes her
think that maybe there's no such thing as too young and maybe she
and Christopher are forever—and that night she got so distracted
thinking about her boyfriend and the way his eyes squint when he
laughs and the way her heart thumps when he puts his arm around
her and slips it into the pocket of her jeans that she forgot all about
her list.

In the middle of the night, she woke up from a nightmare slick with
sweat. She couldn't remember anything about the dream, but she
couldn't fall back asleep. So she turned on the light and pulled out her
journal again, and added one more thing to the list, something she
would never have confessed to her French teacher or Christopher or
anyone else, especially not Tate, who wanted to save the world.

Things I Like:
being normal

"But why me?" she asks again, as the car speeds toward the
Mississippi River. In three more hours, they will reach the most
sacred spot of the Cahokian people, and Sarah will swear herself to
her new fate. Three more hours—then there's no turning back. "I still
don't understand why they would pick me."

Her mother doesn't talk while she's driving: she prefers to focus all
her attention on the road. So it falls to Sarah's father to turn around
and reassure his daughter. "Because you're brilliant and kind and
wonderful," he says, and she can tell from the set of his face how much
he hates this, and how much he's trying to hide it.

Tate refused to come.

"None of that crap is my problem anymore," he said through the
closed door of his room. He doesn't leave his room unless he has to,
nor will he let anyone in. "Have fun, little sis."

Sarah's phone buzzes for the third time in an hour. It's her best friend, Reena, wanting to know how her big date night went. Last night was the one-year anniversary of the first time Sarah kissed Christopher Vanderkamp. Christopher planned a romantic dinner for them, and Reena will want every detail.

Yesterday afternoon, Reena came over to help her choose an outfit for the date. "Not that one," she sniffed at the ruffled black dress Sarah pulled out first. "You want him thinking make-out sessions, not funerals."

Sarah put the dress back on its hanger and held up a lime-green skirt for Reena's inspection. She knew Reena liked this one—Reena was the one who had picked it out.

But her best friend wrinkled her nose. "It just doesn't look like you."

"You told me that was a good thing!" Sarah reminded her, laughing. "You said that's why I had to get it, so I could transform myself into a 'sexy beast.'"

Then they were both giggling.

"I have most certainly never uttered those words in my whole life," Reena said, with as much dignity as she could muster while snorting with laughter.

"Did so."

"Well . . ." Reena shrugged. "Who told you to listen to everything I say?"

"Pretty sure *you* did," Sarah said. "You tell me that basically every day."

"Then listen to me now." Reena climbed off Sarah's bed and rifled through her closet, pulling out a pair of worn purple corduroys and a long black shirt. It was Sarah's favorite outfit. "Wear this."

"You always tell me that makes me look boring," Sarah reminded her. Reena prefers bright colors, wild patterns. All year, she's been begging her mother for permission to dye her hair blue. Anything to make her stand out.

Reena grinned. "Apparently, Christopher Vanderkamp *likes* boring."

Sarah elbowed her best friend; Reena whacked her gently with a pillow. "Christopher likes *you*," Reena reminded her. "It's been a year—you don't have to pretend to be someone else for him. He just wants you. Smart, wonderful, dependable, maybe ever-so-slightly boring Sarah Alopay."

"You think?" Sarah asked. After all this time, she still couldn't quite believe that someone like Christopher wanted someone like her. "It's just . . . he's so amazing."

"Yeah, and fortunately, he's smart enough to realize *you're* amazing," Reena pointed out. "It's what makes you perfect for each other."

Sarah agreed to wear the purple cords; she promised to call Reena in the morning and tell her everything.

And when she said it, she really believed she would. Even though she and her parents were supposed to leave the next day for the sacred ceremony. Even though her stomach was churning, thinking about how much everything in her life was about to change—and how she couldn't tell Reena or Christopher about any of it.

She put on the cords. She put on the black shirt. She brushed a light layer of silver shadow across her eyelids and put on the pink lip gloss Christopher liked, the kind that tasted like bubble gum.

Then she rushed to the bathroom, bent over the toilet, and threw up. She couldn't do it.

She couldn't face him across the table, smile, tell him how happy he made her, pretend that everything was fine. She couldn't lie to him like that.

So she lied to him another way.

"I am so sorry," she told him on the phone. "I was feeling fine a couple hours ago, but now my stomach is just, like, *Nope, don't think so.*"

It wasn't *quite* a lie, because every time she thought about the future, her stomach flipped somersaults all over again.

"Is this . . ." He hesitated. He'd been doing that a lot, lately. Ever since Tate got hurt, ever since she'd gotten the offer from the elders, there were so many things she couldn't say to him. He could tell she was holding something back—so he started holding back too. "Is this about your brother? Because if you're not in the mood for a whole big thing, I could come over, we could watch one of those terrible movies you insist on loving—"

"They're not terrible!"

"I love you, but anything called *SlasherFest Summertime Fun, Part Three* is a terrible movie."

"It's *Slasher Summer Camp Fun, Part Four*," she corrected him, thinking, *He loves me, he loves me, he loves me.* "And it's *awesome*."

"I'm just saying, we don't have to do this whole dinner thing. I just want to see you. Cheer you up."

Sarah sighed. "Look, I know I've been kind of weird, lately—"

"Dude, he's your brother. I get it."

Christopher thinks that all her bad moods, all the new distance between them, are about Tate's injury. And she lets him think it.

Which isn't fair to anyone.

But it's easier.

"I want to see you too," she said, thinking, *I love you too*, but she couldn't say that, not with what she was about to do. How could she promise herself to him when she was about to promise herself to the Cahokian line? "But I'm really just sick, I swear. Unless you want me puking all over your precious Converse—"

"Enough said."

Sarah smiled. Nothing was more important to Christopher than his sneaker collection.

"Rain check?" she asked.

"Just try to get out of it. I dare you."

She hung up the phone, wondering if she'd made a mistake. Maybe she could have just told him the truth. But how, exactly, would that work? Christopher was cute and rich and the star quarterback on the JV football team; he was sweet and funny and endlessly understanding. But no way would he understand if she told him she was a descendant of an ancient civilization and she was about to devote the next six years of her life to training for Endgame, just in case the Sky People returned and decided it was time for the end of the world.

No, even Christopher wouldn't understand that, and she couldn't expect him to.

He sent her a sweet text this morning, with a GIF of a dancing gorilla to make her smile. He's been trying to so hard lately to make her smile. She hates disappointing him.

Sarah puts the phone away. She doesn't want to lie to her best friend any more than she wanted to lie to Christopher. It's easier just to ignore her for the day. Once she gets back home, once she's officially sworn in as the Player and starting on her new life, then she'll decide how to deal with her old one. She slips in her earbuds and turns the music up as loud as she can stand it: Arcade Fire, Christopher's favorite band. Sarah closes her eyes and tries to lose herself.

It's a six-hour drive from Omaha to Collinsville, Illinois. They make it in eight—Sarah's mother is a *very* careful driver.

It's midnight, and the historic site is closed to tourists. The council, of course, has a man on the inside, and so everything is prepared for them. Sarah and her parents rush through the gate, though Sarah's father laughs and says there's no point in hurrying.

"After all, they can't start without you," he says, and Sarah tries to laugh too.

Her parents are doing the best they can to pretend that this is an occasion for pride and joy—and that they're not remembering the last time they were here, hand in hand with their precocious preschooler, Tate stumbling over the oath that would indebt him to his people for life.

One thousand years ago, these acres were home to the continent's first and greatest civilization. For more than half a millennium, the Cahokian people ruled over their teeming metropolis—and then, mysteriously, vanished. Nothing was left of the city but three square miles of grass and soil mounds, the largest of them 10 stories tall.

Nothing was left of the civilization or its people but a handful of survivors, and a story handed down through hundreds of generations. A story of a bargain made with the Sky People. The Cahokians would receive power and technology, enough to rule over the young nation for centuries. In return, when the Sky People asked, the Cahokians would hand over a precious resource: 1,000 of their children.

The Cahokians ruled, as planned. After 500 years, the Sky People came back, as promised. They demanded payment—and the Cahokians refused.

For the first time in 10,000 years, a human civilization waged war against the creatures from the sky. They fought bravely—and died horribly, all of them, the civilization annihilated with a single blast, only a handful of survivors left to tell the tale.

These survivors, travelers who returned home to find everything they knew and love destroyed, were sentenced to a humiliating punishment of their own: the Sky People reached into their minds and obliterated the true name of their people.

Hundreds of years later, Europeans conquered the continent and assigned a new name to the vanished people: Cahokia. The New World has no idea there are survivors of the ancient civilization, that the Cahokians lived, haunted by its past glories and defeats.

The Cahokians had been forced to forget their name, but they remembered their history, and they struggled on in secret, determined that their bloodline should survive.

By now, most North Americans have Cahokian blood running through their veins; their survival now depends on Sarah's willingness to fight.

It is said that across the world, the sacred sites of the other 11 ancient lines have been preserved: underground temples, secret caverns, hidden passageways that the land developers and tourists know nothing about.

Not here.

The European invaders proved nearly as skilled as the Sky People at obliteration. There are no hidden passageways running beneath the Cahokian mounds. There are only millions of cubic feet of soil raising the earth to the sky, and postholes showing where the ancient people once erected Woodhenge—an arrangement of wooden posts that symbolized the Earth and the four cardinal directions, used to communicate with the gods.

Sarah's people have erected new posts for the night, and now she stands at their center.

The eldest of the elders is before her, a 6,000-year-old stone in his hand.

Sarah recognizes the stone; she's seen it every day of her life, hanging from Tate's neck. It belongs to the Player, and always has.

If she goes through with this tonight, it will belong to her.

She won't be the normal one anymore, the one who takes shortcuts on her homework and scarfs pizzas with her best friend and has nothing more important to think about than whether Christopher will ask her to the school formal. She won't be a backup anymore. She'll be the Player, and the lives of her people will rest on her shoulders.

If she goes through with this, she'll claim what was once her big brother's future—a future that scares her, of violence and danger and pain, all the things she never wanted for him and wants even less for herself.

And he might never forgive her for it.

Sarah's phone buzzes in her back pocket. The elder looks at her, pointedly, and Sarah wonders whether the old man has ever even seen a cell phone. She wonders what he would say if she asked him to pause the ceremony for a moment while she texts Reena back. *Hey, it wasn't my idea that the Player should be a teenager,* she would like to tell him. *What did you expect?*

But of course she can't do that.

Add it to the list of things she can't do, now.

Sarah is suddenly having trouble breathing. A hot flush rises in her cheeks. Somewhere, far away, Reena is hungry for gossip; somewhere, far away, Christopher is worrying about his girlfriend's supposed food poisoning. She wants to run away from this, run home to them, maybe just run, and keep running until she leaves everything and everyone behind, until there are no more hard decisions to make, only the sound of wind in her ears and the thump of ground beneath her feet.

She doesn't run.

"Put out your hand," the leader of the Cahokian elders commands her. Sarah does, and he lays the ancient stone on her open palm. It feels warm to the touch, and almost seems to pulse with her heartbeat, but she tells herself that must be her imagination.

The old man says several words in the ancient language of the Cahokian people. "Do you forswear all else?" he asks her then, in English. The same question has been asked of every Player for a thousand years.

There are countless reasons to say no to this question. There is Christopher; there is Tate. There is everything she wants for herself, and everything she's afraid of. Countless reasons to say no, and only one reason to say yes.

But that one reason trumps all the others.

Her family; her people. All the Cahokian lives that have been lost, and all those hundreds of thousands more that could be, when Endgame comes. They need a champion.

Sarah came to this place still unsure how she would answer the ancient question. Half expecting she would lose her nerve, back out at the last moment. She has always trusted logic, and her logic tells her that this is a foolish choice.

But there's something in her, something deeper and wiser than logic, something reaching for her destiny.

The elders chose her for a reason. She doesn't understand what it could possibly be. But some part of her—that sure, steady part beneath rational thought—feels certain that they were right. That this is the right choice for her, and for her line. The Cahokian people need a champion, and that champion should be, must be, Sarah Alopay. The stone burns her palm; she grips it tight, feeling suddenly connected to all those generations of Players long dead, woven into the fabric of Cahokian history. She can feel them out there, the Players of the past, dead and alive. They're watching her, waiting for her to join them. All except Tate. She can't feel him at all. "Do you pledge yourself to the survival of our people, and to the ancient oath?" Sarah's parents have warned her not to swear unless she's completely sure. That there's no going back.

They don't spell out what the punishment would be for breaking her oath, but Sarah is Cahokian, and every Cahokian knows that promises made to the Sky People are not to be lightly broken.

Too much is at stake.

Too many have already died.

She closes her eyes, breathing in the soil and the sky. She hears the echo of Tate's screams and can almost feel the touch of Christopher's fingers grazing her lips, asking permission to kiss her for the first time. She feels something else, an insistent vibration in her hand, and for a moment she thinks it's the phone again, Reena breaking in at the most inopportune moment.

But it's the stone, waiting for her answer.

"Yes," Sarah says, because her people have summoned her to duty, and she's been raised to believe that this is a call that demands an answer. She repeats the words that she's carefully memorized. "Yes, I swear. I swear to take your lives onto my shoulders. I swear to serve the Cahokian people to the best of my abilities and beyond. I swear to Play."

Players are supposed to have time to learn their craft. Time for training in weapons, meditation, languages, code cracking, pain tolerance, physics and computers and bomb making. Time to understand their responsibilities, then find a way to make their Playing their own.

Sarah has no time.

No one knows when Endgame will come: it could start tomorrow.

She's not ready.

As days of grueling training turn into weeks, she's unsure she'll ever be ready.

So are her trainers.

At Sarah's school, there's a student trying to become a professional gymnast. She hits the gym for long hours before and after school, stays up all night trying to get her homework done, never has a free second for extracurricular activities, or friends and family, or any kind of life. Though she seems happy enough with her back handsprings and her array of trophies. Sarah has always pitied her— she doesn't know what she's missing.

Sarah *does* know. Her new schedule demands she wake before dawn for a 10-mile run and calisthenics, then cram in as much of that week's subject—ancient Greek, hydrodynamics, explosives defusing—as possible before school. She sleepwalks through the day, stealing every free period and lunch hour she can to zip through the homework she no longer has time for at home. Then, after school, it's straight to the training center for martial arts and firearms, a brief meal with her family or, if she's lucky, Christopher and Reena, then more studying, then merciful, if brief, sleep.

Those are the easy days.

Some days she spends in seclusion, learning to withstand the burn of hot coals on her soft flesh, or trekking through wilderness with neither food nor water, depending on her wits and the bounty of nature to keep herself alive and find her way home.

She's starting to feel like she lives at the training facility, a nondescript building only 10 minutes from her house, its lease owned by the Cahokian elders, its interior filled with workout equipment and weapons stores. She spends more time with the experts employed by the council, steely-eyed trainers who treat her like a machine, than she does with the people she loves.

More weeks pass, and her reflexes sharpen; her muscles harden; her skin grows insensitive to touch, her system inured to pain. Sometimes she feels like she's turning to stone.

The new skills come easily to her, as everything always has, but the trainers are unsatisfied.

They're always telling her how much harder her brother worked, how much more he wanted it, how they can tell her mind is somewhere else.

They're right.

"What happened?" Christopher asks in alarm the morning she comes to school with a black eye. He raises a finger to the purpling bruise, but she ducks his touch.

"I walked into a door," she mumbles.

The lies are getting lamer.

Eventually, he's going to get tired of this and break up with her. Or she'll do it first and put them both out of their misery.

That's probably the right thing to do, but she can't bring herself to consider it. She's not that strong.

"Sarah . . ." He puts his arms around her, and she almost loses it.

For two months, she's stayed steady, she's made herself hard; she's lied to Christopher and Reena so she can steal time for her training; sometimes she's even lied to her trainers so she can steal time for Christopher and Reena. She's told herself that this isn't so bad, that she can do it, that any day now things will get easier, life will get calmer, Tate will start speaking to her again, everything will start to seem normal again, even though it never can be. She's told herself that being the Player is no different from being a starting forward on the soccer team or being president of the honor society—just a few more things on her to-do list, no biggie. She's walled up the truth, locked it away, but now, in Christopher's arms, she feels the walls crumbling. A crowd swirls around them, students grabbing things from their lockers, hurrying off to class, chattering and buzzing about all the important problems of junior high life. Sarah feels a sudden surge of hate for them, how easy they have it, how little they understand. She breathes deep, breathes in the smell of Christopher's soap, tries her best to block them all out. Pretend that she and Chris are the only two people that matter. The only two that exist. He whispers in her ear. "Sarah, if something was going on with you, something at home, or wherever . . . you'd tell me, right?"

She feels the sting of tears, knows that if she holds on to him much longer, she'll lose it completely. She's so tired—of lying to him and to herself that she can do it all. But if she lets herself collapse, if she lets him be the strong one and hold her up while she cries, there will only be more questions, and more lies.

"I told you, everything's fine." It comes out more harshly than she intends, and Christopher recoils. She angles her face away so he can't see the sheen of tears in her eyes. She spots Reena picking her way through the crowd, waving eagerly as she approaches. The open, trusting look on her face makes Sarah's heart clench. "I'm late for homeroom," she says brusquely, and before Christopher can stop her, she rushes away.

She gets better at making up excuses.

Intensive French lessons in preparation for an imaginary summer abroad, a nonexistent international math competition to study for, a doctor's appointment for Tate, a surgery for Tate, rehab and therapy for Tate—it's easy, at least, to make up Tate-related excuses, because Reena and Christopher know how angry and miserable and damaged he is, if not why. They are endlessly kind and understanding, and Sarah hates herself for lying to them.

And even then, even after all she's given up and all the energy she's thrown into her new mission, it's still not enough.

"Honey, your trainer's a bit concerned about something," Sarah's father says, as the four of them dig into his Sunday special: spaghetti and meatballs. It used to be Sarah's favorite part of the week, but now she's usually too busy for Sunday family dinners, and Tate almost always eats in his room.

"Which trainer?" Sarah asks, mouth full of pasta. She has a different trainer for each specialty—which means that even after nearly six months, they still feel like strangers.

Her parents exchange a glance. "Well . . . all of them," her father admits.

"Oh."

"They think you're too distracted," her mother says. "That you're not focused enough on your training."

"Are you kidding me?" Sarah feels like she's going to explode. "I'm giving *everything* to this! What more do they want from me?"

"Last weekend you went to the mall with Reena when you could have been working on your Chinese," her mother points out gently. "And I know you've been staying up late talking to Christopher on the phone when you need your sleep"—she held up a hand before Sarah could interrupt—"and I understand: you're juggling a lot; you're doing the best you can. But your trainers have suggested we make a few changes. Maybe it's time to rethink the question of school—"

"No," Sarah snaps. "No way. I'm not dropping out of school."

"It would just be for a year or so, until you get your feet under you," her father says. "And it's not exactly *dropping out*. You already know everything they're teaching you anyway. Your lessons here would—"

"No!" Sarah feels like a child having a temper tantrum, and wishes she knew how to let herself go that way, wishes she *could* have a temper tantrum, fists pounding, tears streaming. Then they would know how she feels, and they would stop this. "I'm giving everything I can to Playing, but I can't give up my whole life. Tell them, Tate."

Tate flinches, like he's surprised they know he's there. Like he was hoping he'd turned invisible.

"No comment," he mumbles, and fidgets with his eye patch. The doctors say he's ready to be fitted for a fake eye, but Tate refuses. He doesn't want to pretend everything's normal, he says. And he doesn't want to give his family, or anyone else, the luxury of pretending either.

Sarah presses on. "*You* didn't have to drop out of school. You graduated."

He shrugs. "Lot of good it did me."

He's 18 now, and was expecting to spend the next couple of years focused solely on Playing. Sarah knows he never looked any further than that. Certainly not toward college, or a career. Tate has only ever wanted to Play. Now he lies in bed, listens to music, and promises his parents he'll figure out what to do with his life. Someday.

"You're not your brother, honey," her mother says.

Tate snorts into his spaghetti. "*That's* for sure."

Sara doesn't know whether she wants to cry or use her new krav maga prowess to flip over the table and jam a fork into his neck. But either way, she's lost her appetite. She pushes back from the table and rises to her feet. "Thanks for dinner," she tells her father, in a tone that says, *Thanks for nothing*. "But apparently, I've got work to do."

She's standing by her locker when a shadow falls over her. Strong arms scoop her up and two hands press over her eyes, shutting her into darkness.

She flinches.

"Guess who."

She recognizes Christopher's warm voice just in time—she was about to flip him over her shoulder and slam him to the floor. She's tensed for violence all the time now; her trainers have taught her to always be searching the shadows for enemies, to always be on alert for those who want to destroy her.

They have nothing to say on the subject of those who only want to love her.

She wants to warn Christopher not to sneak up on her again—that she's more dangerous than he knows, that she's forgotten how to play games that don't end in death. Instead she says, "Hey, stranger," then fakes a smile and twists around so they're face-to-face.

He kisses her.

A year and a half ago, Christopher was just the surprisingly hot rising star on the football team who'd sprouted up six inches over the summer and was the first boy in their class to sport actual muscles. Sarah had gone to school with him since she was little, but she barely knew him. She and Reena spent hours on the phone, giggling about the cute tufts of hair that curled over his ears, the cute way his shirt was always rumpled and his socks never matched, the cute sparkle in his emerald-green eyes, the crooked front tooth that made his smile *extra* cute . . .

Then he asked Sarah out for pizza, and they held hands under the table, and he walked her home and, just before sending her inside, asked if he could kiss her. After that, he wasn't Christopher-the-cute-guy-in-math, anymore. He was *Christopher*, the guy she could tell anything to, the guy who could always cheer her up when she was sad, the guy with the bottomless eyes and the soft lips and the Christopher smile, who she could keep kissing for the rest of her life.

She intends to.

Behind them, Reena clears her throat. Loudly. "Get a room, guys."

Christopher grins. "If only."

Sarah blushes. They haven't done much more than kiss yet, but when he looks at her, when he *touches* her . . . she's thought about it. A lot. The bell rings for first period, saving her from further teasing.

"You still up for Sam and Louie's after school?" Christopher asks, tucking a strand of hair behind her ear. It's their favorite pizza place, and the three of them used to go there a few times a week . . . before.

"Oh, crap."

"You forgot," Reena says accusingly.

"I . . ."

"We haven't gone for pizza together in *forever*," Reena complains.

"Okay, drama queen. It's been like a week," Sarah says.

Christopher squeezes her hand. "It's been like three weeks," he corrects her. "You promised."

She did promise . . . but she also promised her firearms trainer that she would double her training time this week.

"I can't, guys. I'm so sorry. Tate has an appointment with this eye specialist and I promised I'd go with him to the appointment. You know how it is."

Reena and Christopher exchange a look. Sarah pretends not to see it.

"Yeah," Reena says. "We know how it is."

"I'll text you when I get home?" Sarah says. "Both of you. Okay? Promise."

"Yeah. Promise. Whatever." Reena walks off to class without another word. Sarah searches Christopher's face, trying to figure out if he's mad at her.

"I would if I could," she tells him. "You know that, right?"

He kisses her again, soft and sweet, and she closes her eyes and lets herself fall into his embrace. It's so warm, so comforting, that it's not until she's seated in English class pretending to listen to the teacher drone that she realizes: he never answered her question.

"No!" Shelly shouts, as Sarah again tries to reassemble the AR-15 assault rifle in under 60 seconds and fails. "Again, and do it right this time!"

"Sorry, sir." Sarah sighs, taking the weapon apart and laying each piece neatly on the table.

Shelly is a short, stout Cahokian and retired marine who's in charge of making sure Sarah knows everything there is to know about guns and can hit a bull's-eye with her eyes closed. She prefers shouting to talking and makes Sarah call her "sir."

She thinks Sarah doesn't have what it takes to be the Player.

Sarah knows this because Shelly says so, constantly.

Sarah stares at the pieces of the gun, trying to piece them together in her mind so her nervous fingers will know what to do.

"You waiting for an engraved invitation?" Shelly asks, and clicks the stopwatch. Sarah scrambles for the barrel jacket, fumbles the magazine, and drops it on the floor with a loud clatter, and Shelly slams her hand against the table. "Forget it! This is a waste of time if you're not even going to try."

"I am trying, sir," Sarah says in a small voice. She's been screwing up all afternoon, firing shots several inches from the bull's-eye, forgetting her safety goggles, trying to load the sniper rifle with the wrong kind of bullets.

"You say that, but your mind is somewhere else," Shelly accuses her. It's true. Her mind is at Sam and Louie's, with Christopher, biting into a steaming slice of mushroom pepperoni and groaning at one of his terrible jokes.

"I'm sorry, sir."

"If you want me to tell your parents you can't handle this . . ."

In the silence left behind the trainer's threat, Sarah feels a glimmer of hope. What if she can't measure up? What if the council deems her unworthy, and replaces her with someone else?

What if she simply stopped trying, and let it go?

But something in her—the same impulse that made her agree to Play in the first place—rebels against the idea.

"I said, I'm *sorry*," she says forcefully, and, without waiting for permission, begins piecing the gun together again.

This time, she gets it right.

She assembles and disassembles the weapon 10 more times, her movements nimble and machinelike; then, after a quick break for food, she spends an extra three hours in the gym, working the punching bag and practicing her tae kwon do. Even when her martial arts trainer goes home for the night, Sarah keeps at it, only giving up when her muscles are screaming so loudly she can't bear to aim another kick.

Well past midnight, she stumbles into bed, thinking, *See? I can handle this,* and it's not until morning that she checks her phone and sees the flood of text messages from Christopher and Reena.

She forgot them, again.

Christopher doesn't text her back. Reena doesn't text her back. And when she sees them at school, they won't talk to her.

Sarah finally pins Reena down in the girls' bathroom. "What's going on?" she asks. "Are you seriously this mad I forgot to text you last night? I'm sorry, okay? I went to bed really early."

"Oh, yeah?" Reena's washing her hands. She watches Sarah in the mirror. "Long, hard doctor's appointment with Tate, yeah?"

"Well . . ." Sarah hates using her brother as an excuse like this. "Yeah, actually."

Her best friend whirls to face her. "You know, if you're cheating on Christopher or something, that's an asshole move, but you could at least trust me enough to tell me about it. I'm supposed to be your best friend."

"Wait—what? Why would you think I could ever cheat on Christopher?"

"I don't know, how about because you're constantly sneaking off and lying about it?"

"I told you, I was—"

"At a doctor's appointment. With Tate. I know. Except for how we saw Tate at Sam and Louie's, drunk off his ass in the middle of the afternoon and chowing down on a whole pizza all by himself."

Sarah doesn't know what to say. Her mind is too crowded with confusing, disturbing facts.

Reena and Christopher went for pizza without her? Like, on a date? Tate's getting drunk? In the middle of the afternoon?

They know she was lying? They think she's been lying this whole time?

"Don't bother," Reena snaps.

"What?"

"I know you're just trying to come up with another lie."

"Am not."

"Sarah, we've been friends since we were eight years old. I know you.

And I know when you're trying to lie to me. Not that you used to do that."

"Fine," Sarah says. "No more lies."

There's a silence between them.

Because what's she supposed to say now? The *truth*?

"I'm not cheating on Christopher," Sarah says. "I wouldn't do that. If you know me as well as you say you do, then you should know that."

Reena sighs. "Yeah. Of course I know that. But then what . . . ?"

"I can't tell you."

"Are you freaking kidding me?"

"You don't want me to lie to you, fine. But I can't *tell* you. It's complicated and . . . can you just trust me for now?"

Unexpectedly, Reena pulls Sarah into a hug. "I wish you could just tell me what's going on with you."

Sarah buries her face in her friend's shoulder and blinks back tears. "Yeah. Me too."

Reena steps back, all business again. "Whatever it is, you better not dump Christopher before the formal. I've spent way too long planning this double date."

"The . . . formal?"

Reena rolls her eyes. "The spring formal? Only the most important event of the year? The dance we bought dresses for six months ago? The dance that's *this Friday*? Even you couldn't forget—"

"No," Sarah says quickly. "Of course not." She doesn't like that: *Even you.* As if Reena's expectations have sunk so low. And maybe they should have, because of course she's right.

Sarah did forget.

"It's going to be an amazing night," she promises her best friend. "I swear."

Reena talks to Christopher for her, and whatever she says works. He agrees to cut class and meet her under the bleachers that afternoon. Neither of them has ever cut class before. They're good kids; they follow the rules.

Sarah is so tired of rules.

"I'm sorry," she tells him again, curled up in his arms on the dewy grass. "I'm sorry I'm sorry I'm sorry."

"You said that already," he says. "And I said I forgive you. And I trust you. Can we get back to the kissing now?"

"And I'm going to make it up to you—"

"On Friday, at the formal. I know. You said that too. Multiple times."

"I just want to make sure you know that I would never . . ."

"Sarah." He cups her chin in his warm hands. Their eyes meet. "I do know. Sometimes I just feel like . . ."

"What?"

"Like you're so far away. Like even when you're here with me, you're really somewhere else. Or you wish you were."

He's partly right—she is somewhere else. These days she's always somewhere else. When she's with Christopher, she's thinking about fighting moves or ancient Cahokian mythology; when she's with her trainers, she's thinking about Christopher.

"I don't wish I were anywhere else but here with you," she tells him, and it's the truest thing she's said in a long time.

When she gets home that afternoon, her parents are both in the kitchen, waiting for her. They have an elderly woman with them, her weathered face covered in scars. Sarah recognizes her as one of the council elders: Juliana, a former Player herself.

Sarah wonders at the scars, where they came from, and whether when she grows up her face will bear similar marks. She's never thought of herself as a superficial person, but she doesn't like the idea that her Playing will permanently mark her for all the world to see.

She's already had to explain away bruises and sprains—more lies for Christopher—but at least those heal and fade.

Every time she looks at Tate, she's reminded that some wounds don't. She can't remember the last time a council member visited their home. Whatever this is about, it can't be good.

386

"What's going on?" she asks.

"Sit down, honey," her father says.

She shakes her head. "Tell me what's going on first."

Juliana points to a chair and says, with the imperious confidence of someone who's used to having her commands followed, *"Sit."*

She sits.

"This is the situation," Juliana says. "We've received troubling reports of your progress, or lack thereof. We wish you to withdraw from school and focus solely on your training. You will come with me back to Illinois and we will provide a suitable—"

"What? No!" Sarah cries. She looks at her parents. "Are you just going to sit there? *You* think that's a good idea?"

"Sarah, your training is important. The stronger you get, the more likely you are to . . ."

Sarah knows how to fill in that blank.

The more likely you are to survive.

She tries not to think about Endgame, and what it would mean. She doesn't even like to think about the trials of pain and strength and endurance that she knows to be in her future, as every Player must meet them. It was a pain trial that destroyed Tate, and he was so much stronger than she is, than she could ever be.

"I won't do it," Sarah says.

Juliana looks untroubled by the argument. "But you must."

She doesn't make an ultimatum. She doesn't say, *If you want to Play,* because they both know there is no *if.* Sarah swore the ancient oath. She agreed to do this, and that means doing whatever the council deems right. No matter how wrong they might be.

"There must be something else I can do," Sarah insists. "Something to prove I don't need to throw away my entire life and go with you."

Training in Illinois, away from her family, away from her friends, away from Christopher. No school, no future, no love. Just fighting and working and Playing.

She doesn't think she could survive it.

"There is perhaps one thing," Juliana says, and something about the way she says it makes Sarah wonder whether this hasn't been the point of the visit all along. "Your first trial. The trial of the wolves. I understand you've been putting it off."

"She's not ready," her mother says loyally.

"There's no hurry," her father says.

The trial of the wolves is, traditionally, the first of the many trials the Cahokian Player must undergo. The Player spends the night alone in the woods, at the heart of a wolf pack's territory—and either survives or doesn't. Tate did it when he was nine. He needed 102 stitches when it was over, a fact that he never got tired of bragging about.

Sarah doesn't want to do it.

Sarah is afraid.

"You'll do it Friday," Juliana says.

"But—"

She can't do it, and she certainly can't do it on *Friday*. She can't miss the formal, not after everything she's screwed up. But she also can't exactly tell Juliana that a junior high school dance is more important than the council's wishes.

"You'll do it in three days' time, and prove to me that you're committed to this task, this life. Or you will fail to do so, and you will come away with me."

"You're telling me those are my only two options?" Sarah says.

"I am."

But there is only one option. She can't leave Christopher. She can't leave her family, or school, or her life.

Sarah takes a deep breath. "Then I'll do it. Whatever I have to do."

Upstairs, safe in her room, she cries.

She can't seem to stop crying.

She doesn't know whether she's more afraid that her friends will be mad or that the wolves will tear her to shreds; maybe she's just afraid that she can't do this, have everything she wants and needs. She's terrified that she's going to have to choose.

"Would you stop being such a damn baby?" Tate throws her door open, then slams it shut behind him. It's the first time he's come to her room since the day of the bees. It's the one time she doesn't want him there. But still, for just a moment, her heart leaps at the sight of him. She keeps forgetting that he's not the old Tate anymore, the one she could always count on.

"You don't understand," she says, wiping at her dripping nose. "The council says—"

"I know what the council says, and it's your job to do whatever it is, don't you think? Isn't that what being the Player is all about?" His lips twist cruelly, and she knows what he's thinking. That the council said he couldn't be the Player anymore, and like a good Player, he obeyed.

"You have nothing to cry about," he snaps. "You have no idea. And if you can't hack this, you should admit it now, and save everyone a lot of trouble."

"Do *you* think I can't hack it? That I'm not as good as you? As strong?" She knows what he thinks, but she wants to hear him say it out loud, to her face.

"They picked me, not you. That's all I'm saying."

"They picked both of us."

"Yeah, well, they make mistakes. And if you think your sad little 'relationship' is more important than the fate of the world, maybe they did."

"Screw you, Tate." It pops out before she can stop herself. He looks as surprised as she is. For so long, everyone in the family has been tiptoeing around him, trying to be kind, give him time and space, let him bite their heads off. But she can't handle it anymore.

"Why did you even say yes, anyway?" he asks. "You act like you don't have a choice. I'm the one who has no choice."

"Maybe that's why I said yes."

"For me?" he sneers. "What, to carry on the family legacy? Don't do me any favors."

389

"No." She wishes that *were* why. It would make sense, then; it would be easier. She loves Tate, would do anything for him, and if she thought Playing would fix him, would make him happy again, then she would Play forever. But it's not fixing him. Sometimes it seems like nothing will fix him. And what she can't admit, what maybe neither of them can admit, is that her Endgame has nothing to do with him anymore.

"What, then? You just want to prove that you're better than big brother? Got sick of me getting all the attention?"

"No!" she cries. "Stop it!"

"You don't even know why you're doing it, do you?" He shakes his head. "Bad move, little sister. You can't Play without a reason to Play. That's a good way to end up dead."

"How can you . . ." She's crying again now, too hard to talk. How can he say it like he doesn't care?

"Stop crying!" he shouts.

She does, abruptly, not because he told her to, but because she's suddenly angry. Too angry to cry—too angry to not finally say exactly what she thinks. "You're not the only person allowed to have emotions, Tate. You're not the only one in the world with problems."

"No, but I'm the only person in this *room* with problems," he says. "One of us has an amazing chance to be the savior of her people, to pledge her life to the survival of the Cahokians, to be a hero—and is throwing a sulk because it might mean missing a stupid school dance? The other of us has *nothing*, do you get that?" He's shouting now, angrier than she's ever seen him. "Nothing."

"That's your choice," Sarah says, not sure whether her heart is breaking for him or for herself. If he won't leave her room, then she'll leave, and leave him here alone, which is what he deserves. "You *choose* to have nothing. I hope you enjoy it."

Tate's right about one thing. She doesn't know why she agreed to Play. But she *did* agree. That's what matters now . . . isn't it?

Her relationship isn't more important than saving the world. She can't let it be. If it's true that she can't have both, that she has to choose one life or another, it's no choice at all.

She texts Reena and Christopher, tells them both that she's sick and can't go to the formal after all. Then she takes a hammer to her phone and throws the pieces in the trash.

She doesn't go to school the next day, or the one after that. She doesn't talk to Tate. She doesn't think about Christopher.

She trains.

She meditates.

She studies the wolves.

And when Friday comes and the sun dips below the horizon, and all her friends are squeezing themselves into fancy dresses and straightening their hair, Sarah Alopay ventures into the woods.

Into the woods: There are no trails, no campgrounds, no safe havens for sweet young girls. There is only darkness, the whisper of wind through the leaves, the rustle of footsteps, the eyes blinking from the shadows.

Sarah builds a fire, as she's been taught to do. She could spear a squirrel, roast it on a spit, tear its meat off its bones; she knows how to survive. But this is one night, and hunger is no concern. This night isn't about survival skills, about lean-tos and water filtration or navigation by the stars.

This night is about the wolves.

The wolves, it is said, are a friend to the Cahokians.

The wolves, it is said, are drawn to the Player, by her power and her need. They know a test is in order, and so they offer it, a challenge red in tooth and claw.

Sarah doesn't believe in such things.

At least, she doesn't think she believes in such things.

But here's what she knows: for generations, every Player has ventured into these woods for a night, and every time, the Player has met the wolves.

She knows there are creatures lurking in the shadows, watching her. She knows they will come for her, and she knows they will be hungry. One hour passes, and another. Sarah stares into the fire, imagining the faces of the people she loves dancing in its flames. Imagining that her world is burning, will burn, unless she can stop it. She loses herself to the vision, can see the skies set aflame, buildings blazing, bodies falling. She can see Reena, older and even prettier, Reena in a graduation cap, Reena with cartoon shock on her face and her arm torn away above the elbow. She can see the dirt explode beneath Tate, crushing him against earth and stone. She can see Christopher's body, lifeless and cold, blood pouring from a neat hole at the center of his forehead.

You don't even know why you're doing it, Tate accused her, and it was true. She'd agreed to be the Player because an inner voice had told her it was the right thing to do; she'd listened, she'd obeyed, but she hadn't understood.

Now she does.

She can, in those endless moments of flickering fire, see Endgame, and she knows it is coming for her. Knows these things she sees are promises of what may come, if she can't find the strength to stop it from happening.

She is the only one who can stop it from happening.

She has to Play, not just for her line, not just for her promise, but for the people she loves the most. She thought Playing was tearing her away from them, but now she sees that Playing will be the only thing that keeps them alive.

She knows, now, what is to come.

She knows she can never give up. That as much as she loves her friends and family, that's how hard she will work to save them.

She knows this as well as she's known anything, and then the certainty slips away as quickly as it came, as she blinks herself back to these woods, this night, and sees the wolves.

Five of them have come for her, surrounded her. Gray fur, black eyes, white fangs.

She feels like they're judging her. Weighing whether or not she's worthy.

"I don't care what you think," Sarah says. The wolves growl, and inch closer. "I don't care what anyone thinks. I can do this. I *will* do this." As she says it, she finally knows it to be true.

As she says it, the largest wolf leaps on her.

They drop to the ground together, a snarling tangle of slashing claws and wild limbs. Sarah slams her skull into the wolf's nose, and as it howls in pain, she shoves her fist down its throat as far as she can, far enough that the wolf struggles to breathe. Fangs tear at her skin, and somewhere, deep in the back of her mind, there is pain. But she thinks only of the wolf, its gaze fixed on hers, its lungs heaving as it struggles to free itself of her fist, and as she ducks and dances past its lashing paws, Sarah curls her own fingers into claws, strikes at the wolf's face, and rips its eyeball out of its socket.

A howl of pain and rage shakes the night, and Sarah howls along with it, all her pain and fear and fury unleashed into the dark, and with a mighty heave she flings the wolf's shuddering, spasming body toward its pack.

"Go ahead," she dares them. "Come at me."

But the wolves whimper and lower their front legs, touch their noses to the ground in submission, then back away into the woods.

She's covered in the beast's blood as well as her own, she's sliced and scratched and shivering with aftershock, but she's smiling. Then, alone in the woods, wolves circling, blood dripping from a hundred painful wounds, she's laughing.

She won.

Sarah sleeps soundly, flanked by three wolves, who guard her against the night. She can feel it, their desire to protect: they've judged her, and found her worthy.

She's judged herself, and concluded the same.

When she hikes out to the rendezvous point, she expects Juliana to collect her, or maybe her parents. But instead, it's Tate behind the wheel of his rusted Pontiac. He hasn't driven since he lost his eye—she's not even sure he *should* be driving. But she gets in without a word.

"Are you okay?" he asks, and she knows from the concern in his voice that she must look worse than she feels.

"Most of it's not my blood," she says, and they drive.

Tate concentrates on the road. "I'm glad you're okay," he says, without looking at her.

"Could've fooled me," she mumbles.

"That council lady's gone, in case you were wondering. She had some kind of dream, then said something about not wanting to argue with the wolves. You get to stay. That's good news, right?"

"Just because I'm bleeding, you don't have to pretend to care."

"Sarah . . ."

He stops for a long time. Sarah fingers the stone pendant hanging from her neck. As always, it warms to her touch. The stone knew before she did. It belongs to her. Whether or not this is how it was supposed to be, this is how it *is*. What was Tate's is now hers, and maybe neither of them likes it, but there's no way back.

She can't tell him that, though. He's her big brother; he should be able to figure it out.

"I was jealous. Before. When I yelled at you. That's why. I wasn't mad. Just . . . jealous." It's like every word hurts him more.

She wants to tell him it doesn't matter, that she loves him, that she forgives him, that he can do anything he wants if it will make him hurt less.

But she can't let him hurt her so that he can hurt less. That's something else she understands now.

"It wasn't fair," she says. "I didn't want this, any more than you did."

He's still fixed on the road. "I know."

They drive the rest of the way home in silence, and when they arrive, he pulls the car around back.

"Why are we going in this way?" she asks, as they slip through the kitchen door.

"You're a complete mess," Tate says. "You don't want them seeing you like this."

Sarah figures that "them" must be their parents, and maybe Tate's right; maybe they've spent enough time worrying about their child. So she lets him lead her upstairs, and after she showers off all the blood, she sits on the edge of his bed while he disinfects and bandages her wounds. He's very gentle, and it's clear he knows what he's doing. She realizes now how little she knew about his training—she never asked him the hard questions, like how much it hurt, or whether he was afraid. Whether he ever regretted a choice he'd made when he was too young to know better.

They're questions she can't ask him anymore, even though the answers matter more than ever.

But there's something she can say. She's done with being afraid.

"It's my fault, what happened to you," she blurts.

He freezes. "What?"

"Not my fault, I mean, but I knew something was wrong, I *knew* it. And I didn't stop him. Samuel. I could have made him stop the trial, if I'd had the nerve. I could have saved you."

Tate sits down beside her on the bed. He takes her hand.

"You can't be afraid to say what you think, to speak up for what's right. Not anymore. You know that, right?"

Sarah nods. She's never felt so small.

"But Sarah, you have to know it's not your fault. I *chose* to put myself in that room."

"Yeah, when you were four years old," she says. "What did you know?"

"Then, and every day after that," Tate says. "Being the Player, it's not just like you sign your name on the dotted line and then you belong to your destiny. You *make* your destiny. Every minute, every choice, you build the life you want. The kind of Player you want to be. What happened in that shed, it's no one's fault. It just happened. And it happened because of what I chose. Do you get that?"

She thinks about the woods and the wolves, about how she had no other option but to face them—but that facing them was still her choice. Playing was the choice she wanted to make. The only choice love will let her make.

"I do," she told Tate.

"Good. Now brush your hair, put on something that looks nice, and go downstairs."

"Why?"

"There's a surprise for you down there. To prove it—that you get to choose. I was wrong before, when I made it sound like you had to choose one or the other, your old life or your new one. You don't have to Play like I did, Sarah. Or like anyone did. This is yours now."

"Do you really believe that?" she asks, so desperately wanting it to be true.

Tate nods.

"But what does that have to do with whatever's downstairs?"

He gives her a mysterious smile, and even with the pirate patch, he looks like the old Tate again. "Oh, did I tell you? I figured out what I'm going to do next."

"As in tonight?"

"As in for the foreseeable future," he says.

This is more than she hoped for. Maybe he finally filled out some of those college applications their mother has been stacking on his nightstand. Or even got a job. Anything would be better than wallowing.

"What is it?" she says, hoping he can't read the eagerness in her voice. Now the smile widens into a grin she hasn't seen from Tate in months, mischievous and sparking with joy. "I'm going to help you, little sis. Help you Play. Not that you'll ever Play as well as me . . ." He says it teasingly, without any of the bitterness of the last months, and she feels free to tease him back.

"Not as well as. *Better.*"

Tate nods, and presses his fingers to her forehead. It feels like a benediction. "Better."

Sarah puts on a dark green dress that sets off her auburn hair, layers foundation on her face to disguise the worst of the scratches, and goes downstairs. She stops cold at the bottom of the stairwell, and gasps. The living room is festooned with streamers, the stereo is playing her favorite song, and standing in the center of the room, his arms wide as if waiting for her to step into them, is Christopher. He's always looked especially good in a suit.

"What are you—"

"Questions later," he says. "First . . ."

Then she's in his arms, swaying to the music, drowning in his kiss.

"You're not mad? About the formal?" she says, once she's able to pull her lips from his.

"I was," he admits. "And Reena . . . she was about ready to march over here and burn your house down, I think."

"Oh God, Reena." She's forced herself not to think about any of it, but now it all comes rushing back to her in a tidal wave of guilt and panic. Has she lost her best friend?

Christopher sees it in her eyes, and kisses her once on the forehead, then once on each eyelid. As he does, she can breathe again. "Don't worry," he says. "Tate explained it to her just like he did to me. Oh, and when we're done here, she says you better text her back or she'll kill you."

Sarah grinned, thinking that would be slightly difficult, given the state her cell phone was in. Then the full meaning of Christopher's words sank in. "Wait, so, Tate . . . explained it to you? Explained what, exactly?"

"You know, about the tryouts for the national soccer squad—how you've been training like a maniac, but you didn't want to tell us about it until you knew if you made it, because you didn't want to let us down if you failed. Which is insane, by the way, because you could never let me down even if you didn't make it. But of course you made it!" He wrapped her in a hug so tight she could barely breathe. "I'm so proud of you, do you know that? Proud of me, too." He laughs. "I can't believe I'm dating one of the ten best soccer players in the country."

"Tate told you that too?" she whispered.

"Yeah, he said they had some last-minute tie-breaker tryouts last night. That that's why you missed the formal. And you made it." He looks radiant, and she loves him for being so happy for her, and tries not to hate herself for the lies. "Promise me you won't forget me, now that you're such a big deal," he says. "I know a lot's going to change now, with all the extra training and traveling, but promise me we'll find a way to make this work."

"I promise," she says, leaning her head against her shoulder, and she's not talking to him. She's talking to herself—swearing to herself that she'll lie to him only as much as she needs to, and only to spare him the terrors and sorrows he can't handle. She promises herself that she will give everything she can to her line—but not everything she has, not everything she *is*. She will choose the life she wants, which means choosing both lives, both halves of herself. The part of her that cares about school, that wants to be a good friend to Reena, that wants to lose herself in Christopher's arms, that's the part that will sustain her through what is to come. That's the part that will give her strength, and she won't give it up. She promises herself, and Christopher, that she won't have to.

"Was this your idea?" she says. "The streamers, the suit—like a formal of our own, right?"

He pulls her closer in. She loves the way she fits so perfectly against his chest, the way his arms make her feel so safe. "Right. Wish I could take the credit, but it was Tate's idea."

It was the only answer that could have made her even happier than she already is.

"Can we dance again?" she asks.

Christopher restarts her favorite song and then wraps her again in his embrace, singing along softly in her ear. He has a terrible, off-key voice, and it makes her love him even more. *Six years,* she tells herself. Six years to survive, to fight, to work, to Play, to find a way to hold on to this—to *him*—no matter what. Six years of sacrifice that will all be worth it, if it means saving him and Reena and Tate from those horrors she saw in the fire. The specifics of the vision have already faded, but the message of the vision is still clear: *Play the game, or you will lose everything and everyone you love.*

Six years of Playing, and then they can begin the rest of their lives together. It doesn't matter what destiny wants for her. It doesn't matter what she saw in the flames last night: so much blood, so much death.

Life is choice, and Sarah chooses to have it all.

ENDGAME IS REAL. ENDGAME IS NOW.

SEE HOW ENDGAME BEGINS:

MARCUS LOXIAS MEGALOS

Hafız Alipaşa Sk, Aziz Mahmut Hüdayi Mh, Istanbul, Turkey

Marcus Loxias Megalos is bored. He cannot remember a time before
the boredom. School is boring. Girls are boring. Football is boring.
Especially when his team, his favorite team, Fenerbahçe, is losing, as
they are now, to Manisaspor.

Marcus sneers at the TV in his small, undecorated room. He is
slouched in a plush black leather chair that sticks to his skin whenever
he sits up. It is night, but Marcus keeps the lights in his room off. The
window is open. Heat passes through it like an oppressive ghost as
the sounds of the Bosporus—the long, low calls of ships, the bells of
buoys—groan and tinkle over Istanbul.

Marcus wears baggy black gym shorts and is shirtless. His 24 ribs
show through his tanned skin. His arms are sinewy and hard. His
breathing is easy. His stomach is taut and his hair is close-cropped and
black and his eyes are green. A bead of sweat rolls down the tip of his
nose. All of Istanbul simmers on this night, and Marcus is no different.
A book lies open in his lap, ancient and leather-bound. The words on
its pages are Greek. Marcus has handwritten something in English
on a scrap of paper that lies across the open page: *From broad Crete I
declare that I am come by lineage, the son of a wealthy man.* He has read
the old book over and over. It's a tale of war, exploration, betrayal, love,
and death. It always makes him smile.

What Marcus wouldn't give to take a journey of his own, to escape the
oppressive heat of this dull city. He imagines an endless sea spread out
before him, the wind cool against his skin, adventures and enemies
arrayed on the horizon.

Marcus sighs and touches the scrap of paper. In his other hand he holds a 9,000-year-old knife, made of a single piece of bronze forged in the fires of Knossos. He brings the blade across his body and lets its edge rest against his right forearm. He pushes it into the skin, but not all the way. He knows the limits of this blade. He has trained with it since he could hold it. He has slept with it under his pillow since he was six. He has killed chickens, rats, dogs, cats, pigs, horses, hawks, and lambs with it. He has killed 11 people with it.

He is 16, in his prime for Playing. If he turns 20, he will be ineligible. He wants to Play. He would rather die than be ineligible.

The odds are almost nil that he will get his chance, though, and he knows it. Unlike Odysseus, war will never find Marcus. There will be no grand journey.

His line has been waiting for 9,000 years. Since the day the knife was forged. For all Marcus knows, his line will wait for another 9,000 years, long after Marcus is gone and the pages of his book have disintegrated.

So Marcus is bored.

The crowd on the TV cheers, and Marcus looks up from the knife. The Fenerbahçe goalie has cleared a rainbow up the right sideline, the ball finding the head of a burly midfielder. The ball bounces forward, over a line of defenders, near the last two men before the Manisaspor keeper. The players rush for the ball, and the forward comes away with it, 20 meters from the goal, free and clear of the defender. The keeper gets ready.

Marcus leans forward. Match time is 83:34. Fenerbahçe has yet to score, and doing so in such a dramatic way would save some face. The old book slides to the floor. The scrap of paper drifts free of the page and slips through the air like a falling leaf. The crowd begins to rise. The sky suddenly brightens, as if the gods, the Gods of the Sky themselves, are coming down to offer help. The keeper backpedals. The forward collects himself and takes the shot, and the ball blasts off.

As it punches the back of the net, the stadium lights up and the crowd screams, first in exaltation for the goal, but immediately afterward in terror and confusion—deep, true, and profound terror and confusion. A massive fireball, a giant burning meteor, explodes above the crowd and tears across the field, obliterating the Fenerbahçe defense and blasting a hole through the end of the stadium grandstand.

Marcus's eyes widen. He is looking at total carnage. It is butchery on the scale of those American disaster movies. Half the stadium, tens of thousands of people dead, burning, lit up, on fire.

It is the most beautiful thing Marcus has ever seen.

He breathes hard. Sweat pours off his brow. People outside are yelling, screaming. A woman wails from the café below. Sirens ring out across the ancient city on the Bosporus, between the Marmara and the Black. On TV, the stadium is awash in flames. Players, police, spectators, coaches run around, burning like crazed matchsticks. The commentators cry for help, for God, because they don't understand. Those not dead or on their way to being dead trample one another as they try to escape. There's another explosion and the screen goes black.

Marcus's heart wants out of his chest. Marcus's brain is as hot as the football pitch. Marcus's stomach is full of rocks and acid. His palms feel hot and sticky. He looks down and sees that he has dug the ancient blade into his forearm, and a rivulet of blood is trickling off his hand, onto the chair, onto his book. The book is ruined, but it doesn't matter; he won't need it anymore. Because now, Marcus *will* have his Odyssey.

Marcus looks back to the darkened TV. He knows there's something waiting for him there amidst the wreckage. He must find it.

A single piece.

For himself, for his line.

He smiles. Marcus has trained all of his life for this moment. When he wasn't training, he was dreaming of the Calling. All the visions of destruction that his teenage mind concocted could not touch what Marcus has witnessed tonight. A meteor destroying a football stadium and killing 38,676 people. The legends said it would be a grand announcement. For once, the legends have become a beautiful reality.

Marcus has wanted, waited, and prepared for Endgame his entire life. He is no longer bored, and he won't be again until he either wins or dies.

This is it.

He knows it.

This is it.

ENDGAME IS REAL.
ENDGAME HAS STARTED.

ENDGAME IS REAL. ENDGAME IS NOW.

ENDGAME
THE CALLING

JAMES FREY

AND

NILS JOHNSON-SHELTON

Twelve ancient cultures were chosen millennia ago to represent humanity in Endgame, a global game that will decide the fate of humankind. Endgame has always been a possibility, but never a reality . . . until now. Twelve meteorites have just struck Earth, each meteorite containing a message for a Player who has been trained for this moment. At stake for the Players: saving their bloodline as well as the fate of the world. And only one can win.

HARPER

An Imprint of HarperCollinsPublishers

WWW.THISISENDGAME.COM

BEFORE THE CALLING.
BEFORE ENDGAME.
THEY TRAINED TO BE CHOSEN.

Don't miss the thrilling prequel novellas that follow the lives of the 12 Players before they were chosen as the one to save their ancient bloodline—and win Endgame.

Read the first three novellas in one paperback:
Endgame: The Complete Training Diaries.

HARPER
An Imprint of HarperCollinsPublishers

W W W . T H I S I S E N D G A M E . C O M

PRAISE FOR ESTELLE LAURE'S
THIS RAGING LIGHT

"*This Raging Light* is a funny, heart-wrenching, and soulful read as Lucille
develops her own personal family, bloodline or not.
It's not one you'll soon forget."
—*Bustle*

"Her first-person narration is lyrical, akin to that of a Francesca Lia Block
character, but there's an undercurrent of roughness in her voice. . . .
Heartbreakingly hopeful, lyrically told."
—*Kirkus Reviews*

"Estelle Laure's prose is utterly gorgeous, even as it lays out the story of a girl
dealing with the failings of her parents, death, and her own insecurities."
—*Book Riot*

"Feverish with suspense and charged with emotion, *This Raging Light* is a
striking debut from a writer to watch. More than a love story, it's a poetic,
insightful, and ultimately hopeful exploration of loneliness and connection."
—Laura Ruby, Printz Award–winning author of *Bone Gap*

"Estelle Laure's *This Raging Light* might be YA,
but it's got plenty of grown-up appeal."
—Entertainmentweekly.com

"In an assured debut, Laure gives Lucille a fierce stubbornness that
keeps her going. . . . The characters are well drawn, and Laure effectively
depicts the adrenaline rush of love."
—*Publishers Weekly*

"Lucille's fresh, first-person voice spills over with metaphor,
poetically capturing her emotional landscape with force and fury,
frantic love and absolute exhaustion."
—*Shelf Awareness*

"Laure's debut is brilliant and not to be missed."
—RT Book Reviews

"Lucille may not take down a beast or assassinate any super bads,
but she's what heroines look like and love like in real life."
—*Justine* magazine

"[Laure] has a raw, authentic voice and a passion for storytelling."
—Matt de la Peña, Newbery Medal winner, Pura Belpré honoree,
and award-winning YA novelist of *The Living* and *Mexican WhiteBoy*

"The narrative rings authentic, especially as Lucille wrestles with
romantic pangs. Thankfully, there's enough wry humor to balance
the worry and poignancy. Above all, you'll love steadfast Lucille
and keep caring about what comes next."
—*Atlanta Journal-Constitution*

"Lucille is a steel-strong, deeply human heroine
fighting against impossible odds."
—B&N Teen blog

"Readers will be seduced by the love affair budding between
Digby and Lucille as much as she is. The characters are believably flawed,
but eminently likable, leaving the reader with hope for humanity."
—Montana Public Radio

"Laure's debut stands out for her keen understanding
of the spectrum of human emotions, and her ability
to put tough feelings into beautiful prose."
—*Horn Book*

"Estelle Laure writes with power and lyricism—
but more than that, she writes honestly from the heart.
Definitely a writer to watch!"
—A. M. Jenkins, Printz Honor–winning author of *Repossessed*